PRAISE FOR DIXIE LYLE

A Taste Fur Murder

"A delightful, funny mystery filled with eccentric and colorful characters, be they humans, animals, or spirits. Dixie Lyle will entertain the reader page after page!"
—Leann Sweeney, *New York Times* bestselling author of the Cats in Trouble mysteries

"A clever new series that deftly blends cozy mystery with the paranormal, and that is sure to please readers of both genres . . . *A Taste Fur Murder* is original and witty, with a twisting plot that contains more than a few 'shocks'."
—Ali Brandon, author of the Black Cat Bookshop mysteries

"An enjoyable read for cozy fans." —*RT Book Reviews*

To Die Fur

"Blends pet cemeteries, animal spirits, and a cast of zany human characters . . . those who read paranormal mysteries will enjoy." —*RT Book Reviews*

Marked Fur Murder

"The sort of wild and wacky mystery that could only come from the pen of Dixie Lyle . . . I think you'll enjoy the ride."
—*Bookwyrm's Hoard*

ALSO BY DIXIE LYLE

To Die Fur
A Taste Fur Murder
Marked Fur Murder

A DEADLY *tail*

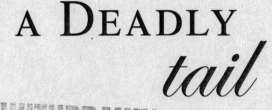

DIXIE LYLE

St. Martin's Paperbacks

This is a work of fiction. All of the characters, organizations, and events portrayed in this novel are either products of the author's imagination or are used fictitiously.

A DEADLY TAIL

Copyright © 2016 by Dixie Lyle.
Excerpt from *Purrfectly Dead* copyright © 2016 by Dixie Lyle.

For information address St. Martin's Press, 175 Fifth Avenue, New York, NY 10010.

ISBN: 978-1-250-07843-8

Printed in the United States of America

St. Martin's Paperbacks edition / February 2016

St. Martin's Paperbacks are published by St. Martin's Press, 175 Fifth Avenue, New York, NY 10010.

10 9 8 7 6 5 4 3 2 1

This is dedicated to my friend Deni Loubert,
a real-life ZZ (though not as rich).

1.

Let's just get this out of the way right now: My life is weird. And I don't mean just in the "I have weird hobbies" or "I have weird friends" kind of way. Oh, no. I mean, yes, I *do* have weird friends, but they only account for a certain percentage of strange in the weirdness equation that is my existence. Which, if you were going to break it down, might look a little like this: *ghost dog plus reincarnated cat times graveyard haunted by animal spirits divided by rich eccentric boss with multiple oddball interests (including her own private zoo) minus any spare time for the gal who has to oversee it all and solve any problems that might crop up.*

Got your head wrapped around that? Too bad, because there's more. But maybe we should drop any attempt to define this as a mathematical problem, because pretty soon we're gonna get into supernatural integers and crime scene algebra and then this breakdown turns into the nervous kind and I have to start all over.

So.

Let's just start out with the scene that greeted me and

my dog as we arrived for work on Tuesday morning, at the sprawling estate that holds the Zoransky family mansion. It was October, a very chilly day, and the iron bars of the front gate that swung open for my car when I arrived were furred with frost.

The front lawn was overrun by zombies.

[I say, Foxtrot,] said a deep, cultured voice in my head. [The front lawn appears to be overrun by zombies.]

That voice was my dog, Whiskey. He looks like an Australian cattle dog, sounds like a barrel-chested butler, and is actually composed of ectoplasm—the stuff ghosts are made of. This allows him to shift his form into that of any canine breed, all of which seem to be normal dogs to any observer. He and I converse telepathically, though often I just talk out loud.

"Zombies, you say?" I answered. "How unusual. I thought they preferred the warmer weather—" And then I noticed something strange and slammed on the brakes.

[Indeed. Though the lower temperatures would no doubt help with the rate of decomposition, and Halloween *is* fast approaching—]

"Whiskey. Shut up for a moment about the walking dead. What the heck is *that*?" I stared out my window at what the animated corpses were milling around, under, and in some cases on.

At first glance it seemed the zombies were attending a yard sale. Gardening implements, power tools, bicycles, furniture—all this and more was strewn about. But it was how it was all *displayed* that was truly bizarre: Rakes and shovels were lashed together into angular frameworks; bikes featured weed whackers attached to the front like some sort of jousting lance; chairs had been carefully arranged into a maze, some sections covered by tarps that turned them into tunnels. I recognized bits and pieces of

ZZ's various hobbies over the years, ranging from scuba tanks to mountain-climbing gear to snowshoes. Bright-green loops of garden hose overhead connected some pieces to others, and a path made of old roofing tiles meandered throughout.

"That," I said, "was not there last night."

Whiskey studied it with me. Australian cattle dogs (sometimes called blue heelers) often have one blue eye and one brown, and their coats are a combination of black-and-white brindle with yellow; Whiskey's overall appearance gave the impression that he wasn't so much a single dog as a transporter accident between a golden retriever and a Border collie.

[I assumed it was simply part of the set. It's not as if I've read the script.]

"I have. This isn't mentioned." I sighed and took my foot off the brake. "Plus, I recognize a lot of that stuff as ZZ's. How much you want to bet the director talked her into upping her contribution?"

Whiskey snorted. [Dogs do not gamble. But even if you're correct, what is this construct supposed to represent? It looks like some sort of obstacle course. Are the zombies supposed to chase people through it? Is there some sporting aspect of undead cannibalism that I've failed to grasp?]

I pulled into my regular parking spot beside the house. "Well, there's usually a lot of chasing and fleeing in zombie movies, so it almost makes sense. Except this movie is supposed to be a period piece, and most of that stuff is post-twentieth-century. I guess I'll just have to talk to the boss and find out."

My boss—in this case—is Zelda Zoransky, the owner of the estate and all-around bon vivant. ZZ practically invented the word *eclectic,* and she takes every opportunity to prove it. Her latest obsession was something called steampunk, which was mostly a reimagining of Victorian fantastic literature through a more modern lens. The indie film she'd agreed to let shoot on the grounds and in the mansion was called *Sherlock Zolmbes,* about Sherlock Holmes fighting off a horde of the undead while trapped at a country estate. It didn't have a large budget, but the director was passionate about the project and ZZ thought it sounded like fun.

"Fun" for ZZ always meant plenty of headaches for me. As her personal assistant, my job meant translating whim into reality. Chaotic as that generally was, adding in a film crew tripled everything—but I was managing. It was, after all, what I was paid for.

I took another look at the undead horde before I got out of the car. They weren't so much milling around as huddling and clutching paper cups of coffee, looking even more haggard and unhappy in the cold than zombies usually did. They must have been up awfully early to get through makeup and wardrobe, and now they had to stand around in the dawn chill dressed in nothing but rags and latex prosthetics. A couple of them were trying out some "Thriller" dance moves to keep warm, while others watched and laughed.

The first person to greet me at the door was wearing a black-and-white fur tuxedo: Tango, my feline other partner. Currently on her seventh life, she also communicated with me via thought. *<Morning, Foxtrot.>* Her mental voice always reminded me of an old torch singer, all raspy and worldwise. Her attitude wasn't far off, either. *<Have you noticed the front lawn?>*

"Yep. Covered in zombies, just like yesterday. Only they appear to have decorated, too."

<Oh, that wasn't them. It was Keene.>

Keene was our semi-resident celebrity, a guest at the house so often he should have his own room. ZZ liked to host salons: She invited various interesting people—politicians, scientists, actors, musicians—to stay here and enjoy the amenities, with the only rule being everyone must attend the nightly dinners. The one thing Keene enjoyed more than being a rock star—which he was—was a lively, slightly inebriated conversation with intriguing people. Except sometimes the phrase *slightly inebriated* was replaced by *definitely high, fairly wasted,* or *ohhhhh, man.* Regardless of his level of intoxication, though, he was always charming, funny, intelligent, and mostly polite.

"Keene's responsible for that?" I shook my head. "Well, better than trashing his room, I guess. Doesn't look like he wrecked anything, though it is quite the mess. Any idea what he was trying to accomplish?"

Tango gave her head a slow shake. *<You got me. It was entertaining to watch, though—for a while. Then I got bored and stopped.>*

[Of course,] replied Whiskey. [I'm sure you're echoing the words of every cat who was ever present at a significant event in history: the eruption of Vesuvius, the moon landing, the parting of the Red Sea. "The lava/stupendous feat/miracle was somewhat interesting, but then I got bored and wandered off."]

Tango started to clean one white paw with her tongue. *<Meh. Volcanoes are overrated, the astronauts didn't even have a cat with them, and when it comes to that much water, who cares what it does? Piled up or not, it's still wet.>*

"Hang on," I said. "The parting of the Red Sea? That actually happened?"

I looked at Whiskey. Whiskey looked at Tango. Tango rolled her eyes.

<You're the one who brought it up,> she said to Whiskey. *<You give her an answer.>*

I turned my look into a stare. "Well?"

[Ahem. My reference was purely on the basis of a shared social metaphor, to wit, *the parting of the Red Sea.* I did not mean to imply any personal knowledge of such events, or their possible historical accuracy.]

Big surprise. Despite their post-life status, both of my two companions were extremely tight-lipped on any metaphysical subjects. I'd found out a few things on my own, but was still mostly in the dark on the true nature of the Universe.

Mostly.

"Good morning, dear," said the corpse shuffling its way down the staircase that led from the main lobby to the second floor. "Slept well, I trust?"

"Better than you, from all appearances," I said to ZZ. "Though possibly not as long."

ZZ grinned at me with a horrible mouth. "Oh, you know how I am before I've had my coffee. Haven't the makeup people done a simply *gruesome* job?" She did a little pirouette on the bottom step, showing off the lovely (if rotting) Victorian dress she was wearing. Lots of crushed velvet and stained lace. In return for letting them use the grounds for filming, ZZ had insisted on being cast as one of the zombies.

"They have. And speaking of gruesome jobs—what, exactly, is the explanation for that elaborate hodgepodge on the front lawn?"

"Now, Foxtrot—you knew the film crew was going to make a mess. It's just what they *do.* Don't worry, it's all temporary."

I took off my coat and hung it up on the coatrack just inside the door. "It's not the movie equipment I'm worried about. It's that bizarre *thing* that—well, that appears to have grown there overnight." Only my boyfriend, Ben, knew the truth about Whiskey and Tango, so I couldn't tell my boss that the cat had just ratted out the rock star.

A puzzled look crossed her decaying features. "I'm not sure what you're talking about, dear. Why don't you show me?"

I opened the door and let her look for herself. "See? I could be wrong, but I don't really see an elliptical trainer being used as a prop in a Sherlock Holmes movie."

ZZ took a few steps forward, stopping at the threshold. Tango rubbed against her legs, purring. "Oh, my. I have no idea what this is all about. I suppose we should talk to the director."

"I'm on it," I said. "Any idea where he is?"

"He popped in while I was still in makeup, said he was going to grab some breakfast. Check the dining room."

[Foxtrot.] Whiskey's voice inside my head was urgent. I glanced down at him and saw that he was staring through the doorway, both ears up, eyes wide and alert. [Something's wrong. Follow me.]

He bolted outside. "Whoops," I said. "Not the squirrel thing again? I thought you'd gotten over that." I sighed and grabbed my coat again. "Sorry, boss. If I don't corral him immediately, he'll tree the damn critter and go into a barking frenzy that will last for hours. It's like he's convinced they're all plotting against him."

"Go ahead, dear. I'll talk to Mr. Trentini."

<They are, you know,> Tango said as I stepped back out, closing the door behind me. *<Plotting against us. They're like ninjas, only more evil and with bushy tails.>*

"Yes, I'm sure that's where they store all the extra evil,

in their tails. Never trust anything that looks like a rat with a toilet brush stuck up its butt, right?"

<You'll take me seriously when they learn how to make nunchuks. Oh, yes, you will. And I will laugh, and laugh, and laugh . . . >

I had to jog to catch up to Whiskey, and right about then I reached the limit of Tango's telepathic range. Or maybe she just got bored with the conversation and wandered off; she's like that.

Whiskey had slowed down, his nose to the ground. "What's up, pup?" I asked as I got closer. "Little Timmy fall down the well again?"

[Please stop making that reference. It's demeaning to a great performer.]

"What, Lassie? I'm surprised you even know who that is."

[I have friends outside of work, you know.] He continued around the corner of the house, sniffing intently.

"Wait. You know Lassie? The actual Lassie? I thought she was—"

[Dead, yes. As am I. Though I'm considerably less fictional.]

We were beside the house now, on a little paved path with a birdbath to one side. I picked a scrap of duct tape off a rosebush, frowning; they'd been filming here yesterday, and hadn't done a very good job of cleaning up after themselves. The fake gore they'd liberally splashed around was still evident, now in frozen lumps and rivulets that made the birdbath look more like a well-used ritual altar than a wildlife spa. The paved path was the same; a huge, reddish-brown stain covered the path and the grass on either side. I wrinkled my nose. "Yuck. If it weren't so cold, I'd get the gardener out here with a hose. Is this what you were worked up about?"

[I'm afraid so.] Whiskey sniffed delicately at the stain, then sat back on his haunches and looked at me solemnly. [This is not what it appears to be, Foxtrot. Or—more accurately—it is.]

My eyes widened, and I took an involuntary step back. "You mean this is . . . real? No way. I was here when they filmed that scene, and it was just Hollywood make-believe. Nobody actually got torn to pieces."

[Much of what I smell is corn syrup, food coloring, and cocoa powder, to be sure—a common stand-in for blood. But not all of it.]

I swallowed. "How much is . . ."

[Human? A great deal. All from the same person, and in quantities that mean they couldn't possibly have survived.]

I looked around, feeling queasy. "So this is an actual, genuine murder scene?"

[Unknown. All I can guarantee is the presence of a large amount of blood.]

I took a deep breath. "Is it . . . anyone we know?"

[I don't recognize it, but I spent yesterday in relative isolation.] His tone was decidedly cooler, due to the fact that he'd been shut in my office for most of the previous day; the director had insisted both Whiskey and Tango be locked away in case one of them inadvertently wandered into a shot. "Nothing ruins a zombie movie like a dog trying to lick a shambling monstrosity's face," he'd said. "Except maybe a cat cleaning herself while the zombie apocalypse happens a few feet away."

I let my breath out. Nobody Whiskey knew personally (which meant, more or less, anyone I knew, too) was dead. Maybe this was some sort of zero-budget cost-cutting measure? I'd worked for a band once that seriously floated the idea of making their own fireworks out of road flares to save money on their stage show.

"How fresh is it?" I asked. "Could it maybe be—I don't know, from a blood bank or something?"

He got to his feet, put his head down, and nosed around some more. [Definitely not. It's only a few hours old, at most. And there are other scents, as well—scents that indicate the body was not entirely intact.]

I sighed. "Death *and* dismemberment? Thank you for not going into detail. So, the next obvious question is— where *is* the body in question?"

[I believe I know. If you examine the grass closely, you'll see that something fairly large was dragged in that direction. The ground is too frozen to hold tracks, but there is a scent trail—one that is all too familiar.]

"You mean of the killer?"

[I mean of the one who moved the body. Come with me and I'll show you.]

He trotted away, pausing every now and then to sniff the ground and make sure he was still on the right track. I followed.

We didn't go far. The trail led to a low, tarped trailer beside the tennis courts, sitting on a flat area the film crew was using as a temporary parking lot.

There was a hand sticking out of the edge of the tarp.

I got closer and peered at it. "Huh," I said. Then I grabbed the edge of the tarp and pulled it back.

The trailer was full of body parts—fake ones, that is. Arms and legs and torsos and the occasional head, all props made for the movie.

All except one.

About the only thing that gave it away was the clothes it was wearing—a nondescript black tracksuit and running shoes. The other body parts were all either in Victorian rags or unclothed, but this particular corpse seemed to have jogged through a portal from the future, just in time to be decapitated.

Whiskey stood on his hind legs and peered over the edge of the trailer's lip. [No head or hands on the victim,] he noted.

Strangely enough, all the artificial grisliness that surrounded it made it easier to look at. "Okay, I'm no forensic pathologist, but even I can see they weren't removed cleanly. The edges are all ragged and uneven."

[As if they were chewed? Precisely. And not just chewed, either—but swallowed, as well.]

"You mean—oh, no. Not zombies. Not real, live—okay, not-so-much-alive—creatures that have risen from the grave with an insatiable craving for after-midnight brain-flavored snacks? Because, I'm sorry, I did *not* sign up for that. Supernatural weather spirits, ghosts, even the odd animal deity I can handle, but I draw the line at the zombies."

It's funny how demeaning it is to have a dog roll his eyes at you. I suppose it'd be worse if they actually left his skull, but the condescension was bad enough. [No, Foxtrot. Zombies, inasmuch as I know, are not real. However, you are correct on one count: The brain was in fact consumed. As was the skull itself, and the hands.]

Suddenly the scene in front of me seemed a lot less fake. I pulled the edge of the tarp back into place. "The entire *head* was eaten? What do we have around here that would possibly—oh."

[Yes. I've already picked up his scent, which is not exactly subtle. After stashing the body here—presumably to finish later—he went in *this* direction.] Whiskey was already trotting away, nose to the ground, and I went after him. I knew I had to inform the authorities, but I wanted to check out our primary suspect first.

The trail led straight to the menagerie, which is what ZZ calls her private zoo. She's always been keenly interested in the welfare of animals, so the residents here aren't on display or for her amusement; they're here because they have no place else to go. We do our best to rewild them whenever possible, and take good care of the ones who aren't capable of surviving on their own. We have snakes and warthogs, big cats and small monkeys, hippos and birds and crocodiles.

Crocs are one of the few critters we house that could do that to a human body, but they like to stick their kills under rocks or submerged trees to ripen; I had a hard time imagining one pulling a body into a tarped trailer.

But it wasn't a crocodile we were tracking. It was something much nastier—something that occasionally liked to eat crocodiles, or even chow down on *other* animals who ate crocodiles. As far as this beast was concerned, the words *food chain* and *buffet* meant the same thing.

"I can't believe this," I muttered. "If he actually got out and killed a guest, we are in big, big trouble."

[We don't know that for sure. It might have been a random jogger.]

I groaned. "How is *that* any better? A man is *dead,* Whiskey. He died on the grounds, and one of our animals *ate* him. That much seems clear."

[I'm not so sure. Yes, he's an opportunistic predator, but attacking and killing a human being seems . . . out of character.]

"Right," I snorted. "Because he's so genteel and refined. Just look at the name he gave himself."

[Ah. Well, that *is* unfortunate. But animals do have a sense of humor, you know . . .]

We arrived at our destination, a sturdy, concrete-floored, high wire-fenced pen with a big mound of dirt in the middle. Our suspect was presumably inside his burrow, asleep.

"Hey, Owduttf," I said loudly. "Get your beady-eyed little carcass out here!"

Owduttf is from South Africa, but—despite how it sounds—the name isn't of Dutch origin. It's an acronym for "One Who Does Unspeakable Things To Foxtrot," and our resident honey badger refuses to answer to anything else.

Yes, we have a honey badger. For those of you unfamiliar with the species, they are basically a meaner, tougher, hungrier version of a wolverine. All a wolverine has to deal with are cougars, bears, and the occasional moose; the honey badger has to face down everything from lions to king cobras, and not only does so but will also steal food from the first one and gulp down the last. It gets its name from the fact that it likes to raid beehives to eat the larvae inside—and when I say *bees,* I'm talking about African killer bees, the kind that go into a murderous frenzy when anything even comes close to their nest. But hey, when you've got a craving, what are you gonna do?

I heard sounds of movement from inside the mouth of the burrow, and then Owduttf shuffled out. He's not much bigger than a house cat, with a wide flat head and a broad white stripe that covers his back and the top of his skull. He stopped in the entrance and yawned, showing a mouth full of sharp teeth. Then he looked at me, blinked, and made a chuffing noise.

"Um," I said. Having cornered my suspect, I realized one very obvious fact: I didn't speak Honey Badger, and neither did Whiskey.

[What do you suggest we do? Search the premises for damning evidence?]

"You first."

I've never seen Whiskey afraid, but that doesn't mean he's stupid, either. [Surely you jest. I may be composed of ectoplasm, but that won't stop him from trying to eat me. In fact, he'd probably enjoy the challenge.]

"You're probably right." I frowned, then dug out my cell phone. "I think this is about as far as we can take this, pooch. We can come back later with Tango and question Owduttf, but right now we have to report that body." Tango was my translator, fluent in hundreds of animal dialects. "I'll tell the police you led me to the body, then here. We'll sort out the details as we go along—"

And that was when I heard the explosion.

I turned, and saw a plume of black smoke rising from the roof of the mansion.

2.

Twenty-four hours previously:

[I really don't understand why I have to be locked up like some sort of prisoner,] Whiskey huffed. [Can't you simply explain that I'm well trained?]

I swiveled my office chair away from my computer and put my hand on his furry head. "Nope. We're dealing with a first-time director here, and he's doing his best to put the *neu* in *neurotic.* I've worked with guys like him before; a rational argument just doesn't cut it. He needs to have his hand held, his little superstitions catered to, and his ego stroked. Most of all, he has to feel like he's in control—any and all chaos must be found, bound, and locked away. In this case, that means you. Sorry."

Whiskey put his head down on his paws and looked forlorn. [Very well. At least the cat isn't being allowed to roam free, either.]

"Um. Yeah, about that—"

His head snapped up and those mismatched brown and blue eyes glared at me. Sometimes he switches the two colors back and forth, which he says is just absentmindedness but I think he does deliberately for the unnerving effect. [You're not telling me that the *cat* has her freedom?]

He made the word *cat* sound like a euphemism for an unspeakable act of depravity.

"Sort of? I mean, she's definitely not supposed to be running around free, but I've hit a few snags vis-à-vis actual implementation of the process." When I'm caught in a flat-out lie, I sometimes revert to corporate-speak as a defense mechanism—which is stupid. It's like treading water when you realize a shark is circling you. It might buy you a little time, but does nothing to reduce your profile as an Unhappy Meal.

[You mean you can't catch her.]

"I mean I can't catch her."

[Foxtrot. I am a dog. No matter how much my appearance may vary, that singular truth remains at the core of my being. I can be ferocious or affectionate, playful or stoic, but I am always loyal. I do my duty, no matter how unpleasant; I am dependable, I am trustworthy.]

"I *know* you are, sweetie, but this wasn't a choice on my part—"

[Not my point. A cat . . . a cat is chaos unbridled. A cat is mischief wrapped in deviousness. A cat is the embodied potential for disaster on four silent paws. They are impulsive, contrary, self-centered, and oblivious to consequences. Letting one wander unchecked anywhere is practically a crime unto itself, but caging a canine while freeing a feline is more than merely injust; it's madness on an unthinkable scale. Never forget the root of the word *catastrophe*.]

I stared. "Wow. That was . . . impressive. Off the cuff, or have you been saving it for a special occasion?"

[Dogs do not have *cuffs*.]

"Good point. Well, I'm working on it, but she's wily. Cat flap's locked and all the windows are shut, but this place has a lot of doors. She's currently trapped inside, but I'm not sure exactly where."

[Hmmph. If you'd let me out of this room, I could find her for you easily enough.]

I thought about it. "Nah, I don't think so. The dynamic between you two is tense enough without adding a whole escaped-prisoner/collaborator thing to it. But thanks for offering."

[I live to serve.]

I winced. "I'll bring you a nice steak from the kitchen, okay? And I'll make sure Tango stays in the house, at the very least."

[I suppose that will have to do.]

His accusing gaze followed me as I left, but I knew he'd forgive me quickly once he got his teeth into that steak. Whiskey, being a ghost, has no need for food, but that doesn't mean he's incapable of enjoying it. And since ectoplasmic digestion leaves no waste products, I don't even have to worry about walking him afterward.

ZZ's mansion is pretty great, as far as workplaces go. As a professional assistant I've plied my trade in tour buses, corporate boardrooms, and everything between, but I especially like the feel of the Zoransky estate. I mean, it has the oak paneling and antique furniture and cut-glass sconces you'd expect in a sprawling Victorian house, but it also has stuff like a mobile automated booze dispenser that ZZ uses to serve drinks at dinner, or experimental postmodern art sprouting up in the garden next to the carefully tended flower beds. It's an interesting mix of the old and the new, like a dignified old lady undergoing a second childhood. Which is, I suppose, a good description of ZZ herself—minus the dignified part. She came of age in the sixties, and I think she views the whole growing-old-with-grace thing as an obvious trap. It's not that she's devoid of dignity, she just refuses to be a slave to it. It's one of the reasons I love working for her.

But having ZZ as a boss also means living in a state of perpetual flexibility. No battle plan survives contact with the enemy, and no schedule survives contact with ZZ. The film production was making things especially fluid, since we were not only providing them with a place to film but housing and feeding the cast as well. Crew members were staying at a small motel in town; ZZ had said she'd be glad to put everyone up, but the producer, Maurice Rolvink, had insisted on the separation. "It makes for a less stressful environment, overall," he'd told me, though I couldn't see how cramming four people per room into budget accommodations was less stressful than staying in a mansion. Then I realized that Rolvink was dividing the word into *over* and *all,* and guess which side of the adjective he put himself on?

But it wasn't my job to complain on behalf of somebody's else's employees, so I didn't. Besides, it made my job easier—my job, and the maids', and the chef's.

The chef in question has dark eyes and sandy-blond hair and rugged features, none of which has anything to do with how well he cooks but is definitely relevant to being my boyfriend, which he is. When I popped into the kitchen to see how Ben was doing with breakfast, he looked up from a big skillet of something omeletty and grinned. "Hey, Trotsky! Joining us for breakfast? Got some oyster mushrooms and Brie that are just dying to meet you."

I came over and gave him a quick kiss. "Can't, you know that. Breakfast is hummingbird time."

He moved the pan onto a different burner. "Hummingbird?"

"Yep. Caffeine and sugar, slightly diluted by hot water. By the time our guests have finished their eggs, I'll be vibrating too fast for the human eye."

He laughed. "Okay, okay. Nice of you to flit by while you're still visible."

I refilled my mug from a kettle of hot water and tossed a tea bag in it. "You're chipper this morning. I thought chefs hated breakfast."

"Only the unimaginative ones." He used a spatula to carefully lift the omelet onto a plate. "Me, I look at it as a challenge. Despite the fact that most people seem to either eat exactly the same thing every morning or skip the meal altogether, I refuse to surrender. My goal at the break of every day is to make something so good that *it* becomes the diner's new default breakfast."

I considered this. "So, you're trying to make something so good they'll ask for it over and over again."

"That's the idea."

"Thereby depriving you of the chance of making something new. Seems self-defeating."

He grinned, speared a forkful of what he'd just made, and held it up to my mouth. "Nope. Just means the bar keeps getting set higher."

I took a bite. Chewed. Frowned. "Dammit. Now I have to have this every morning, and I don't even know what it is. Pureed angel wings? Divine eggs *à la fromage*?"

He studied me curiously, much the way Tango will sometimes study an unusual bug. "Hmmm. You should never, ever try to describe food to other people. I don't mean that as a general statement, I'm talking about you specifically. I think I've found the one thing you're terrible at."

"Oh, I'm terrible at lots of things. I'm just really, really good at concealing that fact."

<Except from your boyfriend. Or any random person who happens to be strolling past.> Tango casually sauntered up, then regarded me with narrowed eyes. *<Anyway,*

I refuse to believe that food is any good until you've proven it.>

Ben sighed. He's the only other human in the household who can hear Tango and Whiskey, and that's because he's not entirely human himself; he has the blood of an ancient race of weather spirits called Thunderbirds running in his veins, and can whip up a storm, tornado, or blizzard as easily as he can make toast. "And why should I have to prove anything to you, furball?"

She cocked her head to one side. *<I'm a cat. Everybody knows that when it comes to food, we have the highest, most exacting standards. So while Foxtrot may just gobble down anything you put on her plate, I'm clearly the one you need to impress.>*

Ben smiled and shook his head. "You would deign to try my most unworthy cuisine, O black-and-white one?"

<Maybe. We'll see.>

Ben put a little of his creation on a plate. "I'm not sure what's more unbelievable—that you think snobbery is a viable strategy to get food, or that I keep falling for it."

He put the plate on the floor in front of her, and she bent her head to sniff at it. *<Falling, nothing. You're just following the natural order.>*

"Of what?" I asked. "The gourmet sensibilities of domesticated mammals?"

She took a delicate bite of Ben's offering. *<No. Recognizing a superior life-form, and demonstrating the proper respect. If your kind hadn't been capable of learning it, we would have wiped you out long ago.>*

It can be difficult—if not impossible—to detect the difference between Tango's casual ruthlessness and her sense of humor. Sometimes I think there isn't one.

"Well?" Ben asked after she'd taken a second bite. "How is it?"

<Too much oregano. Keep trying.> She twitched an ear and wandered away.

Ben shrugged. "Back to the frying pan, I guess."

"What, you're going to accept her verdict over mine?"

"Her complete lack of tact means she's the most honest critic I have. You, on the other hand, are somewhat biased."

"Aw. That's the sweetest thing you've said to me all day." I grabbed my mug of tea and headed for the door. "And now I've got to check in with the film crew. I hope they're as biased about your food as I am—but not for the same reasons."

As it turned out, they were all more than happy with the buffet Ben had laid out on the long dining room table—they'd eaten every scrap and guzzled back the coffee like caffeine-deprived camels about to embark on a six-month desert journey. I found Consuela and made sure she kept the urns outside full; they'd need the fuel for the long day. Not that the days were particularly long this time of year, but a film production starts before dawn and goes until after dark.

Then I went outside. It was chilly, not quite freezing: there was no wind to speak of (thanks to our resident weather wizard, though nobody but me knew that), and the sun, still low on the horizon, was wintry but bright.

On one side of the lawn was a crowd—a stagger? a shamble?—of zombies. There was something extra-eerie about the way they stayed put, calm and patient, waiting for instructions. A few were getting into character by swaying back and forth or making zombie-faces, but mostly they just stood there, a bunch of corpses at a bus stop for the afterlife.

The camera equipment and lights were all set up on the other end of the lawn, the presence of the zombies making the whole thing feel like some sort of standoff between a group of monsters and the high-tech mad-scientist army opposing them, the towering arclights and elaborate camera lenses about to spew forth deadly beams of energy.

But not until the woman throwing the fit between the two got out of the way.

I could easily hear her all the way from the front door. Considering the size of the lawn, that was impressive; you could play football on it and still have room for spectators on either side. The director, Fortunato "Lucky" Trentini, was obviously taking full advantage of that green expanse, or was at least trying to. Despite his nickname, though, he was currently being assailed by a monster even older and nastier than the undead: the Hollywood diva.

"—are you kidding me? Is that what this is, some kind of joke? THIS IS MY CAREER!"

The woman in question was Natalia Cardoso, the so-called star of the movie (and yes, writing what she said in all caps is necessary. Italics, while conveying a certain forcefulness, do not fully express the kind of bug-eyed fury I'm talking about here) was demonstrating not only her acting ability but her vocal range. I'm talking screaming, spit flying out of her mouth, arms flailing like Kermit the Frog on meth. Too bad it was about the only convincing performance she seemed capable of; once the cameras started rolling her eyes glassed over and her flesh grew bark.

Which is not at all a nice thing to say. But Natalia was not at all a nice person, so much so that every time I dealt with her I had to frame it in my mind as a personal challenge. So far I hadn't let her score any points off me, but the woman was abrasive enough to clean stainless steel.

I listened for a moment—mostly gauging saliva velocity and verbal intensity—then slipped my best professional smile into place and headed toward Hurricane Nat.

"—it was supposed to be lunge, swipe, miss, not lunge, grab, yank! That's a completely different scene!"

Trentini was in his twenties, with a black puffball of curly hair like an ink-stained dandelion. He wore a down-filled blue parka and jeans, thick-framed black glasses, and a look of desperation. "Come on, Natty. It was a mistake, okay? These are amateur zombies, all right? We spent more on their makeup than their paychecks. You tell them to shamble and stumble and moan, they do okay—anything more than that, we're rolling the dice. I'll have a word with them, make sure they understand what we're trying to do in this scene."

She gave him a look that would have made a death ray fall in love. "That's not good enough. One of those brain-dead idiot morons actually *grabbed* me. I want him *gone*."

Trentini's voice was low and reasonable; Natalia's was not. This was a performance, all right, but it wasn't for the director; it was for the benefit of the poor belated and be-latexed extras over by the undead bus stop. She wanted them to know that they were expendable and she wasn't, and she wasn't going to be subtle about it. Personally, I think Trentini could have made a better movie by just giving her a chain saw, telling her one of them got her latte order wrong, and then following her around with a camera.

I know what you're thinking: None of this was my problem. I had my own potential disasters to worry about, so why borrow trouble from somewhere else? Was I such a masochist that I had to fling myself blindly into the whirling blades of whatever crisis was currently revving its engine?

No.

But it *was* my job to keep things running smoothly and the guests happy. And while I prefer to prevent calamity whenever possible, sometimes all you can do is wait until the storm passes—and have lots of warm blankets, soup, and first-aid supplies on hand. Which was, more or less, what I was preparing to do.

At the moment it was a matter of timing. I did my best to match my pace to her seethe, and did pretty well; she ramped up at a fairly predictable rate. Critical detonation in five, four, three . . .

"—I don't *care* if you don't know who it was! Make one of them admit it!"

Trentini shook his head carefully, as if he were afraid it was about to fall off. "How? Threaten to take away their brain rations?"

Two, one . . .

"You think this is a *joke*? That's *it*! I am not shooting this scene until you deal with the problem!"

Boom.

She spun around in her ripped Victorian gown—which, admittedly, was made to spin—and stormed off as I arrived. She ignored me completely, which was just about perfect as far as I was concerned.

I glanced back at her, pretending to be mildly puzzled but really just waiting for her to get out of earshot. When she'd stalked far enough away, I smiled at the director and said, "Mr. Trentini. Just came out to let you know that our maintenance people have dealt with the electrical problem, so you shouldn't be having any more outages. Lunch will be Vietnamese spring rolls with rice noodles and lemongrass chicken, and our regular masseuse is dropping by at three. I know you're busy, but she's willing to do a ten-minute back and shoulders right here on the lawn. I'm setting up a heated tent to one side and she's bringing her own chair. Oh, and I tracked down that craft beer you were raving about yesterday—there'll be a case on ice in your room by five."

He looked at me blankly, and for just an instant I wondered if I'd read him wrong. Some people—okay, many people—will react to being yelled at by immediately finding someone else to yell at, and even being nice to them is no guarantee they'll react the same way.

"Foxtrot," he said. "Will you marry me?"

"Can't," I said with a grin. "Too busy. You know how much planning a wedding takes?"

"Yes, I do." He sighed and rubbed his forehead with one thumb and a forefinger. "Because I'm married to the devil. And by married, I mean chained for eternity, and by devil I mean this project—"

"Lucky! Lucky, I gotta talk to you!" The man yelling at us from over by the cameras wore a bright orange puffy coat with a white fur-lined hood. As he jogged toward us, Lucky turned his face away and murmured, "And him."

I checked the buckles on my professional smile, made sure it was still firmly strapped in place. Yep. "Mr. Rolvink," I said pleasantly.

He stopped just short of us and leered in my general direction. "Foxtrot! You know, it's not too late to take me up on my offer. I could make you a *star*." He said this with absolutely no trace of irony or even playfulness; his delivery was more of the car-salesman, I'm-being-so-sincere-it-hurts sort. He had a tan that came out of a bottle, a body that came from a personal trainer he mentioned at every opportunity, and the worst comb-over I've ever seen. If he just shaved his head, he might be passably attractive—in a purely physical way—but those stringy, greasy strands plastered over the top of his skull were the tonsorial equivalent of a horrifying five-car pileup. I kept expecting to see a fleet of tiny police cruisers and ambulances come zooming along his hairline and screech to a stop on his forehead.

"Thanks, but I'm happy with my current position in the solar system," I said. "Besides, you already have a star. Though she seems to be burning a little hot this morning—"

Rolvink turned his attention to Lucky, like I was a TV channel he was bored with. "Lucky, Lucky, Lucky. You have to treat Natalia right. She's very . . . *passionate* about what she does, y'know?" He raised his eyebrows in a hey-you're-a-guy-so-of-course-you-do way. "You just need to *channel* that. She's gonna turn in a great performance, I guarantee it. Didn't she ace the finale you shot yesterday?"

"She killed it, yeah," said Lucky. I got the feeling he and Rolvink were using the expression in very different ways, but I kept my mouth shut.

Rolvink chuckled and clapped him on the back. " 'Course she did. And we're still on schedule, right?"

"More or less," Lucky sighed. "We'll wrap primary shooting tonight, do a few pickup shots tomorrow and the next day—mostly zombie stuff, maybe a few scenes with Tervo. He's got some ideas for a different take on what we did before, and they sound interesting. It's about his character's motivations—"

"Yeah, no, I don't think so. Get what you need today, all right? I mean, *we* can stick around for a few days so you can edit footage, but I gotta send the crew home after tomorrow at the latest. These union guys don't work cheap, you know?"

What he wanted was to enjoy ZZ's free hospitality for a few more days while cutting costs wherever he could. Not really surprising, considering the film's budget, but not good news for me.

Lucky frowned. "I thought we were okay on the financing. You told me—"

"I know what I told you. Just wrap things up, okay?" Rolvink's voice suddenly had that strained, overly polite, not-in-front-of-the-kids tone; he didn't want to discuss this in my presence.

Lucky, though, wouldn't take the hint. When he wasn't behind a camera he came across as nervous and unsure of himself, but that changed when he was on set. Directing called for many different skills, but the most important was the ability to be in charge; try to take that away and you're in for a fight.

"Is this about that blogger's article?" Lucky asked. "Look, you can't listen to people like that. You pay attention to every negative opinion that pops up on the 'Net, you'll make yourself crazy. We have nothing to worry about—"

"Do I *look* worried?" Rolvink said, holding his hands wide and smiling. To anybody else, maybe not—but he did to me. I'm used to working around people in high-pressure environments, and I've developed a very fine sense of when that pressure is starting to get to someone. Rolvink wasn't about to blow, but I could see how hard he was trying to look calm and relaxed. I wasn't fooled.

Neither was Lucky, but there wasn't much he could do about it. "I'll . . . get it done," he said quietly.

"Great, great." Having gotten what he wanted, Rolvink's interest in Lucky's side of the conversation blew away like smoke and he turned his attention back to me. "And what about you, beautiful—got a little downtime coming?"

I'm very detail-oriented, so I catch things other people don't. And in that instant when Rolvink mentally dismissed Lucky and focused on me, I saw what's called a microexpression cross the director's face. Microexpressions are very fast, sometimes lasting only one twenty-fifth of a second, but you can catch them if you're really paying attention. They often reveal an emotion the person is trying to hide, or sometimes an emotion so buried the person isn't aware of it themselves.

The emotion I saw on Lucky Trentini's face was rage.

"You ever wanna hit the hot tub," Rolvink continued, "I'm sure your boss could dig up a bikini for you. Or you could go without—wouldn't matter to me."

Normally, I'm unfazed by being hit on. I've had more passes thrown at me than an NFL player, and even the highly inappropriate ones can usually be dealt with by deliberately ignoring them or deflecting them with humor. Most guys will get the hint and back off, and if they don't I politely excuse myself and leave. Should someone try to prevent me from leaving, it becomes a very different situation and I respond much less politely. Very rarely have I found myself in a situation where it went beyond that, and in every single case it went very, very badly for the other person involved. Being tough is an attitude, not a physical attribute, and the very worst person to have angry at you isn't somebody large—it's somebody smart.

I am pretty damn smart.

But Maurice Rolvink was my least favorite kind of sleazeball: the kind that wouldn't give up. His game wasn't so much to get me in bed—he knew his chances of that were zero to minus zero—as to just get a rise out of me. He'd approach, spout some clichéd pickup line, watch for my reaction and then try again. It was less annoying than it was tedious, like swatting at a cloud of bugs that just refused to go away. I guess he figured that he could eventually wear me down to the point I'd snap at him, which he would consider a victory.

Sadly, he had no idea who he was dealing with.

"Oh, Mr. Rolvink," I said. "You *know* I'm not waterproof. Besides, immersing me in water above one hundred and three degrees would invalidate my warranty." I gave him my blankest, emptiest smile and waited for his response.

As I expected, he blinked and then laughed. "Ah, Fox, you're a riot. A robot, right. This is a zombie flick, remember? Not sci- fi."

I could have schooled him on all the different genres zombie movies can fit into, but tossing information at guys like Maurice is like throwing peanuts at a snake; it's mildly entertaining, but all you're really doing is wasting peanuts and annoying the snake. What I actually wanted was a good exit line, and now I had it. Of course, I had to throw in a few hammy robot steps, but once I was moving I just kept going.

That was the plan, anyway. But then Rolvink called after me, "Hey! What's that cat doing out here? I thought I said no animals on set!" And I came to an abrupt, jerky halt before I'd gone more than ten feet.

I saw a black-and-white blur disappear into the bushes beside the front door. *Tango,* I thought with exasperation. Of course she'd gotten out; nothing could stop a determined feline.

Tango! I called mentally, but she wasn't answering. I saw movement, then another blur of black-and-white as she sprinted out of the bushes and around the corner of the house. I scowled and went after her.

When I turned the corner, she was gone.

3.

It's useless to chase a cat. They are faster, more agile, sneakier, and can go places you can't. However, I thought I knew where Tango was headed. So I didn't try to catch her—I just paused and then changed direction, as if I'd suddenly thought of something I needed to do over that-away, but there was no hurry in actually doing it. Much like a cat.

I made my way around the far end of the house, and down the little path, and around the pool, and finally over to the tall wooden gate in the hedge that divides the grave-yard from the rest of the estate proper.

I may have mentioned the presence of an animal grave-yard previously, and what with all the other weirdness it's entirely possible it slipped right by you. Don't blame your-self, it's my fault.

So. Here's the thing.

The animal graveyard in question is not only right next door but technically part of the grounds, since ZZ owns the land. Also, it's really big; at more than fifty thousand plots of varying shapes and sizes, it's been the final destination for many a beloved pet for over a hundred years. Except *final destination,* as it turns out, is not exactly accurate.

See, animals have their own afterlives. And because the universe is actually a much fairer place than most people think, pets who die can reunite with their former owners once *they're* dead, too (or, you know, the other way around). They accomplish this through portals, grave-site gateways that let the animals pop out of their afterlife and hop, scamper, crawl, or fly over to a portal into the human one. This is made possible by having the graves of so many different species (including urns full of human cremains) all in one place. Not so much for mystical reasons, either: it's more like building a train station at the spot where a bunch of different railway lines intersect.

Now, I know what you're thinking. Pet cemetery plus zombies equals horrific outcome (not to mention massive copyright infringement). But that's not how the Great Crossroads works, not at all; it's all about love surviving death, not shambling monstrosities clawing their way out of the ground. Virtually all the ghosts in the Great Crossroads are simply travelers, on their way from their own special paradise to visit a much-loved person in another; that's about as far from a stomach-twisting horror story as you can get.

That being said, there are exceptions.

We call them prowlers. Lost spirits, not quite wild, not quite domesticated. They're drawn to the Crossroads by the activity and the emotion, but they're too confused or wary to actually cross over into whatever animal heaven they belong in. They hang around like homeless outpatients at a bus station, and sometimes they can be unpredictable—even violent.

Standing right at the threshold, blocking my way, were two people—one of whom I knew quite well, the other of which I'd only met online.

"Foxtrot!" Keene beamed at me. He's a great beamer; he's got one of those wide, toothy smiles, framed by dimples and topped by eyes that practically twinkle with mischief. The bushy, rock-star hair helps too, but he'd be boyishly cute even with a shaved head. "Yemane just got here. I had to show him the graveyard, first thing."

The other one was Yemane Fikru. The name was Eritrean in origin, which was kind of odd for a blue-eyed, blond man with dreads and a reddish-orange beard. When I'd asked him about it online, he'd told me it was a chosen name, meant to reflect his beliefs as opposed to his genetic heritage. He wore an oversized bright-blue T-shirt, black yoga pants, and sandals, and didn't seem cold at all.

"Hey, Foxtrot," Yemane said, putting out his hand to shake mine. "Nice to finally meet you. Great place you have here." His grip was firm but gentle, and he put his other hand over mine for just a second before breaking contact. He wasn't beaming quite as broadly as Keene, but his smile was warm and open.

"Thanks, but it's not mine—I only work here. Which means if there's anything you need, just let me know. I aim to please, and I'm a pretty good shot." It's one of my standard introductions, but most people don't react the way Yemane did: He shook his head and laughed.

"No, I don't mean the house," he said. "I was talking about *this.*"

He swept his arm around, indicating the graveyard. "It's amazing. I can *feel* its significance."

Normally when people make statements like that I have to make a conscious effort not to roll my eyes, but Yemane appeared sincere; the look on his face was just short of rapture. Then he seemed to catch himself, and turned back to me with a wry grin. "I mean, obviously it's significant to the people who buried their pets here. I just—I can tell it's a special place. A . . . *Great* place."

He put just enough emphasis on the word that I could hear the capital letter. I nodded, but tried not to show anything other than bland agreement. "Yes, it's quite impressive. Over fifty thousand animals are interred here, and the cremated remains of more than two hundred people are right alongside their pets."

I was waiting to see if he'd make some sort of veiled comment about crosses or roads, but he didn't. He just nodded back, looking solemn. "That's a lot of souls. Must be quite the responsibility."

A responsibility that happened to be mine, though only a select few were supposed to be aware of that—and Yemane definitely wasn't on the list. "I . . . guess so," I said. I really didn't know what else to say.

Fortunately Keene is never at a loss for words, and he jumped right in with, "Lucky that's not your domain, eh, Trot? You've got enough on your plate as it is—including a zoo full of animals still among the living. But not to worry; Coop's got matters well in hand."

Cooper was the graveyard's caretaker, the one who cut the grass and maintained the graves. He and Keene got along just fine, mostly because Coop was an old hippie and Keene was . . . well, let's just say an enthusiastic fan of chemical recreation.

"I can't wait to meet him," Yemane said. "I'm sure he has some incredible stories to tell."

"You two will get along like a house on fire," Keene said. "Most likely a greenhouse, if I know old Coop."

"Don't take up too much of his time," I said. "He's still got a job to do." Which made me sound like a real buzzkill, but if Foxtrot wasn't my middle name—which, technically, it wasn't—then it would probably be Responsibility.

"We'll stay aware," said Yemane. He said it as if I'd just warned them about voracious bears in the woods and he was assuring me they wouldn't get eaten.

"Come on then," said Keene, motioning to Yemane as he stepped into the graveyard. "Let me introduce you to my muse. You and him will get along famously, I'm sure." He wasn't talking about Cooper now, but the ghost of a nocturnal primate named Jeepers, the only galago buried here. Keene liked to hang out at his graveside when he was stuck on a new song; he claimed the bush baby was a kindred spirit who helped him through creative tough spots. I'd seen Jeepers myself, though I'd never talked to him.

Yemane still stood at the threshold to the graveyard. He took a deep breath, exhaled, then slowly took a step inside and stopped. Nothing dramatic occurred, but he looked around as if seeing the place for the first time. "Far out," he murmured.

I couldn't help myself; I looked around, too. Ghosts had this brilliance to them, the colors of their coats or feathers or scales so sharp and vivid they looked like a special effect. Even black or brown seemed to shine.

What my eyes took in was this: a slow, stately line of brilliant green iguanas, trundling along; a tightly scrunched-together herd of hamsters flowing over the crest of a hill like some sort of ever-shifting white, orange, brown, and black quilt; a huge Great Dane with a coat of black chrome, bounding over (and through) headstones with glee, tongue lolling out of his mouth like a gleaming pink neon slug; and a single blue-and-green parrot perched on a headstone, feathers glowing as if lit from within, seemingly amused by all the activity.

Rainbow Bridge, nothing. It should be called the Rainbow Turnpike.

"Foxtrot," Yemane said softly. "Before you go—I wanted to ask you something."

"Sure. What is it?"

"I saw a cat when I got here. A black-and-white one."

"Oh, that's Tango. Yeah, she lives here, has the run of the place. Though actually, at the moment, we're trying to keep her indoors so she doesn't screw up any of the filming."

"Yeah?" Yemane said. "I thought saw her run into the graveyard just a minute ago."

"Really?" said Keene. "Funny, I completely missed that."

"What's your question?" I asked.

"Uh—just wanted to know if she lived here, that's all. I love cats. But she seemed kinda skittish."

Which is when I finally spotted a feline form, peering out from behind a headstone just beyond Keene and Fikru. *Aha,* I thought. *Gotcha, kitty!*

And then I realized it wasn't Tango at all.

The resemblance was remarkable, right down to the white almost-question-mark on her face, but after the first shocked second I realized I was looking at an entirely different tuxedo cat.

A dead one.

None of the animal spirits are actually bound to the graveyard, but the regulars rarely venture beyond its boundaries. It wasn't unheard of for a ghost to show up near or even in the mansion, but it wasn't something that happened often.

And I'd never seen it happen with a cat.

I suppose I'd always assumed it was a territorial thing, with Tango claiming the grounds for her own; while she's still among the living, she could see animal spirits as well as Whiskey or I could.

By *skittish* Fikru clearly meant *not-among-the-living*, because obviously he'd seen the ghost kitty and not Tango. Which he really shouldn't have been able to do—but at least he wasn't seeing the daily parade of spectral animals I was. Or if he was, he was doing an awfully good job of hiding it.

"Well, thanks for letting me know," I said. "I'll keep an eye out and try to herd her back inside. Have you been up to your rooms yet?"

"We'll head up presently," Keene said. "Going to have a bit of a wander around here first. All right?"

"Sure. Anytime you're ready." I performed Standard Professional Exit Number 2, the Nod and Smile While Turning, and walked briskly away.

Tango's ghostly twin was probably just another deceased feline, one who decided to investigate the nearest house while between portals. Sure. If my middle names were Foxtrot and Responsibility, then your average cat's was Curiosity and Impulse. It all made perfect sense.

But why had Yemane been able to see it?

I went into the house via a back door, the one that opens into the kitchen. Ben wasn't around, and neither was Tango. I decided to make myself another mug of tea while I was there.

The door opened and a woman strode in, cursing under her breath. She was short, stocky, and dressed entirely in black. Her makeup was more restrained than gothic, and her hair was long, black, and braided. She had a huge steel coffee mug in one hand, a backpack in the other, and murder in her eyes.

"Hey, Catree," I said. "How goes the war?"

"I'm gonna nuke the site from orbit," Catree snarled.

She headed straight for the espresso maker. "It's the only way to be sure."

Catriona Christie was my counterpart. What I did for ZZ, she did for the director. Normally, that would give her the title of production assistant—but that wouldn't be fair or accurate. Catree was also their special-effects guru, in charge of everything from pyrotechnics to prosthetics. She was the one who made the fog roll in, the guns bark, and the zombies' heads explode. Right now she looked like her own was about to do the same.

"I hear you," I said. "You don't actually *have* nukes, right? Because that would require massive amounts of paperwork, and I really don't have time for that."

She grinned at me as she dropped her pack on the floor and set about expertly assembling an espresso. "Nah, that stuff's a pain to work with. Give me good old-fashioned high explosives, any day. Or concentrated acid. Or maybe just cyanide."

I dunked the tea bag in my mug of steaming water. "Sounds like you have someone specific in mind. Or are you just feeling slaughtery in general?"

"Little of both. Yes, there's someone I'd cheerfully give a grenade without a pin right about now, but there's no guarantee it'd be the *same* person in an hour."

"You like to spread the mayhem around. Give everyone a chance."

"Hell, yes. An equal-opportunity maniac, that's me."

I liked Catree. She understood the pressures of doing a job like mine, juggling a million different variables, dozens of volatile personalities, and every possible way they could intersect to produce a crisis. None of her current crankiness would be on display while she was actually working; it was a sign of respect and camaraderie that she felt comfortable enough with me to show how she was really feeling. Over the last few days we'd become more than friends—we'd become allies. I could go to her for just about any information about the film production, and she could come to me for just about any resource I could lay my hands on. Between us, we kept two intricate, unstable organizations functioning, and most of the people who belonged to those groups were blissfully unaware of that fact.

"This production is doing its best to kill me," she announced cheerfully as she poured the first shot into her mug and started making another. "But it's gonna have to work harder. Three days in and I can still form coherent sentences. That's some kind of ribbity-dibbity-doodad, gazunga?"

I leaned back against the steel counter and took a sip of my tea. "Oh, you've hit gazunga? Haven't gone *there* in a while. Not since that time on tour with Slotterhaus, probably."

She raised an eyebrow. "You toured with Slotterhaus? Man, that's hard-core. I'm assuming you weren't a groupie."

I shuddered. "Definitely not. More like a groupie wrangler, which meant trying to deflect the ones that were underaged, likely to overdose, or actually psychotic."

"So, just about all of them."

"Pretty much. Mostly I handed out room keys to hotels from our previous stop, along with directions that made no sense. 'Yeah, the Hotel Pompadour, just off the interstate. Tell the concierge Becky sent you.' They'd wander off with stars in their extremely dilated eyes, and I'd never see them again."

She considered this as she pulled and poured another shot of espresso. "Hmm. I'd say that was cruel, but the souvenir—and the tale—they wound up with was probably better than anything Slotterhaus could have given them. If half the stories I've heard are true."

"Depends. Which stories have you heard?"

"The swimming pool, the motorcycle, and the bungee cords?"

"True."

"The twenty-three strippers?"

I rolled my eyes. "That one always gets exaggerated. It was seventeen."

"The bar mitzvah, the soccer mom, and the butterscotch schnapps?"

"Unfortunately. Had to work pretty hard to keep that one out of the papers."

I eyed the enormous metal mug she kept adding shots to. "Uh, just exactly how much espresso are you planning on drinking? Because I think you've already got enough to make a three-toed sloth do gymnastics."

"That reminds me of a joke. Knock knock."

"Who's there?"

"Coffee."

"Coffee who?"

"Who cares? COFFEE."

"That's pretty—"

"*COFFFFFFFEEEEEEEE.*" She made her eyes go wide and turned her grin up to full lunatic.

I studied her for a second and said, "That's part of the punch line, right?"

"Punch line? I know no punch line. I *am* gonna need an IV drip, though—got one handy?"

I shook my head. "I specialize in logistics, not technical support. And we both know you could build one in about two minutes, anyway—probably with what's in the magic backpack." I motioned with my mug toward the pack on the floor. It seemed to be composed entirely of duct tape and bumper stickers, though Catree claimed there was actual canvas some unknown number of layers deep. It was festooned with carabiner clips in various bright colors and sizes, and had numerous zippered pouches zap-strapped to it, too.

"Right!" said Catree. "That reminds me—I brought some cool stuff to show you." She picked the bag off the floor, unzipped a pouch, and pulled out—a hand. A very life-like one, with bits of gory redness at one end and cracked, dirty fingernails at the other. "Check it out," Catree said, offering it to me as proudly as a toddler with a frog.

I took it. It was heavier than I expected, but the level of detail was remarkable—it even had fingerprints.

And then it grabbed me.

Yes, I shrieked. And yes, I instinctively flung it away in some random direction. Then I glared at Catree, who was giggling maniacally. "Oh, man . . . the look on your face. That one's an evergreen, it never gets old."

I laughed despite myself. "Okay, you got me. Remote control?"

She showed me a keyfob-sized device she'd palmed when she opened the pack. "Servos powered by lithium-ion, activation via Bluetooth. Fully—ahem—digital."

"And—ahem—handcrafted, too?"

"Absolutely. Ahem. My handiwork, of course."

"Okay, the puns are bad, but you know what's really getting out of hand? Saying *ahem* every time."

"Yeah, I think you put your finger on it."

"Can we stop now?"

"Oh, get a grip. *Ahem.*"

I made a mental note to work out some sort of devious, clever revenge—hey, I do have access to a shape-shifting dog and a bunch of ghosts—and then changed the subject.

"Okay, you win the pundit award. Got anything else to show me?"

"Sure." She retrieved the hand, stuck it in her pack, and then rummaged around and pulled out a Tupperware container. "Here we go."

"I'm no fool," I said. "*You* open it."

"I intend to." She pulled the lid off, then reached in and used her thumb and one finger to gently pull out . . .

A cube-shaped cloud.

It was about the size of a child's wooden block, perfectly square, and looked exactly as if someone had filled a soap bubble with smoke, convinced it to grow four corners and six flat sides, then popped the bubble without the smoke noticing. Impossibility, cubed.

She set it down on the counter. It didn't jiggle or shimmy the way gelatin would have, and it was faintly translucent in a very smoky way.

I reached toward it, then stopped. It seemed incredibly delicate, like even looking at it too hard would make it dissolve. "Can I touch it?"

"Sure. It's stronger than it looks—a lot stronger. Watch this."

Her giant metal mug was now at least half full of pure espresso. She set it squarely on top of the cube, which took its weight as easily as a coaster. "See?"

"Wow. What is that stuff?"

She lifted the mug and took a sip. "Ah, nectar of the gods . . . it's called aerogel. One of the lightest substances on Earth, and incredibly robust structurally. Go ahead, touch it."

I did, putting one fingertip on the top where the mug had rested. It wasn't even warm. "It doesn't feel like a gel. More like Styrofoam."

"It's derived from a gel, which is where the name comes

from. I like the other terms for it better: frozen smoke, or solid air. Isn't it great?"

I picked it up carefully the way she had. It weighed almost nothing, like it wasn't really there. "Wow, again. What do you do with it?"

"All kinds of things, from sports equipment to super-capacitors. NASA used some to collect space dust from a comet. Me? I just like to look at it. Reminds me of why I got into this business in the first place."

I frowned and put the block down. "To collect space dust from comets?"

"To use science to make magic." She stared at the block, and for an instant she seemed a little sad. Then she popped it back in its Tupperware container and snapped the lid in place. "Some days I need to look at it longer than others."

"Ah. Today's one of those days, huh?"

She stuck the Tupperware back in her pack. "Nah, not really. Natalia Cardoso's a pain, but I've dealt with worse. Of course, most of them were actually talented, as opposed to just sleeping with the producer."

"Really? I'm shocked. What a shocking piece of shock-ing news that has totally shocked me. Also, I'm shocked. Shockingly."

Catree hoisted the backpack over one shoulder. "Yeah, she may as well wear a T-shirt with CASTING COUCH IS COMFY on it. Maybe I'll get one printed in Japanese and give it to her."

"I like that. Tell her it says QUEEN OF THE ZOMBIES—I think she'd accept pretty much any title that implies she's in charge."

<Are you talking about me?> Tango did that feline ninja thing, where they appear seemingly from nowhere. She claims she can't actually walk through walls, but I'm not convinced.

"Hey, Tango," Catree said. She bent down and stroked Tango's back, running her hand all the way to the tip of her tail. Tango stretched luxuriantly and began to purr. "On the other hand, I also get to work with Jaxon Nesbitt. Who really shouldn't even be here."

"Why not? I thought he had talent to burn."

"He does. The question is, why is he burning it here? The last indie film he was in got nominated for an Oscar, and when this wraps he's signed to do a big Hollywood film for megabucks. Honestly, he's so much better than this flick I'm starting to wonder who *he's* sleeping with."

"I'm guessing that's not uncommon for Mr. Nesbitt."

Catree giggled again. "Yeah, he's easy on the optics, that's for sure. Too bad he's not a little more social."

Jaxon Nesbitt had spent most of his time holed up in his room: He came out for filming and the obligatory dinner gatherings, then vanished again whenever he wasn't needed.

I shrugged. "He obviously values his privacy. Or maybe he's conducting satanic rituals in his room. Either way, as long as he doesn't burn the place down it's none of my business."

"Yeah, well, thanks for the go-juice. Gotta run." Catree was out the door before she even finished her sentence, which is just how people in our line of work say good-bye. It might seem rude but it's actually a sign of respect, acknowledging how busy we both are by not wasting any time with acknowledgment.

It's a Zen thing. I'd explain further, but I don't have the time.

<*Hey, Toots. I want to go outside.*> That was Tango's version of a polite request.

I shook my head. "No can do, kitty. Strict orders from the director that all animals have to stay indoors and away from being underfoot."

She stared at me in that unblinking feline way that makes you wonder what they're thinking. In my case, though, I knew. *<Oh, you'll listen to a director? Here's some direction for you. Open the door and let me out.>*

"No."

<Let me out.>

"No."

<Me. Out.>

"Stop it."

<Out.>

"That's not going to—"

<OUT.>

"There is no way—"

<OUUUUUUUUUUUUT.>

Ever heard a cat yowl? Yeah. Ever had one yowl in your ear? How about *between* your ears? It's just about as annoying as you might think, except you *can't* think.

Cut it out! I thought back at her, as loudly as I could. *I'm doing this for your own good. There are explosives and big pieces of machinery and all sorts of equipment out there. I don't want you to get hurt.*

<Plus, you're just doing your job, right?>

I frowned at her. That had almost sounded reasonable. "Well, yes. The guests are my responsibility, so I have to make sure they're happy—"

<You have other responsibilities, though.>

"You mean the graveyard? I don't see your point."

<You have two jobs. I only have one—looking out for the Crossroads. My single responsibility plus your half responsibility is greater than your other half responsibility.>

When did my cat learn how to do math? "Doesn't matter. You and Whiskey being unavailable for a few days shouldn't . . ."

<Shouldn't what? Leave the Great Crossroads com-

pletely unprotected and unpatrolled? Or are you going to keep an eye on it twenty-four seven while doing your other job, too?>

Dammit. She knew exactly which button to push, and right now she was mashing the SENSE OF DUTY one repeatedly with a dainty white paw. "Look, it's not like there's been anything unusual happening. The only spirit I've seen lately has been a single, very ordinary ghost cat."

I knew as soon as I said it that I'd made a mistake.

<What ghost cat?>

"Just your run-of-the-kitten-mill ghost cat, prowling around the front door. Ran away as soon as I spotted it, right back to the graveyard. Nothing unusual about it, probably just curious."

<Uh-huh. This ordinary ghost cat—what did it look like?>

"Um. Well . . . a bit like you, actually. Black and white."

Her voice in my head was as silky as her fur. *<I see. How much like me, exactly?>*

I gave up. "Pretty much the same. Even had the little question mark between your eyes."

<That's not a question mark. You say this doppelgänger was snooping around my front door? And you let it escape?>

"I *tried* to chase it—"

Tango gave her head a quick shake of annoyance. *<You tried to chase a cat. A ghost cat. How'd that work out?>*

"It got away."

<Amazing. I sure am glad you're the one in charge, what with your bendy thumbs and giant brain. Wouldn't want to trust poor, klutzy me with something as dangerous as a doorknob.>

"Okay, okay. You have your strengths, I have mine. But let's not get carried away. How is this a problem?"

<It's a problem because there's a ghost cat running around that looks like me, in my territory. What if it's not a cat at all?>

That brought me up short. Whiskey's a shape-changer, but he's not the only one. Thunderbirds can shift between human and avian forms, and apparently so can their biggest enemy—a nasty creature called an Unktehila. We'd never met one in the flesh, but supposedly they can look like just about anything.

Including Tango. Or a honey badger.

"Look," I said, "if there's a shape-shifting monster roaming around the grounds, there's even less reason to let you out."

<Shape-shifting and mind-controlling. Don't forget about the mind-controlling.>

Right. Unktehilas also supposedly had this big crystal implanted in their heads that let them influence people's minds, making them a paranoid's worst nightmare come to life. "I didn't forget. And like I said, no way are you going outside."

<Yes, I am—I'll even bet you a bag of catnip. See, you're not getting it, Toots. You need to send me out to investigate. If it is the Big Unk, we're in serious trouble and have to know right away. If it isn't, there's nothing to worry about.>

"But you can't—"

<Take it on? Of course not. This is a mission that calls for stealth, cunning, and keen observation. Now, out of the three Guardians of the Great Crossroads, which of us best fits that bill?>

She had me, and she knew it. "Promise me you'll stick to the graveyard and stay away from the film crew," I said.

She gave me a pitying look. *<Right. There's a supernatural snake-beastie scampering around disguised as*

me, and you think I'm going to waste my time with a bunch of Hollywood wannabes. Gimme some credit, Toots; I take my image a lot more seriously than that.>

I walked over to the kitchen door and opened it. "Just stay safe."

She strolled out with her tail high, as casually as . . . well, a cat. *<Sure. I'll take that bag of nip Ben keeps on the shelf beside the walk-in freezer; it's the good stuff. Later.>*

A few words on the subject of croquet:

It evolved from a much older game called lawn billiards, a sport in which you tried to fling large wooden balls through a central ring with giant spoons. This eventually gave way to hammering them through metal hoops instead, which probably both reduced the number of ball-related injuries and killed the craze for gigantic teacups. This game was called *Paille Maille* in France (derived from the Latin roots for "ball" and "mallet") and Pall Mall when King Charles II of England imported it as something fun to do on those huge palace lawns. Commoners love to imitate royalty but usually can't afford to; hitting a ball with a club, though, was something pretty much anyone could do. It became so popular that a London street wound up being named after the sport—the Pall Mall—and apparently sucking up to the monarchy like that paid off: The street itself became a very upscale, happening place that everybody else wanted to copy, including an American cigarette company that named their new brand after it. Which is why, the next time you take a big, cancerous drag on that Pall Mall, you can console yourself by remembering it was named after a game in which you try your best to hammer someone else's ball before they hammer yours.

While the Zoransky estate isn't anywhere near Palace

of Versailles size, it does feature some impressive expanses of grass. Both the front and back lawns take up a considerable amount of real estate, and croquet often happens. ZZ's son, Oscar, is a bit of a hustler with the hoops, and has relieved more than one of our guests of their folding money.

Keene is one of his victims. However, rather than holding a grudge, Keene's decided to take the approach that he's paying for lessons, and cheerfully loses to Oscar over and over again. But each time he loses by a little less, and even Oscar admits that someday he won't lose at all. In the meantime they have a lot of fun while drinking entirely too much, which is something they're both very good at.

"I say," Oscar remarked as I strolled up to them on the back lawn, "I believe you're blocking my wicket." Oscar often sounds like he was born in the British Isles—he wasn't—but it gets especially pronounced when he has a wooden mallet in his hand.

"Yes, no wicket-blocking, please," Keene added. He wore a long woolen overcoat, a furry white hat with ears that stood up, and fingerless gloves.

I stepped out of the way while Oscar lined up his shot. "Awfully chilly for outdoor sports, don't you think?" I said. "Frosty, even."

"Nonsense," said Oscar. He was dressed just as warmly as Keene, in a heavy overcoat, gloves, and a woolen hat. "Many activities take place in weather just such as this. Football, for instance."

" 'Course, this doesn't involve as much physical exertion," Keene said. "Or contact—except between balls."

"Yes, you're fond of pointing that out," said Oscar. He swung and knocked his ball through the next hoop. "Tell me, when is your thirteenth birthday? I'd like to get you a nice poster you can hang in your bedroom."

"Also, we have the advantage of alcoholic incentives," Keene said. "Through the hoop and over the gums, look out stomach, here it comes!" He pulled a small flask out of his pocket and unscrewed the top. Oscar did the same. They raised their respective drinks to me.

"Chin chin," said Oscar.

"To the Queen," said Keene. "Freddie Mercury, now there was a chap who knew how to rock." They both drank.

"Do you do that on every turn?" I asked.

"No, just when someone hoops," said Keene. "We maintain strict sportsmanly protocols at all times. No peeing on the field, either."

"I see," I said. "You guys are starting awfully early, aren't you?"

"All part of my strategy," said Keene. "Having proven he's my better when it comes to skill, I plan on beating Oscar through sheer endurance. Staying power, that's my secret weapon. Can't tour thirty cities in forty days if you're going to let a little thing like exhaustion stop you."

"Marathon croquet?" I said. "Interesting. Maybe I should call the Olympic committee."

"Don't bother," said Oscar. "Croquet hasn't been played in the Olympics since 1904, and even then it was an American bastardization called Roque. Why they dropped the first and last letters of the name I'll never know."

"It's just what you Yanks do," said Keene. "Take a perfectly good English word like *spanner* and mangle it into a wrench. Bloody annoying, it is."

I shook my head. "Well, be advised that the film crew may need this location later in the afternoon. They're using the front lawn for most of their shots, but that may change."

"Ah, yes, the zombies," said Keene. "I was having a word with the director earlier, and he said he might use my idea of having one of them be dispatched with a croquet mallet. Fits right into the theme, he said."

Oscar said something dry and dismissive in reply, but I didn't really catch it. I was staring at the ghost dog.

Unlike Whiskey, who's indistinguishable from the living article, this canine was definitely deceased: A collie, it had the brilliant, glowing sheen that most spirit animals seem to possess, its brown-and-white coat gleaming a luminescent bronze and pearl. It was trotting along next to the hedge, and did no more than glance in my direction before disappearing around the corner of the house much like the cat had, though it was heading in the opposite direction.

"Excuse me," I said. "Something I need to take care of right away." I strode off after it, though I wouldn't have been surprised if it was gone by the time I rounded the corner.

It wasn't, though. It was still moving at a steady pace alongside the house, and when it got to the far edge it stopped, peering around the corner.

I walked up to within a few feet and stopped, too. It was a beautiful dog, with the kind of calm elegance some collies just seem to exude. I didn't quite know what to do next; I could try to talk to it—all ghost animals seem to share a common tongue—but I was afraid if I did it would bolt.

Then I realized I was close enough to my office that I could probably talk to Whiskey in my head and he'd be able to pick it up. *Whiskey,* I thought. *Can you hear me?*

[I can. Has your shame at my unjust imprisonment become so great that you can no longer communicate with me face-to-face?]

More like I need your help and I'm willing to shamelessly ask for it.

[I live to serve.]

That would be more guilt-inducing if you were actually alive. A condition, by the way, also shared by the deceased collie I'm currently looking at. Any idea why one would have wandered away from the Crossroads and onto the estate?

[Not really. Is there something unusual about said collie?]

Not as such. It's just that this is the second animal ghostie I've encountered on the grounds today, and the other one bore an amazing resemblance to Tango.

[Does this one resemble me?]

Sure—if you were a regular spirit and posing as a collie. Otherwise, not so much.

[Maybe it smells like me.]

Maybe, but how would I know?

[You wouldn't. Does this suggest a possible course of action in your immediate future?]

Hold on there, Nosy. I'm not letting you out unless I absolutely have to. Right now all Lassie is doing is standing there watching.

[Watching what?]

Uh . . . I can't actually tell, since it's around the corner of the building. The film crew, I guess.

[Fascinating. Perhaps its former owner was an ersatz zombie as well.]

[No,] said a new voice in my head, [but he worked with a few.]

The collie turned his head to look at me. His mouth was open in a friendly doggy smile, and his warm brown eyes seemed slightly amused.

[Hello,] he said. [Hope you don't mind. It's been a long time since I was on set—I just couldn't resist taking a look.]

4.

Now:

Whiskey and I sprinted for the house. Most people would run away from an explosion, but not us. Like EMTs, fire-fighters, and cops, we'd been trained to head toward the disaster. Lucky us.

There was a house-sized black cloud over the mansion now, with a few trailing wisps emanating from the chimney. My detail-oriented brain noted that the little roof over the chimney that kept out the rain was gone, and a few seconds later I heard a metallic crash off to my left as we sprinted through the garden. Conclusion: The explosion had occurred in one of the fireplaces, channeling the blast up through the chimney like the barrel of a gun. The little tin roof had been the bullet, and what was left of it was now in pieces on the ground. Hopefully not on top of a guest.

Tango! I shouted telepathically. *Are you all right?*

<*What the Cat Shampoo was that?*> I didn't know where she was; she sounded angry and scared, but not hurt. <*Can't a feline enjoy a little catnip without being bombarded by artillery?*>

[She's fine. Stoned, but fine. Let's concentrate on searching for wounded.]

That's my dog—concerned, but pragmatic. Triage first, then we'll sort out the details.

We pushed our way through a crowd of gawking zombies and got to the front door just as ZZ, the makeup people, and the household staff came stumbling out. "Anybody hurt?" I yelled. "Anybody missing?"

ZZ headed straight for me, coughing. For a frozen instant I thought she'd been horribly maimed, but then I realized she was still made up as one of the walking dead. "Foxtrot!" she wheezed. "What—what was that?"

"One of the fireplaces blew up, I think." I did a quick head count and saw that Maurice Rolvink and Natalia Cardoso were the only ones not accounted for. Shondra Destry, our head of security, was on her cell phone, either talking to emergency services or calling in the marines; she's ex-military, so this sort of thing is right in her wheelhouse.

Ben rushed up to me, his face grim, and said, "Something blew up. You think there might be a fire?"

From the look on his face, I knew that was Thunderbird-code for *Do you think there should be a brief but intense rain shower in our immediate vicinity?*

I gave my head a brief shake. "Let me check. Two people might still be inside."

"How about Tango?'

<They did it. They finally did it.> Tango sounded even more disoriented, as well as something else. Melancholy?

Did what? I asked.

<Made it illegal. I didn't think they would, but they did. And now they're coming for me.>

Just calm down. Who are they *and what did they make illegal?*

<The Catnip Cops!>

I didn't have time for Tango's freakout. *You're fine.*

Go outside. If you're already outside, stay there. "Come on, Whiskey. Ben, you too." I headed for the open front door, and to their credit neither my dog nor my boyfriend protested or asked questions, just trooped right along behind me. I knew Shondra would have come with me if I'd asked, but I wanted her outside doing crowd control and keeping an eye out for any further danger.

There was smoke and dust in the air, but it wasn't too bad. I grabbed a fire extinguisher from the foyer—yes, I know where each and every one is located on the grounds—and looked around.

"Second floor," Ben said. "That's where it happened."

"How do you know?"

"Air talks to me. Right now, it's complaining that a whole bunch of it got pushed out of the way upstairs."

Cautiously, I crept up the stairs. Plaster crunched underfoot, and there were little swirling things in the air—bits of shredded paper and cloth, most likely. I could smell charred wood and melted plastic and something I couldn't identify.

[Trinitrotoluene. Or as it's more commonly known, TNT.]

"Dynamite?" Ben said. "That's not what I was expecting."

"Me either," I said grimly. So much for my working theory that somebody had tossed something volatile in one of the fireplaces by accident.

We reached the second floor, which was darker and smokier. No power, of course. Most of the light was coming from a doorway at the end of the hall that was missing its door, the remains of which were leaning against the corridor wall. A chilly breeze blew toward us—the blast had blown the windows in the room out. I'd have to make sure the back lawn was cleared of broken glass—

And then I realized that there was someone under that door.

I rushed down the hall, set down the fire extinguisher, and knelt. It was Natalia Cardoso, which made sense; it was her room that had blown up. She must have been outside when it happened—it looked as though the door had shielded her from the explosion itself, but had then torn free of its hinges and slammed her against the wall.

I checked her pulse. Still alive, but unconscious. "Help me move the door off her," I said to Ben. Once we got that out of the way, I checked her more thoroughly. She was bleeding from a cut over her eye, but I couldn't find any broken bones. She might have internal injuries, of course, but her breathing seemed normal. I pulled out my phone and called an ambulance, while Ben grabbed the fire extinguisher and took care of the few small fires guttering around the room.

I peered through the doorway. It looked like the blast had destroyed the wall directly above the fireplace, as if a bomb had been placed on the mantel. There had been a clock up there the last time I checked, but I was pretty sure I'd remember if it had been wired to a stick of dynamite. Because, you know, I have a *terrific* memory—

"Um," I said. "Ben? There's something else you should probably know about before the police arrive. Not because it directly involves you or anything, but just—you know, FYI."

Ben glanced over at me and gave the extinguisher one last burst at a stubbornly smoldering piece of wreckage. "What?"

"Whiskey and I found a body on the grounds this morning. It had been—partially eaten. Probably by our honey badger."

Ben stared at me. "Well, haven't we had a busy morning. Who was it?"

"I don't know. Those parts weren't . . . there."

He nodded, obviously trying to process this new information. "The honey badger. Of course. Well, you did try to tell me just how evil he was, though this is really taking it to the next level. What *I* want to know is, who taught him how to make a bomb?"

"That's one theory . . ."

"Wait. It's so obvious. He's been talking to Wile E. Coyote. I mean, what with all the talking animals around here, doesn't it make sense that they'd network?"

[I'm not sure if he's being facetious or just in shock.]

I looked around at the blackened remains of the room. "I'm not sure he isn't right . . ."

"Lieutenant Forrester," I said.

"Ms. Lancaster," he replied. Forrester was a cop on the Hartville police force, which was too small to support a full-time detective but could afford one willing to pull double duty as a uniformed officer in a patrol car as well. I wasn't sure how the police union felt about that, but Forrester seemed okay with it. Today he was in plainclothes, which meant a dark-blue suit and tie. He'd gotten rid of the dreadlocks he used to wear, which I suppose made him look more professional. Too bad; I liked them.

"You're really trying to fast-track my career, aren't you?" Forrester said as he surveyed the blast damage. "Now I'll have to take night courses in bomb disposal, too."

I almost made a joke about killer homework, then thought better of it. I'd already shown him the body, and neither of us was really in the mood for humor. "Sorry. At least the blast didn't kill anyone."

"Yet," he said. "Natalia Cardoso is comatose and the hospital doesn't know if she'll pull through. Has Maurice Rolvink been located?"

"No. But his cell phone is still in his room, along with his wallet. I think we might have already found him, if you know what I mean."

Forrester nodded, his face gloomy. "Yeah, the corpse fits his description. But there's no identifying marks on it, including fingerprints. We'll have to wait for DNA results before we know for sure. What are your thoughts on this, Ms. Lancaster?"

I hesitated. "I'm no detective. But if the body in the trailer does turn out to be Rolvink, the bomb might have just been insurance. Apparently he and Natalia were spending time together."

"So she might have been collateral damage. Pretty cold-blooded, since she was almost certain to have been killed along with Rolvink."

I shrugged. "I don't know. But neither of them was terribly popular, at least around here. Natalia was a full-blown diva and Rolvink was—or maybe still is—an arrogant womanizer."

Forrester eyed me neutrally. "Sounds like you're putting yourself on the suspect list."

"Me? I'm the one who has clean up this mess. Or, you know, hire the people that are actually going to do it."

He sighed. "I know, I know. You're too busy to blow people up. You'd probably just outsource it."

"So I couldn't be an assassin, but I'm capable of hiring one?"

He smiled. "From what your employer tells me, you'd probably contact a dozen, interview six, and then take bids on the job."

I pretended to look offended. "I never take bids. I'd average the quotes and take the third from the top."

"Why that one?"

"The highest quote is always overpriced. The second highest is good, but never as good as they think they are. Third from the top is competent, experienced, and just a little bit hungry. The rest are playing it safe or desperate."

"See? This is why I asked for your thoughts, Ms. Lancaster. You always have an excellent grasp of the facts."

"It's what I'm paid for. Speaking of which, if you're done talking to me I should really get back to it."

"Go ahead. I'll be in touch later with some questions."

I nodded good-bye and left. Most of the explosions I dealt with were more metaphorical than actual, but the process of cleaning up the aftermath was surprisingly similar: make sure everyone was okay, assess the damage done, figure out what needed to be fixed immediately and what could wait, then get in touch with the appropriate professionals and start collecting quotes. The part of my brain in charge of making lists—which was at least a third of my cerebellum—had already started listing all the lists I needed to list. Listy, list list.

But I couldn't listen to my list-lust, because there was something much more important I needed to do first. Just to appease that part of my brain, I put it on a list of its own with only one item:

1. Question the honey badger.

Because, despite the overwhelming circumstantial evidence that pointed to Owduttf chowing down on the corpse, Tango's mention of the Unktehila had me questioning that theory. What if the honey badger was being framed?

What if Owduttf had eaten some of the remains, but wasn't the killer? What if the head and hands had been removed for another reason, and the chewing done afterward?

However, while I am able to converse with animal spirits, holding conversations with living beasties is beyond my abilities. Fortunately, Tango is fluent in the tongues of many species, including Honey Badger.

But first I had to find her.

I took the back stairs down to the main floor, which was unfair to all the people waiting to talk to me but utterly necessary. *Whiskey!* I called in my mind. *Have you located our erstwhile kitty?*

He replied right away. [I have. She's in the cabana, cowering under a pile of towels.]

<*I am not cowering! I'm recovering.*>

I headed straight there. Thankfully, at this time of year the cabana didn't see a lot of use, which is probably why she picked it.

The door was ajar. I poked my head inside and saw Whiskey lying on the floor by what I can only describe as a mountain of towels. The last time I'd been in here they'd all been neatly stacked and on top of a wicker table; now it seemed they'd been turned into some sort of fluffy termite mound.

"She's under there?" I said.

[She's under there.]

"Tango? It's okay. You can come out now."

<*Well, of course I can come out. Why wouldn't I be able to come out? I can come out anytime I want.*>

Nothing happened.

"Um. Tango? Why aren't you coming out?"

<*I don't feel like it.*>

I sighed and sank onto a wicker chair. "Right. Okay. Do you want to talk about it?"

<Talk about what? There's nothing to talk about and I'm definitely not hiding from anything and I'm perfectly comfortable under this gigantic pile of heavy, smothering fabric.>

[That sounded suspiciously like a request for help.]

<Then you should get your suspicion sensor checked. It was a bold statement of independence.>

[From a cat hiding under a pile of towels.]

"Whiskey, you're not helping. Tango, I need you. Now. We've got a honey badger to interrogate and I have to do it before Forrester figures out where the missing body parts have wound up."

<I am not hiding. It's just—that was some powerful nip, okay? The invisible mice almost got me.>

"Invisible mice?"

<Yeah. They're all over the place, but you can only see them when you've taken some really, really good catnip. Usually you can just chase 'em away, but this time they were armed.>

"*Armed* invisible mice. Armed with what, cocktail toothpicks?" I knew I shouldn't be encouraging the direction this conversation was taking, but sometimes after diving into the rabbit hole all you can do is fall.

<I wish. They went medieval on me—swords, spears, axes. But the catapults were the worst.>

[Shouldn't that be mouse-apults?]

"Again, not helping. Tango, I can assure you that there are no legions of invisible warrior mice in the immediate vicinity."

<How would you know?>

Well, she had me there. "Look, those mice weren't real. You were hallucinating."

<Prove it.>

[Oh, this should be good.]

I scowled at him. "No stuctural damage, kitty. Shouldn't tiny siege engines leave dents in the wall? I have observed no such dentage."

<Well, of course not. Superballs don't leave dents, they just boing all over the place.>

"Superballs. You mean those little bouncy things you get from vending machines?"

<Is that where they come from? I always wondered.>

[The real mystery here is where invisible mice carry spare change.]

"No, the real mystery is why I put up with either of you—one's a dope fiend and the other's just a fiend. Now come on out—it's time to go to work."

A black-and-white head emerged from under the towels and looked up at me through slitted eyes. *<Not gonna happen, Toots. Honey Badger is a tricky tongue at the best of times, and I'm not exactly at the top of my game, here. So unless you're okay with Owduttf's usual carnivorous lechery mixed with random gibberish, you really should let me get a little rest, 'kay?>* Her head disappeared under the towels again.

I groaned, but I could tell I wasn't going to convince her. Well, maybe I couldn't interrogate our resident appetite on four legs yet, but at the very least I could make sure Owduttf stayed put.

I hoped.

You might think it would be difficult to get through a crowd of confused and frightened actors, film crew members, domestic staff, and houseguests, and normally you'd be right. The fact that pretty much all of them knew me as the person to go to when they had a question or a request made this even harder, and the police presence just put a cherry on top of the pressure cooker.

So I didn't go through the crowd, I went around them. Out the back, behind the cabana, along the hedge, between the tennis courts and the stable, down the path only the gardener uses, and through a side gate onto the zoo grounds. Easy peasy, only a little squeezy. With Whiskey's nose to alert me to anyone coming toward us, we managed to make it to the honey badger pen without getting caught—though my cell phone was buzzing like a hive full of frustrated bees. I switched it to silent mode and put it away. ZZ would be upset that I wasn't answering, but I had to take care of this before anything else and I couldn't exactly explain my actions: *Oh, yeah, sorry I wasn't around to do my job during the emergency, but I had to discuss the dinner plans of our South African badger. No, I wasn't scheduling it as an activity, it was more along the lines of an exit interview. Yes, I could explain that in further detail, but believe me, you wouldn't enjoy it.*

Whiskey and I headed for the menagerie's clinic, a blocky one-story building painted a bright green. I strolled through the front door and found Caroline, our resident vet, giving eardrops to a skunk. The skunk wasn't happy about it, but Caroline seemed unfazed.

"I hope she's descented," I said.

"Me, too," said Caroline cheerfully. "What's up, Foxtrot?"

[The skunk's tail,] Whiskey noted from the doorway. [She is *not* pleased. I believe I'll stay outside.]

"The honey badger's getting out at night," I said.

"What? Not again. I just finished putting all that work into a new enclosure." The skunk in her arms was making quite the racket, alternating between hissing and squealing like a pig.

"I know, I know. But somehow, he is. I have it on reliable authority."

"Did your reliable authority tell you how he's doing it, or where he is now?" She carefully put three more drops in the skunk's ear, then deposited the animal in a small wire-mesh cage on the floor. It glared at her resentfully and squealed some more.

"He's back in his pen. And no, I don't know how he's doing it."

Caroline frowned. She was a plump, pretty blonde who put the health and safety of her animals above everything else. "So he escaped, was seen, and now he's returned on his own? Do I want to know what he was up to while he was out?"

"No. Plausible deniability is your bestest friend."

She sighed. "Okay. I'll give his compound the once-over. You think ZZ's willing to spring for a guard tower, spotlights, and a twenty-four-hour security detail?"

"Unlikely. But security cameras might be doable."

"I suppose. As long as he doesn't eat them."

The skunk had finally quieted down, still hissing now and then but mostly whimpering. Caroline glanced down at her and said, "Oh, come on, it wasn't that bad. You'll thank me when those ear mites are gone."

[I doubt that,] said Whiskey when I walked out the door. He was waiting for me on the sidewalk, sitting erect with his ears perked up. [I may not speak Skunk, but I know profanity when I hear it.]

I kept walking, and Whiskey got to his feet and followed along behind me. "Hopefully Caroline can put a stop to Owduttf's nighttime rambles. Right now I've got a billion other details to take care of."

[Like uncovering who used high explosives on the house?]

I shook my head. "I can't even think about that at the moment. Every single person who works, lives, or visits the mansion is going to want something from me the second I enter their field of vision, and almost all of them are going to have to wait until after I take care of all the absolutely essential details first: electrical, plumbing, structural integrity. Once those ducks are lined up, then I can start thinking about secondary effects: smoke damage, water damage, broken windows and appliances. I will no doubt have to hold the hands of anyone who was shaken up—those who still *have* hands, anyway—probably book a few hotel rooms and maybe even schedule some counseling sessions. All while trying to whittle down the—" I broke off, yanked out my phone, and brandished it at Whiskey. "—twenty-seven phone calls I need to respond to immediately."

[Please don't brandish that at me. You know I don't approve of brandishing.]

"Sorry." I put the phone away. "Suddenly feeling a little stressed."

[That's understandable.]

The first person I had to deal with, of course, was ZZ.

"Foxtrot!" she said as I walked in the front door. She'd removed the zombie makeup and Victorian garb, and was wearing a bright-purple plush bathrobe. "Thank goodness! Where were you? I've been trying to reach you for the last hour!"

It was more like forty minutes, but pointing that out wouldn't exactly endear me to her. "My phone battery died," I said. "I couldn't get to my spare because it was in my office and the police had that blocked off so I went to my car and then got sidetracked by talking to one of the film crew who needed to go off-site but the police wouldn't let them leave and now here I am. What do you need?"

She blinked. "Well, let's see. My house is broken. Is somebody going to fix it?"

I took a deep breath, and smiled. "I have top people on it. *Top* people." Which wasn't true, precisely, but was about to be.

Then the next few hours sort of blurred by. Which isn't to say all the various, intricate, interlocking details of those hours were blurry; oh, no, they were sharp and clear and very, very numerous. It was the time itself that seemed to rush past in a great, shimmery wave, one punctuated by many mugs of tea, a hundred or so phone calls, and an endless parade of worried, confused people marching through my office.

But I got it sorted.

By the time dinner was in sight, I'd pretty much broken the back of the crisis. Things were far from over, but all the necessary parts had been set in motion; all I had to do now was make sure it kept moving. Damages had been assessed, contractors had been contracted, schedules had been adjusted, and the nervous had been reassured. All in a day's work for the mighty Foxtrot, slayer of cataclysms.

The police had finally left, after cordoning off the room the blast had occurred in. Maurice Rolvink was still missing.

I stood up, stretching and yawning. My brain was buzzing from all the caffeine, but also the aftereffects of a major adrenaline high. That's the thing about emergencies; when they're happening every neuron you've got is firing like mad, and when it's over you crash. Hard.

I didn't want to crash. I wanted to figure out exactly what was going on that had produced an explosion, a coma, and a corpse.

Rolvink. Was that his body Whiskey and I had found? And if it was, did Owduttf kill him? Why were the head and hands gone? Who blew up Natalia Cardoso's room, and why?

I'm something of a research fiend, and I do a certain amount of background work on each of ZZ's guests. I already knew Maurice Rolvink was a producer, one who specialized in low-budget, direct-to-video B-movies. That was the easy-to-access stuff; now it was time to dig a little deeper.

So I sat right back down, and I dug.

Some time later, I heard a scratching at the door and a whine. I rubbed my eyes, got up, and opened the door to let Whiskey in. He brushed past me with a disapproving look. [I've been out there for five minutes. Were you asleep?]

"No, no, just preoccupied. Why didn't you braincast me?"

[I did. I got absolutely no response, which is why I asked if you were asleep.]

"Huh." I sat back down, and Whiskey jumped up on the couch. He's allowed; ectoplasmic fur doesn't shed. "Sorry. Guess I was just really focused on what I was doing."

Whiskey sniffed the air delicately. [Ah. Hot on the cybernetic trail, are we? I can smell the search engine.]

"You cannot. Google does not have a scent."

[I was referring to you, not the computer.]

"I refuse to believe that how I smell changes when I'm doing research."

He yawned. [I'm not surprised; humans simply can't appreciate olfactory nuance. What's got your medulla oblongata in such a frenzy?]

"Maurice Rolvink." I tapped the screen of my laptop with a fingernail. "I knew he was sleazy, I just didn't know *how* sleazy."

[And now you do?]

"Listen to this. Twenty years ago he was selling used cars. Fifteen years ago, he was running his own mail-order scam out of Honolulu that was shut down by the feds. He didn't do any time, but several of his employees did. Ten years ago he hit it big with his own online gambling site, which tanked about two seconds after he sold it for far more money than it was worth. Hard to say where the money went, but he seems to have spent the next few years partying hard with some very questionable people, most of whom had a lengthy criminal record. Seven or so years ago he got interested in low-budget film, which he seems to have stuck with until the present day."

Whiskey put his head down on his paws. [So he's finally found a legitimate business to invest in?]

"Not so much. In economic terms, movies are an exotic beast; they spend bunches of money on bunches of things, and they do it very quickly. Independent films don't have a lot of oversight, and I found at least one article speculating that organized crime might be using that to launder money."

[I must confess I don't understand exactly how that would work.]

I swiveled around in my chair. "Okay, let's say you're a criminal with a lot of money you need to hide. You pose as an investor—or multiple investors—and give the money to a film company. The company spends every dime on a gajillion different things, at least on paper—in reality, the producer cuts the actual budget to the bone and pays the money right back to the investors through shell companies that claim they provided various services: catering, carpentry, travel, wardrobe, props, even special effects. It doesn't matter if the movie makes money or not; if it does it's a bonus, and if it doesn't it's still accomplished its purpose."

[You think he was doing that with this production?]

I frowned and leaned back. "I don't know. But if he

were, it would raise a bunch of possible reasons someone might want him dead. Maybe he was cheating his investors. Maybe he was informing on them and they found out. Maybe someone from his past decided to get revenge for an old injustice."

I got to my feet. "Come on. Tango has to be recovered by now; let's go find her and see if we can pry a few answers out of Owduttf."

We found her downstairs, zonked out on an ottoman in the study. "Hey, kitty. Rise and shine—time to go to work."

She opened her eyes and blinked at me sleepily. *<What, now? I'm busy.>*

"Yeah, sawing logs. Come on—we've got a honey badger to interrogate."

<You sound grumpy. I hate it when you're grumpy.>

I sighed. "Sorry. I'm under a lot of pressure."

<Well, don't take it out on me. I have problems of my own, remember?>

"Oh, for—your problems are not problems. They are non-problems, is what they are."

<You wouldn't say that if you were a cat.>

"If I were a cat, I wouldn't say anything. I'd spend all my time napping, eating, playing with cat toys, and being adored. Which, come to think of it, is pretty much what you do when you're not complaining about your nonexistent problems."

She sat up, then stared at me accusingly. *<I don't think you understand the seriousness of the situation. There's a cat casually strolling around in my territory. And there's nothing I can do about it!>*

"Because he's a ghost, you mean? Or because he's a famous ghost?"

She sniffed in a clearly offended way. *<Famous, right. That was a long time ago and nobody alive today even*

remembers him. It's not like he actually did *anything, anyway.>*

I shrugged. "Technically, I guess he didn't. But I don't understand why you're getting so upset; he's a ghost, and you deal with those all the time. Are you afraid he's going to take your job or something?"

Her eyes narrowed. *<I'm not afraid of anything. There are some things I hate so much that the only way I can express that hatred is to leave as fast as possible, but he's not one of them. I just don't like him, that's all. He's . . . sneaky.>*

"Wow. A cat calling another cat sneaky? That's like a ninja telling another ninja that they wear too much black. And one of them is named Pot and the other one Kettle, only it's in Japanese."

<Whatever. I don't trust him.>

"What I just said."

She yawned, exposing tiny white teeth in a pink mouth. *<Okay, okay. Let's get this over with.>*

5.

We trooped up to the pen and stopped. Owduttf wasn't outside, which meant he was probably asleep inside his burrow at the center of the big mound of dirt. I hoped.

"Okay, let's do this," I said. "Hey! I'm back! Get out here, I want to talk to you."

Tango translated what I said into Honey Badger, a language that consisted mainly of chuffing, snorting, and grunts, with a few gruff *kry-ya-ya* sounds thrown in. After a short pause, we heard Owduttf's reply.

[Did he just pass gas?] Whiskey asked.

<*I'm not sure how to translate that.*>

A moment later Owduttf himself appeared at the entrance to his burrow, blinking sleepily. He had bits of straw stuck in his fur, too, all of which made him look adorable in a Charles-Manson-in-a-bunny-suit sort of way.

He replied and Tango translated: <"Hello, Foxtrot. You brought the smaller one that talks for you this time. Too bad. The other one would have made a better meal.">

"I think even you'd find Whiskey hard to swallow,

Owduttf. Though you do seem willing to eat just about anything."

<"Not true. I don't care for rocks. Much.">

"How about human hands and heads?"

He tilted his broad head just slightly. <"Depends. Are you offering?">

"Only if you're up for seconds."

<"Seconds are good. So are thirds and fourths and whatever comes after that.">

"How about firsts? How were those?"

He yawned, revealing jaws lined with short, sharp teeth. <"First what? I've lost track of what we were talking about. I'm hungry.">

So much for subtlety. "Owduttf, did you eat parts of a human being last night? Specifically, the head and hands?"

He appeared to consider this. <"Maybe. I eat so many things, I don't always remember what they were. Why do you want to know?">

I scowled. "Because eating people is not something you're supposed to do!"

As soon as I said it I knew I'd made a mistake. This was a cunning, voracious predator I was talking to, not a misbehaving child—scolding him wasn't going to do anything but let him know I was angry. Which I was; I could deal intellectually with the idea of a person dying, but somebody getting eaten pushed some pretty primeval buttons in my hindbrain. In fact, they were so primeval they weren't even buttons, just levers made from bamboo lashed together with vines and jammed into my gray matter.

But getting angry wasn't going to make him cooperate. Bribery might, though—it had in the past. "Look, I'm not blaming you, I just need to find out what happened. Tell me and you'll get a treat."

<"Tell you what happened to the head and the hands? Because it sounds like someone ate them.">

"Actually, I'm more interested in—"

<"I doubt if there's any left, is all I'm saying. If they were as tasty as they sound, they probably went pretty fast.">

I rubbed my forehead with one thumb and a forefinger. "I don't care what happened to them. I mean, I do care, but what happened to the person they belonged to is what I'm really after."

<"Oh, I see. Never mind the head and hands, you want to know about what they were attached to.">

"The owner of said body parts, yes. Do you know what happened to him?"

Owduttf shuffled out of his burrow and up to the edge of the wire fence. <"You mentioned a treat?">

"Absolutely. How about a nice whole chicken?"

He squinted at me suspiciously. <"The last time you said that, you gave me something that didn't have a head, feet, or feathers, and was empty on the inside. Try again.">

"How about a package of nice raw bacon? Extra greasy."

<"Hmmm. Yes, that will do. What happened to the body was, I hid it.">

"I already *know* that."

<"Then why did you ask? Are you trying to trick me?">

"I'm not trying to trick you. I'm just trying to find out what happened *before* you ate the head and the hands."

<"Who said I ate the head and hands? You *are* trying to trick me. Just for that, I'm not going to tell you where I hid the body until you give me the bacon.">

"I already know where you hid the body!"

He turned up his snout and gave a little dismissive snort.

<"Sure you do. That's why you're going to all this trouble, to find out something you already know.">

This was getting me nowhere. "Look, I'll give you the bacon. I'll give you *two* packages of bacon. Just tell me one thing—*did you kill him?*"

<"Oh, no. I'll tell you where the body is—after you give me *both* packages of bacon—but that's it. I'm hungry, not stupid. I'm not admitting I killed, removed, or ate *anything*.">

And with that, he turned his back on me and shuffled back inside his burrow.

The front lawn was still a chaotic mess; the bizarre arrangements of gardening implements, sporting equipment, and other random objects had been left exactly where they were. With the day's filming canceled, the film crew had returned to their motel rooms in town; the household staff was in a state of shock and just trying for a semblance of normality, which meant sticking to routine tasks and responsibilities. The huge mess on the front lawn wasn't anyone's responsibility, per se; nobody on staff had "dismantle and put away gigantic, sprawling jumble of miscellaneous junk" as part of their job description. Which meant, I supposed, that it fell to me.

Well, I may not have known what it was for, but I knew who built it. I went searching for him, and discovered no one had seen him all day; one of the maids informed me that he'd gone back to bed after the police had left.

I paused in front of Keene's door. Whiskey looked up at me. [What are you waiting for?]

"Just preparing myself, mentally. There's two different methods of dealing with hungover rock stars, and I'm trying to decide which one to use."

[Are you sure he's hungover?]

"It's after four and he's still in bed. No, correction: It's after four, and he went *back* to bed after a bomb went off. He either had a *very* late night or he's mixed up his medications again."

[What are the two methods?]

"Cautious and quiet or bright and cheery. The first one gets used when I think there might be firearms present. The second is mostly for petty revenge."

[Does either apply here?]

"Not really. Keene's vices don't include guns, and I'm more intrigued than annoyed about the front lawn. However, I do need to make sure he's actually awake." I went with a brisk knock instead, and waited.

"G'way," came a muffled groan from the other side of the door. "Sleepin'."

"It's Foxtrot. I need to talk to you—open the door, please. But put on some pants, first." Keene liked to do many things naked, and sleeping was one of them. Don't ask me how I know that.

"Mumble *fargin* no fish plang."

"I strongly disagree. Now open the door or I'll sing your number one hit."

"Aaaaah! You evil wench . . . you wouldn't *dare*."

"With full musical accompaniment. I have it on my phone, you know."

[I don't understand. Why would reminding him of his greatest achievement be considered a punishment?]

I grinned. "*You've* never had to play it at every single concert you've ever performed."

No sound from within. I pulled out my phone, called up the music file, and cranked the volume to high.

As soon as he heard the catchy opening riff, he moaned in anguish. "For God's *sake* . . ."

I belted out the opening lyrics in time with the song: "Oooh-hoo, crazy baby, do you, crazy baby, feel blue, crazy baaaaaabeeeeeeee . . ."

He flung the door open. I was expecting some full-frontal revenge nudity, but I was disappointed; he was wrapped in a fluffy bathrobe that seemed to be made entirely from Muppets. "Please don't do that," he croaked. "Pretty sure it's against the Geneva Convention." His five-o'clock shadow was closer to six forty-five, his eyes were open about as wide as a newborn kitten's, and he had the kind of epic bed-head he'd probably write a song about later.

"The Geneva Convention?" I said, turning off the music. "Is that where you were? No wonder you're tired, what with the jet lag and Swiss cheese overload and cuckoo clock smuggling. Mind if I come in?"

He raised a single finger. "Don't," he managed.

"Don't what? Come in? Turn on the lights?" I asked as I brushed past him and turned on the lights. Whiskey trotted in after me.

"Engage me in lively conversation," he muttered. "Ah, buggeration. Too late." He closed the door and slumped against it.

Whiskey promptly jumped up on the unmade bed and made himself comfortable. [Just ensuring he doesn't crawl back under the covers, you understand. And I thought you weren't going to do bright and cheerful.]

This is only half strength. Full B and C involves flinging open the drapes and giggling in delight.

"I can hear you, you know," Keene said.

Both Whiskey and I froze.

"Your thoughts. I can hear them," Keene repeated. "And what you are both thinking right now—much too loudly, I might add—is that this is all a terrible, terrible mistake.

This is not the singer you were looking for. You're going to go now."

I relaxed. "Nice try, Jedi. But before we do, there's some splainin' you need to do."

He squinted in my general direction. "Splainin'? Splainin'? I'm not sure I'm ready for that. Is that a drug, a sexual position, or a new dance?"

"None of the above. I just want to ask about the free-form sculpture you built in the front yard."

He shook his head. "Pretty sure those words were in English, but they made no sense. Is it possible you mixed up the order before they left your mouth?"

I glanced around the room. "I did not fairly sure I am. But it looks like you may have done a little mixing yourself last night." I spotted an empty tequila bottle, a half-empty basket of grapefruits, and dozens of little silver nitrous oxide canisters—used.

"Untrue. Base lies. I've been sound asleep and have the lack of new tattoos to prove it."

"Never mind that. I want to ask you about last night, when you apparently decided to create some sort of pop-art masterpiece in front of the mansion."

He staggered over to the bed and sat down beside Whiskey. "No idea what you're talking about, Trot. Truly. The last thing I remember is Oscar finally admitting defeat in our croquet marathon, and tottering off to bed. Then it's all dark blankness, excepting the occasional vivid nightmare." He put his head in his hands. Gently, as if he were expecting it to fall off.

"You mean like something blowing up?"

He raised his head to look at me. "How'd you know? Also, there were zombies. And police constables."

"That was no dream, that was part of the house exploding this morning."

"Ah. Should have known. The lack of naked purple women alone was a massive clue."

"So you don't remember your little project?"

He tried to blink, but it just looked as if he were shrugging his eyes. "Not a moment. Sorry. Did I do anything I'm going to have to pay for?"

[I'd say he's paying for it right now.]

"Too early to tell." I sat down beside him on the bed, and Whiskey promptly crawled over and put his head in my lap. "But if it turns out the boom in the room was caused by that thing you built out on the lawn—then you're going to be looking at a pretty hefty bill."

His head dove back down into his hands. "Agh. There may have been chemicals involved, but I tend to stay away from anything that might be combustible. Well, *too* combustible. All right, *combustible* isn't the right word. Blowy-uppy."

"That's two words, and technically they aren't. Words, that is."

"I'm sorry, Trot, really I am. I think I may have gone a bit overboard last night."

[Yes, in the sense that the *Titanic* may have had a bit of a problem with ice.]

I frowned. "Yeah. Haven't seen you quite that wasted in a while."

"And you still haven't." His hands muffled his voice, but I could still hear the defensiveness in it. "I save my worst depredations for when you're not around."

"I wish you wouldn't. Better to do that stuff when I'm available to fix it, instead of just having to clean up the aftermath."

He raised his head, then flopped backward onto the bed and stared at the ceiling. "I'm afraid that's impossible, love. I understand that you're very proactive and adaptive and supercapable, but I'm more of a train-wreck-as-performance-art sort. Which is to say, if I actually possessed the wherewithal to schedule these sorts of bollocks, I probably wouldn't commit them. Probably."

"So what brought on this latest bout of bacchanalia? Are you celebrating, trying to distract yourself, or just doing what comes naturally?"

"There's nothing natural about *me,* Trot. I am a creature of artifice and illusion, a badly organized tangle of affectations, neuroses, and addictions. In short, a mess."

I glanced down at him. "Kind of hard to argue with that, Sparky. At the moment, anyway."

"I know, I know. Perhaps that's what the thing on the lawn is."

"Not following."

"My offspring. A mess, created by another mess. I shall call it Junior, and teach it the ways of the world, and leave it my rapidly dwindling fortune when I eventually succumb to the ravages of my lifestyle."

[I don't think he has a clear grasp of what he's made—though for someone who can't remember its creation he's certainly formed an immediate attachment.]

Artists come in three categories: ignoble, metaphoric, and sentimentary, I thought back. *A writer told me that.*

I patted his knee and stood up. "Before you go drawing up a new will, maybe you should take a look at your construct. It might jog a few brain cells, give you some idea of what you were trying to accomplish."

"Certainly. I shall attend to it, forthwith." He punctuated this statement by jabbing a forefinger at the ceiling, which would have been more convincing if his other arm hadn't been draped over his eyes.

"Uh-huh. Come on, Whiskey. Just make sure you're up for dinner—ZZ gives you a lot of leeway, but that rule stands firm. Unlike yourself."

"If you're going to insult my manhood," he said, "you can see yourself to the door."

We did, and I closed it quietly behind us.

I'd just sat back down when there was a knock on my office door. Shondra, our head of security, opened it without waiting for my reply—a sure sign that she was annoyed and had something on her mind.

"Foxtrot," she said from the doorway. "We need to talk."

"Sure," I said. "Come on in, have a seat. What do you need?"

She came in and closed the door, but stayed on her feet. "Peace of mind. Why did you disappear right after the bombing?"

Whoops. I might be able to smooth-talk my way past ZZ, but Shondra's bullshit detectors were military-grade. "There was something I needed to take care of, and I knew I was about to get bogged down in a million urgent decisions. I had to do it then, or it wouldn't get done."

She crossed her arms. Shondra keeps her hair very, very short, and probably cuts it with the gaze she was aiming at me. "And what was this thing that was so urgent it took precedence over a goddamn *terrorist attack*?"

I put my hands up in defense. "Whoa. This wasn't a terrorist anything, okay? Something blew up and somebody died, true, but there's nothing to suggest this was political."

"Not my point. Answer the question."

I'd have a better chance of deflecting a bullet than Shondra's attention. "I can't."

"Why?"

Because I had to make sure a possibly homicidal South African badger didn't escape from his pen to kill another guest while my telepathic, multilingual cat was too stoned to help me interrogate him about a previous murder, and saying that out loud would be problematic in terms of our professional relationship.

I sighed. "I just can't. If I told you *why* I can't it would reveal *what* I can't, and I just told you I can't do that. You can understand that, can't you?"

"If you thinking saying *can't* half a dozen times in a row is going to make me go away, you're wrong."

"Can't blame me for trying."

"Sure I can."

Well, this was getting me nowhere. "Look, Shondra. I have a lot of responsibilities, and sometimes they conflict. This was one of those times. I swear, if I could tell you, I would—and you'd laugh, most likely, about what I'm actually hiding. About the only thing I *can* tell you is I'm not doing this for myself."

She kept that hard stare pointed in my direction for a few more seconds, then glanced away. "No, you never are, are you? It's always somebody else's needs getting taken care of. The first thing you did when you got there was run right into the damn house. So I guess I have to give you a pass. This time."

She turned around and walked back to the door, then paused with her hand on the knob. "One thing, though, I need for you to hear. All right?"

"I'm listening."

"I've got your back, whatever it is. You can trust me."

"I know. Thank you."

She nodded without turning around, pulled the door open, and left.

[That was difficult for you.] Whiskey's tone was sympathetic.

I reached for my mug of tea, realized it was empty, and set the mug back down. "Yeah. I hate lying to Shondra. I hate lying to anyone who trusts me, but I don't have a choice."

[Not a viable one, anyway.]

"Wait a minute. Sure I do! I'll just tell her I was using my telepathic, multilingual cat to interrogate a South African badger about—oh, no, hang on, I already ran that scenario in my head."

[How'd it go?]

"About how you'd expect. Confusion, irritation, demands for clarification, slowly dawning realization, shock, pity, sadness, steely-eyed determination to help, notifying the authorities, denial, nervous laughter, running, screaming, crying, sedation, observation in a controlled environment, eventual release under close supervision."

[I see. Not really optimal, then.]

"Not really, no."

I got to my feet. "Come on. I've been doing this for too long—I need to stretch my legs. Let's go see Ben."

ZZ was passionate about her dinners. They were the focal point of the salons, a chance for her guests to laugh and chat and debate about anything and everything. You know that old question, *If you could choose any three people to have dinner with, who would they be?* She asked herself that question, a long time ago, and decided two things: first, that the parameters were too limited, and second, that the answer never stayed the same for very long. So when she invited people to stay with us and catered to their every whim, she had one ironclad rule: You had to show up for the evening meal. You didn't have to drink, you didn't even have to eat—though we provided plenty of both—but you did have to show up. And as long as you were interesting and didn't actually throw any punches, you'd probably get invited back.

I had a standing invitation to attend any of these dinners, and often did; watching celebrities discuss anything from quantum physics to the Kama Sutra was always entertaining, especially when the people talking were frequently experts on the subject. ZZ liked a bubbling mix of the famous, the brilliant, and the socially conscious, and it was my job to make sure everything ran smoothly—from specialized diets to personal preferences, I scrutinized every aspect of the menu, the seating arrangements, and the decor. Comfortable decadence lightly overlaid with formal elegance was the preferred ambient environment, and I'd gotten very good at tweaking it.

A big part of this, of course, was the food. Normally Ben and I met every afternoon to discuss what was going to be served that night, but today had been anything but normal. I left Whiskey in my office and ducked into the kitchen to see what Ben had prepared; I knew it would be good, but felt guilty I hadn't had the time to talk about it with him.

"Hey, Trot," Ben said. "You okay?"

I walked over and gave him a quick kiss. "Hanging in there, Thunder Boy. Something smells wonderful."

"That would be you. But yes, dinner is coming along nicely."

He gave me a quick rundown on the soup and salad courses, then unveiled the main dish, a spicy jambalaya. "I didn't want to do anything too meaty," he told me. "You know, with all the fake rotting flesh everywhere."

<Rotting flesh?> Tango's voice, though I couldn't see her. *<Don't say that around the dog. We'll all drown in drool.>*

"I don't think he actually likes eating decomposing meat," I said. "Just rolling around on it."

"Can we not discuss this in my kitchen?" Ben asked.

Tango appeared from under a table, yawning and stretching her hind legs one at a time. *<Yes, it's a disgusting subject. In fact, let's just agree not to talk about dogs, ever again.>*

"As if you could stop," I said. "You get more pleasure complaining about canines than you'll ever admit."

She sat down and stared up at me impassively. *<I don't complain, I point out the obvious. Sadly, there are some who just can't seem to grasp the basic facts of reality, so I'm forced to remind them. Over and over again.>*

Ben shook his head. "Sounds like quite the burden, Tango. I don't know how you find the strength to go on."

She gazed up at him and blinked once, very slowly. *<Skritches help.>*

Ben grinned and got down on one knee to comply. If you think you've heard loud purring before, you need to hear it inside your head. It's sort of pleasant and sort of not; on the pleasant side, it's a very happy, rhythmic, soothing sound, almost hypnotic. On the other, it's a little like having a vibrator stuck between your ears.

"Well," I said, "I can see you've got everything under control here—"

<Can't talk. Skritches.>

"Uh-huh. I guess I'll get ready for dinner myself then."

"Oh?" said Ben. "You're staying? Is it the cuisine or the chef?"

"They're both irresistible, but no. I just feel like there's a lot going on and I need to keep an eye on things."

Ben frowned. "Unlike the rest of the time, when you blithely ignore the problems around you and do nothing to fix them?"

I reached down and mussed his hair. "Aww. What a sweet yet sarcastic thing to say. Yes, I am a control freak, and on a day when a bomb goes off *and* a headless corpse is found on the premises, I'm allowed to be a little obsessive."

<Yeah, that's the spot. Right therrrrrrrrrrrrrrr.>

I looked down at Tango and grinned. "Everything all right with the world, now? Not worried a spectral kitty is going to sneak in here and steal your skritches?"

The purr sputtered and stopped. A pair of feline eyes stared up at me accusingly. *<Oh, sure. Bring that up just when I'm getting my purr on. Thanks a lot.>*

"Whoops. Sorry, my bad. But really, he's a ghost—the only skritches he's getting are from other postmortem types."

Ben straightened up as Tango began to pace. "What ghost are you two talking about?"

"Unsinkable Sam," I said.

<Unthinkable Scam, you mean.>

Ben looked puzzled. "Who's Unsinkable Sam?"

<A con artist.>

I gave Tango a look. "A cat who bears an uncanny resemblance to Tango. Well, the ghost of a cat, anyway— and a famous one, to boot. I spotted him yesterday and followed him to the graveyard, where he disappeared."

Now Ben looked intrigued. "Famous? How so?"

<Oh, here we go. I'm going to take a nap. Don't wake me when you're done.> She strutted off to her current favorite sleeping spot, the top of Ben's desk in his tiny office.

"Unsinkable Sam," I said, "was a navy cat, in World War Two."

"The navy had cats? I thought they used seals."

"This was a long time ago before seals were invented and also shut up. Sam wasn't called Sam, then."

"What was he called?"

"I don't know. Something German, probably."

"This story has barely left the ground and already I'm confused."

"I know you're part bird, but try to stick with nautical metaphors for this one, okay?"

"Aye, aye, Captain."

"Much better. Now, this cat was aboard a battleship on its very first mission. I don't know why; maybe they thought he'd bring them luck."

"Did he?"

"Not so much. The battleship was named the *Bismarck*."

Ben shook his head. "Wait. He was in the *German* navy?"

"Briefly. Then he was in the Atlantic Ocean. But the ship that sank the *Bismarck,* the *Cossack,* rescued him."

"He was rescued by a Russian ship?"

"No, a British one. Are you even paying attention?"

"I'm on the edge of my seat. And then?"

"Then they gave him a new name. Either they didn't like the old one or never bothered to ask any of the survivors what it was, which I suppose is understandable: *Hey, guys that survived after we blew up your ship and killed most of you—anybody remember what the cat's name is?* Not in the best of taste."

"No. So they called him Unsinkable Sam because—"

"Oskar."

"Say what now?"

"Oskar. With a *k*. That's what they named him. I'm guessing they threw the *k* in there to remind him of his German heritage, which is the least you can do when you just sank somebody's battleship."

"You've really drunk a lot of tea today, haven't you."

"That wasn't even a question. I know, because I heard

a period instead of a question mark. Also, I can see through time."

"Finish your story before you start vibrating so fast you disappear. They named him Oskar?"

"Yeah. Which, instead of appeasing his German former owners, apparently just ticked them off. A few months later they sent a U-boat to torpedo the *Cossack*. Killed a hundred and fifty-nine British sailors, but not good old Oskar. He escaped, once again."

"He lived through the sinking of two different ships?"

"Who said that? Nobody said that. Are you even listening?"

"Sorry, Captain. Please, carry on."

"Oskar and the rest of the survivors were picked up by the HMS *Legion*. The British were quite annoyed by this point, so they did the unthinkable: *They changed his name.*"

"Those *bastards.*"

"Don't mess with the Brits, I always say. They could have just dropped the *k,* but they took it all the way—and so, Unsinkable Sam was born. Er, christened. Baptized?"

"Is it safe to ask questions yet?"

"Absolutely not, and don't think I didn't notice that was a question. From there, Sam moved up in the world—he was a symbol now, and as such took up residence on a veritable floating palace, the aircraft carrier *Ark Royal*. I can just see him, posing proudly on the prow of the ship as it thundered majestically through the waves, a huge, unstoppable juggernaut of British military might ready to unleash destruction from its battery of guns or squadrons of dive-bombers."

I paused. He waited a moment, then cautiously said, "That's . . . impressive?"

"Not so much. It was sunk, too—submarine again."

"And Sam?"

"*Angry but unharmed* was the official description when he was pulled from the wreckage by the crew of the HMS *Lightning*. Can't say I blame him; all those unplanned baths must have really been getting on his nerves by that point . . . anyway, that was more or less the end of his maritime career. He retired to a sailor's home in Belfast."

"More or less?"

I feigned innocence. "Excuse me?"

Ben smiled. "You said *more or less*. What's the kicker?"

I smiled back. "No kicker. Except that—as far as we know—Sam lived on three different ships and traveled on two others."

"The two that rescued him from the drink."

I picked up an apple from a bowl on the counter and considered it. "Yep. And neither of them survived the war, either. Five ships, five new additions to Davy Jones's locker. Dead or not, you wouldn't get me on a boat with him."

<Exactly!>

Tango stalked back into the kitchen, her tail twitching. *<You can't seriously believe that was all coincidence.>*

I took a bite. "How should I know?" I said around a mouthful of apple. "All I know is what Eli told me."

"And what did our resident spooky white crow have to say on the subject?"

I finished chewing and swallowed. "That cat you were looking for? Unsinkable Sam. Google it."

"That seems unlikely."

"Yeah, unearthly albino bird spirits usually head straight to Wikipedia. Surprised me, too."

Tango sat down and regarded both of us sternly. *<I'm telling you, that cat is bad news.>*

I leaned down and put my hands on my knees. "For anyone in the maritime field—well, except maybe shipbuilders—yeah. But we're nowhere near a shoreline, Tango; even if Sam were some sort of nefarious seagoing monster, he picked the wrong place to skulk. What's he going to do, haunt the Jacuzzi? See if he can sink an inflatable drink tray?"

<I'm not saying I know what he's up to. But he's up to something—and I'm going to find out what it is.>

And with that she stalked away once again, her tail in the air. A nice exit, ruined only slightly by her dropping to the floor after a few steps and taking another nap.

"A famous deceased feline, huh?" Ben said. "Well, the Crossroads pulled in Edison's elephant, so I shouldn't be too surprised."

"That's more or less what Eli told me," I said. I crunched into another bite of apple. "You know, after we talked about Lassie showing up."

Ben raised his eyebrows.

"Sorry," I said. "Didn't I mention that?"

6.

"Welcome, everyone," ZZ said. She sat at her usual place at the head of the table, wearing an elaborate Victorian gown; it looked authentic, until you really studied the floral pattern of the fabric and realized the tiny flowers were actually manga versions of Sherlock Holmes. "I know it's been a most distressing day, but I want to assure everyone that we're perfectly safe. The gas mains have been checked and there's an investigative team up there right now doing all sorts of tests to figure out what happened."

"I'll tell you what happened," Oscar said. He took a liberal sip of his drink. "Part of our bloody house blew up, that's what happened."

I glanced around. Natalia Cardoso and Maurice Rolvink weren't there, of course, but neither was Keene. I suspected he'd just gone back to bed—behavior ZZ would normally frown on, but this hadn't been exactly an ordinary day.

Jaxon Nesbitt laughed. He had a movie star's laugh, with lots of big white teeth and sparkling eyes. "Yeah, that was crazy. I'm still half deaf."

"Really?" I said. "You were that close to the blast?"

"Up in my room rehearsing my lines," said Jaxon. Despite what he'd just claimed, he didn't seem to have any trouble hearing me.

"I was outside with the crew," Lucky said. "Poor Natalia."

"Yes, poor Natalia," said Maxwell Tervo. He was the actor playing the villain in the movie, a tall, thin man with a high, wispy widow's peak of blond hair. He had one of those highly mobile faces with slightly exaggerated features: wide mouth, beaky nose, large, deep-set eyes. He looked genuinely sorrowful, but who can tell what an actor's really feeling? It's like trying to figure out if a cat killed a mouse because she was hungry or just in the mood to kill something. You have to watch her for a while, and really pay attention.

Of course, in my case you could just ask her, but that's no guarantee of a proper answer. Or in Tango's case, no guarantee of an answer that doesn't wind up blaming you for her food bowl being half full.

"I was in the menagerie, myself," said Tervo. "Contemplating a porcupine, in fact."

"Pointy, aren't they?" said Oscar. He signaled the drinks trolley with the push of a button, summoning a robotic cart made for us by one of ZZ's former guests. "I was still abed, I'm afraid. The guesthouse is far enough from the main building that I simply thought it was part of the production. In fact, I was on my way to complain when I saw the smoke and realized something wasn't right."

It's funny how people have this impulse to share where they were when a disaster occurs. Some kind of deeply buried survival instinct is what I think, a compulsion to not just record a moment when things went terribly wrong but compare notes later, so the whole group can figure out how to prevent it from happening again. It's related to the urge to ask for details about how someone died—a cousin, probably, one of those relatives you hung out with when you were younger and always got into trouble together. The Morbidities; they make the Addams family look like the Brady Bunch.

"I was in the graveyard," said Yemane Fikru. "It's an amazing place." He looked directly at me when he said this, and I had the distinct impression he wanted to say more.

"I was in the gardens," I said, which was almost true. "Running from one errand to another, as usual."

"I was in makeup," said ZZ. "About to have my artificial gore removed. I'm just thankful it wasn't replaced by the real thing."

We all fell silent for a moment, picking at our salads. Many of us, I was sure, were thinking the same thing: Where had Maurice Rolvink been, and in what condition? And where was he right now?

"Keene claims to have been asleep," said Oscar. "Which is entirely possible, considering how late he was up last night."

"Oh?" I said. "You were up with him?"

Oscar shook his head. "Not as such. We parted company around midnight, when I decided our friendly croquet tournament was verging on the obsessive. But I've heard reports from the film crew he was hard at work at five AM, and I suspect during the entire interval between."

"Hard at work?" said Fikru. "At what?"

"I thought you'd know," said Oscar. "He's your compatriot, is he not? I can't make head or tails out of what he built."

"You mean that thing out on the lawn?" Fikru asked. "Keene did that?"

"You sound surprised," said ZZ.

"I'm not sure what to think," said Fikru. "I mean, I

know what he's like—but I also know he's trying to follow a more spiritual path."

"Keene?" said Oscar. He sounded like a man who was just confronted by a tiny green alien in his martini where he expected an olive. "Forgive me, but the only spirits he believes in are the same ones I do. Chin chin." He held up his glass to demonstrate, and took a drink to punctuate the remark.

"Well, spirituality can take many forms," ZZ said. "Keene's a very creative person, and not exactly conservative. It makes perfect sense to me that any awakening of his higher consciousness would take an unorthodox shape."

"I tend to agree," said Tervo. "It's not about following set rituals, it's about a connection to the divine. You can find that in the most unexpected places."

"Very true," Fikru acknowledged. "You sound as if you're speaking from personal experience."

At many dinner parties, bringing up the subject of personal belief systems would be frowned upon; ZZ's parties were different. She encouraged discussion of just about anything, and never shied away from controversy.

Tervo glanced around, but nobody looked uncomfortable. "I suppose I am," Tervo said. "I had a most strange experience several years ago. I was undergoing difficulties in my relationship, for a variety of reasons. Foremost among these was the amount of money my occupation was bringing in, which wasn't much. After much acrimony on both sides, I had decided to end things. This was rather difficult, as we had been together for a number of years and in fact I'd hoped to marry her."

"Always a tough situation," ZZ said.

Tervo nodded. "Yes, but that's only tangential. What happened was that I decided to tell her the next day, but we'd been invited to a party that night. It was to be the last social event we ever attended together, though neither of us knew that at the time. Due to the stress, I drank more than I should, and spent most of the event avoiding her. She left early, clearly angry and confused. I can't say I blame her.

"All this is merely preamble, however. I couldn't face going home to her, and so I stayed and continued to drink. In my emotional and drunken state, I even confided to several other partygoers that I was leaving her the next day, as if seeking some sort of approval. Perhaps I even received it; I don't recall.

"The party was within walking—or should I say stumbling—distance from our home. Eventually, I left and made my way in that direction. I was overflowing with emotion, deeply sad and yet relieved; as hard as the journey had been, I felt as if it was almost over. I'd come to a crossroads in my life, and I had made my choice."

Tervo fell silent for a moment.

"You chose your art," Jaxon said.

Tervo's smile was sad. "Yes. There was more to it, of course—there always is—but that was the crux. She'd made it clear I had to start bringing in some money, and I can't blame her for that. Art demands a certain selfishness, and always exacts its price. It would be easy to portray her as the selfish one, the hardhearted pragmatist who couldn't recognize the value in what I did—but that was not the case."

He looked around the table, at each one of us in turn. "She was an artist, too, you see. She was simply better at it—or at least, better at keeping the money coming in. I suppose that's what hurt the most."

He shook his head, as if to clear it. "I apologize if this is dragging on. But it's important to set the stage, as it were, for what happened next.

"It was a warm summer night. The street I walked along was dark and deserted, only the streetlights providing any illumination. As I walked, my mood lightened; the world seemed full of potential, the darkness an empty slate waiting for me to write on it. The only sound was the distant noise of traffic . . .

"And then I heard the clicking."

Tervo raised his water glass and took a small sip. "It came from the other side of the street, quick and steady. *Click click click.* I stopped, looking for the source, and after a moment spotted it: a dog on the sidewalk across the road, perhaps fifty feet ahead of me. The noise was its claws on concrete as it trotted along."

"What sort of dog?" I asked.

"A stray, I thought at first. Lean, gray, sharp-eared— and in fact, not a dog at all."

"A coyote!" ZZ said with delight.

Tervo smiled back. "Yes. Shy and secretive creatures, almost never seen during the day and rarely even at night. I expected this one to bolt as soon as it noticed me.

"But it did not."

Tervo stopped to take another drink of water. He was, I realized, a natural storyteller.

"Well, what did it do?" Lucky asked.

"It crossed the street to my side," said Tervo. He put the water glass down on the table and studied it for a second, as if he thought it might suddenly do something unexpected. "Most unusual behavior for a coyote. It stopped, still fifty feet away, and we regarded each other for a second.

"Then it sat down."

"How intriguing," Oscar murmured.

"Indeed. It plainly had no fear of me, and seemed to be waiting for something. It was at that moment I had my . . . I want to say *epiphany,* but that doesn't seem accurate. It wasn't so much a realization as a recognition, combined with a burst of alcohol-fueled inspiration. I knew a bit about the Native American myth of Coyote, the trickster god, and in that moment of recognition it seemed to me that we were kindred spirits, he and I; that we both dealt in the creation of illusion, and that we did so as much for our own enjoyment as the enjoyment of others. Storytellers, in other words. And—one storyteller to another—I felt compelled to acknowledge that mutual bond with a suitable offering."

"You performed for it?" ZZ asked.

"I composed an ode, a brief poem, on the spot and recited it. I wish I could remember what I said, but it seems the coyote took those words with him when he left. I remember the tone of it, more than anything; respectful but wry, neither solemn nor serious. I bowed my head when I was done, and when I raised it he was gone."

"What do you think it meant?" Fikru asked.

"I took it as a sign that I had made the right decision. The next day I ended my relationship, and less than a week later I landed the biggest role of my career."

Lucky Trentini grinned and raised his glass. "To storytellers," he said.

"To storytellers," we all agreed, and joined him.

After we drank, Lucky said, "Not to diminish your wonderful, magical story with grubby facts, but more and more animals are becoming part of urban life. Coyotes are a lot more common than people think."

"It's true," ZZ said. "Anyone care to hazard a guess at how many of them live in a big American city like Chicago?"

"Dozens," Jaxon said.

"I'll go as high as a hundred," Lucky added.

"I'll see your hundred," said Oscar, "and raise you the same amount. Two hundred."

"Okay, I'll play along," said Fikru. "Nature is always more abundant and adaptable than we give her credit for. I'm going to go all out and say five hundred. Chicago's a big place."

I actually knew the answer, but I didn't want to steal my boss's thunder. "No idea," I said. "Um . . . forty-two."

ZZ gave me a little smile that told me she knew I was lying through my teeth. "Two thousand," she said quietly.

"Really?" Jaxon asked.

"Amazing," said Fikru.

"That would explain the dearth of roadrunners," said Oscar.

ZZ has three large flatscreens in elaborate frames on the walls of the dining room, and now she used the remote in her hand to switch them from the Monets they were currently showing to a website about urban wildlife. "They're the only predator that's doubled their range in North America despite being widely hunted. They started out in the suburbs, but in Chicago they did so well there wasn't room for all of them. Coyotes are highly territorial, so new generations were forced into the only available real estate: the city itself."

"You're still talking about mainly residential areas, though, right?" Lucky asked. "Not downtown."

"No," said ZZ, "I'm talking about the entire city, downtown included. They're very, very good at keeping themselves hidden. In their natural habitat, they come out during the day and at night; in the city core, they're strictly nocturnal. They navigate high-traffic streets and rarely get hit by vehicles. They used to call them ghosts of the plains, but now—"

"Ghosts of the cities," Tervo said. "Yes. That seems appropriate."

"Hmmm," said Lucky. "That'd make a pretty good documentary. Depending on who did it, of course."

"Well," said ZZ, "National Geographic has already done some pretty amazing work on the subject. They even captured a few Chicago coyotes and put cameras on them. I'll see if I can find some of the footage . . ."

While she fiddled with the remote, Consuela served the soup course. "There we go," ZZ said at last. We enjoyed an excellent clam chowder while watching a coyote's-eye view of late-night streets bounce and jerk past—a combination that wasn't all that popular after a minute or two.

"Okay, enough of that," ZZ announced, returning to the non-mobile Monets. "Inducing motion sickness in my guests during dinner is the last thing I want."

"Thank you," Fikru said. "I have to admit, it was starting to get to me. At least all the shots were low to the ground—if those cameras had been attached to eagles, I'd have to leave the room."

"Acrophobia?" I asked.

"Absolutely," Fikru said. "I stay on the ground floor whenever I can. Been that way since I was a kid."

"Not me," said Lucky. "You have to be fearless to direct movies. Know who my idol is? Werner Herzog. Any director whose advice includes *always carry bolt cutters with you* and *there's nothing wrong with spending a night in jail if it gets you the shot* will always be my personal hero."

"Everybody has fears," Tervo said mildly.

"Sure," Jaxon said. I noticed he'd been doing more drinking than talking for a while. "Actors, especially. We just know how to *use* that fear."

"Exactly," said Tervo. "Any strong emotion you can—"

Jaxon interrupted him. "Insecurity is the worst, though. Right? Right. I mean, if you're afraid of heights you can just not go anywhere high. But some things you can't get away from."

Oscar raised his glass. "In my experience it depends on how fast they can chase you, and the manner of transport with which you make your escape."

"Especially with eighty-proof fuel in the engine," ZZ said with a disapproving glance. She had nothing against drinking, but I know she wished Oscar did a little less of it.

"My point," said Jaxon, "is that actors are some of the most insecure people alive. About our talent, about what people think of us, and most of all about our careers. Know what I say when aspiring astors ack me—sorry—aspiring *actors ask* me, for advice? Water wings. Buy some good-quality water wings, 'cause you're gonna be treading water for the rest of your life."

"Quite true," said Tervo. "Though some of us are better swimmers than others."

I was pretty sure Tervo meant that as a compliment, but I could be wrong; in any case, Jaxon took it as a slight. He didn't get angry, not visibly, but he turned to Tervo with an even bigger smile and said, "And some of us are terrified of drowning. 'Specially when you've been in the pool for a while, right? Somebody tosses you a life preserver, you grab that sucker, no matter *who* threw it. Or what it's attached to."

"Maybe we should change the subject," Lucky said. Directors need many skills, but defusing conflicts between clashing egos is high on the list.

"No, no," Jaxon insisted. "There's this line you have to

walk when you're an actor, between taking risks and chickening out. I just wanted to make it clear which side of the line Mr. Tervo is on."

"Are we dropping the swimming metaphor, then?" Oscar asked. "We seem to have moved on to line-walking and poultry."

Jaxon ignored him. "I've seen your contract, Tervo. Two sequels? Really? Why don't you just wear a collar with your name on it?"

Tervo met Jaxon's eyes, but neither smiled nor got angry. "I don't have the luxury of youth, Mr. Nesbitt. I have a family and bills to pay. If you're fortunate, one day you'll understand that."

"Oh, I understand it just fine, Mr. Tervo," Jaxon said. "What I don't understand is why you agreed to do two sequels for *no money*."

Tervo didn't reply for a long moment. Nobody else at the table said a word. Finally, Tervo dropped his eyes and said, "You may have seen the contract, but you obviously didn't read it. I *am* being paid for all three films—in fact, I'm being paid in advance. One lump sum as opposed to staggered payments."

"Really?" Lucky said. "I had no idea—Maurice wouldn't tell me a thing."

Jaxon was looking smug, Tervo was looking defensive, Lucky was looking curious but concerned.

"I've had some . . . financial difficulties," Tervo said. "I confided in Mr. Rolvink and he proposed this arrangement."

"Awfully generous of him," Fikru said.

"Generous?" said Tervo. "Hardly. I'm locked in to a three-picture deal for barely more than the salary for one. If I didn't need the money so badly, I would have thrown the contract in his face. As it is, I can only hope all three are made quickly enough that I don't starve to death in the meantime. Excuse me." He abruptly stood, turned, and strode out of the room.

"For a chap afraid of starving to death," Oscar said, "he certainly left at a bad time. Here comes the main course."

Everyone turned their concentration onto their food, easing the tension and providing an excuse to change the subject. Fikru started talking about a South American drug called Yopo that tribes shot up their noses using the equivalent of blowguns, and pretty soon the conversation had wandered so far from the subject of actors' paychecks nobody even tried to drag it back.

But it made me wonder: Exactly how serious were Maxwell Tervo's financial troubles—and what would happen if the producer of those movies suddenly turned up dead?

7.

After dinner I popped back in to my office to finish up a few things before I headed home. Whiskey sat in front of my desk and waited, while Tango sprawled bonelessly on the couch.

<Lassie, huh? Big deal.>

[As I'm tired of explaining, Lassie was a fictional character. This was simply one of the dogs who played Lassie in the television show. His name is Pal.]

<I thought Lassie was a she. As in Lass—*ee.>*

[Acting. A skill you wouldn't understand.]

<I understand plenty. Cats are natural-born actors.>

Whiskey snorted. [Please. The essence of acting is to see the world through someone else's eyes. Cats are simply too self-centered to even attempt this.]

<Well, you're at least partly right. Cats don't attempt anything. We decide, and then we act.*>*

[That's not what I meant by *acting*.]

<I know exactly what you meant. You meant pretending to be someone else. Cats are extremely good at pretending to be someone else. In fact, I've been pretending to be

someone else for this entire conversation, and you haven't even noticed!>

"I don't think that's how it works, kitty."

<Kitty? Who is kitty? I am the Archduchess Perfecta von Turtleneck.> She sat up and looked around regally. *<Bring me the royal catnip. I feel a craving.>*

[That's not acting. *This* is acting.]

Whiskey can shape-change really fast when he wants to. He went from being a bright-eyed blue heeler to a squat, pudgy bulldog in an instant. The voice inside my head that accompanied this was thick and even more British than usual. [We shall fight them on the streets, we shall fight them in the parks, we shall fight them in the pet shops. And we shall never surrender.]

Tango's sniff was the epitome of dismissal. *<Oh, please. Changing form isn't acting, and neither is that ludicrous excuse for an accent. Acting is all about* attitude.>

Whiskey shifted into a German shepherd. [Vell, you haff plenty of zat, fraulein. Such a shame you don't haff ze skill to go vith it, jah?]

<For Bast's sake. That is the most atrocious . . . stop, just stop. Do you have any idea what it's like for an actual language expert to listen to you mangle an accent like that? Do me a favor and change into something that's mute. A mimehound, maybe.>

"Technically, that would be a dog that hunted mimes. Not that I'm saying that's a bad idea."

Whiskey reverted to his usual form. [My point is that acting is a very fluid, reactive process. The feline mind is simply too stubborn to be anything other than what it is, a fact you're usually proud of.]

Tango's eyes narrowed. *<I'm proud of everything I do. That weird thing you do with your face when you feel . . . what's it called again? Sheem?>*

[Shame.]

<*Yeah, cats just don't get that.*>

Whiskey rolled his eyes. [How can you possibly claim to be a great actor when you admit there's an *entire emotion* you don't understand?]

<*Easy. I was acting.*>

Whiskey growled in exasperation. [You can't—that's not—it doesn't even—]

<*See? That's the kind of reaction only a truly great performance can provoke.*>

"Oh, there's a whole lot of provoking going on, that's for sure."

[Look, let me make this as simple as possible: Numerous dogs have had long, successful careers as actors, both on television and in films. Name *one* cat.]

<*Morris.*>

[Putting a bowl of food in front of a cat and filming it eating is not acting.]

<*Garfield.*>

[Is a cartoon.]

<*The Cat in the Hat.*>

[Is *another* cartoon.]

<*Salem, in* Sabrina the Teenage Witch.>

[*Was* a comic book. Graduated to being portrayed by an animatronic puppet—which, while stiff, unconvincing, and more than a little creepy, was *still* a better actor than a cat.]

I sighed. "Guys, guys, guys. You're both missing the obvious."

I spun my monitor around so they could see it. "Grumpy Cat and Ceiling Cat," I said. "Along with a few hundred thousand others. Sorry, Whiskey—on the Internet at least, cats rule."

To my surprise, Tango gave her head an annoyed shake. <*Yeah, not so much, Toots. Taking pictures when we're not at our best and showing them to the world? That's not acting, that's just cruel.>*

[I have to concur. Posing an animal—even a cat—in a humiliating costume with a childish caption is hardly art.]

I frowned. "An issue that you two agree on? Wow. Obviously, I am on the wrong side of this. My apologies." I made a mental note to dump a certain file in the digital trash as soon as possible.

[Clearly we are not going to resolve this with facts, as you refuse to recognize mine and are countering them with nonsense. I will have to settle for Foxtrot recognizing the superiority of my argument—]

"Whoa! Slow down there, speedy. You're not dragging me into the middle of this."

<Yeah, especially since she agrees with me.>

I cocked an ear to one side. "Did you hear that? That scraping noise? Like a tortured soul's fingernails on the floorboards as she's slowly pulled to her doom . . . Me, now, middle of this."

<Glad you're on board. And I'm going to up the ante by saying not only are cats better actors than dogs, we're better at the whole movie thing in general. What do you see up there on the screen before the feature starts? Is it a schnauzer? A Great Dane? A dalmation? No. It's a lion, a great big honking full-maned King of the Beasts.>

[That's only for certain movies, not all of them—and you're not suggesting the lion is the one who actually *made* those films, are you?]

<You can't prove he didn't is all I'm saying. Ooh, I thought of another one—the Lion in The Wizard of Oz.>*

[Man in a furry suit, with makeup. While I will concede that lions are large and fearsome predators, I'm skeptical of their ability to sing and dance.]

<You're skeptical cats can do anything. If I told you a

cat could make a better movie than a dog, you'd sneer at that, too.>

[You're mistaken. A dog's facial musculature makes it quite difficult to sneer and laugh at the same time.]

"The things you learn as life's grand pageant rolls along," I murmured. "Come on, guys, wrap it up. Mommy wants to go home and get horizontal with the latest John Connolly novel and a cup of chamomile."

Whiskey cocked a skeptical eyebrow at me. [Please don't refer to yourself as *Mommy*. You don't have the requisite breasts.]

"What a disturbing yet insulting thing to say. Too big? Too small?"

[Too few.]

<Also, not hairy enough. Tell you what, Whiskbroom—I'll prove it to you. I'll make a movie myself.>

I was still recovering from the previous remark, so it took me a second to digest what Tango was saying. "Wait. Make a movie? How?"

<Please. All I need is somebody with a camera phone, a story idea, and some actors. You can provide the first, the second will be a breeze, and the third is practically taken care of.>

[Is it? What are you planning on doing, recruiting talent from the film being shot here?]

<Nah. I was thinking more of drawing on the retired side of Hollywood Boulevard.>

[Oh, no.]

<Why not? I mean, if Lassie's already hanging around, pining for her—sorry, his—glory days, there's gotta be more out there.>

[And how are you planning on getting them to show up on film? They're *ghosts*, Tango.]

<Details, details. Hey, anybody remember the name of that hamster that had his own show? I used to love that guy.>

Whiskey put his head down on the carpet and covered his muzzle with one paw.

I had expected the police to be gone by the time I came in for work the next morning, but there were still police vehicles parked beside the house and yellow caution tape blocking off large parts of the yard—including the section containing the free-form sculptures erected by Keene. Lucky Trentini was waiting for me at the front door with a large white mug of coffee in one hand and a worried look on his face. Actually, it was pretty much the same look he always seemed to wear, so maybe it wasn't so much worry as general angst.

Whiskey and I strolled up. "Morning, Lucky. How are you today?"

"I'm—not good. Not good." He gestured with the coffee mug. "Just look at this mess. I have reshoots to do, and I need this space."

"I'll see about getting it cleaned up as soon as possible."

He shook his head morosely. "I know you're good at what you do, Foxtrot, but unless you've got some serious clout with the cops, I'm not gonna hold my breath. They seem to think all this stuff is somehow related to the explosion or the body, I'm not sure which. None of my people are being allowed anywhere near it."

I nodded in sympathy. "I see. But isn't being without your female lead going to put a serious crimp in your shooting schedule anyway?"

He took a sip of coffee and stared glumly at an exercise

bike balanced on top of an empty planter. "No, not really. Mainly I need some more zombie crowd shots— Natalia's scenes are all done."

"How's she doing?" I already knew, having called the hospital this morning, but I wanted him to know I cared enough to ask.

"Good news, thank God. Vital signs are all strong and healthy. The real question is whether or not there's brain damage. Brain damage, for God's sake, on the set of a zombie movie. The Internet's gonna have a field day with it."

I winced. "Yeah. I think I saw a few media vultures hanging around the front gate when I drove in. They're circling, but haven't landed yet."

"My Twitter feed is practically screaming at me for information. I posted a brief message last night, but I'm gonna have to give them something more, soon. I just don't know what I'm supposed to say."

I shrugged. "I can get some extra security down here if you want. Stop them from scaling the walls, anyway."

"I can't afford that. This production is bleeding money every minute we're not filming, and the guy with the credit card is missing in action. Maybe permanently."

I remembered the conversation Rolvink had with Lucky about money. "Right. Rolvink wanted you to wrap things up early, didn't he?"

"Yeah, but it wasn't because we were over budget. I think he was more worried about his financial backers than anything else."

I frowned. "Worried? Why?"

Lucky hesitated. "Maybe I shouldn't say anything, but—I got the feeling some of the money wasn't exactly clean. Frankly, those sorts of questions are the kind you don't ask. You might not like the answer, or what sort of accent it's delivered in. Which is not meant to be an ethnic slur, because the country I'm talking about is Criminal-istan."

"I see. You think that might have something to do with what happened to him?"

He shrugged. "Could be. Maybe he's dead, maybe he just decided to cut his losses and run. The last conversation I had with him, he said he was looking at taking on another investor."

"An investor with the last name of Zoransky, perhaps?"

He shook his head. "No, actually. He said he was going to talk to Keene's friend, Yemane Fikru."

I blinked. That was a surprise—I didn't think the two of them had anything in common. Well, other than . . .

Lucky saw the look on my face and nodded. "Drugs, yeah. He didn't share any details, but I could tell what he was thinking. Guess it didn't pan out, though."

"Guess not," I said. "Well, as far as the paparazzi go, ZZ values her privacy, too. I'll talk to her, see what I can—uh-oh."

"Uh-oh? That's not a good sound. *What* uh-oh, *why* uh-oh—oh."

Whiskey, I thought. *Do you see that?*

[I do. Do you want me to round him up? I *am* wearing the form of a cattle dog.]

Not yet.

What we were discussing was the sudden—but not entirely unprecedented—appearance of an ostrich on the front lawn.

"There's an ostrich on your front lawn," Lucky said. "Which is probably the *least* strange thing that's happened since I got here."

"That's Oswald." I sighed. "He's not even supposed to be outside, let alone roaming free. I knew I shouldn't let him have that subscription to *Lockpick World,* but it was Christmas and I just couldn't bear the look in those big, sad eyes."

Oswald is our resident escape expert—or was, until Owduttf made his break. I honestly don't know how Oswald does it; I've tried getting Tango to ask him, but he always plays dumb. Which means he's either a criminal genius or just too dumb to understand what he does is impossible.

We stared at him. He stared at us. He was about twenty feet away from the first yellow ribbon of crime scene tape, and every time it fluttered a little his head would jerk to it for a second, then back to us.

"Careful," I said quietly. "Don't spook him. You wouldn't believe how fast he can run."

"Oh, I'd believe it. I've seen *Jurassic Park* at least a dozen times, and looking at those legs right now I have no problem in believing birds are descended from dinosaurs. The *T. rex* in particular."

He had a point. Ostriches have incredibly powerful legs tipped with claws, and they're sharp enough to disembowel a human or even kill a lion. They can sprint at over forty miles an hour, stand up to nine feet tall, and weigh over three hundred pounds. They prefer running away to fighting, but they can also be aggressive and territorial.

Oswald looked at the tape, then back at us. Tape, us, tape, us.

If he crosses that tape, I thought at Whiskey, *he could compromise the whole crime scene. Which, Lucky's complaints notwithstanding, is probably a bad thing.*

[If I'm going to intercede, I'll have to get between him and the tape. I can't do that as long as he's watching us.]

Go around the house and try to sneak up on him from the other side.

"Whiskey, circle and contain," I said. He turned and trotted casually away from us, but not before sending me a parting thought: [Circle and contain? Really? That's what you come up with?]

Shut up. I'm trying to sound like a professional dog-talking person.

[Redundant-talking person is more like it.]

"Wow," said Lucky, watching Whiskey disappear around the corner of the house. "Your dog is really well trained."

"Yet strangely impolite," I said.

Which is when Oswald took one big step closer to the tape.

"No!" I said. "Don't do it, Oswald. Do not—"

He looked at me and blinked with absurdly long cartoon eyelashes. And took another slow, deliberate step.

"No. Bad bird. *Bad* bird. Stay. Do not move."

"You do realize you're scolding poultry," Lucky pointed out. "Giant poultry, but still."

Oswald studied me with those gigantic eyes. Two inches across, the biggest peepers of any non-aquatic animal alive. I stared into them and thought as hard as I could: *Oswald. Please. Just stay where you are and I'll bring you a whole bag of nice, juicy crickets—*

Big, round eyes as innocent as a toddler's. And just as ready to see how far he could push me.

One more step. Right up to the edge of the tape.

Whiskey! Don't—

Which is when my dog chose to tear wildly around the far corner of the building, barking his head off. If Oswald had been just a few feet farther away from the tape, it might have worked; as it was, it just drove the ostrich right where I didn't want him. He tore through the yellow tape like a sprinter at the finish line, and bolted right into the modern art exhibit Keene had turned the lawn into.

Whiskey skidded to a stop and looked to me for guidance.

"Don't just stand there!" I called. "Get him out of there!"

Which was exactly what Whiskey wanted to hear.

My dog may be dead, but that doesn't mean his instincts are. According to him, whatever breed he's currently embodying colors his outlook as well as his abilities; when he's a Newfoundland dog, for instance, he's powerfully attracted to water. And blue heelers—or Australian cattle dogs, as they're also known—have been bred for generations to chase and herd cattle.

When there are no cows around, I guess an oversized chicken will do.

Of course, Bessie's top speed is considerably less than an ostrich's. They even race them in some places—ostriches, I mean, not cows. Apparently Oswald had some sprinter in him, as he tore around the lawn like a greyhound after a rabbit, a length of yellow plastic wrapped around his neck as if sporting a jaunty scarf. Whiskey tore right after him, barking crazily.

"Circle and contain! *Circle and contain!*" I hollered.

[Stop yelling that! It doesn't *mean* anything!]

Well, stop barking like a maniac! It's not helping!

[I can't help myself! *Oh Gods this is glorious!*]

So much for the sanctity of the crime scene. Amazingly, neither of them crashed into anything during their crazed dash around the impromptu obstacle course—though at one point Oswald did make an impressive bound right over a pyramid of yoga balls lashed together with duct tape.

"Get him out of there!" I called. "Herd him back toward his pen!"

[Yes! Yes! Give me instruction! Use the word *herd* again!]

Okay, that made me distinctly uncomfortable—but it seemed to work. Whiskey managed to get Oswald headed in the right direction, which unfortunately was straight toward us. I knew he'd veer away, but Lucky wasn't as experienced in the habits of enormous runaway feather dusters. He shrieked and dove to the side, splashing coffee all over the place.

As I expected, Oswald darted to the left at the last second (though that's probably not the right verb for a creature his size; *javelined* is more accurate), his huge, two-toed feet ripping clods of dirt out of the lawn as he cornered. Ernesto was going to be some annoyed when I told him he had to fix that.

[Can I make him do a lap around the house before getting him into his pen? Please please please?]

No! Curb your damn instincts and corral him already!

[Okay, okay!]

I watched them disappear behind a hedge, then leaned down and helped Lucky up. "Are you all right?"

"Fine, fine. Just embarrassed. You remember what I said last night about directors being fearless? I wasn't scared, I was just doing my impression of somebody who's scared. You know, in case I ever have to communicate that to someone I'm directing. What with me being a director, and totally devoid of fear."

"Totally," I agreed. "Though not entirely devoid of a thin layer of coffee, I'm afraid. Or a broken mug."

He looked at the white handle of the ceramic mug he still held, though the mug itself was no longer attached. "Yeah. Well, easily remedied. Don't you have to, uh, go after them?"

"Whiskey's got it under control. But I should give Caroline a call and let her know what's up." I pulled out my phone.

"I'm going to get a new mug of coffee. And a dry shirt."

I gave Caroline the news, and she told me she'd be right down. Then I contacted Whiskey, who told me he'd chased Oswald into his pen and was guarding the open gate. I walked over to see for myself, and got there just as Caroline did.

She looked more apologetic than annoyed. "My fault. I came through here this morning and left it open—Oswald was locked in his house. Sure, he's hard to keep contained, but I didn't think he could defeat a door dead-bolted from the outside."

"He didn't," I said, pointing. I could see the open window from here. "He found another exit."

Whiskey now had Oswald trapped in one corner of the pen and was pacing back and forth in front of him with his head down, his eyes intent. Oswald was watching him with the same blank-eyed look he always wore, an expression somewhere between *inscrutable* and *idiot*.

Caroline and I went over to examine the window. From the scratches and dents on the frame, we deduced he must have pried it open using both his beak and feet.

"Well, let's get him back inside," Caroline said. "Ostriches are native to Africa—they're not built for this kind of cold."

That turned out to be surprisingly easy; we just closed the window, opened the door, and had Whiskey usher him inside. "I'll jam something into the frame from the outside for now," Caroline said. "Until I can install something a little more permanent."

"I'd suggest a cell in low-earth orbit, except I'm pretty sure Oswald would be the first ostrich in history to figure out how to fly. And to invent heat-shielding made from feathers and bird poop."

"Speaking of escapees . . . I've figured out how the honey badger has been getting out. He went old-school—World War Two POW, in fact."

"A tunnel, you mean? But—from where? I couldn't see any evidence of digging."

"Inside the burrow. Down, then out about twenty feet away, under a hedge."

"What? There's a foot of concrete under that burrow!"

"I know. But honey badgers are strong, persistent, and have impressive claws. I mean, *I'm* impressed."

"*The Great Escape,* honey-badger-style," I murmured. "Wait—in the movie, they came up with clever ways to hide the dirt from their digging. How did the badger do it?"

"As near as I can figure, he ate it." She shrugged. "I should have noticed, I know. But he consumed it in small enough quantities that it didn't cause a significant change in the appearance of his droppings."

"So what are you going to do?"

"I've moved him into a temporary cage. We'll have to dig up the floor, put in a layer of steel—not mesh, actual steel—and put earth over it. If he can dig through that, I say we give him a cape and let him go."

"Works for me."

I told Caroline I'd get some estimates for contractors to do the work on the pen, then collected Whiskey and headed back toward the house. Two crises dealt with already, and I hadn't even made it in the front door yet. But now I had a new item on my agenda: talk to Yemane Fikru and find out what sort of deal—if any—the possibly-late Maurice Rolvink had tried to make with him.

Once I was actually inside, I made my usual rounds: to the kitchen, first, to make sure breakfast was going fine. Ben met me at the door with a kiss, which is also part of my rounds. Priorities, you know.

"No Tango?" I said, glancing around. "She's usually here patrolling for renegade bacon."

"Haven't seen her for a while," Ben said. "She bolted down her breakfast, muttered something about a casting call, and vanished."

"Well, this should be interesting," I said. I told Ben about the argument my partners had last night and Tango's claim.

Ben grinned. "A movie, huh? With ghost actors? How's she planning on filming it?"

"Beats me. Maybe she's got connections with the ghost of Stanley Kubrick's cat."

Ben shook his head. "Just when I think this place can't get any stranger . . ."

"Speaking of stranger," I said, "how's class going?" Ben was undergoing tutoring in some of the finer points of being a Thunderbird by Teresa Firstcharger, a fellow weather elemental. Most of the instruction took place in Thunderspace, a mystic dimension where time passed differently, which was convenient when you needed to cram for finals and suddenly five minutes turned into a day and a half. Ben usually went first thing every morning, which meant he'd already put in a full day before putting on his apron. That might sound exhausting, but Ben told me being in Thunderspace charged him up; he always felt great after spending some time there.

"Didn't go today," Ben said. "Teresa's taking some time off. Got a big First Nations conference coming up and needs to focus. Gave me homework to keep me busy while she's gone, though."

"Oh? Let me guess—a ten-thousand-word essay on the history of weather vanes and how they influenced the design of early-nineteenth-century roofs."

"Nope. She wants me to work on my landings."

"Your landings? Is there something wrong halfway up your staircase?" I glanced down. "Hmmm. Hard to tell. Could be banister rot."

"No, I mean my actual landings. When I'm, you know . . ."

"A big bird?"

"You know I hate it when you call me that."

"Oooh. Not a big bird, more of a grouch. Your garbage can leaking again?"

"So, references to *Sesame Street* are your preferred method of flirting?"

"Only when I'm semi-serious. If I'm really into a guy, I'll drop some heavy *Muppet Show* innuendo."

Ben started cracking eggs into a large steel bowl. "That reminds me of a joke. What's green and—"

I held a finger up to his lips. "Stop. I've heard that joke and it's disgusting. Also highly inappropriate in the vicinity of bacon."

"Bacon?" said Catree, walking through the back door with her steel mug in one hand. "Yes, please. Unless I'm being highly inappropriate, in which case pretty please. With extra bacon on top."

"Hey, Catree," I said. "I'm working on the front-lawn problem, I promise."

She spotted a carafe of coffee and filled her mug. "I'm sure you are. But don't rush on my account; I'm getting paid for my time regardless. And I think our producer is past caring—I just hope his last check clears."

I frowned. "You really think the body I found is his?"

"Let's see. They're having trouble IDing it, so it must be mutilated pretty bad. That pretty much fits in with the fantasies of everyone who ever met the man, so chances are good. Plus, I'm an optimist."

"Doesn't sound like he was real popular," said Ben.

"Maybe among invertebrates. I think he must have been part slug, because mostly what he produced was slime. There's a school of thought that leans more toward the snail side—some sort of metaphor about the shell and callousness—but I never bought into that. Nope, garden-variety slug all the way."

"You're obviously not worried about being blamed for his death," I said.

"Or *am* I?" she asked, trying to look mysterious. "Maybe I'm trying to deflect suspicion by pointing out the obvious. *Maybe* I'm so confident in my evil scheme I can openly proclaim my loathing. *Maybe* I know there are so many people who feel the same I'll just disappear into the crowd. Or *maybe* I'm just really, really impulsive and unable to keep my mouth shut."

"I won't tell if you won't," I said. I grabbed a muffin from the counter and took a bite. "Seriously, he couldn't have been *that* universally hated."

Catree shook her head. "You didn't know the guy. I think even Natalia despised him, and she was sleeping with him. If that corpse turns out to be someone else, I'll bet you a vat of coffee and a grilled cheese sandwich Rolvink killed him to fake his own death and skipped the country with every dollar he could embezzle."

Ben looked puzzled. "A grilled cheese sandwich?"

"Hey, I *love* grilled cheese sandwiches."

I leaned on the counter and took another bite of the muffin. "How about the director? Rolvink's financing his project—Lucky can't bear him too much ill will."

"No? Word is, Rolvink really screwed him on the financial end. If this film makes any money, it'll all go into Maurice's pocket. If it doesn't—well, I heard Lucky put up his house as collateral for some of the financing. Been in his family for generations."

"And if Rolvink goes missing?"

Catree shrugged. "Depends on if the money went missing, too. If Rolvink just drops dead, the production goes ahead—believe it or not, this isn't the first time something like this has happened in the movie biz, and the contracts have evolved to deal with every possibility. These days the apocalypse could occur and there'd be multiple clauses on how each and every facet would affect production: *If the party of the first part is raptured, all agreements between the licensee and the guarantor shall still be valid, unless the party of the second part is killed by a plague of frogs.* And so on."

Interesting. Even if Rolvink was dead, the movie wasn't. Like the zombies it was portraying, it would lurch along until someone came along and shot it in the head. Or it ate them.

Okay, maybe it wasn't that much like a zombie.

"Well, this is pleasant, but I have to get to work," I said. I gave Ben a kiss, Catree a wave, and strode away while pulling out my phone. Whiskey, as usual, trotted along behind me.

"You're being quiet," I said to Whiskey as we headed for my office. "You didn't even chime in when I mentioned Tango's new project to Ben. I thought for sure you'd have a few choice comments to make."

He sniffed. [You thought incorrectly. Dogs prefer to confront an opponent honestly, rather than talking about them behind their back. Human beings have an idiom for doing such a thing, I believe; you call it being *catty.*]

"Which, ironically enough, you're sort of doing right now by pointing that out."

He gave me one of those worried looks dogs do so well. [That was not my intention.]

"Don't worry about it, doggy. I'm just yanking your chain."

[I'm not wearing a chain. Or a collar, for that matter.]

I sighed. "Never mind. Let's just—"

I stopped dead. Farther down the hall, blocked by police tape, was the bombed room. That was still off limits, but the other rooms had been cleared for use.

Including the room next to Natalia's, the one Rolvink had been staying in.

"Whiskey, have you ever had an idea so obvious that when you thought of it, you immediately felt stupid because you didn't think of it earlier?"

He considered this. [No.]

"Well, prepare for a new experience. Maybe the police are having a hard time telling whether or not that corpse belongs to Maurice Rolvink, but *you* could tell in an instant."

[That's true—if I'd ever met the man. You were keeping me locked up in the office, remember?] That accusing look was back on his face again.

"Let's try not to dwell on the past. You may not have met him before—but you can still meet his *stuff*." I walked toward the door of Rolvink's room, pulling out my master key as I went.

Whiskey didn't follow. I glanced back and saw that he was still standing there, the oddest expression on his face: it's hard to describe, but I'm going to go with confused embarrassment as opposed to embarrassed confusion. "Whiskey?"

[Foxtrot. That reaction you mentioned a moment ago?]

"Yes?"

[I believe I'm having it.]

I grinned. "Don't take it too hard. We had a bombing right on top of finding a corpse; that tends to tax the crisis-management protocols. You wind up paying so much attention to the actual emergency and its aftermath that anything not stamped URGENT in bright-red letters gets shuffled aside for later. My brain just informed me that now is, in fact, later."

[So it is. Shall we?]

I unlocked the door and opened it. "After you, my dear bloodhound."

[That won't be necessary. My current nose is more than enough to identify a simple human scent.]

A brief word about Whiskey's olfactory abilities, and that word is *phenomenal*—which, at four syllables, isn't brief at all. But it is accurate, and not just because his talent at shape-shifting also grants him the skills of the breed he's emulating. No, what's really amazing is his access to a supernatural library of smells, an olfactory repository that holds every aroma and odor ever experienced by any dog's nose, ever. It's an awfully handy—or nosy, I guess—tool if you're an investigative sort. Which we definitely are.

Whiskey paused at the threshold and took a first, tentative sniff. [Hmm. Still a lot of charred wood in the air, but I think I detect something familiar . . .]

"Inside," I said, softly but urgently. "I don't want any nice police officers wandering out and seeing us being all Sherlocky."

[Very well.] He stepped into the room and I stepped after him, closing the door behind me.

Whiskey immediately went to the suitcase lying open on the bed. He jumped up and sniffed at the clothes. [Yes. These were worn by the man whose body we found. His scent is all over this room.]

So Maurice Rolvink was dead. But who killed him—and how?

8.

While we were there, we did a quick search of the room for anything that might tell us more. The police had already done that, of course, and about all we learned that they didn't know was the brand of Natalia's perfume.

[There's not much of it, though,] Whiskey reported. [I don't believe she spent much time here.]

So if what Catree told me was true, Rolvink and Natalia went to Natalia's room for their little trysts as opposed to the producer's. That said something about their relationship; Rolvink wasn't letting her get too close. They may have been sleeping together, but they weren't exactly a couple.

We slipped out of the room, locking it behind us, and continued on to my office. I had some thinking to do.

"Let me bounce a few things off you," I said to Whiskey once I was seated behind my desk and he had taken his usual spot (well, usual when Tango wasn't occupying it) on the sofa.

[Please don't. Just because I'm made of ectoplasm

doesn't mean I don't feel pain. Also, it seems rather pointless.]

"Don't be so literal. I meant ideas, doofus."

[Carry on.]

I squinted at him suspiciously. My dog's ability to grasp human idioms is not exactly consistent, and seems to vary depending on his mood. He's not the only one with a chain that gets yanked.

"Okay. We know Rolvink wasn't a popular guy. If he was killed by the one of the guests, as opposed to our resident bee-poop eater *slash* bodysnatcher, then we might not be looking at a single murder—we might be looking at two murder *attempts,* only one of which succeeded."

[But Rolvink was already dead when the bomb went off.]

"Yes. Which suggests that the two killers may have been working independently, neither one aware of the other's plans. One plants a bomb and sets it to go off when they think Rolvink will be in Natalia's room, while the other actually stalks and kills Rolvink."

[A man so despised that people are competing to eliminate him? Perhaps.]

"There are other possibilities, of course. The killer sets the explosive, then learns that Rolvink won't be there when he's supposed to and kills him in person, instead."

[And the bomb?]

I shrugged. "Maybe the killer can't get back in the room. Maybe they hate both Natalia and Rolvink and always planned to kill both of them. Maybe . . ."

[Maybe they suffered a blackout and forgot they'd planted a bomb in the first place.]

I raised my eyebrows in disbelief. "Seriously? Come on. First of all, Keene's not even a suspect—what's his motive? Second of all, planting a bomb takes planning and precision—it's not the kind of thing you do while wired out of your skull."

[But turning the front lawn into an obstacle course is?]

"Yes, actually. One shows poor impulse control and a touch of manic delusion, while the other is obsessive, sociopathic, and violent. Which, weirdly enough, is also a pretty good description of the two basic kinds of serial killers: disorganized and organized."

He put his head down on his paws. [That still doesn't explain what that monstrosity is or why he built it.]

"Well, maybe we can figure it out. Deductive reasoning, right? It's what we're good at."

[I see little reason in Keene's creation, or in trying to understand it.]

"You never can tell what's important in a mystery, Whiskey. You have to pay attention to all the information, especially the stuff that doesn't make sense. More often than not, that's what solves the case."

[Let's get back to the bomb. What do we know about it?]

"Well, let's see. I got a good look at the room before the police closed everything off, and it looked like the bomb was on the mantelpiece, just over the fireplace." I frowned. "No, wait. That's not quite right. There were bricks all over the room. If the bomb had been on the mantel, the bricks would have been blown backward, into the chimney itself. I mean, I'm no explosives expert, but doesn't that make sense?"

[I suppose. Wouldn't they have fallen through to a lower fireplace as well?]

"Yes, and that didn't happen. Lots of soot and ash blasted through, but no bricks. Which can only mean one thing."

[The bomb was in the chimney.]

"And that gives us a timeline. The night before the big boom it was cold, and the fireplaces on both the first and second floors had blazes in them. That means the bomb had to be placed afterward, late enough that the fires were out and before the next morning."

[Obviously. Which means someone gained access to Cardoso's room in the middle of the night.]

I nodded. "And was able to do so without waking her up—or maybe because they knew she wouldn't be there."

[Which raises many questions, but answers none of them.]

I leaned back in my chair. "Yeah, but at least we have a starting point. We need to find out if any of the guests were out of their rooms during the night."

[Well, we already know one was. We even know what he was doing, though not why.]

"You're right. And if anyone was likely to have seen something in the wee hours, it's the guy that was hauling exercise equipment out of the storage room at three AM . . ."

We found Keene in a little nook just off the dining room, clutching a cup of tea and staring blankly out at his handi-work. He wore a pair of rumpled red silk pajamas, over-sized plush slippers in the same color, and the beginnings of a wispy beard. He glanced blearily at me when I pulled up a chair and sat down next to him. "Not you again," he said.

"Good morning to you, too. Don't worry, I've dialed the cheerfulness down a few notches. How are you feeling?"

"Like I just slept for sixteen hours but forgot to lie down."

"Ouch. Well, now that you've seen your creation again for the very first time, what do you think? Anything coming back to you?"

He took a slow sip of tea and considered the view. Looked all the way to the right, winced, then looked to the left. "Huh. Is that an inflatable walrus?"

"I believe so. You paid a little visit to the cabana at some point."

He gave his head a single, careful nod. "Well. Junior out there does bear a certain resemblance to myself, there's no denying that. Same carefree attitude, lack of moral inhibitions, and a certain flair for the inexplicable. But my lawyers tell me I really must insist on a DNA test to be sure."

"I was hoping you'd say that."

He raised an eyebrow at me. "I'm not going to like your explanation of why you said that, so I'm going to pretend you didn't. Care to join me for a late breakfast of tea, a picture of some toast, and more tea? The toast is optional."

"Maybe later. First, you're going to change into some warmer clothes, and then we're going to take a little tour of your masterpiece."

He groaned. "But it's bloody *cold* out there. I'm *English,* love; my blood's as thin as the ethics of a music executive. I go out there, I'll develop little icicles in my arteries. I can feel them forming already."

"The only thing forming in your bloodstream is a picket line of antibodies demanding overtime pay and better working conditions. Besides, you were fine while building the thing."

"Then I was riding a rocket ascending into the heavens. Today I'm lying in a smoking crater and trying to disentangle myself from the shredded remains of a parachute. That's not the right frame of mind to go traipsing round the hinterlands."

"You'll be fine. Fresh air is the best thing for you right now."

"No, an iron lung in a sensory deprivation chamber is the best thing for me right now. Preferably one filled with warm tea, whiskey, and just a touch of morphine."

"Quite a contraption. Sort of like the ones out there."

He gave a huge, eye-rolling sigh. "You're not going to give up, are you?"

"I covered for you last night at dinner. You owe me."

"Ah. Well, when you put it like that—"

"I'll give you twenty minutes. Don't make me come back there and play 'Crazy Love' again."

"You are a cruel taskmaster, Foxtrot Lancaster. I shall be very cross with you later, when I have the energy."

"No, you won't."

He got to his feet. "I *might*. Just a bit."

"Off you go."

He shuffled off, muttering and trying to look as pathetic as possible.

"And don't forget your mittens!" I called after him. "It's kinda cold out there!"

I'm not sure what his reply was, but it sounded fairly obscene and very British.

[Do you think he'll actually come back?] Whiskey asked.

"I predict he'll be about forty-five minutes, which is fine with me. We have to give him something."

[Agreed. How about euthanasia? He'd probably thank us.]

As I expected, Keene was back in three-quarters of an hour. I spent the intervening time answering messages on my phone, making a list of things to check on once the contractors started work, and tweaking the maids' schedule to accommodate Consuela's upcoming trip to visit her mother.

When Keene finally showed up, he was showered,

shaved, and dressed. His attitude wasn't exactly buoyant, but he gave me a grudging smile as he came down the stairs.

"Happy?" he asked. "I'm vertical, mobile, and reasonably lucid."

"I'll give you the first two. Number three you're gonna have to prove."

I handed him a down-filled parka and slipped my own on. "Come on, English. If you start to turn blue, we'll send Whiskey back for . . . well, whiskey, probably."

"Bit early in the day for that, don't you think? Straight, anyway."

We trudged outside. The grass was crunchy with frost underfoot, but it hadn't snowed yet.

"I see Oswald got loose again," said Keene, eyeing the two-toed gouges in the lawn. "Silly bugger. He'll freeze his tail feathers off in this."

"Oswald shares the twin attributes of cunning and blind optimism. He has absolutely no idea what he's going to do once he's out, but he's equally sure it will be something wonderful and worth all the effort. Kind of inspiring, in a lunatic sort of way."

Keene glanced at me sidelong. "Do I detect an undercurrent of not-so-subtle insinuation? A possible comparison, even?"

"Between you and a deranged ostrich? I don't know . . . could an oversized, legally insane turkey have made *this*?"

We stopped in front of the first installation. A dozen or so hula hoops, all of them wrapped in iridescent tape, were stretched around the frame of an electric treadmill, as if the machine itself had decided to get some exercise but hadn't figured out where its hips were.

"Interesting," Keene said. "It makes a statement, doesn't

it? Unfortunately, that statement is *giffnetz the floogle spring,* and that's only a rough translation."

"Sparking any memories?"

He frowned in concentration. "Perhaps . . . no, no, that's a memory from a ski trip in Jamaica."

"You can go skiing in Jamaica?"

"You can go skiing anywhere—it all depends on how much time you're willing to spend getting to the bottom of the hill. Also, you may be interpreting the word *trip* incorrectly."

We walked to the next one. "Ah," Keene said. "Yes. Yes, of course."

"You remember?"

"Not at all. But I do recognize my style. The rake lashed to the wheel of the overturned mountain bike—that's me all over. And the birdbath with the miniature trampoline on top? I might as well have signed it. Wait, what's this?"

He stooped and picked up something from beside the birdbath: a wooden ball with a red stripe. "I . . . think I recall something. Something about . . . *croquet.*"

He walked back to the bike and placed the ball on the inside curve of the rake's tines. Then he gave the bike's pedal a quick turn with his hand; the rake, lashed to the wheel, spun halfway around and stopped, flinging the ball toward the birdbath. It hit the trampoline and bounced, landing a few feet away.

"It's not an obstacle course," Keene said. "It's a croquet field."

"Extreme croquet?" I said.

"No, that's something else. This is more like . . . *enhanced* croquet. That's the phrase that just bubbled up from the murky depths of my mind."

Whiskey sneezed. Since he's an ectoplasmic being

that's not technically alive, he's immune to colds, allergies, and just about anything else that might make you sneeze; I'm pretty sure he does it on purpose, and it's the approximate equivalent of rolling your eyes and swearing at the same time. He claims it's just an instinctual reflex, but I have my doubts.

I looked around the grounds with a new perspective. "I think I'm starting to see the pattern here. Where would you say the start is?"

"Um. Over there?" We walked to one corner of the lawn and examined the structure present; it was the one with the inflated walrus, as well as several empty flowerpots and two garden hoses laid out side by side. "Yeesssss," Keene said slowly. "The tusks are the wicket. Then it goes between the garden hoses, which form a roller-coaster track of sorts going over the flowerpots . . ."

"Eventually heading toward the second wicket, over *here*."

We traced the route around the yard, figuring it out as we went. "Congratulations, Keene," I said. "You've invented a brand-new sport that nobody has ever conceived of before, ever. But for some reason, I'm convinced it's missing something. Hmmm, what could it be . . . wait, I know! A windmill! For some bizarre reason, I'm convinced this course needs a miniature windmill."

He gave me a look. "Yes, yes, we have mini golf in Ye Olde Englande as well, though we usually call it something else."

"Something erudite and sophisticated, no doubt. Putting on The Ritz, maybe? Or the Delicate Application of Force to a Small Ball in Order to Propel It Through an Intricate Maze of Preposterous Objects?"

"Crazy Golf."

"I like mine better."

Whiskey whined. I noticed he was staring fixedly at the wooden ball Keene still held in one hand, his eyes following it as Keene idly tossed it from one hand to another. "Keene," I said. "Either throw that thing or put it down. You're making my *dog* crazy."

[I'm fine. I'm fine. I'm fine. JUST THROW IT, ALREADY!]

Keene looked at the ball in his hand. "Oh. Sorry." He gave it a good toss and Whiskey took off after it so fast I thought he was going to catch it before it hit the ground.

"Working dogs," I said. "Smart as all hell, but they're bred to *do* stuff. Showing them a ball and not throwing it is like waving a small coastal village at a Viking and then not letting them plunder it."

Whiskey was already back with the ball, which he dropped at Keene's feet before sitting back with an expectant look on his face. [Again?]

"An obsessive-compulsive Viking, with boundary issues," I said. "Whatever you do, don't pick it up. You could be here all day."

[That is a scurrilous lie. I am under no compulsion whatsoever to repeat that performance and OH GOD, YES, THANK YOU!]

I gave Keene a pitying look. "Now you've done it. He'll follow you around for the rest of the day."

Keene shrugged. "I know a bit about compulsive behavior. Consider this a down payment on my karmic debt."

"I have enough on my plate without doing metaphysical bookkeeping for your soul, thank you very much."

I paused, thinking about what I'd just said. "On the other paw, who knows? Maybe Whiskey's Catholic. He could put in a good word for you with Saint Francis."

[You're not seriously suggesting I communicate with a being that may or may not exist at the behest of a drug-addled YES YES YES YOU'RE THE BEST I LOVE YOU]

"Yeah, you're definitely racking up the karmic points, there. If the regular place won't have you I'm sure you can find a spot in doggy heaven."

[Foxtrot! You are coming perilously close to violating our strict oath of nondisclosure YES! AGAIN! I HOPE THIS NEVER STOPS WOOF WOOF WOOF WOOF]

I giggled. "*Man,* is he having a good time. I think I've finally found the canine equivalent of catnip. Dognip."

Keene smiled. "It's nice, isn't it? Truth be told, one of the reasons I love visiting here is because of your animals. Can't have any of my own, of course; wouldn't be fair. I'm hardly ever home and you can't drag a cat or a dog along on tour. The road's no place for a pet."

We strolled toward the next installation, Whiskey continuing his manic dash-and-return, Keene continuing to throw the ball.

"There are other options," I pointed out as we walked. "Something small and portable?"

"Nah. Rodents and birds are too high-strung. Fish are out of the question. About the only thing that fits the bill is some sort of lizard or snake, and my repertoire doesn't have enough heavy metal in it to justify either."

"Hmmm," I said. We'd come to what seemed to be the last wicket, if we were interpreting the course correctly. It abutted a hedge, and in fact seemed to extend into it. "The menagerie is on the other side of this hedge. Did your inspiration extend itself all the way into an animal enclosure?"

"I honestly have no idea. But yes, it does seem to go in that direction. Shall we?"

"I suppose we should."

We went around the hedge as opposed to trying to go through, Whiskey trotting alongside us with the ball in his mouth and a hopeful look on his face, and found ourselves behind a building. "Speaking of reptiles, this is where we house ours," I said. There was a ladder propped up against it, one of those extending aluminum ones that you can adjust the height on. The reptile building was only one story high, so the ladder wasn't fully extended.

"No," said Keene, staring at the ladder. "It's not."

"Excuse me?"

"Snakes. This is the building that houses the snakes, right?"

"Well, yes. Snakes are reptiles, so they're in there, too."

Keene shook his head and looked mortified. "Oh, you ridiculous lump of quasi-intelligent protoplasm. A night of epic overindulgence, and this is what you choose to remember? *This* is what qualifies as worthy of our memoirs?"

[What is he babbling about?]

"What," I said, "are you babbling about?"

"Snakes and ladders, Foxtrot. This was to be the last wicket, the ultimate goal of the game. An existential pun, of sorts. Snakes and bloody ladders." He looked dejected. "It's not even properly British. We call it chutes and ladders, which makes a lot more sense. I mean, you slide down a snake's gullet you're not coming out the other end, are you?"

"You're sure? You actually remember doing this?"

"In a blurry, memory-of-a-dream sort of way, yeah. Much as I hate to admit it, this deformed mutant is my offspring. I throw myself on the mercy of whatever legal entity presides over croquet-related desecration of property."

"That would either be the Red Queen or the grounds-keepers. Personally, I'd hope for the Red Queen—all she'll do is chop off your head."

[Well, I'm glad we arrived at a logical conclusion to our endeavors. Now, is he going to throw the ball again or not?]

It didn't look like it. Keene walked over to the ladder and sat on one of the lower rungs, looking glum. "I'm no fan of blackouts, Foxtrot. What good is having fun if you don't recall any of it? Plus, there's the horrible uncertainty that goes along with the experience. I always worry that I've done something unspeakable that will come back to haunt me later . . ."

I wanted to reassure him that wasn't true, that nothing he did during his blackout could be *that* bad.

But I couldn't.

9.

Keene, Whiskey, and I went back to the house. I had Consuela bring us some tea and a plate of the biscuits Keene likes. Whiskey reluctantly left the croquet ball outside and sprawled at my feet looking morose.

Get that expression off your face, I thought at him. *You had your fun, didn't you?*

[I am an ectoplasmic being. I do not require *fun*.] He looked up at me with sad puppy eyes to see if I was falling for it. I wasn't.

"So you were out there all night," I said to Keene. "I'll give you this much—for a decadent sybarite, you sure have a strong work ethic."

Keene was staring out the window at his handiwork again, apparently deep in a morose-off with Whiskey. "Blue-collar upbringing," he said distractedly. "My parents wanted me to make something of myself."

"Well, you definitely made something. And now that you know what you were trying to accomplish, is anything else coming back to you?"

He frowned. "Perhaps. There was a great deal of rushing

around, I remember that much. A sense of purpose, and a certain amount of glee."

"What about people? Do you remember seeing anyone else awake at that hour, or talking to anyone?"

His brow furrowed. ". . . Yes. I do. That woman you're always chatting with, the one with the braids. I remember seeing her."

Catree? She wasn't staying on-site, she was bunking at the motel in town. "Are you sure?"

"Not entirely, no. I didn't speak to her or anything, not that I remember. But I do have this image of her with a great bulging backpack, striding along in the moonlight; I think I was hauling flowerpots at the time."

"So it *is* coming back to you."

He rubbed his chin with one hand. "Bits and pieces. Coming across that ladder jarred something loose, somehow. I also remember seeing a flashing blue light and not knowing what it was . . . I'll have to do some thinking, see if anything else shakes out."

"All right. Call me if you do, all right? I've got to get going—got a million things on my to-be-done-already list."

He stopped me as I was getting up. "Trot. You don't think I had anything to do with—well, any of the nastiness of the last few days?"

"In the sense of causing any of it? Of course not. But you might have *seen* something important, which is why I'm being so persistent about this. Now sit there, drink your tea, and don't think too hard. It'll come to you."

And that's where we left him, still staring out the window, his tea growing cold in front of him.

I wasn't terribly surprised when Lieutenant Forrester called.

"Ms. Lancaster. I was wondering if you would do me a favor."

"That depends, Lieutenant. While I'm definitely in the favor-granting business, I do expect a little quid pro quo. What do you need?"

"Your organizational abilities. I require a little sit-down with everyone who was on the grounds the night before the explosion. I could just show up and start barking orders, but I thought things would go a lot smoother if you'd introduce them to the idea first."

"Oh, you want me to do some *scheduling* for you? Why, Lieutenant—are you flirting with me?"

A short pause, during which I wondered if I'd gone too far. Then: "No. But I will if that'll get me a little cooperation."

"Oh, you silver-tongued devil. How can I resist a line like that? All right, I'll set them up for you. Half an hour each okay?"

"That'll be fine. Please let them know this is strictly routine, none of them is being singled out, and we're just gathering data."

"Don't spook them, right. Now, here's what I want in return: information."

"You know I can't comment about an ongoing investigation." He sounded more amused than annoyed.

"Please. I'm not a reporter, I don't care about anything juicy. I just want an idea—a general idea—how much longer the daily routine is going to be disrupted around here."

"The bomb squad wrapped up their investigation this morning. Homicide is releasing the crime scene later today. When that's done you can start putting everything back in place."

"Thank you so much. That's really all I needed to know." This, of course, was a lie.

People lie all the time. Good people, bad people, smart people, dumb people. People lie on purpose and by accident. People lie by omission, addition, and fudging. People lie for the best of reasons and the worst of reasons, and often don't even realize what they're doing. Lies are the bugs hiding in the cracks of the world; universally present, mostly despised, and utterly necessary. There's also the whole reproducing-like-crazy angle, but that leads into the what-a-tangled-web-we-weave metaphor, which brings spiders into it and they're technically not even insects, so let's just put down the analogy and back slowly away, all right? No one needs to get hurt, though some of you *are* probably annoyed by now with this long, rambling digression.

My point (and, as Ellen DeGeneres likes to say, I *do* have one) is that lying is not the one-dimensional, evil activity it usually gets labeled as. It's one of the fundamental ways we exchange information.

Heh. No, that's a lie.

Sounded good for a second, though, didn't it? And that's the essence of a good lie. Surround it with actual facts, then slip in the falsehood. Which doesn't make you unreliable or a bad person, it just means you're in a situation where telling a lie is a better option than telling the truth.

Better for who, you ask. That would be where the whole good-or-evil thing would come in, and since my lie was in service of the greater good I didn't have any moral qualms about lying to a police officer. Nope, no qualms for me. I was completely and absolutely devoid of qualmage.

"So," I said to Lieutenant Forrester, an actual member of law enforcement who could totally shoot me, "you IDed Rolvink's body, huh? Any idea what killed him?"

There was a pause. "Who told you that?"

"A fellow grape. Not sure what their name was—all us grapes on the grapevine look the same, to me—but they seemed like a reliable source. You know, for a talking grape."

"Fair enough. Just tell me it wasn't one of my own people."

"It wasn't one of your people."

"That's not very convincing."

"Oh, you wanted convincing? I can do convincing. I can even drop hints, if you know what I mean."

"Not always, no. All I can tell you is this: It would be really, really helpful if we could locate the missing parts of the body."

Uh-oh. I knew where those parts had ended up, and I didn't think they'd prove all that useful in their current form. I'm no forensics expert, but I couldn't see whatever was left after passing through the digestive tract of a honey badger containing much in the way of relevant information.

"Sorry, can't help you there," I said. "But if they turn up on the grounds, I'll make sure to let you know. Is there any place in particular you think I should look?"

"If I knew that, we'd be looking there already."

"Let me put it another way. Was this a middle-of-the-night event, or did it happen while people were still up and around? The first could have happened pretty much anywhere, while the second needs seclusion."

He sighed. "I see what you mean. It's entirely possible some of your guests were still awake when it happened, so you might keep an eye out for any concealed places that smell strongly of bleach."

"I'll do that. In the meantime, I'll schedule those interviews for you and call back—shouldn't take more than an hour, tops."

He thanked me and hung up, leaving me to ponder what I'd learned. If they really needed the head and hands for cause of death, that meant they hadn't learned it from the rest of the body. That ruled out a bunch of possibilities, including poison, heart attack, or simple bleeding to death. Most likely it had been some kind of head trauma, but with the head gone that was difficult to narrow down. Gunshot? Sharp object? Blow to the skull?

Calculating time of death is tricky; usually the coroner's dealing with a range rather than a concrete moment, and that range can be a few hours long. From what Forrester had told me, it sounded like he'd narrowed it down to sometime between seven thirty—when dinner had ended, and the last time Rolvink had been seen alive—and whenever everyone (except Keene) had gone to bed.

It wasn't much, but it was more data than I had a moment ago. And I could use the pretext of scheduling the interviews to ask a few questions of my own.

The first person I intended to talk to was Catree—I needed to know if Keene's memory of seeing her was accurate, and if so what she was doing on the grounds in the middle of the night. But you know the old joke, the one about how to make God laugh? Turns out you can more or less replace *God* with *a cat* and it turns out exactly the same. Which won't come as a surprise to anyone who's had a cat, ever.

In case you haven't heard it: How do you make God laugh? Tell him your plans.

Whiskey and I ran into Tango at the foot of the stairs, where she was being appreciated by Yemane Fikru. Appreciation meant lots and lots of stroking her while seated on the bottom step, with Tango blissed out in his lap.

I stopped halfway down the stairs. I could hear the purr

from there, both in my ears and my head. *Wow. Sounds like he's really got the touch.*

No verbal response, just the steady rumble of a very happy cat. Needless to say, Whiskey couldn't let that go unremarked.

[Oh, dear. Somebody appears to be trapped under a chain saw. Which they forgot to turn off.]

The only response from Tango was to stretch out even farther, spreading her toes as wide as she could. Her claws extended, too, but only for a second at the very limits of her stretch. Completely coincidental, I'm sure.

"Hi," Yemane said. He was dressed in another baggy T-shirt and sweatpants, his long blond dreads spilling out from under a red-and-green knit cap. "Not in the way, am I?"

"No, not at all. I see you found Tango. Not so skittish now, are you, kitty?"

<PURRRRRRRRRRgowaym'busyRRRRRRRRRRRRR>

[A rusty chain saw, at that. It's a wonder it works at all.]

Yemane shook his head, his dreads swaying. "No, this isn't the cat I saw. Pretty close, but definitely not the same one."

"Oh. Well, I'm going to go out on a limb here and say this one is far superior."

[But badly in need of engine maintenance.]

The purr slowed, sputtered, and died. Two feline eyes opened just a crack to look at me. *<Okay, that I gotta respond to.>*

[Hmm. A *speaking* chain saw. How bizarre—]

<Not to you, toilet-breath. Do you know how offensive that phase is to cats?>

What phase? "So, Yemane—I hope you're settling in okay. Haven't seen much of you."

<Out on a limb. *It reinforces the old stereotype of cats getting stuck in trees. Cats don't get stuck in trees. It's a myth.*>

"Yeah, been doing a lot of meditating. Started out in the graveyard, but had to move to the gardens."

"Oh? Why is that?"

[Cats have been getting stuck in trees since trees were invented. Ever seen a dog stuck in a tree? No, because we understand what trees are for: bulletin boards. That and producing sticks.]

Yemane stopped stroking Tango and looked up at me. "Too much going on. The psychic atmosphere is, like, *intense.* Not in a bad way, just really powerful and constant. Like standing next to an electrical plant and hearing that hum down in your bones."

<*Cats were* made *to climb trees. It's one of the reasons we have actual claws instead of those giant, dirty toenails on the ends of your paws. We use them to get into trees, and we use them to get* out *of trees.*>

I put two fingers to my temple and rubbed. I'm good at multitasking, but sometimes having a mental conversation and an audible one at the same time was a bit much. "Too much mental noise, huh? I can relate to that. Well, I think you'll find that the gardens give off a much mellower vibe."

[You'd think that would be the case, wouldn't you? And yet, time and time again, firefighters have to be summoned to rescue some hapless feline who's unclear on the concept of *reverse.*]

<*A cat is never hapless. We're hap-rich. We're hap-hap-happy. We have so much hap that large hap corporations are hiring us to oversee their hap operations.*>

[Firefighters are often accompanied by dalmatians. Would you like to know what a dalmatian calls a cat? Not smart enough to be a squirrel.]

"Actually, I had to leave there, too," Yemane said. "I know this is going to sound a little weird, but—well, do you believe in ghosts?"

"Absolutely."

He looked a little surprised. "Yeah? Well, animals have spirits, too. And your graveyard is full of them—maybe a little too full."

I kept my voice neutral. "And you know this because?"

"I've seen them. I know how that sounds, but I really am sensitive to other realms. And you have ghosts wandering through your yard."

This was not a problem I ever expected to have. Not only was the ability to see ghosts rare, the ghost themselves didn't tend to roam. There were exceptions to both rules, but I'd never had to deal with both happening at the same time.

"I'm . . . not sure what I can do about that," I said carefully. "But I'm sorry if any part of our environment is making you uncomfortable. Is there anything that would help?"

He shook his head again, and Tango took the sudden movement as an excuse to jump off his lap. "Nah, it's fine. I'm not sensing any hostile intent or anything, it's just a bit much. Been chilling in my room. I could sense that they were still around, but I put out a *do not disturb* vibe and they respected that. They were still there, but they didn't *manifest,* if you know what I mean."

I thought what he meant was he couldn't see them, but since I didn't have that luxury—if there was a spook present, it was plain as day to me—I wasn't sure. "I think I understand."

"Anyway, I've adjusted my psyche. Keene and I are going to do a little exploring later, see what we can see. It's cool."

"Sure. Say, were you around for his big construction project?"

He looked blank, so I told him about the front yard and what Keene had done to it.

"He did that? I thought it was part of the movie." Yemane shook his head. "No, sorry. I was around for the first part of the croquet game, but competitive sports really isn't my thing. I spent the afternoon in the graveyard and the evening in my room. Sacked out early, around eleven."

"Oh, that reminds me. The detective in charge of the investigation is coming back for follow-up interviews. He's asked me to liaise for him, so this is me, liaising. Shouldn't take long at all—when's good for you?"

We arranged a time, I thanked him, I turned to go—then stopped and turned back. "Oh. One last thing. Did Maurice Rolvink ever track you down? He asked me if I knew where you were and I couldn't tell him. Wanted to talk to you about some sort of business proposition?"

Fikru just looked at me for a second. I'm good at reading people, but at that moment he was a complete and utter blank—no signals at all. Anyone entering the room at that moment would have sworn I was alone.

Then he spoke, and the blankness was gone. "Yes, he did. He wanted to know if I could obtain a large quantity of illegal drugs for him, which he would then dilute and sell at inflated prices. I told him I was a shaman, not a drug dealer, and wasn't interested. He immediately stopped being interested in *me* and left."

"Ah. Are you going to tell Lieutenant Forrester that?"

Fikru smiled. "Why shouldn't I? It's the truth . . ."

After talking to Yemane Fikru, I tried to call Catree—I collect phone numbers more avidly than autograph hounds hoard signatures—but she didn't pick up. That was unusual; like me, she's expected to be more or less available all the time. Of course, like me, she's also sometimes too busy to answer her phone.

I disconnected without leaving a message and put the phone back in my pocket. What I really wanted was to talk to her in person, but I couldn't do that if I didn't know where she was. I decided my best course of action was to roam the grounds with Whiskey and Tango, and see who we ran into. I could arrange interviews and gather information at the same time, and sooner or later someone would point me in the right direction.

Or I could just ask my partner with the supernatural nose to find her for me—

That's as far as I got with that thought, because of the goats.

They were exploring Keene's croquet course. And by exploring, I mean practicing goat mountaineering techniques.

Goats love to climb, and for an animal with hooves instead of claws, they're awfully good at it. I should probably add at this point that these were spectral goats, probably from a petting zoo or something, goats that got plenty of affection and attention when they were alive but were now definitely dead. If they were living goats, they would no doubt be trying to eat the structures as well, but ghosts don't (generally) have much in the way of appetites.

"Um," I said. "We've been invaded. By goats."

Whiskey studied them intently, his herding instincts springing to attention. [I could take care of that.]

<Oh, never mind them. They're just extras,> Tango said as she strolled up.

"Extras? As in, you've already filled your quota of goats for today and these are left over? Or extras as in *oh my God*

*Tango you cannot fill the front yard with deceased ungu-
lates you plan to use in your new film.*"

<*Don't get their hopes up. They still have to audition.*>

[Audition? You don't audition to be an extra.]

<*Maybe not in the* canine *film world. We cats have
higher standards.*>

You know what else goats love to do? Jump. Climbing
and jumping and eating whatever they could find; it's like
they evolved living on the side of a mountain or something.
But now, having accomplished the primary goal of
evolution—which was to die in order to make room for
something better suited to surviving—they were free to do
whatever they wanted. At first glance that simply appeared
to be *more* jumping and climbing, but ghosts can do things
living beings can't. A dead shark can swim through the air
as easily as the ocean; a dead bird can fly right through a
closed window without smacking into the glass.

And dead goats can jump really, really far.

I watched one bound from the frame of a rowing machine to the handle of an upended wheelbarrow to the
very tip of a spade leaning against a lawn chair. It paused
there, unconcerned, looking totally at ease and highly improbable.

"*Goats on the Moon,* as rendered by Salvador Dalí," I
murmured. "All it needs is a few melting clocks."

<*Please. They're extras, not the stars. And this picture
already has a director, thank you very much.*>

Another goat bounded gracefully over my head, landing
on the miniature trampoline and not bouncing at all. "I'm
beginning to understand why Mr. Fikru was complaining about all the psychic traffic noise. Tango, you've got
to keep these spirits inside the boundaries of the Crossroads."

<Me? I'm the director, not a cattle dog. Honestly, this is definitely a job for a cattle dog. If only we had one. Cattle dog, that is.>

[Stop saying *cattle dog*. I'm already uncomfortable with the fact it has the word *cat* right in it without hearing it from *your* brain.]

"Besides, these are goats, not cows. *Ghost* goats. I'm not sure Whiskey even *could* herd them."

[Now you're insulting my professional abilities? After that demonstration with the ostrich?]

I bowed to the inevitable. "Okay, pooch. Have at them."

The words were hardly out of my mouth before Whiskey took off like a rocket, barking madly and charging right at the nearest goat, which was standing beside a weight-lifting bench and trying to gnaw at the padding with non-corporeal teeth; I guess habits sometimes die harder than appetites.

Cattle dogs are trained to herd all sorts of animals. Unfortunately, Whiskey now found himself in a situation that seemed specifically designed to frustrate him, as goat apparitions could do two things most livestock couldn't. First, we were in a large space that was full of tall, precarious perches that the goats could reach easily and Whiskey couldn't; the goat he rushed toward leapt straight up and then stared at him from the top of the wicket, which was made from a portable basketball hoop.

Second, these goats could talk.

If I wanted to converse with a living animal, I needed Tango's translation skills—but the dead share a common telepathic tongue, one that cuts across species boundaries. I may not always understand what they're trying to tell me, but the concepts themselves come across as recognizable words in my head.

{Ahem,} said the goat.

"Bark bark bark bark bark!" barked Whiskey. But what he was saying mentally was [Go! Go go go go go go!]

{Go where?}

"Bark bark bark barkety bark!" [Over there! Over there! Over there!]

{Why?}

Whiskey stopped barking and stared at the goat with the kind of intensity only a working dog in the unrelenting grip of his instincts can manage. [Because I said so! Do it now! Do it now!]

{Will you please stop repeating yourself? It's really irritating.}

A goat perched on another wicket called out, {What's he want?}

{Says he wants me to go over there.}

{Why?}

The goat standing on the rim of the basketball hoop hopped to the top of the backboard. {No idea. Seems pretty upset about it, though.}

The second goat decided to join the first one, bounding from his wicket to the hoop where the first one had been. This produced a frenzy of barking: [No no no no no no no!]

The new goat peered down at Whiskey. {Hmmmm. You're right, he does seem rather overwrought. Perhaps we should ask him why. Excuse me?}

Whiskey paused. [What?]

{What's all this barking about? What's so important over *there*?}

The first goat chimed in. {Yes. And if it's so important, why don't *you* go over there?}

Whiskey gathered his control and his dignity and sat down. [Ah. My apologies. I was simply following the dictates of my instincts and attempting to guide your actions through the direct intervention of loud vocalizations.]

{Barking, you mean.}

[Well, yes.]

The first goat snorted. {You could have just asked. *Excuse me, would you mind moving in that direction, please?* Is that so hard?}

[I suppose not.] Whiskey was beginning to look a little mortified. [Um. Would you?]

{Would we what?}

[Mind moving along, in that direction. Please.]

The second goat squinted at him suspiciously. {You still haven't said why. I question your motives.}

{As do I.}

{Hullo, fellows! What's up?} said a third goat, bounding over to join the other two. {Looks like jolly good fun, whatever it is!}

{Oh, hello, Nigel,} said the first goat with a marked lack of enthusiasm. {Reginald and I were just discussing why we should go "over there."}

{Why? What's over there?}

{Well, that's the bloody question, isn't it?}

{Is it? I thought the question was *why* we should go over there. Hope I'm not presuming about my own inclusion in this little excursion, ha ha ha.}

[If I might interject? My sole purpose in getting you to move "over there" is in having you *not* be "over here."]

{I'm not sure you can define such an action in purely negative terms—oh, hello, Phillip. Geoffrey. Randolph.}

More and more goats were joining the first two, bouncing from wicket to wicket like hyperactive kangeroos in a trampoline factory, until they landed on top of the backboard or the rim of the hoop. Normally their combined weight would have toppled the entire structure over by now, but since they were spirits they could safely ignore restrictions like that. When they ran out of actual room, they just stood on one another.

"I always wondered how high you could stack a bunch of ghostly goats," I muttered. "Said no sane person, ever."

[. . . if we could get back to the matter at hand,] said an increasingly desperate-sounding Whiskey. [It's really quite simple. You're all *here,* and I would like you to be *there.*]

{We grasp the essence of the situation,} said Reginald huffily. {What we are trying to ascertain is the purpose behind our requested exodus. Isn't that right, Tim?}

{Absolutely, Reggie. Seems a bit presumptuous to me.}

{Say, fellows! Why don't I go over there and check things out? Make sure there's no large predators lurking in the underbrush, ha ha ha.}

{*Great* idea, Nigel. Off you go.}

Nigel bounded off cheerfully, leaping from wicket to wicket as if they were craggy mountaintops. When he got to the one farthest away, he yelled back, {I'm here, fellows! Seems hunky-dory to me!}

{Too soon to tell, Nigel! Stay there and keep your eyes peeled!}

{Roger that!}

[Let me elucidate,] Whiskey tried again. [It seems—]

{I'm back!}

{Yes, Nigel, we can see that. Bit unclear on your instructions, were you?}

{No, no, just missed being in the thick of things. I can see your reluctance in making the trip; somewhat remote, that place is. Nice to be home.}

{It's nice to see you, too, Nigel. Even though, at the moment, I can't see much of anything due to your standing on my eye.}

{Sorry, Tim.}

By this point Tango was lying down, her paws tucked beneath her. "Enjoying yourself?" I asked.

<You have no idea.>

Confronted by the spectacle of a mountain of goats, Whiskey remained resolutely calm. In one sense, he'd accomplished exactly what he'd set out to do: All the goats were in one place. Being vertical as opposed to horizontal was a mere detail; the important thing was, they were *listening* to him.

{I don't know, Nigel, I think it tastes more like tin can than garbage pail to me.}

{Not as crunchy, though.}

{Not as such, no. But then, nothing is.}

{*So* true.}

[As I was saying,] Whiskey interjected. [Now that you're all together, I'd really appreciate it if you'd—]

{Oh, not this "over there" business again.} Ever seen a goat roll his eyes? With those slitted pupils they have, it's quite something to witness. {This is getting quite tiresome. We sent one of us over, didn't we?}

[Well, yes, but he didn't stay.]

{I could go again! I don't mind a bit!}

{Thank you, Nigel, but that won't be necessary. You've done your part.}

[It's just that you moving along would be terribly helpful.]

{Would it? In what way?}

[In the sense that you would no longer be here.]

{I'm back!}

{Oh, hello, Nige. Haven't seen you in a dog's age. How've you been?}

{Can't complain. It's the isolation that bothers me the most, you know?}

{Oh, I understand. Don't know how you do it, meself.}

A whine escaped Whiskey's throat. Nigel peered down at him. {What's the matter with him?}

{No idea. Bit high-strung, I think. Tad obsessive, too.}

[Not at all. I'm just not used to having explain myself to those I'm herding.]

{No? What's your usual approach?}

[Dashing about barking wildly.]

{Really? And that's effective, is it?}

[Not recently, no.]

{I have a question!}

{Yes, Nigel?}

{*Why* do you want us to stay here?}

There was a pause.

{Nigel?}

{Yes, Tim?}

{Please stop talking.}

{You got it, Tim!}

[Look, it's really very simple. You're here for the film, correct?]

{The film? Ah, yes, the film. That's why we're here, all right. We are definitely here *for the film*.}

Whiskey glanced back at me in despair. Poor doggy. But a cattle dog is nothing if not persistent. He asked the next, inevitable question.

[Do you have any idea what a film actually *is*?]

{I'm back!}

{Sorry, Nigel. Did you leave? I'm afraid I didn't notice.]

{No, I just enjoy saying it. Everyone's always so happy to see me when I do.}

{It's because we're fondly anticipating your next departure, Nigel.}

[Can we focus, please? FILM. We were discussing your understanding of what it actually *is*.]

{No need to get testy. It's an easy question to answer, after all. It's . . . }

The pause went on and on. I started to wonder if Tim had forgotten the question and Whiskey was going to have to start over.

{ . . . a very thin layer of something on top of something else. Often flexible, sometimes tasty, occasionally chewy. Watch out for the chewy, brightly colored stuff, though. Pretty sure that's what killed me.}

{Oh, are you dead, Tim? My condolences.}

{Thank you, Nigel. Also, you might as well know: You're dead, too.}

{I am? But I was only gone a minute!}

On the ground, Tango had gotten to her feet and was now studying the scene intently, her ears cocked forward. *<He's gonna blow.>*

"Give him a little credit. He's doing pretty well, all things considered—"

And that's when Whiskey lost it.

10.

"Wow," I said. "I don't think I've ever seen you lose it like that."

Whiskey and I were in the small paved area where the film crew parked their vehicles. The trailer we'd discovered the body in was gone now, taken away by the police to be combed for clues, but there were still plenty of other vehicles there, including a few large equipment trucks.

Whiskey glanced at me contritely. [Once again, I'm sorry. But everyone has their limits.]

"I know. But it didn't accomplish much, did it? You morphing into that gigantic—what was it, again?"

[Irish wolfhound.]

"Irish hellhound, more like. You changing into that and then leaping right at the pyramid of goats—well, you scared them, that's for sure."

[Yes. Scattering them to the four winds, which is the exact opposite of what I was supposed to do.]

I couldn't argue with him there. Apparently enhanced croquet was also ideally suited to apparitional Ping-Pong bowling, as the goats bounced madly from wicket to wicket like cloven-hoofed inflatable ten-pins after being struck by a wiry-haired Celtic juggernaut.

It was a spectacle Tango should have taken great delight in, but in all the chaos she just slipped away without a word. I wasn't sure if it was because she thought she'd ultimately get the blame for creating the mess in the first place, or because she just didn't want me to see her convulsed with laughter. Maintaining the feline mystique and all that.

[In any case, they did eventually leave.] He stopped to sniff at a car tire.

"True. I just hope no one saw you change shape. An Australian cattle dog running around a lawn barking crazily at invisible animals I can explain—an Irish wolfhound, not so much."

I stopped. "Did you hear that?"

[Yes. A thump, from inside the back of that truck.]

I moved closer. The truck in question was a battered white cargo van, the kind that looks like someone just nailed a white box to a flatbed. Now that I looked at it, I could see the back door—the type that rolled up into the roof—was cracked open at the bottom. A tiny wisp of vapor escaped from the opening, indicating the interior was warmer than the outside.

"Hello?" I called out.

I heard footsteps, and then the door rolled up with a clatter. "Oh, hey," said Catree. "Welcome to my Fortress of Solitude. Unlike Superman, though, I *will* have to kill you to keep its location private."

Behind her, the walls on either side were lined with tall steel shelves bolted to the floor, leaving a wide aisle in the middle. The shelves were stacked with transparent plastic bins that looked like industrial Tupperware, each of them sealed with a brightly colored lid. Warm air wafted out of the interior, and I could smell coffee.

Catree was dressed in her usual mostly black outfit, with high-top sneakers and a down-filled, multipocketed vest over a long-sleeved sweatshirt. She shook her head and said, "Sorry, was that too soon? I got thrown out of a sensitivity class once for making cannibal jokes to a vegetarian."

"That doesn't seem that bad."

"She was in a wheelchair. And I may have used the word *vegetable* in a questionable manner."

"I'm not going to ask you to explain that. So . . . are you going to invite me in, or am I interrupting something?"

She hesitated, then shrugged. "Sure, come on up. But you should probably leave Whiskey outside; there are chemicals and things he shouldn't be sticking his nose into."

[Every one of which I can identify from twenty feet away. I'm safer in there than either of you.]

Yes, but she doesn't know that and I want to put her at ease. "Whiskey, stay here," I said firmly, and hopped up into the truck.

Catree rolled the door shut behind me.

"Sorry for the secrecy," she said, strolling past me to the rear of the truck. "I guard my little refuge fiercely. Most of the crew don't know what I've got back here, and I'd like to keep it that way. The stars have their trailers, and I've got mine. But unlike theirs, nobody knows mine even exists."

Another shelf stood at the back of the truck, at a strange angle. Catree slipped past it, and I realized it was a door, its hinges hidden. I stepped past it as well, and Catree reached out and swung it carefully closed.

The space she'd carved out for her inner sanctum was small, but very efficiently laid out. A small table that folded down from the wall currently held a laptop, a desk lamp, and her coffee mug. A heater hummed quietly under the table. A shelf at head height was occupied by a microwave, a Keurig coffeemaker, and a tiny fridge. I could see a bag made of bright-yellow meshwork hanging from a sturdy hook below the shelf, and realized it was a hammock. There was another hook mounted on the far wall, letting it be strung diagonally across the room.

Catree offered me the one seat, a folding chair with pillows duct-taped to it. "Not really set up for visitors," she said.

"I'm honored. So this is where you come for a little break?"

She leaned against the wall. "It is. You have something similar, or do you just self-medicate?"

"I did, once upon a time." I used to hang out in the graveyard to get a little peace and quiet, but that wasn't the case anymore. "These days I mostly just huddle in a corner and weep."

She nodded sagely. "That works, too. My corners aren't terribly large, but I do have four. Feel free to use them."

"Thanks, but I'm holding up okay right now. Actually, I was hoping I'd run into you. I tried calling, but—"

"Sorry about that. The cell reception out here is terrible, and by that I mean my phone was turned off. With the production on hold, I figured I could get away with it for an hour or two. What do you need?"

A reason you were here in the middle of the night, I thought, but kept it to myself. "Help answering a question. One of the other guests saw someone on the grounds early the same morning I found the corpse. Needless to say, the police are extremely interested in talking to said person."

She picked her large steel mug up from the table and took a sip from it. "What's your question?"

"Was it you?"

She met my eyes without any guilt. "Yep. I've been bunking out here since the second night. The motel Rolvink put us in was one step up from a craphole, and he was making us share four to a room. I need my space, Foxtrot; I deal with gotta-have-it-yesterday deadlines, hair-trigger tempers, and overinflated egos all day every day, and if I don't have someplace to go to depressurize I explode. Hasn't been a problem so far, but I'm reluctant to let the Catree out of the bag, so to speak."

There we go. An innocent explanation that made perfect sense, delivered without hesitation or shifty eyes. Everything was fine.

Except.

"So," I said casually, "what were you doing in the wee, small hours?"

She raised her eyebrows. "Do you see any bathroom facilities in here?"

"Oh. Uh, that's probably not something you should mention to the gardener. Or ZZ. Or, really, anyone that isn't me."

"Wasn't planning on it. Am I in trouble? Because I was . . . careful."

I winced. "Stop right there. No, you're not in trouble. But Lieutenant Forrester is coming back this afternoon to do follow-up interviews, and if this gets back to him he'll want to talk to you. Might be better if you approached him."

"Sure, I can do that. Thanks for the heads-up."

Then there was an awkward moment of silence.

"Well," I said.

"Right," she said.

"I'll give you a call later." I got to my feet, she opened the swinging shelf-door, and a minute later I was back in daylight.

"You'll keep my secret?" she asked, one hand on the pull-down of the door.

"Absolutely," I answered.

She nodded, then yanked. The door rattled shut.

Whiskey was sitting right where I'd left him. He joined me as I walked away. [Did you learn anything interesting?]

I shrugged. "Not really. She says she's been sleeping here because she likes her privacy, and didn't deny being out on the grounds when Keene saw her. Said she was answering the call of nature."

[Her nature compelled her to roam the grounds in the middle of the night?]

"It's a euphemism, pooch. Means she was peeing."

[What an odd way to put it. Not to mention it being untrue.]

I stopped. "What?"

[The grounds are large, but human urine tends to be pungent. I've been from one end of the yard to the other over the last few days, and I can reliably report that no human being has urinated anywhere in it.]

"Are you sure? She said she was . . . careful."

[If by *careful* you mean not a drop touched the ground, I concede that I could be mistaken. But if she was going to be that cautious, why go outside at all?]

It was a good question, one I didn't have an answer for. But it was Whiskey's next inquiry that really stumped me.

[About those chemicals she was so worried I'd get into—there was quite the heady mix that drifted out when the door was open, but while you were inside I took the time to carefully sort through my impressions and compare them against my olfactory library. Among the identifiable scents were nitric acid, sulfuric acid, sodium sulfite, and toluene.]

"So? She does special effects. I'm sure she's got all kinds of esoteric compounds in there."

[The chemicals I just listed can be combined to form one compound in particular: trinitrotoluene.]

Or, as it's better known, TNT.

I wasn't really surprised.

Catree was smart and well educated. She played with all sorts of chemicals and electronics, and had even demonstrated a few to me. Of *course* she knew how to make a bomb, and of course she already had the materials at hand. None of that meant she was actually responsible for the blast that put Natalia Cardoso in the hospital, just as her lack of affection for Maurice Rolvink didn't mean she'd killed him.

What was more troubling was the fact that I didn't *want* it to be true—so much so I was worried it might be affecting my judgment.

She was a lot like me: focused, hypercompetent, able to juggle a dozen tasks at once with a grin on her face. I liked her—more important, I respected her.

Could she have killed Rolvink? Or planted the bomb? Absolutely.

But if she had . . . she wouldn't have been sloppy about it. The body wouldn't have been discovered a few feet away from her little secret hideout. The explosion would have either killed its target or gone off harmlessly, depending on what she was trying to accomplish.

And there wouldn't have been any traces of TNT in that trailer.

It was right about then that I had a lightbulb moment, though what it illuminated was more embarrassing than insightful. I'd been avoiding thinking of Catree as a suspect not because of the similarities between us, but because of the mistakes the killer had made. An evil version of me? No problem. But an incompetent one? No, no, *hell* no.

Human beings are weird, weird animals.

The realization made me feel better, though. Catree hadn't hidden her distaste for Rolvink, either, another dumb move even an inexperienced killer wouldn't make. If anything, the evidence pointed at someone trying to frame her—but maybe that was giving the killer too much credit. Other people on the film crew might have access to that trailer, and the know-how to make a bomb.

I didn't have enough data yet. Time to go dig up some more.

I found Lucky and Oscar talking in the study. I stopped at the doorway, Whiskey at my heels, and waited for a break in the conversation.

"—really, it's about the criminalization of poverty and the inevitability of revolution," Oscar said. He crossed one leg and took a sip of tea from the china cup he held. "And of course, the unholy hunger of the living dead."

"Discussing the movie?" I said, stepping into the room.

"No, a modest proposal of my own," Oscar answered. "Within the genre, but taking a subtly different approach."

"Yeah, it's not bad," admitted Lucky. I imagined he got a lot of pitches for movies, but he actually looked interested. "Got kind of a Robert Rodriguez feel to it."

"Thank you," said Oscar. "As I was saying, due to the shortage of ammunition the hero often employs a sword. This, combined with his expertise on a motorcycle, should make for quite the action dynamic."

"Kind of a modern-day knight?" I asked.

Oscar frowned. "No, that's the precise opposite of the social metaphor I'm trying to construct. Obviously I'll have to synopsize the premise for you, or I'll be deluged by inaccurate comments."

I smiled but didn't reply. I knew Oscar well enough to

see through his feigned annoyance; he couldn't pass up the chance to double his audience.

"Very well," Oscar continued. "It's set a few years after civilization has fallen due to the dead rising from their graves. Pockets of humanity still survive, especially those in remote locations with stockpiles of weaponry and defensible compounds. One such location is deep in a South American jungle, in the once-opulent mansion of a local narcotics kingpin. These days the high life isn't quite so high, but the kingpin's paranoia, extreme wealth, and proclivity for violence have stood him in good stead; he managed to stockpile an impressive mountain of supplies before the world crashed and burned, and he has a small, thuggish army to help him keep it.

"However, the populace of the local village isn't quite so lucky. Beset by zombie attacks and running low on resources, they're completely dependent on the largesse of the drug lord. This is not an entirely novel situation; before the undead apocalypse, they toiled in his fields, planting and harvesting the illegal product that made him a veritable king. His once-loyal subjects now view their feudal lord with thinly disguised hatred, but there's little they can do.

"Into this desperate, volatile environment strides—or rather, rides—our hero. A biker whose family was devoured by the shambling corpses, he now swears not to rest until each and every one has been returned to the hell that spawned them. His preferred method of dispatching the walking dead is decapitation with a Japanese sword."

Oscar paused. Lucky was leaning forward in his seat, genuinely absorbed. "It might seem," Oscar continued, "that the biker and the drug lord would unite against their common enemy. But there's a problem.

"You see, the drug lord is, by definition, a ruthless capitalist. Having been deprived of his source of income by the minor inconvenience of the world ending, he still seeks to turn a profit. Narcotics may no longer command the sort of price he's used to, but he can grow food instead—he still has the fields and the resources to defend them. Manpower is a bit of an issue . . . but then it comes to him. Who says he has to use *men*?"

I thought I saw where this was going, but I didn't want to steal Oscar's thunder. "You mind explaining that?"

Oscar sipped his tea and smiled. "Not at all. In a pre-industrial society, energy is a highly valued commodity. Much of this energy is generated by simple brute force, often via the muscle power of living beings. But it's the *muscle* part that's important. Living, it turns out, is optional."

"Zombie power!" Lucky said, chuckling. "I love it!"

"Wait," I said. "They're going to use zombies as what, cheap labor? How would that work?"

"Fairly easily," Oscar said. "A zombie that can't bite or grab is virtually harmless. If all you need them to do is pull a plow or even just walk in a circle, that's not hard to accomplish."

"Sure, just dangle some meat on a stick. Don't need to actually feed them, clothe them, or house them . . . okay, that might be possible."

"I'm seeing hamster wheels," said Lucky. "Giant, zombie-driven hamster wheels. You could totally generate electricity like that."

"And our intrepid hero?" I prompted.

"Isn't it obvious? Dedicated to the zombies' destruction, he attacks and destroys one post-life industrial site after another. Terrified by the drug lord's constant threats to zombify them, the villagers come to see the newcomer as a savior rather than a destroyer."

"This has a familiar flavor to it," I said. "Downtrodden

townspeople, evil nobility, lone hero with a blade riding out of the night—"

"Ask him what it's called," said Lucky with a grin.

"Okay, what's the title of this epic?"

"Zomborro."

I considered this. "Well, that's better than *Grave-Robbin' Hood.*"

"Clever," said Oscar. "Entirely different metaphor, though—"

"But your way, you miss out on all the Merry Men: Will Eat You Scarlett, Friar of Human Flesh Tuck, Alan-A-Daily Meal of Brains, Little Papa John, the Inventor of Human Pizza . . ."

Whoops. Thunder, stolen.

Oscar was giving me a smile that let me know he'd cheerfully throw me to the next zombie horde that staggered by. Lucky, though, was looking at me as if I had suddenly sprouted wings made of hundred-dollar bills. "That's *brilliant,*" he breathed. "No problems with copyright, either. Public domain all the way, built-in fan base, archery is hot right now . . ."

"I'd be happy to discuss it at dinner," I said. "But at the moment, I need a little of *your* time." I told them about the upcoming interviews with Forrester. Oscar grudgingly agreed to do his duty, though Lucky took even more convincing.

"Is it really necessary?" he groaned. "Cops make me nervous. I always think they're going to Columbo me about something I did when I was twelve. *Thank you for your time, Mr. Trentini. Oh, there's just one more thing—the DNA analysis on that gum wrapper finally came back and we know you're the one who stole that pack of Bubblicious from Mr. and Mrs. Krakowski's corner store. What size of handcuffs do you take?*"

"You have nothing to worry about," I assured him. "I think they're just trying to figure out who was where when it all happened. You know, in case someone heard or saw something."

"In that case, they're wasting their time. I was working late, I went to bed alone, and then I was asleep. Wait, that's terrible—I have no alibi!"

"You don't need one, Lucky. And I'm afraid this isn't optional. I'm arranging the interviews as a courtesy, but if you refuse to cooperate the police will still want to talk to you. You can have a lawyer present, of course."

He sank back in his chair and looked gloomy. "No, that'll make me look even guiltier than I usually do, which is a lot. Plus, it'll cost me money I don't have to protect me from something I didn't do. Go ahead and schedule me; I'll deal with it in the usual way."

"Which is?" Oscar inquired.

"Complaining, mostly. Worried complaining beforehand, relieved complaining afterward. Hey, it works for me."

And that's when my boss flew through the window and landed on my shoulder.

11.

I have two bosses. Three, if you ask Tango, but to her the terms *cat* and *boss* are interchangeable. My first boss, ZZ, is the one who signs my paychecks.

The other one is the ghost of a white crow named Eli.

Eli is more like my superior officer than my employer, I guess, but it comes down to the same thing: He tells me what to do, and I do it. Unlike ZZ, he doesn't pay me, and unlike my job as an administrative assistant, I'm pretty sure I can't just quit—though I've never actually tried.

But then, Eli had never flown into the house and landed on my shoulder, either.

For a moment I thought both Oscar and Lucky could see him, too; they were looking at me with the strangest expressions on their faces.

"Are you all right, Foxtrot?" Oscar asked. "You seem a bit . . . stricken."

Which was when I became aware that my eyes were open about as wide as they would go and my upper body had assumed a position best described as "bolt upright."

"Hello, Foxtrot," said Eli in his croaky crow voice. "I'm not interrupting anything, am I?"

"I'm fine, thanks," I managed. "Just a sudden chill." Not being corporeal, Eli weighed nothing at all—but somehow, I could still feel his ghostly bird feet on my shoulder.

"Good to hear," Eli said. "It can be quite unsettling to have one's normal routine disrupted. Say, by having one part of your life abruptly spill over into another."

"If you'll excuse me? I have a lot to do," I managed. I got to my feet and quickly left the room. Whiskey came with me, of course, staring up at Eli the whole time.

"What's the problem?" I hissed once we were out of earshot.

"The problem? Let's see. How about you ignoring your duties as Guardian of the Great Crossroads?"

"What are you talking about?" I strode down the hall, looking for a room to duck into. Ah, nobody in the billiards parlor. I stepped in and closed the door behind me.

"I'm talking about *chaos*, Foxtrot. I'm talking about exactly the sort of thing that's not supposed to happen in the Crossroads and currently is."

That was news to me, but I hadn't set foot in the graveyard today—I'd been too busy. I didn't think I'd put in more than a momentary appearance yesterday, either. "Um. Does this have anything to do with the goats?"

"Yes, Foxtrot, it does. But not just the goats. Also the hamsters, and the snakes, and the rabbits, and the parakeets. Let's not forget the rats, the mice, the cats, the dogs, the iguanas, and the fish. In short, just about any creature that can swim, slither, crawl, fly, hop, or walk, and are currently dead but not in their respective Paradise. Would you care to guess what all these animals I just mentioned are doing right now?"

"Going directly from one afterlife portal to another in a calm and orderly fashion?"

Okay, that was definitely crow talons digging into my skin. "No, Foxtrot. They most definitely are not. But perhaps you should go see for yourself."

And with that, he launched himself into the air and vanished through the ceiling.

I stared up at the roof for a second, collecting my thoughts. Everybody gets chewed out by their boss now and then, but this was the most annoyed I'd ever heard Eli. "Maybe we should head over to the graveyard," I said.

[Perhaps that would be wise.]

When we got there, I understood immediately.

"Oh, man," I said softly.

[Tango,] growled Whiskey.

The Great Crossroads is a mystic nexus. That means that out of the over fifty thousand grave sites here, many are actual portals to the afterlives of different species—including humans. This lets the spirits of former pets visit the people that loved them when both were alive, and that motivation is usually so strong it overrides any petty behaviors like aggression. At first glance, the Great Crossroads might seem to be a chaotic jumble of bright colors and constant, random movement, but that's not accurate. Once you know how to look for it, you can see regular patterns all over the place: That slow-moving line over there is a stately parade of turtles; that flock overhead are racing pigeons; the surging, Technicolor carpet to the left are guinea pigs. All of them heading from their version of the afterlife to ours, or back.

Not anymore.

I'm not saying every deceased animal I could see was there for Tango's movie, but the ones that were had clearly been waiting for a while. Many of them were cats. Many of them were dogs.

Some of them were good at waiting.

Many of them were not.

So what does a huge mass of deceased cats and dogs do when they're bored? Just about what you'd expect.

It wasn't as ugly as it could have been if they were all alive; spirits aren't as strongly driven by their instincts as the living. And despite Whiskey and Tango's constant bickering, cat and dog ghosts don't actually loathe each other as a matter of course.

But, as I said—they were bored. And I guess the devil makes work for idle paws as well as hands.

It probably started innocently enough. One dog chasing another, maybe. A cat who bolted. Dormant pack instincts getting riled up, and then . . .

That was the most likely scenario. But I like to think it was a bulldog who looked a lot like John Belushi, standing up and bellowing, *"Food fight!"*

Spectral dogs ran between graves, barking wildly. (In case you're wondering, that translates mostly into "Hey! Hey! Hey! Hey!" with the occasional "What? What? What?" thrown in.) Cats leapt from headstone to headstone, or sometimes just perched on them and looked down disdainfully. A few felines seemed to have gotten into the spirit and were chasing dogs, or stalking smaller game like rodents. The rodents had bunched together out of self-defense into nervous, quivering masses resembling furry, crazy-quilt amoebas, while the usually orderly reptiles were just milling about, aimlessly crawling over everything and everybody. The sky overhead was a constantly shifting kaleidoscope of brilliant-colored parrots, parakeets and pigeons, wheeling and soaring and diving; none of them seemed inclined to land. Nobody seemed to be actively trying to eat anybody else, but I've seen birthday parties for six-year-old sugar junkies that were less crazy. No wonder the goats left.

Tango was nowhere in sight.

[I believe I've located the problem,] said Whiskey.

"Thanks, genius. Any ideas how to fix it?"

[I wasn't referring to the overall disaster. I meant its cause. Look for the pattern overhead.]

I did, though the swirling, multicolored display was a little disorienting to stare at. After a moment, though, I understood what he was talking about; like a hurricane, there was an eye of calm at its center. The birds were circling one particular point, and I knew right away what that point was.

"Davy's Grave," I said. Davy was the very first inhabitant of the graveyard, and his burial plot was in a little valley, flanked by benches. Whiskey and I hurried toward the nearest rise, scattering animal spirits as we went.

The hills surrounding the grave formed a natural amphitheater, and that's where Tango had set up shop. She had a few of the scarier animals stationed around her to form a perimeter, including a crocodile, a warthog, and a porcupine. People keep the oddest pets.

Tango herself was perched on the headstone, while apparently the grave itself was the stage for those auditioning. Piotr the circus bear was doing his usual shtick at the moment, riding a unicycle while dressed in a pink tutu.

<Yes, yes, thank you,> Tango said. <My people will let you know. Next!>

Whiskey and I started down from the top of the rise. We'd only gotten halfway down when we were stopped by an octopus.

{~hold on there, folks~please wait your turn~she's very busy you know~}

Being dead, the octopus didn't have to pay attention to little details like gravity. He drifted in front of me like an eight-armed bouncer, his tentacles waving in a vaguely threatening manner. Many people don't know that octopis are masters of disguise, able to change both their shape and shade. This one was puffed up like a balloon, his color a blazing crimson with bright yellow stripes. It was supposed to be intimidating, but it just made him seem like an animated piñata.

I gave him a look of pure incredulity. "Okay, first? You know exactly who I am and what I do, or you wouldn't be talking to me. Second? You also know that since I'm alive and you're not, I could just walk right through you. And third? Why am I still talking?"

{~no need to be rude~i'm just doing my job~you have no idea how hard it is for a cephalopod to get a speaking part in this town~}

"Move it, Eightball."

The octopus reluctantly moved to the side, letting us pass. We continued down to the bottom of the hill, where Tango finally noticed us. *<Just a second,>* she told the next applicant, a brightly colored parrot with the odd name Fish Jumping. *<I have to take this.>*

"Yes, you do," I said. "And I don't think you're going to like it much."

Tango cocked her head to the side, like she had no idea what I was talking about. *<Why? What's wrong?>*

"Awk!" the parrot blurted. "Not a clue! Not a clue!" *I do apologize for that outburst,* the parrot thought at me. *While I have, in the past, periodically made such impulsive statements, I assure you said tendency is now completely under control—*"Awk! Lying through my beak! Lying through my beak!"

"What's wrong?" I said. "While you're busy setting up

your own private post-life Hollywood, the lobby of your agency is hosting a special how-to-stage-a-riot episode of *Ghosts Gone Wild*. Or hadn't you noticed?"

Tango shot an accusing glare at a large, brightly colored angel fish hovering beside her right shoulder. <Is *this true, Miss Stripey?*>

{~i don't know~possibly~i'll look into it~yes that seems to be the case}

<*I'm disappointed in you, Miss Stripey. You're supposed to keep me apprised of any and all developments.*>

{i'm also supposed to stop anyone from bothering you unless they have an appointment~i felt sure you would be bothered by a riot~also they didn't have an appointment~}

<*Hmm. Hard to fault your logic. Okay, you can keep your job. Now tell me about this riot.*>

"*I'll* tell you about this riot, Tango. It's what happens when you disrupt the normal routines of a bunch of animal spirits by cramming them all together in a single space with nothing to do but wait. After a while, they tend to make their own entertainment."

<*Oh. Well, nobody ever said creating art was easy. Don't worry, I'm almost done.*>

"How much is almost?"

<*Just casting a few supporting roles. I've already got my star.*>

I had a pretty good idea of who that would turn out to be, but Tango surprised me. <*Him,*> she said with a flick of her head.

I turned to look, and saw Pal, the erstwhile Lassie, sprawled out at the foot of a tree.

[You've cast a *canine* in the leading role?] said Whiskey. His voice sounded like it couldn't decide between suspicion and outright disbelief.

<*Star power. What are you gonna do?*>

[Aha! So you admit dogs are better actors than cats!]

She gave him a cool glance. *<Better? Of course not. But popular culture is all about appealing to the lowest common denominator, sweetheart. You can't get much lower or more common than a dog.>*

[But—your original point was—did you just call me *sweetheart*?]

<Sorry, the lead's already been cast. But I might be able to find a small part for you—something involving peeing on a tree, maybe. Play to your strengths.>

[I have no interest in participating in this debacle, other than observing it from afar and taking satisfaction when it implodes. Which it currently seems to be in the throes of doing.]

I looked down at Whiskey and frowned. "Sorry, pooch. I need you to take a more active role—by which I mean undoing the mess on the other side of the hill."

[Are you sure? My encounter with the goats was less than successful.]

I reached down and stroked his head. "Yeah, but this time you'll have help. Deceased goats may not give you the respect you deserve, but dead dogs will. You're the alpha male of this entire graveyard, remember? I want you to form a canine Order Patrol, using the spirits of every working dog you can find. Then put 'em to work."

He understood immediately. [Ah, the authority of an organized force. I'll get right to it, shall I?]

"Forthwith," I agreed, and he leapt to his feet and sprinted toward the top of the hill.

But he never arrived.

I was used to hearing all sorts of ghostly animal noises in the graveyard: barks, yowls, screeches, birdsong. But there was one sound I didn't hear very often, and I heard it now: the thumpity-thump of spectral hooves.

Whiskey skidded to a standstill halfway up the rise. The hoofbeats got closer as the unseen animal thundered its way along the slope on the other side.

And then it crested the hill, and came to a stop.

It was a golden horse with a white mane—a palomino. Like all spirit animals, its natural color glowed as if lit from within. And it had a rider.

Not on its back, though. Front paws perched on the horse's broad golden head, back legs straddling the mane, a small black-and-tan dog with twinkling eyes and a panting smile on its muzzle balanced itself confidently. [Hi!] the dog said. [We're here for the *audition*.]

I gaped.

<*Is that Benji?*> Tango said.

"Yes," I managed. "And I think he's riding Trigger."

Trigger, for the woefully uneducated among you, was Roy Rogers's horse. Roy Rogers, for the mid-twentieth-century-singing-cowboy-challenged among you, was . . . well, a singing cowboy. He was wildly popular during his day, starred in over a hundred movies, and had his own radio and TV shows.

But it's his horse that's really impressive.

His birth name was Golden Cloud, but Rogers eventually renamed him Trigger; not just because it sounded cool, but because the horse could follow an instruction as easily as pulling a—well, you know. Trigger could reportedly understand 150 trick cues, walk fifty feet on his hind legs, and poop on command. It was this last feat that ensured his stardom, because it meant he could make personal appearances in theaters and other venues where horses weren't allowed. Not that he was asked to poop as part of his repertoire—this was back in the fifties, you understand. No, it was because he *wouldn't* dump a load of horse apples until told it was okay that made him so be-loved. Well, appreciated.

And now here he was in front of me, in the flesh. Okay, spirit, but still.

Being ridden by *Benji*.

I find it hard to believe there are people who haven't heard of Benji, but in case you're one of the few: Benji was just as big a deal as Trigger. Like Trigger, he had a stage name and a given name (Higgins). As far as pedigree goes, he was a mutt; best guess was a mix of cocker spaniel, miniature poodle, and schnauzer. He was found by an animal trainer named Frank Inn at the Burbank Animal Shelter, and Inn soon realized he had star material on his hands.

Higgins started his career in a popular sitcom called *Petticoat Junction*—where he was simply known as Dog. From there he jumped to the movies (the made-for-TV ones, unfortunately) with *Mooch Goes to Hollywood,* which featured talents ranging from Richard Burton to Ed-ward G. Robinson.

Higgins was eleven when he made *Mooch Goes to Hol-lywood*, considered pretty old for an acting dog, and so he was retired. End of his story, right?

Wrong. Three years later, in 1974, came the film *Benji*.

Higgins came out of retirement to the play the title role. If the old adage about multiplying a dog's age by seven to get the human equivalent holds true, that made Higgins *ninety-eight years old* when he made his one and only big-screen film.

(By the way, that adage isn't accurate. For a small dog, fourteen years old is closer to seventy-two in the human calendar—and actors always lie about their age. But still.)

It was filmed on a tight budget, about half a million dol-lars. No distribution company would touch it. The director finally had to form his *own* distribution company to get it into theaters.

And then it made forty-five million dollars, one of the top-grossing films of the year. Depending on whom you believed, it was either the tenth, fifth, or third most profitable flick of 1974.

Benji is a remarkable movie. I saw it when I was a child, and I'll always remember just how amazing the hero of the story was. Higgins (though of course at the time I had no idea that was his real name) didn't just do tricks; he *acted*. He managed to convey real emotion every time he was on screen, and he had an impressive range: from fear to love, from melancholy to pride. The movie's shot mostly from the dog's point of view, and it captures that brilliantly. Alfred Hitchcock was apparently a fan.

And here he was. The dog, not Alfred Hitchcock.

<*Now* that,> said Tango, awe in her voice, <*is an entrance.*>

Higgins launched himself from the horse, ricocheted off two headstones, and ended up almost at our feet. [Sorry I'm late,] he said. His telepathic voice was merry and just a little gruff, like a Christmas elf who used to smoke. [You know what traffic's like in this town.]

<*Ha! Yeah, ain't that the truth. So what can I do for you and the Butterscotch Stallion?*>

[What do you think? We want to jump on board your crazy train. What's a dog-and-pony show without a dog and pony?]

Tango nodded. I'm not sure I've ever seen her do that before. <*Sure, sure, I get it. I can always find room for a talented duo like you two, of course. But I have to be honest: I've already cast the lead.*>

[The lead? You think I wanted to play the *lead*? Ha! No, no, that's a job for a younger dog. I'm a *character* actor; give me a supporting role and I promise you I'll shine. Sure, I'm best known for playing the spunky underdog, but I'd like to stretch my muscles. Maybe even go a little dark—I could do a *terrific* villain.]

He lowered his head and growled.

Okay, imagine a cuteness rocket. Now imagine someone standing on top of that rocket as it blasts through space as fast as a cuteness-based missile can possibly go. Now imagine someone standing on top of that rocket with a gun. (No, neither the person nor the gun has to be cute. I know I'm asking for a lot with this metaphor already.) Now have the person fire a cuteness bullet from the gun, *ahead* of the rocket.

That bullet is how cute Higgins was when he growled.

We laughed. We *aawwwwwed*. We did both at the same time.

And did Higgins take offense? No. He promptly flipped over on his back, waved his little paws in the air, rolled side-to-side, and *kept on growling.* The laughing and *awwwing* amped up.

His timing was immaculate. When he'd milked the bit for all it was worth, he was back on his feet in a flash. [Well? *Terrifying,* no?]

<*No,*> Tango said. <*But you got the part. By which I mean I'll come up with parts for a dog and a horse and then give them to you. Uh, the Big T can act, too, right?*>

[Are you kidding? He's been in more movies than the Hollywood sign. And he prefers Golden Cloud, these days.]

During this exchange, Whiskey had been studying the horse. Golden Cloud seemed less interested in him, though he did spare him the occasional glance.

[I'm an admirer of your work,] Whiskey finally said. [Sir.]

(I'm a horse, son, not a knight—though my first role *was* Maid Marian's steed. GC will do just fine.)

[I've seen your films. Many of them, I mean. Of your films.]

(Have you? Hope you liked 'em okay.)

[I did! Do. My favorite is *The Golden Stallion*. You were so compelling in that! And when Roy actually goes to jail to save your life? The scene where you say good-bye? It always gets to me.]

(Kind of you to say, pardner. It's always nice to be appreciated.)

"Whiskey!" I called. "Sorry to interrupt, but you've got a crisis to handle, remember?"

[What? Oh, yes, that's right. A great honor to meet you, sir—I mean, GC. Er. Good-bye.] And with that, he bolted around the horse and over the hill.

I couldn't believe it. My erudite, levelheaded canine was tongue-tied, and my canine-loathing cat was being charmed—charmed!—by a small, roguish dog. Starstruck, the both of them.

"Okay, Tango. Wrap this up, okay? Eli's not happy, and he's the head of the studio. Tick him off and you won't get anything green-lit."

<*All right, all right. I've got everyone I need now, anyway. Time to go work on the rewrite.*>

[Well,] said Higgins, [I'll let you get back to work, then. Call me when you need me, sweetheart. *Ciao.*]

And with that, Higgins trotted off. Trigger—I mean, Golden Cloud—nodded solemnly at both of us. (Ma'am. Ma'am.) Then he followed his diminutive partner back over the hill and out of sight.

Pal got up and ambled over to us. He stared at Tango for a second without saying anything. Then: [He wants my part.]

<Now, sweetie, don't be like that—>

[Don't you *sweetie* me! That little ham is after my role!]

<Don't be ridiculous. Nobody could replace you—you're the one and only Lassie!>

[Actually, I was only the first to play the role. Though almost all the subsequent ones were my offspring or descendants.]

<My point exactly. You're the progenitor of a dynasty! The most famous, trademarked dog in history! Which reminds me, I need to talk to you about that. There might be some legal issues.>

I sighed, and walked away.

12.

Once I had Whiskey on the job, it didn't take long. Dogs are pack animals; give them a strong leader and directions to follow, they'll fall in line pretty quickly. Whiskey located a number of lieutenants—sheepdogs, collies, blue heelers—quickly, and told them what to do. None of them questioned his authority or complained, because all he was really doing was giving them permission to follow their own instincts. In a matter of minutes each of them was dashing around, barking orders at all the other species to get in line—

Hmmm. Speaking of metaphors, there's a pretty obvious one here.

But this isn't meant to be a political allegory, so I'm just going to put that aside and describe the more ludicrous aspects of the operation. For instance, each of the dogs was responsible for a different kind of animal, but since they were all mixed together the dogs had to continually explain whom they were trying to direct:

[Hey! Form a line to the left! No, not the guinea pigs, the gerbils! Don't step on the mice! Get those ducks in a row! Somebody find a place for that chicken! No, not next to the alligator! Somebody get the anaconda off Alex— Alex, I *told* you you can't just pick them up and drop them in a pile! Keep those turtles moving!]

The most difficult animals to herd were the birds and the cats. The dogs couldn't do much about the birds until Whiskey got the bright idea of enlisting a dolphin's help. Dolphins are fast, agile, and love to play, so this one had no problem zooming around and corralling renegade flyers. Birds—even ghostly ones—aren't used to seeing something that large and fast up in the sky with them.

And as for the cats, Whiskey didn't even try. He told me later that he figured once everyone else had calmed down and resumed their normal activities, the cats would, too; they'd wait just long enough to make it seem like it was their own idea, and then pretend the riot never happened in the first place. Which is more or less what happened.

Tango, the author of this catastrophe, simply wandered off (after convincing Pal his part was still secure), with the stated intention of taking a nap.

"I thought you said you were going to work on revising the script," I pointed out.

<*It's all part of the creative process, Toots. Have a little nosh, find a sunbeam to soak up a few rays and emit a few Z's . . . see what springs to mind.*>

Whiskey would have had a cutting reply to that, but he was busy overseeing Operation: Roundup. I just shrugged and told her to concentrate on less disruptive creativity in the future.

When the dust had settled, I commended my general on a battle well fought. He tried to respond to my praise in a professional manner, but a dog's tail will always give him away. Today was the most fun he'd had in a while— which got me to thinking.

"You know," I said as we walked along, deeper into the graveyard, "all work and no play makes for a pretty dull day. I don't think you and I do this often enough."

Whiskey stopped to sniff at a headstone and gave a stern, official glance at a hamster who seemed to be wandering aimlessly. The hamster abruptly remembered how to aim and shot away. [Put down an insurrection? I should hope not.]

"That was hardly an insurrection. More like rampant untidiness."

[Whatever you wish to call it, it's over now. We shall have to be vigilant to make sure it doesn't happen again.]

"Sure. Think we could do that and maybe chase some sticks at the same time?"

His head snapped around and his ears grew points. [Sticks? Plural? Or are you simply being ungrammatical?]

I grinned. "I was thinking more along the lines of a single stick thrown multiple times, but if you'd prefer more than one I think we can work something out."

He panted happily. [That sounds splendid. How many sticks? A dozen? Perhaps two? I can tell you where to find some fine examples in the brush over by the west wall.]

"Uh, let's try to keep this manageable, okay—"

Which is when I saw Maxwell Tervo.

He was standing by himself, at a grave. He wore a long black greatcoat and a bowler hat, an outfit from the movie; I remembered him telling me at dinner that he liked to keep costumes from his various roles as mementos. The grave had a brass urn mounted on the headstone, one that held human cremains; that meant this grave was also a portal to the human afterlife for any animal spirit who cared to use it.

"Hello, Maxwell," I said.

He didn't look up. He was staring intently at the headstone itself, obviously deep in thought. I waited.

After a moment he spoke, but didn't turn to look at me. "Ah. Miss Foxtrot, and her constant canine companion. Good day, madame."

"Better than yesterday, anyway. Doing a little epitaph-surfing? Keene says he finds them inspiring."

"Graveyards are always a source of inspiration. I consider them monuments; not to the corpses they contain, but rather to the devices that filled them."

He gestured with his hand. "Over there, a rash of cholera deaths a hundred years ago. Farther down the hill, a carriage accident, three drownings, and the tragic death of an infant. Two suicides flank a soldier's loss, and a host of the elderly surround the unlucky and the unwell. Death, in all its guises, come to visit each and every citizen of this necropolis."

I blinked at him. "Um. You know this is a pet cemetery, right?"

He continued as if I hadn't spoken. "Death is the great instructor, and I his greatest pupil. I come here to study, to learn, to understand. How many of these graves hide the secret victims of murder, do you think? A dozen? A hundred? More? We shall never know for certain, but we can speculate, we can analyze. Over here, the burial plot of a young woman next to her much older husband. Was there a dalliance discovered? Arsenic slipped into a cup of tea?"

"Those are ferret graves. Pretty sure they didn't drink tea."

He finally turned to regard me. His eyes were intense, his expression amused. "You think me mad? Not at all. Pure rationality is an encumbrance to genius, for science by nature is reductive and there are some concepts that must be considered in whole. This is not only the great divide between Eastern and Western philosophies, but my enemy's greatest flaw. He believes that when you eliminate the impossible, what remains must be the truth; but what if the impossible refuses to be eliminated? What if the impossible rises from the dark of the grave and reaches for your *throat*?"

I couldn't take my eyes off his. They were cold with hatred and aflame with passion at the same time. I swallowed.

"Professor Moriarty, I assume?" I managed.

Tervo blinked once, slowly, and his posture relaxed. He seemed to get smaller, somehow, and then he smiled at me. "Yes, that was him," he said. "Since we can't use the grounds, Lucky was talking about shooting a few extra scenes here in the graveyard. I was getting into character."

"Very convincing. Your Moriarty is *scary*."

He chuckled. "Well, thank you. The central conceit of the film is that Moriarty thinks he can beat Holmes with an army of zombies—admittedly a somewhat absurd idea—but I thought the reasoning behind it was interesting. What is the best tool to use against a rational man? The irrational, of course. Though Arthur Conan Doyle already examined the concept in *The Hound of the Baskervilles,* Lucky's taking the opposite approach with this film." He put his hands behind his back and started walking.

Whiskey and I followed. "That the supernatural is real, and therefore Holmes's rational approach is wrong?"

"Yes and no. In the film, the dead do come back to life, but it turns out there are still rules in place. Holmes, while initially refusing to believe the impossible has come to pass, eventually stops denying the evidence of his own eyes and incorporates this new information into his world-view, which allows him to properly evaluate the situation and arrive at a solution. In other words, he displays a true scientific attitude, as opposed to merely insisting the universe follow the status quo."

I nodded. "More like Doyle's Professor Challenger stories, where Challenger fights the scientific establishment with his unorthodox discoveries."

Tervo smiled. "Exactly! But Lucky is attempting something trickier—he's trying to say that sometimes rationality *itself* is not enough, *without* endorsing the principle that all is chaos. A fine line to tread."

"Well, science is a terrific tool. But not every tool can do every thing. You can't slice bread with a garden hose." I paused. "Okay, I guess you could. But I wouldn't want to eat it afterward."

"Indeed . . . I find Moriarty a fascinating character, don't you? A genius intent on proving himself by mastering that darkest and most dangerous part of civilization, the criminal underworld. Not just Holmes's nemesis, but in many ways his counterpart. After all, which is more difficult: solving the perfect crime, or planning it in the first place?"

[It almost sounds as if he approves,] Whiskey commented.

"Are you a . . . *Method* actor, Mr. Tervo?" I asked.

"I suppose I am, though I don't think of it that way. I do believe that in order to truly inhabit a character, you must experience events the way they do. You may not always agree with their methods or goals—or even understand them—but it's essential you *feel* the same way about them. To my mind, in any case."

"I'm sorry I interrupted your process."

"Oh, that's perfectly all right. Once I have a character in my head, I can more or less summon them at will. During filming, I make it a habit to drop in and out of character even in my free time; it's the theatrical equivalent of lifting weights, I suppose."

"That's an interesting way of putting it. But I suppose any muscle gets stronger the more you exercise it."

"Yes. And as with any fitness regimen, the key is a regular routine. Mine is every evening for an hour before I go to bed."

"Must be difficult to maintain during the craziness of a film shoot."

He stopped, looking down at another grave. "It can be. But the life of an actor is always chaotic; if you want any stability at all, you have to learn to impose it. I make it a rule to retire by ten o'clock whenever possible; so far, during this production, I've managed to keep to that schedule."

"Speaking of scheduling . . ." I told him about Forrester and the interview. He agreed to meet and talk with the detective, and we set up a time. I thanked him, then left him there in the graveyard.

When I glanced back, he was staring at another grave, his lips moving silently, his eyes intent.

I went back to my office with Whiskey, sat down at my desk, and did some hard thinking.

[You look like you're doing some hard thinking.]

"It's the frown. Puts the *hard* in thinking."

I picked up my cell phone and called Shondra.

"Shondra? Foxtrot. I was wondering—"

"You need me to pull up the security footage from the cameras at the gates and on the grounds for the night before the bombing."

"Uh—yes?"

"Which you will then go through to determine who was at the house that night."

"Well—"

"None of the guests left the premises. I assume all of the film crew did, but I can't prove that. They used multiple vehicles, and some of them were sealed trucks."

"Thanks. I was just—"

"You do know I get a paycheck, right?"

Whoops. "Yes, you do. And you do a great job. Which is why you are so far out ahead of me on this you just passed me for the second time."

"You know who else gets paid to do this stuff? The police. You might want to let them."

"Absolutely. In fact, Lieutenant Forrester is coming back to do follow-up interviews later today."

"I know. He called me first."

Well, of course he did. She was in charge of security, after all. He would have asked to see that footage, too. "Okay, then. Thanks."

"No problem."

I ended the call, feeling a little uncomfortable. Was Shondra right? Should I just leave this to the police? Unlike some of the other weirdness that had happened at the mansion, the bombing and murder didn't seem to have a supernatural component. I could just leave well enough alone . . .

Ah, who was I kidding.

[Yourself. But only for a moment.]

"Sorry. That was supposed to stay on the inside of my brain."

[Not to worry; most of the time, the integrity of your skull remains intact. Now, what's our next step?]

"Let's review what we have so far. The bomb was planted in the fireplace, after the evening's fire had gone out. Any of the guests—including Catree—could have snuck in and planted it in the chimney late at night. They would have had to have access to Natalia Cardoso's room, and some assurance that she either wouldn't wake up, wouldn't object, or wouldn't be there at all."

[Rolvink had access, obviously.]

"Yes, but he was already dead by the time the bomb was planted. And why would he blow up his girlfriend and leading lady, anyway? It's a lot more likely he was the target and she was just in the wrong place at the wrong time."

[Perhaps.]

The only person I hadn't talked to about Forrester was Jaxon Nesbitt, the star of the film. He seemed a little young to play Sherlock Holmes, but I had to admit he had the talent; I'd seen him in a few roles, and once he was on-screen you couldn't look away. He had that indefinable charisma some movie stars have, a quality that goes beyond looks or even personality. They just seem *bigger,* somehow, regardless of their actual size.

Which was, I was reluctant to admit, the reason I'd put him off until last. Yes, I have plenty of experience dealing with celebrities, but this was different. Jaxon Nesbit was a fantasy that strolled right out of a romcom, and my brain was reacting by having *this* conversation:

STARRY-EYED ME: Oooh! He's so dreamy!

NERVOUS ME: I don't want to do this. He seemed like kind of a jerk at dinner last night.

STARRY-EYED ME: I'll *fix* him! I'll be super-helpful and super-capable and he'll be so impressed he'll *marry* me!

NERVOUS ME: What if he's *still* a jerk?

STARRY-EYED ME: Don't care! Dreeeeeeeeeeeeeammmmyyy . . .

NERVOUS ME: I can't believe you said that. We're such a jerk.

So yeah, hormonal tug-of-war. I didn't want to believe he was a jerk, but I also didn't want him to be too likable. Really, the best option would be to have him talk in a monotone about nothing of consequence while wearing a bag over his head.

So I handled it the same way I'd been handling most of our interactions: over the phone.

"Hello?"

"Hi, Mr. Nesbitt. This is Foxtrot. I was just talking to Lieutenant Forrester, and he'd like to come by and speak with you later today."

"I don't think so. Maybe later in the week."

"It wasn't a request, Mr. Nesbitt. He's talking to everyone that was here when the bomb went off. I've already scheduled all the other guests for their interviews—how does two o'clock work for you?"

"It doesn't. How about four?"

"I can do that. It shouldn't take too long."

"Yeah, whatever." He hung up.

Terrific. Mission accomplished—except, of course, that I hadn't been able to ask him any questions about the night in question myself. If we'd been face-to-face things might have been different, but no—I'd chickened out.

I was going to have do something about that.

What I did was stalk him.

Nesbitt stayed in his room a lot, but he did come out for meals—including lunch. I often eat at my desk, but today I went down to the dining room, where Ben had laid out platters of cold cuts, cheeses, sliced vegetables, artisan rolls, and a huge bowl of fresh Caesar salad. I took a small plate, positioned myself near the buffet table, and ate. Very, very slowly.

Other guests came and went; Lucky Trentini, Yemane

Fikru, and Max Tervo all stopped by to chat and nosh, then went on their way. I picked and nibbled, sipped tea, and tried to stifle my sense of guilt at not accomplishing anything.

And then Death showed up.

Little was grim about this reaper; she wore a long, flowing dress, a wide-brimmed hat covered in flowers, and was showing off plenty of cleavage—bony cleavage, I'll admit, but cleavage just the same. Her dress was a deep scarlet, with a pattern of grinning skulls holding marigolds between their teeth tumbling down the fabric. Death's face was a stylized Mexican skull, with an intricate pattern of red and gold beads outlining the eyes and teeth.

"Hey," I said. "Funny, I thought you'd be taller."

"I'm wearing flats," said ZZ. "Not very authentic, but a lot more comfortable. On the actual day, I'll put on the Cruel Shoes."

I nodded. "The actual day being what—the Rapture? The Apocalypse? Black Friday at Walmart?"

She shook her skull. "The Day of the Dead, Foxtrot. It's only a few weeks away, and I think it's time to start planning a party."

"Oh," I said. "Well, you know I'm always down for a party—I just didn't know if you still wanted to go ahead with that. You know, what with the actual body count around here."

ZZ sat down next to me. "That's exactly why we *should* have a party, Trot. I've been thinking about mortality a lot, and having a bunch of zombies wandering around has made me realize a few things."

"Like what? It's hard to eat soup when you don't have lips?"

She smiled. "No, dear. It's how *ridiculous* death is. Our friends south of the border got it right—death isn't the Big

Bad Wolf at the door; it's the one already in bed and wearing Granny's nightdress. Intimate, inevitable, and absurd. Zombie movies are all about our fear of death, that there's something terrible and beyond our control waiting for us. Day of the Dead celebrations are the opposite. If you can't stop something, why not embrace it? Invite it in for a drink, drag it out on the dance floor, tell it a funny story; maybe it's not so terrible after all. Which is why I'm attending the party wearing this." She gestured, indicating her outfit from head to toe. "*La Calavera Catrina,* the Grande Dame of Death. What do you think?"

I peered at her chest. "Did you get the movie people to do your bust? 'Cause it's kind of amazing."

"Well, they had the time, and they offered. The bones look real, don't they?"

"Sure do. If you were a guy, I'd be making a boner joke right about now."

She laughed. "That's the spirit! Now, if you'll excuse me—I've invited some of the crew to join me in the study. We're going to play charades—any guesses as to the theme?"

"I'd like to take *deceased actors and directors* for three hundred, Alex?"

ZZ grinned and got to her feet. "Do you think you could get some of those little Sugar Skulls here in time for tea?"

"Not a problem. I know a guy. Well, a ghoul. Point being, he can always dig something up."

"Thank you, sweetie." With that she was off, no doubt already planning how to enact *The Wizard of Oz* with an all-corpse cast. My boss, my inspiration, the Crazy Old Lady who signs my paychecks. I really do like her a lot.

Which is about when I overheard the argument.

The Great Crossroads acts as a psychic amplifier, which means that a telepathic entity inside—like an animal spirit, my partners, or myself—can send and receive thoughts at a greater distance than normal. (Yes, I know. *Normal* is not a word that I use often, or at all. Not even quite sure what it means, actually; probably a mash-up of *Norm* and *Al,* two guys who live in the suburbs and never do anything weird.) Anyway, while this thought-amping is often quite useful, it sometimes has odd side effects—like when my own thoughts are wandering and unfocused, and happen to bump into two loud, angry canines having a disagreement: Pal, the erstwhile Lassie, and Higgins, the erstwhile Benji. Being dead had turned barks and yaps into actual words, but the structure of their discourse remained the same:

[You stole my role!]

[How can you steal something when it's been given to you? *How?*]

[You should have stayed where you belong—a park! A *park*!]

[How? How? How?]

[Park! Park! Park!]

Sigh. Sigh. Sigh.

I got to my feet and headed for the graveyard.

I found the two of them staring each other down in a small stand of trees not far from Davy's Grave. The collie and the mongrel had stopped yelling, but their eyes remained locked and they were both growling softly, like two motors idling. Well, 90 percent of communication is non-verbal in humans, so in a species that doesn't have actual language that percentage is even higher. Which gave me an idea of how to break this up without finding a spectral garden hose.

I walked right up to them and said, "Hey, know how I can tell this is a *serious* argument?"

[Because you're not a moron,] growled Higgins. [Unlike certain cross-dressing sheepdogs.]

[That's low, even for you—and you're barely six inches off the ground,] Pal snarled back.

"Nope," I said cheerfully. "It's because it's between two *dog stars*. Get it?"

Both of them blinked. Pal's brow furrowed. Higgins looked puzzled. They both turned toward me.

[What?]

[Excuse me?]

"Dog stars? A *Sirius* argument? Hello?"

Now they were both staring at me with that confused expression. Sometimes the best way to derail an argument is to befuddle both parties; it works equally well with toddlers and stockbrokers, so I figured canines were fair game. Okay, maybe using a bad pun wasn't exactly fair, but it had the desired effect: It forced both of them to think differently, just for a second.

"Never mind. Both of you are being *bad dogs* and I want you to *be quiet*." I glared at them sternly, and suddenly I was looking at two ashamed canines instead of two bickering ones. "You, go over there. You, go over there. I'll straighten all this out in a minute."

Definitely not fair invoking command words that had been drilled into them their whole lives, but the welfare of the Great Crossroads was my responsibility, and with that responsibility came a certain amount of authoritative leeway, too.

I went and talked to Pal first. His version of the story was that there was a rumor going around that he was going to be replaced by Higgins. Higgins, of course, staunchly denied this, though he'd heard the same rumor himself.

Rumors are the bane of a professional assistant's life.

They're like a virus that mutates as it moves from host to host, except it's impossible to track down Gossip Zero. It creates tension and breeds suspicion, and the only vaccine is a healthy dose of skepticism and common sense—which, you know, is notoriously difficult to synthesize in an injectable form.

So you treat the symptoms as opposed to the disease, and hope that eventually the rumor dies a natural death. Which is what I did with Higgins and Pal, assuring both of them that no one, *no one* was closer to the director than me and there was absolutely no way that such a major shake-up could happen without me knowing about it.

Which didn't really satisfy either of them (because they were dogs and the director was a cat and all of us were perfectly aware that the actions of a Ping-Pong ball tossed into a room full of mousetraps were more predictable than the decision-making process of a feline) but we all pretended everything was fine and all problems had been resolved and went on our respective ways. I was going to have to talk to Tango about this later—but first I had a celebrity I had to get back to stalking.

I returned to the dining room, learned that Nesbitt hadn't made an appearance yet, and resumed my place.

Eventually my patience was rewarded. Jaxon Nesbitt strolled into the dining room, gave me a great big smile, and picked up a plate. "Hey, Foxtrot! Not too late for lunch, I hope?"

"No, not at all. Please, help yourself."

There's this weird thing that happens when you meet a famous actor, a kind of cognitive dissonance. Your brain is trying to reconcile this image you have of the person's public persona with the physical reality, and they never match up. The actor is shorter, wider, older. Their behavior is often very different from what you expect—brash comedians can be shy and polite, the charismatic can be abrupt and cold. Working as a professional assistant who often dealt with celebrities, I'd developed a trick to bypass my own preconceptions, and it worked amazingly well: I pretended they weren't who they actually were, but just celebrity impersonators. Other than the constant urge to say, *Wow, you're really good,* it made interacting with them much easier—especially the difficult ones. Having your teen crush be rude to you can do actual emotional damage—none of us are as secure as we think—but someone pretending to be him? That just seems a little sad, especially when you realize he's wearing a toupee and has had plastic surgery.

It doesn't always work. Sometimes, when the celebrity is young and attractive and single, my brain tries to convince me that while the real thing is out of my league, a look-alike was a definite possibility. *C'mon,* my reptilian hindbrain whispers. *Ben will understand. Everybody has that one famous person they're allowed to cheat with, right?*

But this isn't a real celebrity, responds another part of my brain, desperately trying to hold on to the original self-deception.

Shut up! hisses the hindbrain. *Can't you see I'm trying to get us laid?* Then the whole thing breaks down in a mess of contradiction, self-recrimination, and half-remembered teenage fantasies.

Jaxon Nesbitt. Young, attractive, single. Not a teenage fantasy, but only because he wasn't around when I was in the throes of puberty. I could talk to him without making a fool of myself, right?

"So," I said. "You're Sherlock Holmes."

He glanced at me as he loaded up a plate with food. Gave me a movie-star smile, the kind that crinkled the eyes at the corners and showed every gleaning white tooth and highlighted those perfect cheekbones; basically, it did for his face what high heels do for legs, bringing all the good bits into tight focus.

"Uh-oh," he said. "My amazing detective skills are picking up on some skepticism."

"No, no, that's not what I meant," I said quickly. "I think you'll make a great Holmes. I was just wondering what you do to prepare for a role like that."

He added a few cherry tomatoes and a slice of pro- sciutto. "Read, of course. Try to get into his head, see the world like he saw it. You know, considering that he was a fictional character."

"Right. So, Mr. Holmes . . . any insights into our cur- rent situation?"

He laughed. "Oh, is that what this is about? You think I can figure out the murder and the bombing?"

"Can you?" I gave him a smile of my own, one with a challenge in it. Successful people find it hard to resist chal- lenges; meeting them is usually how they became suc- cessful in the first place.

"I can give it at try." He sat down next to me and picked up a fork. "Let's see. Somebody killed an acknowledged sleazeball and blew up our lead actress—who was sleep- ing with him. List of suspects for the sleazeball is long. The real question is, why go after Natalia?"

"You've been thinking about this."

He speared a piece of cheese with his fork and popped it in his mouth. " 'Course I have. We all have. And here's what I think: multiple killers. Gotta be. One went after him with a bomb, the other up close and personal. You're the one that found the body, right?"

"Yes."

"I heard it was all chopped up."

I nodded. I'm not squeamish, but suddenly I had no appetite. I pushed my mostly empty plate away from me.

"Sorry, that must have been disturbing. But whoever did that must have really, really hated him. The person who planted the bomb, though? More cerebral, more cold-blooded. You see what I mean?"

More like the work of a professional, I thought. "I do. Think they were working together, or separately?"

"No idea. Human beings are capable of all kinds of messed-up things. I will say this: The film industry is the only one I can think of that brings together completely different kinds of talent to work together. Brilliant creativity on one end of the spectrum, hard-core engineering on the other. Could two of those people have come together to kill someone they both hated? You tell me."

"What makes you think I have any idea?"

He smiled again, but toned it down a little this time. "If I'm going to play Holmes for you, you're going to have to be my Watson."

"Do I have to? I've read the script."

Watson didn't fare well in the film. In fact, he got zombified early on and Holmes wound up having to decapitate him. The actor that played him had gone home after the first day of shooting.

Jaxon shrugged. "Thing is, Holmes was brilliant at noticing tiny details and remembering esoteric facts, while Watson was better at understanding human nature. Which is the opposite of what we have here—you're clearly a detail-oriented person, while my forte is human nature. If we're going to have any luck cracking this case, we're going to have to play to our strengths."

Was he flirting with me? I think he was flirting with me.

Oh, God. "Well, then," I managed. "The bomb must have been planted after the fires in the hearths had died down, when most of the guests were alone in their rooms. Nobody seems to have an alibi, everybody seems to have a motive. How do we narrow the possibilities?"

"All I have to offer is my own, completely subjective perspective on human nature. Which is as follows." He paused, finished the bite of food he'd just taken, then continued, listing points on his fingers as he went. "Max Tervo: can't be him, he's too straitlaced. Lucky Trentini: can't be him, he's too nervous. Natalia: in the hospital, not a suspect. Keene: bit of a wild card. No obvious motive, but in my experience a guy like that is capable of anything. The one with the weird name—Yiminy Ferkus?"

"Yemane Fikru."

"Him. Clearly Keene brought him along for the drugs. Drugs, Hollywood, and violence have a long history together, so that brings up all sorts of possible scenarios. Rolvink was into some sketchy stuff, you know?"

I did, but I was interested in what Jaxon knew. "Like what?"

Just for an instant, his smile locked up. It was weird, like seeing a movie freeze on a single frame, and then it was gone. "Oh, the usual LA weirdness. Porn, guys with neck tattoos who never take their sunglasses off, suitcases full of cash delivered by steroid junkies with shaved heads and bizarre accents . . . pretty standard, really. I mean, you can't throw a latte in this biz without hitting some kind of freak in the head. Half the people on the crew probably have prison records, and I guarantee none of them had any love for old Maurice."

Catree certainly didn't. "I notice you left one suspect off your list, Mr. Holmes."

He laughed, his absence of concern so overwhelming

it almost seemed forced. Almost—he was a talented actor, after all. "Me? Nah. Totally not."

"Alone in your room, just like everyone else?"

"As a matter of fact, yes. Look, Rolvink was scummy, sure, but no more so than any other algae in the pond—and if you want to succeed in my profession you better be okay swimming in the stuff, because it's not going away anytime soon."

I got to my feet. "Not all of it, anyway. But somebody around here seems intent on cleaning the pool . . ."

13.

And then I got some good news: Natalia Cardoso had woken up and seemed to be okay. I told ZZ I was going to drive down to the hospital to pay her a visit, and she offered to come with me. "Let's have Ben put together a care package," she said. "Nobody's crazy about medical cuisine."

We took the Rolls. Victor, ZZ's regular chauffeur, drove us with the same steely-eyed attention he paid to everything he did. ZZ was oddly quiet, staring out her window while I stared out mine; I found it meditative, just letting the scenery stream past without really focusing on anything, my thoughts flowing along with no particular destination. When this happens, I go with it; sometimes my thoughts wind up arriving in places I hadn't intended—but still places I needed to go.

It seemed as if the bomb could have been planted by anyone. Maybe I should be concentrating on Rolvink's murder instead; it might be easier to pin down the whereabouts of the guests around the time of death, sometime after dinner. Now, how to do that . . .

A bird flew past, beside the highway. Pigeon, I thought, though I wasn't sure. And just like that, my train of consciousness jumped the tracks, smashed through a few memories parked on a siding, and came to a screeching halt at an idea. A crazy, brilliant, almost-impossible-to-pull-off idea.

I *do* enjoy a challenge.

I pulled out my phone. "Sorry, ZZ," I said. "I just remembered something important I have to take care of. Uh, this might sound a little mysterious."

ZZ raised her eyebrows. "Really? How intriguing. Well, you go ahead, dear; I'll try to keep my curiosity in check."

I called Ben.

"Hey, Foxy Socks. How'd she like the basket?"

"I'll tell you later. Right now, I need you to do something for me."

"Okay. What's up?"

"I need you to put someone on the phone, but I can't mention her name."

"Excuse me?"

"I need her help with a linguistics problem."

I glanced over at ZZ. She was staring out the window with a look of feigned disinterest on her face.

"Wait," Ben said. "You want me to put *Tango* on the phone?"

"If you could."

"Why don't you just have me relay a message?"

"Because I'm going to ask *her* to relay a message, and if the message gets filtered through three brains—three very different brains—it might get garbled."

"So this is actually a message for . . . who, exactly?"

"Look, this is hard enough as it is. Is she around, or not?"

"Yeah, she's right here, taking a nap. Just a second."

This whole thing would be a lot easier with telepathy, but I was out of range. I waited, then realized it wasn't exactly like Tango could say hello. "Hi," I said. "I need a favor. You remember that conversation you had with the Venezuelan office worker?"

I heard a meow, but of course I had no idea if it was a yes or a no. "Yeah, the one that had the crush on you. He was really helpful." The Venezuelan in question was a parakeet who lived in the coroner's office, one who'd used his amazing memory to recite some very important overheard information to us. "I need the same kind of thing again. But this time, it has to be a fly-on-the-wall kind of situation. Obviously, we can't use the Venezuelan again, but I was thinking someone from next door. Next door to your place, not the Venezuelan's. Somebody who understands the *spirit* of what I'm trying to do."

Another meow. Maybe it was my imagination, but it sounded incredulous. "Yes, I know you don't have a lot of pull with that group. That's why I want you to get your partner to do it. He's a lot more diplomatic. Get him to recruit someone, put him on the inside, and report whatever they learn. It has to be this afternoon, no later than two. He'll know why."

Ben came back on the phone. "She says she's got it. I hope she's right, because she just took off like a shot."

"Okay, thanks. I'll check in with you later."

I slipped my phone back into my pocket and looked over at ZZ. She smiled and said, "So. How long have you been working for the KGB?"

"No comment. I'm not going to have to kill you, am I?"

"No, dear. But if an embassy blows up in the next week, you and I are going to have a serious discussion about your extracurricular activities."

"Yes, ma'am."

"Don't *yes ma'am* me. I was at Altamont."

"I know. You're not going to stab me, are you?"

"Not right now. I'm not wearing my stabby clothes."

My plan was simple but daring: get Whiskey to convince a ghost bird—one with a good memory—to spy on Forrester during his interviews with the potential suspects, and relay what he heard to one of us. As long as Tango understood what it was I'd asked of her . . .

The visit to Natalia was anticlimactic. She was still extremely disoriented, and kept saying, "What?" every few sentences. When told that Maurice Rolvink was dead, she said, "Of course he's dead. He's been dead for years." Then she asked for a grilled cheese sandwich and a pair of ice skates.

We left the gift basket with a nurse, who told us the disorientation was normal and would probably resolve over the next few days. Then we returned to the Rolls, where Victor was sitting bolt-upright and staring straight ahead, just as he was when we'd left him. I wondered if he actually turned off when people weren't around, or just powered down into sleep mode.

Amazingly, ZZ didn't ask me any questions about my unusual phone conversation. Either she was trying to prove she could mind her own business, or she thought I was pulling her leg and refused to take the bait. I didn't care which explanation was true, as long as she stuck to it.

As soon as we were back at the mansion, I made my excuses and hurried off. ZZ didn't try to stop me, just gave me a mysterious smile of her own. "You go ahead dear," she said. "Those Venezuelans are notoriously impatient."

The interviews were being held in the study, and if Forrester stuck to the schedule I'd made for him, he'd be halfway through talking to Jaxon Nesbitt. I ducked into the billiards room, which shared a wall with the study, and looked around. Empty.

Then I heard Tango's voice in my head. *<Under the table, Toots.>*

I looked. Tango was sprawled out on the floor underneath, her eyes alert and her tail twitching. *<Our spy is inside, listening to every word. I don't know how much his little bird skull can hold, so I'm getting him to recap the high points as they happen. I was going to use Whiskbroom as a backup, but it turns out the bird can't braincast to more than one mind at a time unless he can actually see the being it belongs to.>*

"How's it going so far?"

<Aside from the sporadic outbursts of tactless, unasked-for opinion? Peachy.>

It took me a second to realize what she meant. "Tactless . . . oh, no. Fish Jumping? You're using *Fish Jumping*?" Fish Jumping, the ghost parrot, is usually the soul of formal politeness in telepathic conversation. Unfortunately, though, FJ frequently interrupts himself with a form of parrot Tourrette's, vocally blurting out his true feelings with no inhibitions.

<It wasn't like we had a lot of lead time, Toots. We took what we could get. Here, let me give you a sample: "Ah yes, the lieutenant has just finished asking about Mr. Nesbitt's relationship to the deceased. Nesbitt has nothing but praise for his former employer—Awwk! Don't believe a word! Don't believe a word!">

"I am *so* sorry, Tango—but hey, his comments might actually prove useful. Maybe we can get Whiskey to swap places with you between interviews?"

<You better. Or I'm gonna wind up inventing a way to kill a bird twice.>

I took out my phone and started taking notes.

Okay, it was a weird way to gather information. But it worked, and I managed to call Whiskey telepathically and get him to swap with Tango. That meant calling Fish Jumping into the room, but once the parrot had eyeballed Whiskey and linked to him telepathically, he swooped right back through the wall to his listening post.

I couldn't sit in the billiards room all afternoon tapping away at my phone—but I could get away with doing it on the keyboard in my office, which was still within the range of my partners' telepathy.

So that's what we did. During lulls in the process I did some actual work work, entering data into spreadsheets on my computer or reviewing invoices.

Some choice excerpts: [I believe Mr. Tervo is referencing Mary Shelley in his explanation of why he declined dessert that evening.]

<*Fikru is denying being a drug abuser.* "Awk! Transparent lie! Transparent lie!">

[Oscar is engaging in witty banter about the value of a scotch-based diet. The lieutenant is not amused.]

<*Fortunato Trentini just knocked over his glass of water.* "Awk! Guilty as hell! Guilty as—" *Oh, please, that's hardly an indication of culpability—great, now the parrot's arguing with himself—*>

And so it went.

When the interviews were finally over, I let Whiskey out for a run, gave Tango some kitty treats in the kitchen, and told Fish Jumping he could return to the Crossroads. "Good job, all of you," I said.

And that role your assistant talked to me about? Fish Jumping asked Tango anxiously. *He said he just needed your final confirmation?* "Awk! Desperate plea for attention! Awk!"

<Consider it given. My people will call your people,> Tango said.

But my people are all dead . . .

<So are mine, but they're very *good. Paul can handle all the details.>*

Thank you! I shall speak with him, forthwith. "Awk! Desperation Express, all aboard! Awk!"

When Fish Jumping had gone, Tango gave her head an annoyed shake. *<Guess I'd better head to the set myself and check on things. Being talented is* so *exhausting.>*

I decided I'd go with her, maybe mull over what we'd learned this afternoon.

Mulling, however, would have to wait. By the time Tango and I got there, another crisis was unfolding: Fish Jumping was really getting into it with Paul the octopus. *Now you listen to me, you rubbery-armed aquatic spider! You told me the part was mine!* "Awk! I'm outta control! I'm outta control!"

Paul waved his tentacles in agitation. {~i don't know what you're talking about~calm down~}

You're trying to gaslight me! Telling me one thing then denying it later! I won't have it, I tell you, I won't have it! "Awk! I need a chill pill! Heavy sedation! Awk!"

{~i most certainly did not~that would be miss stripey's job in any case~i only work face-to-face access~}

"Okay, hold on," I said, speaking to Fish Jumping. "I can tell there've been some communication breakdowns. Let's stop pointing fingers—uh, limbs—and fix this. Sound good?"

Fish Jumping hopped from foot to foot, still agitated. *I'm simply not being treated with any sort of respect!* "Awk! I'm a loser! Awk!"

I stopped myself before I could say, *Well, you are a dead parrot.* Unfortunately, once that seed had been planted, it refused to go away. "I get that, Fish Jumping. You're a smart, talented bird with lots to offer, and people don't always recognize that." Inner voice: *You've passed on. You've ceased to be. You've expired and gone to meet your maker—after which you thought you'd try to break into show biz, seeing as how dead parrots are big there.* "But I do. You really came through for us when we needed it, and Tango's happy to return the favor."

I glanced over at her. "Right, kitty?"

Tango sat down and started to clean one of her rear paws. <*Sure, whatever. What was the part, again?*>

FJ stopped hopping, but his feathers were still ruffled. *I thought so as well, and accepted graciously when the offer was made. But now this octopedal recalcitrant denies ever talking to me!* "Awk! Losing my mind! Losing my mind!"

I looked over at Paul and frowned. "You're saying this conversation never happened?"

Despite having eight arms and no shoulders, he still managed to convey a shrug. {i'm sorry but no~i have an excellent memory and no reason to lie~whoever you talked to it wasn't me~}

My built-in bullshit detector is pretty accurate, but it's tuned more toward the human range than the cephalopod or the avian. Still, some things hold true despite species: Lies are always told for a reason, and it's usually a selfish one. Was Paul trying to get the part promised to FJ? Was FJ trying to cash in on a vague promise by insisting it was a firm offer? And when did I become a Tinseltown executive?

I turned back to Fish Jumping. "Okay, I'm going to clear this up, right now. That part is yours. Right, Tango?"

<*Well, I'll have to think about it . . .* >

"Tango . . ."

<Oh, all right, fine.>

Oh, thank you, kind lady! I'm forever in your debt!
"Awk! Back to kissing ass! Back to kissing ass!"

So much for mulling things over. For my second attempt I left the graveyard and went back to the estate; I wound up in the gardens, which are an excellent place for walking and pondering. This time of year there weren't a lot of blooms on the plants, but they were pretty all the same. Something about the spare simplicity of bare branches seemed appropriate to what I was trying to accomplish in my head, too.

What I'd learned from my eavesdropping operation was that out of all our guests—Trentini, Tervo, Nesbitt, Fikru, and Keene—only Keene had a solid alibi for that evening: He was playing croquet with Oscar. Trentini spent most of the evening alone in front of a roaring fire in the study, going over footage on his laptop; Fikru was meditating in his room; Tervo went for a long walk, by himself, in the graveyard; and Jaxon Nesbitt did some reading in bed. The only party animal was Keene, who seemed determined to make up for the rest of them. All of them said that the last time they'd seen Rolvink had been at dinner, where he'd mentioned he was planning on going into town that evening.

Forrester didn't talk to Catree.

So as far as the murder went, Keene was in the clear. The rest of them, not so much—but there was at least one whose story I could verify.

I left my office, checked in on Ben to make sure dinner was coming along nicely, popped my head in on ZZ to check on her latest project—some sort of sculpture, apparently inspired by Keene's monstrosity—and double-checked with Forrester to make sure it was okay to clear the lawn and got Victor and our biweekly gardening crew to start the takedown process.

Then I headed over to the Crossroads.

Tervo claimed he'd been in the graveyard all evening. If that were true, then either he was innocent or he'd killed Rolvink inside the Great Crossroads itself—an event I was pretty sure I'd have heard about.

So I asked around. I questioned guinea pigs, I spoke to homing pigeons. I made inquiries of rats, of gerbils, of mice. I talked to cats, dogs, lizards, and monkeys. I interrogated fish.

In the end, it was the prowlers that came through for me. Prowlers are sort of like transients: They don't quite belong here, but they don't really have anywhere else to go. They usually fall somewhere between feral and domesticated, not really pets but not really wild, either. Often they're from zoos or public aquariums, places they became used to human contact but never really bonded with people.

One of these was Two-Notch, a slightly confused shark. Two-Notch was convinced the Great Crossroads was actually a huge, water-filled tank, and she was in the habit of patrolling its perimeter in a very regular fashion. There was nothing to prevent her from leaving the confines of the graveyard other than her own belief in the existence of invisible glass walls, but that was enough. Funny how often that's the case, even for the non-aquatic.

I found her on one of her endless perambulations, gliding along just inside the fence, about six feet off the ground. I used to worry about her trying to eat other fish ghosts— heck, I used to worry about her trying to eat *me*—but she doesn't seem terribly interested in eating anymore. It's as if her instincts are slowly eroding away, and all she has left is the desire for constant movement.

I caught her eye and waved her over. A shark's mind is

actually very precise; Two-Notch might have been wrong about the existence of that glass wall, but she knew where it was supposed to be to within an inch, and her own depth, heading, and position at all times. Time was a little trickier, but I'd long ago figured out exactly how long it took her to make a circuit of the graveyard and could make a rough estimate from that.

Between what Two-Notch told me and what I learned from other ghost sources, I could reliably put Maxwell Tervo inside the Great Crossroads between just after dinner and ten PM. It looked like he was off the hook, at least for Rolvink's death.

At last, some real progress. I was congratulating myself on my success as I headed back toward the mansion when I heard Tango's mental voice in my head.

<Listen up!> Tango said. *<Everybody has their script parrot or parakeet, right? Good. Go find a quiet corner and rehearse your lines. We'll meet back here in an hour and run through the opening scene. Go!>*

That sounded intriguing enough that I had to investigate. I walked toward Davy's Grave and saw that, sure enough, every ghost actor was paired up with a ghost bird. And as they scattered to the four corners of the Crossroads, I saw that one ghostly pair was hanging back with the erstwhile director: a brilliant blue macaw and a near duplicate of Tango herself.

Unsinkable Sam.

Tango was perched, very director-like, upon a headstone, with Sam looking up at her from the burial plot. They had locked eyes in that way cats have, a stare-off that managed to combine aloofness and alertness in the same posture. *I am completely aware of your every twitch,* that posture said, *and I don't care about any of them in the least.* Was this the big showdown?

It was—but not in the way I thought.

<Look, Sam—you're terrific, you really are. It's just that I don't think you're quite right for the part.>

<What do you mean?> Sam said, his telepathic voice showing a definite German accent. *<I'm a perfect match! We are alike in almost every detail!>*

Tango started to groom one paw. *<Yeah, I know what you're saying. It's just that we've decided to go a different way. Midnight!>*

There are all kinds of animals that come through the Great Crossroads. I've seen armadillos and alligators, falcons and foxes, bears and bats. But this was the first time I'd seen a black panther.

It slunk from behind a mausoleum like it had invented the word *(slunk,* not *mausoleum).* It was a black that gleamed like the highly polished metal body of a hearse, with glowing green eyes. It didn't come to a stop when it reached Tango and Sam, just kept pacing around them in a circle that suggested it couldn't decide which one to eat first.

<Hey,> said Midnight.

To his credit, Sam didn't look cowed at all—not even in the about-to-become-a-burger sense. *<You have to be joking!>* he hissed. *<This? This is what you're replacing me with?>*

Tango continued her grooming, unperturbed. *<Sorry, sweetheart. You're just a little too . . . on the nose. Not your fault. Keep in touch, okay?>*

<You have not heard the last of this,> Sam spat, then turned and stalked away with his tail in the air.

<Ooh,> Tango said. *<Using a cliché for your exit line? Don't put that on your demo reel.>*

I walked up. "Not interrupting anything, am I?"

<Nah. You know the biz. Glad you're here, though; I'd like you to meet my star.>

<Hey,> said Midnight. He had a low, rumbling voice, like a Harley that had learned to talk.

"Your star? I thought Pal was your star."

She snorted. *<That's what he thinks, too. He's just the Big Bad; this is my lead.>*

One of the most trustworthy, beloved animals to ever grace the screen is her villain? Of course he is. "So you cast Unsinkable Sam first? I thought you two didn't get along."

<Oh, I'm past all that. Turns out he was just skulking around because he was a fan—you know what they can be like. Anyway, he's actually a pretty good actor—but when Midnight showed up, I just couldn't resist. Isn't he perfect?>

<Hey,> said Midnight. I thought I was hearing a little Barry White in that voice, too.

"Yeah, he's perfect. So you're using *birds* to help your actors memorize lines? That's pretty good."

<Just stole the idea you used to spy on Forrester and tweaked it a little.>

"Please, Tango. You never use the S word in Hollywood. It's an *homage*."

<Right, right.>

Leaving Tango to her directorial duties, I was almost to the gate when I heard the Voice of Doom.

[The Great Cataclysm approaches,] the voice said. I spun around, because when you hear the Voice of Doom and it's coming from behind you, spinning is clearly called for.

The Voice of Doom belonged to the ghost of a dog.

The ghost was standing on top of a small rise, of which there are many in the graveyard. He was an English setter, with long, silky white hair on his belly and legs, and two large black splotches on his back. His muzzle was white but his head was black, making it look a little like he was wearing a dark mask over his eyes.

The Voice of Doom might have shut me up when I first started this job, but you can get used to all sort of things. "When you say *Cataclysm,* are you talking about actual cats being involved?" I called out.

I thought it was a reasonable question, but the dog stared down at me with pity in his eyes. [Lo, there will be much suffering and gnashing of teeth,] he intoned. [And none will be spared—not the living or the dead.]

And then he turned and darted away.

"Wow," I said as I trudged up the hill. "Spooooooky. Seriously, how do you do that thing with your voice?"

But when I got there, the ghost dog was nowhere in sight.

14.

I made a perfunctory search of the graveyard, but it's a big place—and if a ghost wants to disappear it's pretty easy to hide, especially in a crowd of other ghosts. I sighed and headed back to Davy's Grave to let Tango know of this latest development.

"So anyway, I just saw something weird," I said. "Well, weirder." I told her about the English setter and his ominous pronouncement.

Tango twitched her tail in annoyance. *<Oh, ignore him. Show business always attracts a certain type, you know? Desperately eager to be famous, and not entirely sane. It's like they want to* become *fictional, and are already half convinced they are.>*

"Okay, there's some truth to that," I admitted. "But this is the Great Crossroads, not the Great Crossroads Studio. When I hear dire predictions from a deceased animal, I tend to take them a little more seriously than some guy on the corner with a cardboard sign and a wild look in his eye."

Tango sighed. (Yes, cats can sigh.) *<That's because you're not familiar with this particular sign-carrier. His name is Jim the Wonder Dog.>*

"Jim the Wonder Dog?"

<Yes, Jim the Wonder Dog. I could tell you all about him, but I don't have time to be your Google surrogate right now. Go scratch your research itch—I've got actors to prep.>

My cat knows me all too well. I scurried off to my virtual burrow to nibble away on the rich bounty of the Internet . . .

Jim the Wonder Dog was an English setter in the 1930s. During his lifetime he was studied by psychologists from two different universities as well as a variety of skeptics, but nobody could quite figure out how he did what he did.

And what he did was remarkable. He picked the winner of the Kentucky Derby seven years in a row. He determined the sex of unborn babies, seemed to understand several languages (unlike his owner, who only spoke English), and predicted the victor of the 1936 World Series.

What really struck me, though, is that his owner, a man named Sam Van Arsdale, didn't profit from any of Jim's accomplishments. From all accounts he refused to display the dog for money, and took him to both veterinarians and psychologists in an effort to understand the abilities of his amazing pet.

Jim was a hunting dog, used for quail. His owner claimed he'd flushed out over five thousand birds during his career, an unheard-of total. More than anything, though, he was smart; he could follow just about any command, including orders to pick out a car by the number on its license plate or a person in a crowd by their profession.

And now his ghost was in my graveyard, warning me of an impending disaster.

As soon as I knew what I was dealing with—well, as soon as I knew what kind of weirdness I was dealing with—okay, as soon as I had a general idea what *sort* of weirdness—

You know what? I really didn't know what I was dealing with.

What I knew was that this particular iteration of the unusual had issued forth from a denizen of the Great Crossroads. (Yes, sometimes I use my impressive vocabulary to disguise my actual ignorance. I'm not the only one.) Therefore, in order to gain greater understanding, it behooved me to—okay, that's enough of that. I'm starting to sound like Whiskey on a lecture tour.

I went back to the graveyard.

And arrived just in time to see Tango and her actors preparing to rehearse a scene. They were gathered around as before, her sitting on the headstone she used as a director's chair, listening to last-minute instructions: <*Okay, everybody knows their cues? Good. Places, everybody, please.*>

I strolled up as the animals scattered, resisting the urge to stroke her head; a director needs to maintain a certain amount of mystique. "Tango. Looks like you're almost ready to roll."

<*Just a moment, Toots. Quiet on the set! Aaaaaaaand . . . action!*>

For a moment there was silence. Then Midnight slunk over the top of the hill, black as a shadow and sinuous as an anaconda. He flowed up to a tombstone, disappearing behind it, then darted from that one to another. His great dark head peered out cautiously, his brilliant green eyes alert for danger.

Suddenly his ears perked up. He heard something, though I couldn't—not at first.

Then I did. A low, steady, rumbling, almost like the beating of drums, coming from all around us. Midnight looked left, then right. He snarled.

And then the bunnies swarmed over the hills.

White-furred, pink-eyed rabbits, hundreds of them. A huge, rippling tide of snowy fur, flowing toward us like a gigantic, mutant Angora sweater.

An angry Angora sweater, it seemed. When it reached Midnight, it attacked.

Rabbits are not always the timid vegetarians people see them as. Those big legs aren't just for hopping, and those claws aren't just for digging. In the wild they can deliver vicious kicks and bites in both self-defense and aggression.

What I hadn't realized is that they also knew kung fu.

That's the only way I can describe the fight that followed. Martial arts mayhem, with plenty of kicks, leaps, and punches—though the punches were more like swats, since it was Midnight delivering them. Rabbits flew through the air, buck teeth bared, and were promptly smacked down, up, or back the way they came. There was plenty of violence, but no blood.

When it was all over, Midnight stood panting in the middle of a circle of sprawled white bodies. One or two occasionally twitched an ear or nose, but otherwise they all seemed down for the count.

<Nothing will stop me from reaching my goal,> Midnight snarled. *<NOTHING!>*

<Aaaannd cut!> said Tango. *<Great job, everyone!>*

And with that, all the rabbits came back to life—well, afterlife. Midnight padded over to his director, sparing me only a cursory glance.

<Excellent, really superb,> said Tango. *<I do have a few notes, though. You were a little slow on that last kick with your left hind leg. And while I love—love—that thing you improvised, grabbing the bunny by the neck and tossing it over your shoulder?>*

<Too much?>

<For me? No. For the rabbit? Could be. Hey, Harold—you okay? Head still attached? Nod for yes.>

A large white rabbit looked up and said, (I'm okay!)

<He's okay, it's all good,> said Tango. *<Take five, big guy. When you come back we'll run through the ninja squirrel scene.>*

The panther slunk away. I wondered if he slunk everywhere he went, and if he'd done so when he was still alive. Then I wondered if *slank* was a word, and decided that if it wasn't it should be.

"Wow," I said. "That was certainly . . . action-packed."

Tango drew herself up smugly. *<I know. It's still got a few rough spots in the third act, but it's coming along nicely.>*

"Terrific. So. Jim the Wonder Dog."

<Where?> Tango glanced around.

"No, I mean I know who Jim the Wonder Dog *is,* now. And I have to say, his résumé is kind of impressive."

<Please. He never acted a day in his life. Had a shot at a big pet food gig, but his owner wasn't interested.>

"I'm talking about prognostication, not acting. His uncanny ability to know things he shouldn't have been able to know."

<So he's a know-it-all. Cats know all sorts of things, too—doesn't mean we go around telling *everyone.>*

I couldn't tell if she was missing the point or just being obstinate. "Tango, when somebody who demonstrates the ability to predict the future starts predicting imminent doom and disaster, don't you think it's prudent to pay attention?"

She gave her head an annoyed shake. *<Oh, is that what's bothering you? Look, you know those things I'm not supposed to talk to you about?>*

"Only in a vague and extremely irritating way." *Those things* were the nuts and bolts of how the universe actually worked, which apparently dead pets knew more about than human beings who still had a pulse.

<Well, this is one of them. And while I can't explain how I know, I do know one thing for sure: Jim the Wonder Dog can't predict the future.>

I frowned. "Let's say I take that at face value. If he can't, how did he do all the things he did? And why is he running around proclaiming that terrible things are about to happen?"

Tango yawned. *<Since I wasn't there, I don't know how he pulled off those tricks. Probably wasn't that hard, though; human beings are amazingly gullible. And the reason why he's being all doomsayer of doom is simple: He's a very particular breed of canine known as a gloryhound. Needs constant affirmation, craves praise, has to be the center of attention at all times. Guess who was the first one in line to audition?>*

"J the WD?"

<You got it. And when I turned him down, he whined and bitched and generally demonstrated why all those annoying behaviors are canine-related terms. If he can't get noticed as an actor, he figures he'll get noticed as a prophet. Hey, it worked before, right?>

Tango called out to the spectral octopus that was drifting nearby. *<Hey, Paul; you know a little about predictions, right?>*

The octopus drifted closer. {~i dabble a bit yes~sports mostly~}

<*What do you think of Jim the Wonder Dog?*>

Who knew an octopus could roll its eyes? {~what a fame prostitute~ooh I know the future you should all be scared~ we all want to be loved but he's like a starving orca at an all-you-can-scarf sushi buffet~leave some for the rest of us sweetheart~}

Which is when Piotr, the Russian circus bear, ambled over and joined us. [Da. Is ridiculous, all the terrible moaning and the moping and big sad puppy eyes. He should look on bright side, no? Nobody like dog on big downer.]

I nodded at Piotr. It's hard to argue with the optimism of a dead bear in a tutu. Especially one carrying a unicycle.

"Don't think I've every seen you off that thing," I said.

Piotr put one paw on his chest. [Please. Bear is not defined by accessories. Piotr is complex, has many facets. And sometimes, you just want to feel dirt under your paws, no?]

{~speak for yourself~}

"So that's it?" I asked. "He's a big phony? Nothing to worry about?"

Tango settled down on her paws. <*Plenty of phonies in this biz, Toots. And always something to worry about . . .* >

Which is when I smelled it. You don't troubleshoot for a touring rock band without learning to recognize the aroma of burning ganja, and that's what was currently drifting past my nose. This is not exactly an unusual occurrence in the graveyard; the groundskeeper, Cooper, is an old hippie who probably smokes as much grass as he mows. Nobody much cares, least of all ZZ.

But I also knew Coop's habits, and despite the public's much more permissive attitude these days, the kind of

paranoia that decades of police harassment taught his gen-
eration was hard to shake. He preferred to smoke indoors,
or where he was sure he couldn't be seen; he wouldn't take
the chance of being stumbled upon by some grief-stricken
former pet owner visiting a grave.

The actual culprits came ambling into view a minute
later: Keene and Fikru, passing a pipe between them. I
think it was a pipe, anyway; I don't really keep up with
the latest technological advancements. For all I knew it
was a gadget that broke vegetable matter down into organic
molecules and propelled the result directly into your brain
through osmosis.

In any case, they didn't seem to care they'd been spotted. They waved cheerfully and headed in my direction;
I left Tango on her director's headstone and met them
halfway.

"Care to share?" Yemane asked, offering the pipe. It re-
sembled an elephant carved out of jade, with the trunk
being the part you stuck in your mouth.

"No, thanks," I said. "Not while I'm working, anyway."

"Could have told you that," Keene said. "Foxtrot always
puts other people's fun before her own. Selfless, she is."

"Very true, very true," I said. "Saint Foxtrot, that's me.
I really should ask ZZ for a raise; the price of halo polish
just keeps going up."

"You could always make some extra cash selling snaps
to the craparazzi," Keene said. "Take a few of me passed
out in the Jacuzzi wearing a gorilla mask, that sort of thing."

Yemane frowned. "If you were wearing a gorilla mask,
nobody would know it was you."

"Well, that's what *captions* are for, aren't they? The
point being, I'm available for whatever ludicrous poses you
can dream up. Consider it my penance for the croquet debacle."

"No thanks. That would mean dealing with a tabloid, and I can never get the slime out of my clothes afterward."

"Oh, they're not that bad," Keene said. "For a parasitic, fungus-based life-form, I mean. For a parasitic, fungus-based life-form devoid of ethics, compassion, or any respect for the notion of privacy—all right, they're pretty bad. But at least you wouldn't have to go far; I saw one peeking over the wall this morning. Had a telephoto lens the size of a bongo drum."

My eyes narrowed. If there's one thing—emphasis on *thing*—that I really, truly hate, it's the vultures that prey on celebrities. They embrace the worst in human nature, pervert the idea of the free press, and take no responsibility for the consequences of what they wreak. They devour indiscriminately, like sharks, but ugliness and shame are the flavors they like most. I've encountered my share of them over the years, and I've never met one that could justify what they do beyond "If I didn't do it somebody else would, and I need the paycheck." Bottom-feeding scum, but a necessary evil in an open society.

Of course, this was the first time I'd be dealing with one since I'd acquired my new partners and responsibilities . . .

"Oh, dear," said Keene. "I do believe that's the most frightening look I've ever seen cross your face, Foxtrot. It's like that scene in *How the Grinch Stole Christmas,* when he first gets the idea to give the gift of home invasion to all the Whos."

"Just thinking about my job, and all the parts that I really, really love doing—including those I haven't done yet."

Keene and Yemane glanced at each other, and both of them nodded. "Uh-huh," said Yemane. "A wonderful, *awful* idea. You can almost *hear* it inside her head."

"No, I think that's the pharmaceuticals kicking in,"

Keene said. "Either that, or it's the sound of my own hair growing. What a peculiar noise."

I nodded. "Back at it, huh? I suppose I should take that as a sign you've recovered."

"Yes, well, hair of the pack of dogs that mauled you and all that. I've put my recuperation in the hands of Dr. Fikru, here—though, to be fair, he was somewhat responsible for my condition in the first place."

I raised my eyebrows. "Oh?"

Yemane shrugged. "I'm more of a shaman than a doctor, though I do have a degree in pharmacology. The original plan was to ingest a finely balanced mixture of psychoactive compounds in order to produce a psychically aware but safe experience."

Keene made a dismissive gesture. "Safe. Balanced. Where's the adventure in that? You can't script a chemical indulgence like a bloody vacation planner, can you? *Manic episode at two fifteen, hallucinations at quarter of four, followed by tea*? Bollocks."

Yemane shook his head. "I had something ready, but once I was here I knew I'd have to alter it substantially. The supercharged psychic atmosphere is far too volatile for what I'd prepared—but Keene decided to take it anyway."

Keene looked regretful. "That I did. Was looking forward to some brilliant hallucinations; I might even have had them. Too bad I forgot to press the RECORD button."

Yemane sighed. "That's the benzodiazepine; it can cause short-term amnesia. It was supposed to be there for its relaxing influence, but the atmosphere here exaggerated its effects—just like it did the others."

"Fascinating," I said. "I can't wait to find out which drug inspires croquet mania."

It was meant as a joke, but Yemane took it seriously. "That would be the pramipexole. Non-ergoline dopamine agonist used in treating bipolar depression, restless-leg syndrome, and Parkinson's. It also has both hallucinogenic and sedative properties, which were supposed to produce non-threatening visions. Unfortunately, there's a rare side effect: obsessive-compulsive behavior related to pleasurable activities. Eating, gambling, sex . . ."

I looked at him skeptically. "Knocking little wooden balls through hoops?"

Keene grinned. "I know. Me and all my proclivities, and what does my chemically stimulated brain fixate on? Building a better game of lawn billiards. Could be worse, I suppose; I might have stayed up all night surfing eBay in order to expand my collection of Victorian clockwork clowns—"

He stopped abruptly and looked stricken. "Excuse me," he said, yanking his phone out of his pocket. "I think I have to check something online."

I laughed as he turned away and started fiddling with the device. "So," I said to Yemane, "you mentioned two drugs, both with sedative effects. Neither one sounds like it'd keep somebody up all night, hauling exercise equipment around."

"True. There was also a stimulant component, one strong enough to counteract the benzo and the pramipexole. Unfortunately, its effects were exaggerated, too."

"I take it this is a second attempt to get it right?"

Yemane peered into the bowl of the pipe, then tapped it gently against his palm. A few ashes fell out. "Yes. Something milder, and hopefully more in tune with the essence of this place. Something with the right *resonance*."

"All right, then, I'll leave you to it. Keep an eye on him, will you? Let me know if he has any sudden croquet-related impulses."

"I'll do that."

I walked back to Davy's Grave. Paul the octopus and Piotr the circus bear had left, but Tango was still there. She sniffed the air, then sneezed. *<Ugh. I'll never understand the human need to set things on fire and inhale the smoke.>*

"Really? I would have thought a catnip aficionada like yourself would be more sympathetic."

She yawned. *<It's not the effect I disapprove of, it's the way people get there. Why can't you just sprinkle it on the carpet, mash your face into it, and writhe around like normal folks do?>*

I gave her a mock frown. "Kitty, please. You know we don't use the N word around here. It's *inappropriate*."

<Yeah, yeah.>

"And speaking of inappropriate—there's something happening right now that I really don't approve of. It's happening right at the edge of the estate, involving someone who doesn't really appreciate the idea of personal boundaries."

Her ears perked up. *<Encroaching? I hate encroaching. Let's go show them what we do to people who encroach.>*

I grinned. "I was hoping you'd feel like that. But first, let's do a little preparation—*then* we can go all Border Patrol on their encroaching ways."

It wasn't hard to find him. The paparazzo in question was lurking just behind the back wall, no doubt hoping to get a candid shot of someone through a window or maybe out by the hot tub. He was using an extendable stepladder to get him high enough to clear the wall, and the fact that he'd had the foresight to bring it proved this wasn't the first time he'd done this.

I suppose I should give him some credit for lugging that thing around, especially since he was pretty big himself, but I'm not going to. I mean, if he actually had a heart

attack and fell off the thing, I'd phone an ambulance—
but I wouldn't send him a get-well card in the hospital.

I may not be as stealthy as Tango, but I can be pretty
sneaky when I need to. I managed to get right up to the
base of the ladder without him noticing me; then again,
all his attention was focused on and through the camera
he held. The camera itself was big and black and expensive
looking, but it was the lens that was really impressive. Keene
had been right—the thing looked more like it was designed
to study stars in the sky instead of those with their names
on Hollywood Boulevard. It was white, at least four feet
long, and about the same diameter as a telephone pole. He
had to use a little telescoping stand to hold it up, the bottom of which rested on the top of the stepladder.

"Hey there!" I said, rather loudly.

He didn't scream in surprise, topple off the ladder, and
crash to the ground, for which I was grateful. That would
have been too easy. What he did was glance down at me
and say, "I'm not breaking the law."

This was not a surprise. It's what they usually said.
Sometimes they recited their lawyer's phone number,
which was supposed to sound cool and tough but really
didn't. I'm not the one that's going to be calling your legal
representative, doofus.

"Sure you are," I said cheerfully. "The law of averages,
anyway. What are the odds that you'd have both a ladder
and a camera with you when you encountered a tall, yet al-
luring structure blocking your way? It's almost as if the
universe wants you to see—nay, *document*—what's on the
other side."

He sighed. He looked bored and ever so slightly annoyed. "If you're going to threaten me, you should know
I'm recording this." I couldn't see any obvious recording
equipment, but these days that stuff is so small he could

be wearing it as a tie clip. Not that he was wearing a tie—he was dressed in a camo-patterned parka and matching baggy pants, which didn't so much make him disappear as create the illusion a military zeppelin was hovering ten feet in the air.

"Oh, I'm not here to threaten you—more like *warn* you."

Apparently I wasn't worth his full attention, because he turned back to his camera and resumed his watching. "About what? Legal action? Overzealous bodyguards? Go ahead, I've heard it all."

"Nothing like that. I wanted to warn you about the wild-life."

He turned back to me and frowned. "Wildlife?"

"Yeah. See, we had a chemical spill here recently, and it's affected the local fauna. A bunch of them died, but the ones that didn't went sort of . . . crazy. Like rabies, but without the staggering and foaming at the mouth. Mostly, they just want to eat your face."

Which is when Tango sprang.

She'd been creeping along the top of the wall, picking her way carefully through the overhanging branches. Not a lot of cover from maples or birches this time of year, but there was a spruce that gave her some shelter just shy of Camera Guy's perch. She landed on top of the giant lens, hissing and spitting and doing that cat thing where they basically inflate themselves to twice their size. Her tail looked like the business end of a toilet brush.

Camera Guy bellowed, lurched backward instinctively, and fell off the ladder. The strap around his neck yanked the camera and lens with him. Tango, however, stayed behind; she leapt straight up, then came down in a perfect four-point landing on the top of the stepladder.

Camera Guy landed flat on his back. His camera landed

with an *extremely* satisfying smashing sound right beside him.

I peered down at him. "Ooh. That sounded expensive. Anything else broken?"

He wheezed, his eyes bugging out. He had a scraggly gray beard and acne. "I'll . . . sue . . . ," he gasped.

"I don't blame you. That cat is just *begging* to be litigated. Or did you mean the company that dumped the toxic chemicals that drove her insane? Because we're having a *heck* of a time tracking those fellas down."

He struggled to a sitting position and glared at me. "That animal is a *menace*! I'm going to report this to the authorities and . . . and have her *euthanized*!"

I touched the tip of my index finger to my chin. "Hmmm. Well, she *is* dangerous, that much is obvious. But she's also a *cat,* which means her moods come and go. See?"

Tango had deflated, and now she hopped down a few rungs and stopped. I reached out a hand and stroked her silky black-and-white fur while she butted her head against my hand and purred like an outboard.

Camera Guy had looked pretty pale after he hit the ground, but his face was getting redder and redder. "All right," he growled. "A trained domestic attack cat, huh? Never seen *that* before, but I have encountered worse. Bengal tigers, timber wolves, lions—if it's got four legs and fangs, some celeb's got one for a pet. I don't scare that easy."

"Oh, nobody's trying to *scare* you, Mr. Random Photographer. Like I said, we're trying to *warn* you. Bipolar felines are the least of your worries—you haven't seen what those chemicals did to the raccoons."

Cue the growl.

Imagine a bear that's had a really bad day. Burned his porridge, spilled honey all over his laptop, got served with divorce papers from Mama Bear. Imagine he goes out to a grizzly bar to drown his sorrows, and when he returns to his car someone as smashed all the windows and used the interior for a restroom. Imagine he gets pulled over by Smokey after that, loses his license, and has his smelly car impounded. When he finally gets home he finds that Goldilocks has thrown a kegger in his absence, but it's over now and he's missed all the fun.

The sound that bear makes as he stares down at a passed-out Goldie, lying on a vomit-stained couch in the wreckage of his living room? That's the sound that issued forth from the bushes behind Camera Guy.

His eyes widened. The rest of his body got very, very still.

"Uh-oh," I said. Tango bolted back to the top of the ladder, leapt across to the wall, and tore off in the opposite direction. I let a look of suppressed terror creep across my own face, but tried not to overdo it.

Camera Guy remembered how to talk again, but not very well. "That's . . . that's not real," he whispered hoarsely.

"Shut. Up," I whispered back. "It's vicious, but not that smart. If we move slowly, we might have a chance. Get to your feet, but don't turn around—if you make eye contact it'll attack."

He risked a look behind him. That provoked another, louder growl, and what he saw was enough to make him say, "Oh, my God," and freeze.

"Look away!" I hissed.

"I can't," he moaned. "I just . . . what the hell *is* that?"

"We call it the Dracoon," I whispered.

It was tall, wide, and covered in long, tangled black fur. It had a huge set of powerful-looking jaws and a distinctive black mask across its eyes.

"What do I do?" Camera Guy said under his breath.

"Go back up the ladder—slowly. When you get to the top, jump over the wall. I'll follow you and kick the ladder down before it can chase me."

True to his nature, he didn't insist on me going first. He scrambled up the ladder as fast as he could, dragging his broken camera with him. When he got to the top, he hesitated, but another growl sent him over the wall. He landed with an audible thump and a yelp of pain.

"What now?" he yelled. Not, *Are you all right?* or *Hurry up before that thing eats you,* or even *Don't forget to knock the ladder down!*

"Now you wait right there," I called back. "Our head of security will be here in a minute."

"Is he going to shoot it?"

"No. *She* is going to detain you until the police arrive. You're trespassing."

And then I strolled over and scratched Whiskey behind the ears. "*Who's* a big bad scary dog? *You* are, that's right . . ."

15.

Okay, so tricking someone into breaking the law isn't totally ethical. But when that someone has PROFESSIONAL SCUMBAG—ASK ME ABOUT MY DIRT CHEAP RATES! on his business card, me and ethics pretend we don't know each other.

Shondra collared him beside the house, where he was trying to get a shot through a window with his camera phone. Knowing he was busted, he must have figured he had nothing left to lose.

I arrived as Shondra was proving him wrong. "Ouch," I said as I walked up with Whiskey at my side, now in his normal form. "That looks like it hurts."

Camera Guy glared up at me from the ground. "Let me up! I'll—"

"Sue," said Shondra. "Yeah, I got that. Don't worry, you'll be talking to your lawyer soon enough. Right after they book you, probably." Shondra, in a black turtleneck, jeans, and sneakers, was astride a prone Camera Guy, one hand gripping the wrist she had twisted behind him, the other holding a phone to her ear. She looked like a ninja riding a walrus while on hold with customer service. *Hello, tech support? There's something wrong with my walrus. Yes, I tried jiggling the tusk.*

"Sue?" I asked. "Whatever for? Pretty sure you're the one breaking the law."

"You tricked me! You and that hairy monstrosity in the bushes!"

"I have no idea what you're talking about. The only hairy monstrosity I'm familiar with is this one right here, and he's the *friendly* kind of monster."

Just to drive home the point, Whiskey darted forward and started licking Camera Guy's face enthusiastically. "Eww, don't do *that*," I said. "Germs! You don't know *what* might be living in that beard!"

"Get him off me or I'll sue!"

"Okay," said Shondra to her phone, thumbed it off, and slipped it into a tactical-looking holder on her belt. "Kind of a one-note guy, isn't he? Sue, sue, sue."

"Maybe it's his name."

"Could be. On your feet, Sue." She released his wrist and let him up. He stood slowly, breathing heavily, his face red. Shondra crossed her arms and stared at him levelly. "You and me are going to wait right here until Hartville PD shows up. You try to get past me, I'll put you down as fast as I did the first time."

"Yeah, yeah, this isn't my first time at the dance," he muttered. "Can we at least go inside? It's freezing out here."

"Not even a little bit of yes," I said. "Let you into the house you've been spying on? Let's not forget who the moron is in this situation."

"We'll see about that," he growled.

I nodded. "But while we're waiting, let's have a conversation. What, exactly, were you hoping to get pictures of?

Bloodstains? Zombies? Wreckage? Bloodstained zombies stumbling through wreckage?"

He snorted. "What, the low-budget horror flick? No-body cares about that. I'm here to get photos of Nesbitt—that's what my boss pays me for."

"Even if you succeeded, you'd be disappointed. He's about as boring a guest as it's possible to be. He eats, works, sleeps, and that's about it. I don't think your audi-ence is going to find any of that very entertaining."

"Sure, he's a real choirboy. Except when he's not." He shook his head and laughed. "You have no idea what you have under your roof. And when someone takes a picture—someone like *me*—that exposes what he is, *you're* the ones that'll feel like morons."

And that stopped me.

I believed in the freedom of the press; I just had higher standards for what constituted "press" than Camera Guy did. Taking sensationalistic pictures for a tabloid isn't jour-nalism, it's a violation of privacy. But what if there's an actual story there that the public has a right to know about? Revealing shots of someone in their underwear are one thing; revealing that someone's *stealing* underwear is an-other.

People like Camera Guy might live under rocks . . . but sometimes, they learn things down there.

"Come on, Sue," said Shondra. "We're going out to the main gate to wait for your ride."

After the police came and took Camera Guy away, Whiskey and I went up to my office and I thanked him for his performance. "I don't care what Tango says, you're a natural actor. And what was that thing you turned into, again?"

[A rather unusual crossbreed—only one of them ever

existed, to my knowledge. The mother had both mastiff and German shepherd blood, while the father was a dog known as a puli—that's where the tangled black hair comes from.]

"I was gonna guess Beagle Boy and Rastafarian. So, what do you make of what the shutterbug said?"

Whiskey jumped up on my couch and made himself comfortable. [He seemed to believe what he was saying. Whether there's any truth to his claims is questionable.]

I sat down next to Whiskey and stretched my legs. "Yeah, we have to consider the source. That guy wades in a ditch full of rumor and innuendo every day; pretty easy to grab some mud at random and fling it."

[True. But since he deals with gossip and baseless accusations all the time, his ability to tell truth from exaggeration is probably finely honed.]

"Good point." I frowned. "He could have just been saying that to guilt me—in which case, it worked—but I don't think so. I've heard that tone of self-righteous indignation before, but he had that little note of triumph in his voice, too. That I-know-something-you-don't inflection."

<Infection? Who's got an infection?> Tango strolled through my open door. *<Is it somebody for whom the adjective* mangy *was invented?>*

[Ectoplasmic beings do not get mange.]

<Ah, so you no longer have it? Congratulations.>

[I've *never* had it—]

"Guys, guys. Please. The word I used was *inflection,* all right? And what we're trying to figure out, Tango, is exactly what secret Jaxon Nesbitt is hiding—if any."

<He's a movie star, sweetheart—of course he's hiding something. Unlike cats, who are proud of each and every thing we do, famous actors spend all their time worrying

about whether or not people love them. Kind of like dogs, actually . . . anyway, it means they've turned second-guessing themselves into an art form. Am I going to lose that part because I spend too much time sniffing strange buttholes? Will people still adore me if I hump that guy's leg? Will that rolling-in-roadkill incident come back to haunt me?>

[I had that happen once. Ran into a pet rat in the grave-yard who remembered me writhing on their decomposing corpse.]

There was a pause.

"Sounds awkward," I said.

[You have no idea.]

<She has plenty of ideas, none of which we're discussing at the moment. Point being, an actor's secrets are usually more embarrassing than devastating, and they're all convinced that having those secrets exposed will ruin their careers, which is ridiculous.>

"Maybe . . . maybe not," I said. "What if that secret really could destroy your career, or worse? And what if someone else found out what it was?"

[They would have considerable power over you.]

"Yes, they would. Maybe enough to make an in-demand young actor star in a movie everybody agrees is beneath him."

Tango jumped up on the couch beside us. I stroked her head and she started to purr. *< I get it. Rolvink could have been blackmailing Nesbitt.>*

"Exactly. And that's the kind of thing that can get you killed."

Whiskey put his chin on my lap, and I rubbed behind his ears. [Therefore, the question is: What is Jaxon Nesbitt hiding?]

<Wrong again. The real question is, how are we going to find out what Nesbitt is hiding?>

"Nope," I said, one hand stroking Tango and the other Whiskey. "The real question is how much you two are going to complain when I stop doing *this*."

[She has a point.]

<PURRRRRRRR>

So we snuggled. And we plotted.

And then—of course—we were interrupted.

"You know," I said thoughtfully, "I'm really getting tired of this."

This was yet another on-set disagreement. This time, the strategy session Whiskey, Tango, and I had been halfway— okay, three-quarters of the way—through had been disrupted by a panicky Fish Jumping flying through the wall and loudly proclaiming that there was "*Trouble! Trouble! And I'm a big tattletale! Awk!*" involving Golden Cloud and Midnight.

Putting myself between half a ton of annoyed horse and an irritated jungle cat isn't something I'd normally consider—but in this case both animals were as weightless and unsolid as a politician's promises. And the best way to end a staring contest is usually to give both competitors something else to stare at.

"Ahem," I said. "What's going on, guys?"

(Not much,) Golden Cloud said coldly.

<Hey,> said Midnight. It sounded more like a warning than a greeting.

"Right. It's a non-verbal showdown. By which I mean a contest to see who can be more terse while squinting their eyes menacingly. Normally I'd put my money on the cat, what with the countless generations of highly developed staring genes, but GC here spent his whole life around pretend cowboys, and nobody does that grim, intent look better. I heard that Clint Eastwood actually got a shot glass to crack once, just by looking at it for six hours straight."

Neither of them had backed up, but I was forcing them to deal with me instead of each other, which lessened the tension from fully drawn bowstring to merely taut tightrope, along which I proceeded to stroll casually. "Come on, GC—I know you're a seasoned trouper at this. What's holding up the show from going on?"

Golden Cloud shook his head and snorted. (Backstage gossip, is all. Certain greenhorns can't keep their mouths shut.)

More rumors? I glanced at Midnight. "Oh?"

It's not just domestic cats that can change their attitude at the drop of a whisker; Midnight sank back onto his haunches and started grooming one glossy black paw. It wasn't so much an admission of guilt as a total loss of interest in every aspect of the situation.

I turned back to Golden Cloud. "Okay, two things. First, I'm not going to ask what was said or about whom, because it doesn't matter. You know what show business is like, GC; rumor and innuendo are the uninvited guests that always show up at the party, and anyone who actually listens to them winds up sorry they did so. You *know* that."

(I suppose I do.)

"And second—does *this* look like someone who'd talk behind your back? He barely talks in front of it."

That got me a look from Midnight, and slightly miffed *<Hey.>*

(Point taken. My apologies, ma'am.) And with that, Golden Cloud turned and walked away, his head held high. Midnight yawned.

I scowled and shook my head. If I didn't know any better, I'd swear someone was trying to distract me . . .

In the end, we went with our strengths; Whiskey's nose, Tango's stealth, and my research skills.

<There's a tree outside Nesbitt's window that should give me a good view of whatever he's doing in there,> Tango said.

[I'll see what I can find out by sniffing under his door.]

"And I'll do some serious surfing on the subject," I said. "Okay, gang—let's do some *sleuthing*."

<Have you noticed how she gets all alliterative when she's excited?>

[I find it endearing.]

I love surfing the 'Net. I'm a data junkie, I admit it. For me, doing research is like beachcombing, roaming the infinite length of the cybernetic shoreline and collecting all the shiny bits that catch my eye. Leaping from site to site like a kid jumping from one driftwood log to another, stopping now and then to pick up a bit of sea glass or a perfect shell and cram it in a digital pocket to enjoy later. All of which sounds a lot more romantic and random than painstakingly following link after link, closing an endless succession of pop-up windows, and ruthlessly pestering Google like a four-year-old who's just discovered the word *why*.

But.

Sometimes, when you're roaming the beach, you find things you wish you hadn't. Things that are rotting, or sad, or infuriating. The Internet's reach is wide and deep and drags along the bottom.

And I was trying to dig up some dirt on a Hollywood celebrity.

"Gack," I said. I didn't say it to anyone in particular,

since both Tango and Whiskey had left, but I felt the need to say it just the same.

But while they were out of sight, apparently they weren't out of range: *<I wish you'd stop saying that. It doesn't mean anything.>*

Sure it does, I thought back. *It means this is the seventh time I've had to look away from the screen while pressing the ESCAPE button.*

<Computers have an ESCAPE button? How does that work?>

It doesn't. I'm still here.

[As am I,] Whiskey reported. [Outside Mr. Nesbitt's door, as requested. Scents I have detected thus far are: deodorant, toothpaste, fabric softener, shaving cream, coffee, cream, breath freshener, shampoo, soap, macadamia nuts, hair gel, and a mixture of chemicals commonly found in an over-the-counter muscle analgesic.]

<Thrilling. I've been watching him watch video on his laptop. If you hear me snoring, wake me up, will you?>

I sighed. "Well, I'm not doing much better. He's dated quite a few models and actresses, attended more than a few nightclubs, and has his own fan club made up almost exclusively of women. He likes to surf, and got knocked on the head by his own board in Hawaii last year. Which is where he probably also picked up a macadamia nut habit."

<Is that what those things are he's scarfing down? Yuck. Nuts aren't food, they're what fattens up food.>

[Only if you're talking about rats and mice. Squirrels aren't food. Too fast to catch and too skinny to eat.]

<Plus there's the evil.>

[That, too.]

I found myself on the verge of clicking on a link that promised to reveal One Weird Trick to Make 10K a Month That Podiatrists Hate, shook my head, and pushed back from my desk. "Again with the squirrel hate? Didn't you mention something about using a squirrel in your cinematic opus?"

<Sure. Nobody plays an Evil Ninja better than a squirrel; they don't even have to act. But that doesn't mean I'm going to be turning my back on any of 'em anytime soon.>

[Just a moment. I'm picking up hints of . . . coconut. And pineapple.]

<Don't strain your olfactory nerve, genius. He's putting on some kind of hand lotion. It's got a little palm tree on it, ergo the tropical aroma.>

"The tropics. Must be nice to be able to go there whenever you want. One of the perks of being rich and famous." I spun my office chair in a slow circle as I talked. "Hawaii. White sand beaches. Tanned surfer boys in baggy shorts. Hot tubbing under the stars while listening to the ocean, an umbrella drink in one hand . . ."

I stopped my slow spin and frowned. Something was tugging at my attention, but I couldn't figure out exactly what. Beaches? Stars? Hot—

And then I had it.

I spun back around to my desk and started tapping keys. "Hawaii," I muttered. "Hot tubs."

<Any idea what she's talking about?>

[None whatsoever.]

"Rolvink was fond of hot tubs. And one of the things I dug up about him was that he once ran a mail scam out of Honolulu. He's made at least one film there, too."

[Which means what?]

"Which means it's possible that's where he and Nesbitt met. And maybe where Rolvink learned something about him Nesbitt wants kept secret."

I'd been looking in the wrong places. Camera Guy might have stumbled on something juicy, but he was keeping it to himself until he could turn it into a payday.

But if he could figure it out, so could I.

I looked for the anomaly, the fact that didn't fit. The only thing that stuck out was his surfing accident; he'd gone early one morning by his lonesome, wiped out, and conked himself in the head with his own board. Claimed he woke up on the beach with a bruise on his forehead and no memory of what happened.

Except . . . that was just a little too much like a scene from a movie.

People that get knocked out in the ocean don't wake up on the beach. They drown. But Nesbitt had gone to the local hospital early that morning and reportedly been treated for a mild concussion, which meant he had actually been injured.

I did a little backtracking. It wasn't hard to discover that yes, the Rolvink-produced film *Shark Vixens* had been filming at that time, not too far away.

So what really happened?

I did some thinking, and then some searching: news stories from the area and the time. I focused on accidents, deaths, fires, and crimes. Nothing stood out, so I cast my net a little wider—not in terms of subject, but geographically.

And then I found it.

Farther down the coast but the very same morning, an unconscious woman was found by the side of the road. Hit and run, no suspects. The really interesting thing, though, was one small detail near the bottom of the article, where a police source was quoted as saying, "There's some indication she might have been moved from another location."

Completely circumstantial, of course. But the article gave the woman's name, and a follow-up a week later said she was still in a coma.

Which gave me an idea.

Tango, you still in that tree?

\<Where else would I be?\>

Do you think you could safely jump to the windowsill?

\<Define safe.\>

Being able to do so without proceeding directly to life number eight.

\<Then sure.\>

Good. I'm going to see if I can get him to open the window, and then leave the room. When he does, I'll have more detailed instructions.

\<Requests, *Toots. Cats don't do "instructions."*\>

Right, of course. How silly of me.

I pulled out my phone as I got up and headed for the door. It rang a few times and then went to voice mail. "Hi, Mr. Nesbitt? Just thought I'd let you know our maintenance people are doing a little repair work on the heating system. It might result in your room becoming uncomfortably warm; if so, please open a window and be patient. It shouldn't last long."

\<His phone rang. He picked it up, looked at it, and then put it down again.\>

Somehow, that made me feel a little better about what I was planning to do. I went down to the basement, where the electrical panels for the entire house were, and found the heating controls. It was an old house, but ZZ liked to stay current—no pun intended—when it came to technology, so all the rooms were climate-controlled. They had their own thermostats, of course, but any of those could be superseded if you knew how to operate the master control panel.

I knew.

"Let's see," I muttered. "Warm enough to make him open the window, not so warm as to make him bolt . . ."

I adjusted the settings carefully, then went upstairs to make myself a cup of tea. *Tango? Has he checked his phone for messages yet?*

<*He's doing it now. Now he's getting up and checking that little plastic box on the wall. Now he's sitting down again. It's almost too exciting.*>

Let me know when he opens the window. Whiskey?

[Yes?]

Nesbitt's probably coming through that door in a few minutes. Stay out of the way.

[I shall.]

I made my tea and went back down to the basement.

<*Hey, Toots? He just opened the window. Didn't spot me, though.*>

Okay. When he leaves, wait a minute and then get inside.

This was the tricky part. I had to get him out of the room, but he had to leave his laptop behind. I cranked the heat to his room as high as it could go, then called him again. This time, he picked up.

"Mr. Nesbitt? I'm so sorry, but we're having problems with the heating system. You might want to leave your room for the next half hour or so."

"Oh. This is because of the explosion?"

"It's related, yes. We're also going to have to shut off the house's wireless router for the same amount of time— there's damage to all sorts of infrastructure."

"All right. Guess I'll get a little fresh air."

"Do you like horses? I can get our stablemaster to set you up with a ride."

"No, I think I'll just amble over to the zoo, take a look

around. Been meaning to, just haven't gotten around to it yet."

"All right. I apologize for the inconvenience."

"No sweat." He disconnected.

<He's grabbing a jacket and heading for the door.>

I went up the stairs, tea in hand. *Does he have his laptop with him?*

No. He left it on the table, open.

Perfect.

[He just went past me down the hall. Gave me a nice pat on the way.]

You're on, kitty. I left the basement, made my way through the house to the front stairs, then kept going up.

<No, I'm in. Now what?>

I reached my office, went in, and closed the door. Sat down in my office chair and took a deep breath. "Now I want you to listen very carefully. Reach out and tap a key, any key, on his laptop. That'll keep it from going to sleep."

<Done. Ugh.>

"Ugh? Why *ugh*?"

<He was watching highly unnatural acts on his computer. When I touched a key, things started . . . happening.>

"Sorry about that, kitty. Some humans have . . . interesting hobbies."

<Interesting? This is perverted! I can't believe she's going to—oh, that is just disgusting. Not to mention unsafe.>

"Just focus on the keyboard, okay? Hopefully, you won't have to hit more than four or five keys. First—"

<Why is that thing so long? You'd think wider would be better . . . Oh, she's getting on it. This is the bad part . . . tell me she isn't going to use her hands and her feet—>

"Tango, tear yourself away from the disturbing images and listen to my voice. We're working, here."

<Okay, but—no. She's standing up! The long thing is moving! How can she keep her balance like that? She's going to fall off!>

"I really doubt that, Tango. I'm guessing this isn't the first time she's done this."

<Now there's somebody else doing the same thing, except her long thing was yellow and his has a painting of a shark on it. He's not falling off, either! I had no idea water could even do *that!>*

Which is when the penny dropped and I realized what she was watching. "Tango, it's just a surfing video. Let's get down to business, shall we?"

<Tell me which button to press to make it stop!>

"You know, some cats don't have a problem with water. Some cats even *enjoy* it."

<This is no time for a discussion of the brain-damaged! I'M WATCHING GIANT WAVES TRY TO EAT PEOPLE!>

I winced. "Okay, okay. Here's what you need to do . . ."

I won't bore anyone with the tedious, painstaking process of talking a cat through operating a keyboard. It helped that Tango had a natural facility for language; even though she couldn't actually read, she was pretty good at recognizing letters.

"All right, kitty, we're almost done. Just a few more keys, in this order: K, A, I—"

<A little rectangle just appeared. There's a bunch of words that start with the same letters but then change.>

"That's his search history. We're looking for a word that starts like that and then continues with the letters L, A, N, and I."

<That's the word at the top.>

"It is? You're sure?"

<I'm going to pretend you didn't just say that.>

"Sorry. What are the letters in the next word after that?"

<C, O, M, and A.>

Bingo. "Thank you, Tango. We're almost done—all that's left is to hide our tracks. Now, here's what you do first—"

<It's fine, Toots. I got this covered.>

I frowned. "What, suddenly you're a computer expert?"

<Like I said, I've got it covered. His keyboard, to be exact.>

"Covered with what? What did you do?"

<What comes naturally—I got comfortable.>

Then I got it. "You lay down on top of it. Of course. I hope you realize that in order to make this plausible, you have to stay there until he comes back."

<Yawn. Whatever will I do. I think I'll . . . zzzzzzz>

"Right. Enjoy your nap."

I did a little more Googling to strengthen my theory, then collected Whiskey as I went back downstairs to un-sauna Nesbitt's room. [What did you find out?] he asked as followed me.

I opened the electronics panel and reset the switches I'd monkeyed with. "That the same night Jaxon Nesbitt claimed to have knocked himself on the head with his own board, a woman named Kailani Okole was struck by a hit-and-run driver around thirty miles away. She wound up in a coma."

[That doesn't seem to prove anything.]

"It doesn't. But when the very first item that comes up in Jaxon's search history is her name and the word *coma,* the word *coincidence* starts packing its bags. That search ranking means he didn't just Google that phrase once, he did it multiple times. He keeps going back to see if there's any update on her condition."

[Perhaps she's a friend of his.]

I closed the panel. "If so, she was a brand-new one. I couldn't find any connection between her and Nesbitt online—but I did find her Facebook page. She's young and pretty and likes to party. Oh, and she's an aspiring actress who was very excited about a small part she'd just landed in a local production."

[Shakespeare?]

"Close. *Shark Vixens*—produced by none other than Maurice Rolvink."

16.

Despite discovering that Maurice Rolvink had (probably) been blackmailing Jaxon Nesbitt for (probably) a hit-and-run, I still wasn't much (any) closer to finding out who killed Rolvink. I had plenty of suspects and lots of motive, but nothing really concrete. In fact, what I had was the approximate consistency of Silly Putty, but not as clever. Stupid Putty, if you will.

As I sat in my office, pondering the intelligence of novelty chemical compounds for children, I had an idea entirely uncoupled to this train of thought. The idea was: If I don't start making sense out of all this soon, my head is going to explode. Much like ZZ's chimney.

Except the chimney *hadn't* exploded, not really. Much of the blast had been directed straight up, like the barrel of a gun pointing skyward. The firing chamber of the gun had blown apart when the trigger was pulled, but there was plenty enough force left over to blast the chimney cover capping the muzzle high into the air.

I felt a sudden urge to examine that cover, more out of morbid curiosity than any belief it could provide new information; after all, it had nearly landed on me when it crashed back to earth. I couldn't, of course; the police had taken it away to do forensic things.

The chimney itself, being attached to the rest of the house, was still there, though. I supposed I could go up on the roof and examine it, but I really didn't know what that would tell me. It wasn't as if the bomber had lowered the TNT down the flue—

I sat straight up. I blinked.

Because, of course, maybe he or she had.

It solved one problem neatly: The killer didn't need access to the inside of the room, only the outside of the house. Wait until the middle of the night when the fires in the fireplaces were safely out, and lower the bomb down the chimney on some fishing line or string.

And in the morning, *boom*.

<BOOM!> a feline voice yowled in my head. *<Aaah! It's terrible!>* Tango did *not* sound happy.

"What?" I said out loud. "What's the matter? Did Nesbitt do something to you?"

<No, no—he came in and found me a while ago. I pretended to be alarmed and jumped out the window. No, this is serious.*>*

"How so?"

<Come down to the Crossroads and see for yourself!>

So—muttering about all my impending regrets—I did, stopping only to collect Whiskey along the way.

We arrived to pandemonium.

The previous pandemonium had been on a larger scale, but had mostly been harmless. This was considerably worse.

The squirrels were kung fu fighting.

With, naturally, the rabbits. And the goats. And the guinea pigs. Actually, it was kind of hard to tell exactly *who* they were fighting; they were bounding off every available surface—including bodies—at such a fast and furious rate they made bounding goats seem glacial. It was like watching a barroom brawl erupt at a petting zoo. A squirrel blurred past me, locked in combat with half a dozen bunnies. I couldn't make out any details, just a lot of hyperkinetic movement that went beyond defying the laws of physics to actually giving them the finger.

In the middle of it all, crouched on her director's headstone, was Tango. She looked more than a little freaked out; her ears were flat against her skull and her tail was doing a good impression of a windshield wiper in overdrive.

"Well, this isn't good," I said under my breath. "I wonder what happened?"

Whiskey glanced up at me. [A cat, I believe. A cat happened. One is all it takes.]

If this were an actual movie, as opposed to a haunted graveyard temporarily repurposed as a movie set, I'd be able to bring all the chaos to a halt by putting my fingers in my mouth and whistling really, really loud. But it wasn't, which was actually lucky as I never learned how to do that finger-whistling thing anyway. And despite what the movies tell us, making a loud noise in the middle of a bunch of other people making loud noises rarely makes them less noisy; if anything, it just encourages them to be louder.

"Any ideas?" I asked Whiskey.

[Only one. I'll be right back.] With that, he charged straight at the headstone Tango was perched on.

And into it.

I don't mean he crashed headfirst into the marker; I mean he entered the stone itself, like a diver plunging into a pool. Tango didn't appear to notice, and it didn't seem like a good time to pester her with questions.

Which didn't mean I wasn't going to pester someone else. When confronted with an overwhelming mess, the best approach is to pick one element of said mess and concentrate on unmessing it. I like to tackle the biggest element first, in the firm belief that once you've established a beachhead of order more order will naturally coalesce—or maybe because I'm a masochistic overachiever who's addicted to challenging herself.

A large, ghostly guinea pig barreled straight at my face. I don't think it was any happier about that fact than me, but neither of us had time to react. It passed right through me, of course, and the sensation that produced was . . . unsettling, to say the least. Like the faintest tinge of an ice cream headache coupled with the smell of wood shavings and a sudden craving for walnuts.

The brawl needed to be dealt with, but I wasn't sure how—

And right on cue, the cavalry arrived.

The white iris of an afterlife portal blinked open in the dirt of the grave. Whiskey leapt out—followed by a dog I didn't recognize, a longhaired Irish setter with a coat of blazing red-gold.

The setter glanced around at the ongoing melee.

Then he sat down on the grave, put his muzzle in the air, and howled.

A howl, by its nature, is a mournful sound. Out in the wild, under a full moon, there's an ethereal but inevitable quality to it that seems like a mixture of joy and sorrow. Accepting but defiant somehow, acknowledging life's pain but refusing to submit to it.

But here, in a graveyard full of ghosts, what I heard was very different.

It was a howl that spoke of loss and regret. It ached of the past, of a time long gone. There was a hint of sweetness underneath, but just enough to make the grief even sharper. It was the song of every creature who ever lived who glanced behind them and thought, *Where did my life go?*

It reverberated through the Great Crossroads, through every soul that heard it, and all motion stopped. Everyone listened, and everyone *heard*.

The howl tapered off, its ending somehow even sadder than its start. The dog lowered his muzzle and looked around at all the spirits who were now staring at him.

[This is an important place,] the dog said. [Treat it with the honor it deserves.]

And with that, Davy got to his feet, turned, and walked back through the afterlife portal. It closed behind him and vanished.

Tango was the first to speak. <*Okay, that's a wrap for today. Let's see everybody back here tomorrow at dawn, okay?*>

The crowd dispersed quickly. In a few moments, it was just me, Tango, and Whiskey.

My cat was now sitting upright and looking completely unconcerned. Only a feline could come through a riot and display the attitude *What? I meant to do that.*

"That was *Davy,*" I said. "Davy's Grave Davy."

[It *is* his grave,] Whiskey pointed out. [Considering that, I thought he might be willing to help us out.]

I realized there were tears running down my cheeks, and wiped them away with the back of my hand. "He had . . . quite an impact. And speaking of impact, why didn't you make a big, ectoplasmic *splat* when you dove into that headstone?"

[Information and experience. While the most commonly used portals lead to specific afterlives, you can also use a specific grave to reach a specific soul—if you have the proper clearances, of course.]

<Which, of course, you do,> Tango said, irritation in her voice.

[Yes.]

Her eyes narrowed. *<Right. Go ahead. I'm ready.>*

[Are you? You don't seem to be prepared for much of anything, from what I can see.] Whiskey's mouth was open and his tongue was lolling out in a big, doggy smile.

<You've been waiting for this to happen—a great big disaster that you can blame on me. Well, here it is; go ahead and gloat.>

[Dogs do not gloat. We appreciate. I see little to appreciate here.]

<So that's how you're going to play it, huh? Dogs are so superior to cats that even triumph is beneath you? If you were actually made of meat and bone I'd give you a few scars on that snooty nose of yours, so you could remember me every time you stuck it up in the air.>

"Tango!" I said. "That's enough. I know this is upsetting, but—"

Now her tail was lashing back and forth. *<Upsetting, nothing. This was* planned. *I know sabotage when I see it, and no production tanks this hard without a little help. Rumors are one thing; deliberately planted lies are another. Somebody wanted me to fail, and it's obvious who that somebody is.>*

Whiskey's mouth snapped shut. [You're accusing *me*? Not content with causing a massive disaster all by yourself, you dodge responsibility by placing the blame elsewhere? I wish I could say I was surprised, but this is the sort of behavior I've come to expect from a—]

<Oh, simmer down, stick-chaser. I'm not accusing you.>

"You're not?" I said. "But—"

<Dogs don't have the kind of innate deviousness this

required. Just look at him—a decent mastermind would be chortling with glee right about now, and he can barely bring himself to enjoy his victory. Any second now he's going to offer words of support.>

[I am not!]

<Uh-huh.>

"Hang on. If you don't think Whiskey's responsible, then who?"

<Isn't it obvious? This level of deception and trickery could only be pulled off by a cat.*>*

[She has a point,] Whiskey conceded. [Did you have a particular cat in mind, or are you thinking in more general, overall-evil terms? Either one works for me.]

<Unsinkable Sam,> Tango spat. *<I fired him as the lead, and this is his revenge. It all makes perfect sense— he's been slinking around posing as me and spreading unrest.>*

"Highly unlikely, Tango. Sam's dead, remember? Pretty easy to tell the difference between you and a ghost."

[Not strictly true, actually. Many ghosts confuse the living with the dead and vice versa; it's the underlying reason behind many hauntings.]

I frowned. "But that doesn't quite make sense. I don't know what set off the squirrel/rabbit war and neither Trigger nor Midnight was willing to talk, but Fish Jumping was convinced Paul the octopus told him something Paul denies. Unless you think Sam can pull off a believable impression of an eight-armed, color-changing cephalopod, I think you're missing something."

Tango gave her head an annoyed shake. *<The only thing about Fish Jumping that's brilliant is his plumage. Sure as cats hunt birds, Sam found a way to trick the parrot. And I'm going to prove it.>*

Tango jumped down from the headstone and darted away.

When she was gone, I gave Whiskey a worried look. "Okay, maybe this is me just being paranoid, but—if it wasn't you and it wasn't Unsinkable Sam . . ."

[It wasn't me. Most likely Tango is right, though there is at least one other viable suspect. I don't know how they would have accomplished this, but Sam wasn't the only prominent applicant Tango turned down.]

I nodded. "You're thinking of Jim the Wonder Dog, aren't you? Mr. Doom and Gloom, trying to fulfill his own prophecies?"

[Indeed. While this entire debacle has a definite feline reek to it, dogs are not without their own wiles. Coyotes are canines, too.]

"Sure. So why didn't you point that out to Tango?"

Whiskey didn't say anything for a moment. [If she wishes to find victory in claiming her species is more conniving than mine, it seems tiresome and self-defeating to argue the point.]

"Plus, she needed the win. She was right about you being on the verge of offering support."

[My inclinations lean more toward the strategic than the sly. I'm not trying to manipulate her; I just know she'll be easier to live with if I act in a certain manner.]

I gave him a skeptical look. "Right. You weren't being considerate about her feelings, just pragmatic."

[As always.]

I leaned down and gave him a big hug. "That was just me being practical," I said, and kissed him on top of his furry head. "You know, in case you run out of hugs later and need one."

[Yes, of course. Eminently sensible.]

Then he licked my face. [Just in case you require that when I'm not present,] he explained. I laughed.

"C'mon," I said, straightening up. "If someone *is* trying to torpedo Tango's epic, she needs our help. Let's do a little sleuthing, see if we can figure out what's what."

[Oh? We're investigating a bombing and a murder, and you want to give priority to a case of malicious gossip?]

I shrugged and started walking. "I didn't say priority . . . more like we'll keep our eyes and ears open for anything that might be helpful. Multitask. We're good at that."

[You're good at that. Dogs prefer following one trail at a time.]

We were still amiably disagreeing about it as we got to the nearest edge of the graveyard, where it was bounded by a tall hedge. I knew a shortcut that went right through it, as long as you didn't mind squeezing through a little greenery. It came out right beside the area where the film crew had parked most of their trucks.

Which is how I stumbled upon Jaxon Nesbitt kissing Catree.

17.

As soon as I saw them, I froze in mid-shrubbery. Catree, standing in the open back door of her truck, bending down to give Jaxon Nesbitt a two-handed kiss on the lips. His feet were on the ground, but from the looks of that kiss she could have lifted him right off terra firma through lip-suction alone.

Hold it, I thought at Whiskey. *And stay quiet.*

It might have been intense, but it wasn't lengthy—and as soon as they pulled apart, he took off like a shot and she yanked the door closed. Wham, bam, we're on the lam.

I stepped out of the hedge, Whiskey right behind me. "Well, that was unexpected."

[What did you see?] He raised his muzzle and sniffed. [Ah. Never mind.]

"Catree and Jaxon, sitting in a truck," I muttered. "And though I doubt there was much sitting, I'm pretty sure the next stanza would still rhyme."

[With what?]

"Truck. Come on, let's get out of here."

We retreated back to the graveyard. [So. From your re-action, I take it this is an unusual mating?]

"Yes and no. I guess I'm a victim of my own preconceptions—I'm so used to seeing underwear models on the arms of movie stars that anything else seems jar-ring. What I'm more surprised about is how they managed to hide it so well. I was under the impression Jaxon spent all his spare time in his—"

I stopped. I groaned. I felt extremely dumb.

"In his room with the conveniently placed tree right out-side his window," I finished. "He's a young, fit guy. And young, fit guys who need to be discreet have been climb-ing through windows and down trees to go visit their girl-friends for a very long time. Since before there were windows, probably."

[This alters our list of possible suspects considerably.]

"You're right," I said gloomily. "Now we have to add Catree, and bump Jaxon higher in the rankings. Maybe he's only sleeping with her to get access to her explosives; maybe he's enlisted her actual help."

[Or perhaps it's the other way around: She's concocted a cunning plan to snare a desirable mate.]

I didn't want to admit that possibility, but I had to. She was smart, she was determined, she was fearless—but was she evil? Or at least capable of committing evil acts?

Of course she was—capable, that is. Everyone harbors the potential to do really, really bad things; thankfully, most of us never explore that potential. But an insanely hot lover has been known to make a levelheaded person com-mit insane acts, no matter how smart or determined or fearless they are.

I'd eliminated Tervo as a suspect. I highly doubted Na-talia would blow herself up, and Rolvink wasn't the type to commit suicide. Neither Keene nor Fikru had a motive, but I hadn't definitively ruled either one out. Lucky Trentini was still a possibility, but Jaxon and Catree were looking more and more likely. Time to narrow things down.

Logically, I should have started with the secretive couple, but I wasn't sure how to do that. What I did have, though, was a way to maybe eliminate our resident shaman from the suspect pool; calming the turbulent situation in the Great Crossroads had reminded me that I was good at managing not only eccentric people, but eccentric ghosts. And that some ghosts were just as curious about the living as the living were about them.

"Do me a favor, Whiskey. Track down Fikru and Keene for me. I think they're probably still somewhere in the Great Crossroads."

[Easily done. Follow me.]

We found them, not surprisingly, at Jeepers's grave site. Jeepers was a galago, otherwise known as a bush baby. Galagos had enormous eyes, which was no doubt where his name came from. He was currently present in the ectoplasmic non-flesh and perched on top of Keene's head, though Keene clearly didn't know that. Fikru, though, was staring right at the little primate.

"Hey, guys," I said as I strolled up. "How's the Magical Mystery Tour going?"

"Spectacularly," Keene declared. His pupils were almost as large as the galago's, though considerably redder. "For Yemi, anyway. According to his third eye, we are surrounded by an ever-changing multitude of spiritual splendor, not unlike the aftermath of a terrible fire in a pet store or possibly the nuking of a zoo. But replace all the horrifying bits with niceness. Am I making sense?"

Yemane turned his attention from the top of Keene's head to me. He smiled in that wonder-filled way only the truly stoned can understand, and said, "Yeah. This is amazing. And I can tell you *get* that, you really do. You're just pretending not to."

Uh-oh. Mr. Perceptive was getting a little too close to the truth, as in standing right on it and pointing his finger. "Of course I do," I said. "How could I not?" I met his eyes and smiled back, not in a challenging way but an acknowledging one. As long as I kept things cryptic and nonspecific enough, I could indulge him—and I got the feeling he'd respect my stance.

And then he noticed Whiskey.

He'd met my dog before, of course, but Fikru's mental state had been considerably less altered then. "Wow," he said. His eyes were doing their best to open as wide as Jeepers's, and the look on his face was pure astonishment. "I didn't . . . how could I not have *noticed*?"

Whiskey stared back at him quizzically. Fikru dropped to his knees, then put his hand out, palm up. Whiskey sniffed it politely, then looked at me. [I believe he—]

Sssssh, I thought urgently. I didn't know if Fikru could pick up our thoughts in his current condition—it seemed unlikely—but I didn't want to chance it.

Gently, Fikru put his hand on Whiskey's head. "Amazing," he breathed. "It feels . . . so *real*."

Keene laughed. "Yemi, old man, you are absolutely *gollywonkered*. That dog *is* real. I think."

I had the urge to distract Keene, then get Whiskey to shift form to a Chihuahua and back again really quick. And even though I could have gotten away with it, I resisted the impulse; I had something more useful in mind than indulging a whim.

While Fikru was entranced by the luxuriant ectoplasmic texture of my ghostly dog's fur—to be fair, it *is* silky—I said, "I can see now that you weren't exaggerating your connection to . . . *spirituality*. I'd love to hear more."

Fikru looked up. "I'd be glad to share. It's kinda my thing."

"So I see. That first night, when you were up in your room—you said there were spirits around, watching you. Did you get a sense of what sort of spirits they were?"

"Oh, yeah. Animal spirits, definitely. Let's see . . . there were some rats, or maybe mice. Small and skittery. There was something curious but sort of aloof, which I think was a cat but could have been a snake . . ." He trailed off, either lost in recollection or just lost. Too bad; I was really hoping for something less vague.

"Oh, and a parrot. I thought it was a fish at first, but no, it was absolutely a parrot."

"Wow," I said. "That's *very* interesting. Thank you. I had no idea we had so many nocturnal wanderers in the mansion." Which was true; I didn't sleep there, so I wasn't aware of what went on late at night.

A parrot. That he'd mistaken for a fish.

A Fish Jumping, maybe?

Yemane was still staring at Whiskey as we left. Whiskey, for his part, did his best to act like a completely ordinary, non-supernatural dog: panting, sniffing, even pretending to pee. "Okay, okay," I muttered. "Enough already. If you try to hump my leg, I will be *extremely* displeased."

[Please. I'm delivering a much more nuanced performance. A cat wouldn't have noticed, but I thought you might.]

"I have other things on my mind—like locating a certain parrot with impulse-control issues."

Which we found not ten minutes later, sitting on a head-

stone and preening himself. It suddenly struck me that
Fish Jumping spent a lot of time hanging out in the Great
Crossroads; most spirit animals—other than prowlers like
Two-Notch or Topsy—were just passing through, on their
way from one afterlife to another. Come to think of it, I
saw quite a bit of Piotr, the circus bear, too. I wondered
why.

Maybe I should ask.

"Fish Jumping," I said. He was perched on the head of
a small stone statue of a kitten, and looked up as soon as
I addressed him. "Nice to see you. Got a minute to talk?"

He studied me, then blinked. *Of course, Miss Foxtrot.
I always have time for you.* "Awk! I'm in trouble! I'm in
trouble!"

"You're not in trouble. I just want to ask you about
your . . . *extracurricular* activities." Which, it turned out,
was exactly the wrong way to phrase it.

"Awk! Not my fault! Not my fault!" He fluttered his
wings in agitation. *I know it sounds unlikely, but I swear
the octopus and I had a lengthy conversation about the
part I was up for. I have no idea why he would lie about
it, but that's the only explanation I have.*

"That's not actually what I meant—"

*Oh, this is terrible. People already view me as
unstable—what happens when they think I'm a patholog-
ical liar as well?* Nobody *will want to talk to me!*

And suddenly Fish Jumping stopped being just a punch
line to me.

It's awful, I know, but we all do it. We put labels on
people, especially people we don't know well but deal with
often. We start filing them under easy, two-word descrip-
tives: Delivery Guy, Blond Waitress, Short Plumber. And
the next thing you know, they stop being people and become unpaid extras in the ongoing drama of our lives.

But they're not. They're persons, with their own dramas and history and supporting cast. Even if they've been saddled with a name as ridiculous as Fish Jumping, they deserve respect.

"I'm sorry," I said gently. "I don't think you're a liar. I think you're—obviously—a being of intellect and refinement. I find you a pleasure to converse with, and will gladly do so anytime we meet."

He squinted at me suspiciously. *Really?* "Awk! Really?"

I smiled. "Yes, really. And I'll prove it—let's talk about what *you* want to."

Um. That's very generous of you. I must admit I'm at something of a loss. "Awk! Never happened before! Don't know what to do! Awk!"

I shrugged. "Well, how about telling me about your name? Or is that a touchy subject?"

Ah. No, not at all. It was given to me by a young boy, actually. Joseph was his name. He had some emotional difficulties after his mother passed away, and his father bought me for Joseph as a companion. He wanted a pet that wouldn't expire in a dozen short years, like a cat or a dog, and thought I would be ideal. We spent a great deal of time in a small cabin by a lake, and Joseph loved to watch the trout jump in the evening.

He paused. I realized this was the longest speech I'd ever heard from him without an *Awk!* as punctuation at the end.

Joseph grew up to be a fine young man. I'm very proud of him. He would tell me all his troubles, and I would always listen. It's important to have someone listen to you, don't you think?

"Yes. Yes, I do."

I suppose that's what I miss the most about him.

"So he's still alive?"

Oh, yes. I survived until he was in his thirties, so I suppose I did my job; he had a wife and children, by then. Much happier than when we first met.

"I see. And you can't visit him while he's still alive?"

Ah. Well, let's just say there are rules around that sort of thing, which I'm not supposed to talk about. Still, what's a few years when compared with eternity? Nothing at all. And of course, there's always Paradise, which is exactly as wonderful as one might hope. There's only one thing it doesn't have, really.

"Joseph."

Indeed. So I pass the time as I'm used to, talking to whoever cares to talk to me. I do love a good conversation, regardless of species. "Awk! I'm a blabbermouth! I'm a blabbermouth!"

I had a thought. "Fish, what did Joseph do for a living?"

Oh, did I forget to mention that? He ran a pet store, which I had the run of. Always plenty of chances for a nice chat, there. "Awk! Stockholm syndrome! Stockholm syndrome! Awk!"

A dead parrot from a pet store. Well, that explained why he liked hanging around the Great Crossroads so much; he was used to a mix of different animals. "So you speak more than just Parrot?"

He cocked his head at me. *Not fluently, no. But you can communicate with almost anyone, if you're willing to really pay attention. I got so good at listening to other species that my own vocalizations became more of an afterthought than anything I planned. Now that I've passed on, of course, I speak the common tongue of the dead, like everyone else. I enjoy it so much that I confess I sometimes run on a bit.* "Awk! Stating the obvious! Stating the obvious!"

I thought I understood. Fish had spent his whole life listening to other people's problems, like a cross-species psychiatrist. With all that behind him, he was free to finally talk about his own concerns—but in his eagerness, he was talking a little too much and a little too honestly.

"I understand," I said. "What you do—what you did—is a lot like what I do. Whatever you can to ease the burden others carry."

I suppose. "Awk! She's right, dumb-ass! She's right!"

"Okay, then. I need your help, Fish. I'm trying to find out if a particular person was in a particular place at particular time. I think you might have been there, too."

I'm more than willing to assist, if I can. "Awk! I like to help! I like to help!"

"Good." I told him about Yemane Fikru, meditating up in his room and sensing the presence of spirits watching him—and that one of them was a parrot.

Fish Jumping bobbed his head up and down. *Yes, that was me. I wouldn't dream of imposing my presence during the day, but . . . I do enjoy the company of human beings. Am I in trouble? I followed the proper protocols.*

I was dying to know exactly what those protocols were, but one glance at Whiskey told me that the only thing asking would produce would be a stern lecture from him on Things I Wasn't Supposed To Know Yet.

"No, of course not. You didn't do anything wrong. But you can verify he was in his room all evening? He didn't go out?"

No, he did not. "Awk! Not even once! Not even once! Awk!"

"Thank you, Fish. You've been very helpful. And it was a pleasure talking with you."

He blinked at me. *The pleasure was all mine, madame. Indeed.* "Awk! You have no idea! Awk!"

But I thought I did.

After that Whiskey and I headed back toward the house. Yemane Fikru was definitely off the list, but then he'd never been a prime suspect. Who should I try to cross off next?

[You must heed my warning,] intoned a foreboding yet familiar voice. We were almost to the tall wooden gate that separates the graveyard from the mansion grounds proper, and the voice was coming from behind me. I turned to look back, and there he was: Jim the Wonder Dog, standing again on the crest of the hill, being ominous.

[This,] he said, [is your *last chance.*]

18.

"Really?" I said. "I thought these dire warnings always came in threes, or sevens, or some other mystically significant number."

Jim stared down at us balefully. An English setter can do a pretty good baleful—not as good as a Great Dane, but a lot better than a French bulldog. Several bales' worth, anyway.

[Mock me at your peril. You must take heed—]

I held up a finger. "Hold on. Before I take heed of anything, I need to ask: Did you just say *mock me at your peril* in a non-ironic way? Because the only people who talk like that are old-school supervillains, and I had no idea Dr. Doom was actually a deceased hunting dog under all that armor."

[Your humor is misplaced, mortal.]

"Oh, we're going with name-calling, are we? Go ahead—I always wanted someone to address me as *puny human*. Or are you more of an *impudent whelp!* sort of bad guy?"

He glared at me, trying to amp up the bales but not really succeeding. [That's insulting, you know.]

"What, using *whelp* as an insult? I know, I know, not very PC of me. In my defense, I find that a little snarkiness goes a long way toward getting someone to engage, and getting you to engage—as opposed to intoning a few spooky warnings and then running away—is what I'm trying to accomplish here. Also, once we're having an actual conversation, I can pretty much guarantee you won't leave until you can respond to my comments—because that's how a conversation works—which means that so as long as I keep talking you'll stay put and also not notice that my partner has cleverly circled around behind you and now you can't pull that disappearing stunt again."

Jim glanced behind him. [Oh.]

[Don't try to run,] Whiskey said. He'd taken the shape of a greyhound, but he shifted from that to a muscular Great Dane and then back again. [You'll only embarrass yourself.]

Jim looked like he'd just been caught rooting in the kitchen garbage can. [Well. This is awkward.]

I climbed the rise, stopping a few steps away from him, then crouched down so we were closer to the same height. "I understand—sort of—what you were trying to do. I'm still among the living, so there are certain things I'm not aware of. You figured you could use that to spook me, though I'm still not exactly sure why. What I am sure of is that you're a fake."

Jim had the kind of focused, intent gaze that Whiskey usually wore. [What makes you so certain?]

"Well, I'm fairly intelligent. And when one of my partners who has access to information I don't lets slip that you're a fake—what you do is impossible—I notice. I mull things over. There was even some *pondering* going on.

And the logical conclusion that I've come to is both amazing yet simple: Destiny is *bogus*."

[Bravo,] said Whiskey. [Well done, very clever, and just remember that it was the cat who told you.]

"There's no such thing as fate. There's no big list of things that are definitely, absolutely going to happen. We get to make choices, which means we also have to take responsibility for those choices. We don't get to blame things on some mysterious, all-powerful plan, because we—all of us—are making this stuff up as we go along. *That's* why all your predictions of doom are meaningless; you can't predict what's going to happen because *no one can*."

Jim raised his eyebrows hopefully. [Have you considered, by chance, that I may have confidential—but reliable—information?]

"I have. If so, a smart dog like yourself would have found a way to get a more concrete message to me. The thing is, if predicting the future is impossible now, it was when you were alive, too, which means you were a fake right from the start. No, this prophet-of-disaster stuff is all theater, which fits your history perfectly. You're doing this for the same reason you always did: You love the attention."

Jim's intent gaze slowly faded into shame. He lay down and put his head on his paws. [Very well. I admit it. I missed the adulation of the crowd. I thought perhaps I might recapture some of my former glory, but the director failed to be impressed by my abilities. I concocted this scheme out of desperation; having fooled those around me for years, I thought I might do the same now.]

I shook my head sadly. "Jim, Jim, Jim . . . it was never going to work. None of the other animals take you seriously; it was one of things that tipped me off. I mean, maybe a graveyard full of ghosts is setting the bar pretty high for scary, but if there was any credibility to what you were saying at all, you'd think at least one of them would have gotten nervous."

[It's my performance, isn't it? The cat was right. I'm no good at this.]

Whiskey trotted forward and sat down in front of Jim. [Now, now, old boy—that's not it at all. Personally, I found you *very* convincing. But this business of something terrible coming . . . well, you should have picked something a little less dramatic. It's my job to know when such things are afoot; you sounding the alarm is a bit like telling a fireman how to put out a fire. If there were any smoke on the horizon, I'd be the first to spot it.]

Jim lifted his head. [That's very kind of you. But you know what they say about old dogs and new tricks; I was simply doing what I knew best.]

"Speaking of tricks . . . did you spread rumors among the actors as part of your campaign?"

[What? Of course not. I was going for epic dread, not gossipy backbiting. *A great cataclysm is coming—and by the way, I heard that Chihuahua call you fat.* Not very fear-inducing, is it?]

"Sorry, had to ask. One more thing: How *did* you perform all those amazing feats when you were alive?"

[I just paid attention, mostly. My master would ask me to pick out a particular thing or person, and almost always glance in that direction. Subtle shifts in his posture or smell would also provide hints. And of course, I had a good memory and ear; after a while I learned how to identify quite a few words, which gave me even more information to go on.]

"How about determining the sex of unborn babies? Smell?"

[Of course.]

"Predicting the winner of the Kentucky Derby?"

[Inside information from another dog.]

"Knowing who would win the World Series?"

[My master was a Yankees fan. I just agreed with his preference.]

I felt both oddly elated and a little let down. On the one hand, logic and reason had won the day; on the other, the world was now a little less magical and mysterious. No, wait—I was having these thoughts in the Great Crossroads, with two talking deceased dogs. Magical mystery maintained.

[If you'd like to redeem yourself, I have an idea,] Whiskey said. [Of course, it may require a certain amount of acting . . .]

Jim's ears grew points.

I decided to stay for dinner that night. It was my last chance to see all the suspects together, as Lucky was planning on finishing the final few shots tomorrow and leaving after that. Well, almost all the suspects—Catree wasn't officially on the invite list.

So I changed that.

"Hi," I said, when she answered her phone. "ZZ would like you to join us for dinner tonight."

"Really? But I'm just a lowly engineer. I make stuff blow up and bleed and catch on fire."

"Exactly. Haven't you been paying attention? ZZ's a total science buff. The only reason you weren't staying at the house with everyone else in the first place was Rolvink, and he's no longer in the picture. So stop camping out in your workshop and have a nice meal with everyone; I guarantee ZZ will insist you stay with us before dessert shows up."

"Oh, I don't know. Give up on my comfy hammock and space heater to go eat rich food and sleep in an actual bed? I couldn't possibly."

"You're already walking toward the front door. Aren't you?"

"Yes. Yes, I am."

"I'll see you in a minute."

I wasn't lying to her, either. I'd already cleared her dinner invitation with ZZ, who'd taken even less convincing than Catree: "A special-effects wizard? Of course she's welcome!"

I went back to my office and changed into my evening outfit, a simple black dress and heels. Whiskey studied me as I applied some makeup in a mirror.

[Certain human behaviors never cease to fascinate me. Not satisfied with your own mating and display rituals, you borrow from other species. The brilliant colors of tropical birds, the heady scent of flowers, the bright accents of shimmering scales . . . really, it's like you're wearing a rain forest.]

"I'm not sure that's a compliment or a criticism. And that *heady scent of flowers* you're talking about is my deodorant. I don't use perfume."

[Nor should you. One's own scent should be quite sufficient.]

I peered at my reflection and touched up my mascara. "Yes, well, we humans aren't always as appreciative of natural body odors as you are. I'd prefer people to remember me by my personality rather than my smell."

[To a dog, the two are inextricable.]

I finished up and we went downstairs. The others were just sitting down; I noted with interest that Catree and Jaxon were about as far apart as it was possible to get and still be at the same table.

"And here's Foxtrot," said ZZ, at the head. "Splendid that you could join us tonight, my dear."

"Thank you," I said, and took a seat between Oscar and

Keene. Yemane Fikru was across from me, and Lucky Fortunato beside him. Jaxon Nesbitt was at the end of the table to ZZ's right, and Max Tervo was to her left. Catree was across from Oscar.

"What a lovely gathering," Keene said. Whatever he and Fikru had taken, it hadn't worn off; if anything, they seemed higher than before. "I especially like the fairies on the flying mice, though I wonder what they need them for. Don't they already have wings of their own?"

"Luggage, my dear boy," said Oscar. "Fairies may present themselves as ethereal and unburdened by worldly concerns, but they change clothes at the drop of a leaf. And then there's all the glitter, of course."

Keene smiled dreamily at Oscar. "Oscar's making fun of me. Excellent. He's *so* good at it, don't you think?"

"Oh, dear God," Oscar muttered. "And the floodgates of sentimentality open. It's like defending yourself with a rapier against a scarecrow covered in syrup."

"You see?" Keene said, beaming. "What imagery! What elan! I want pancakes."

"Pancakes," said Yemane Fikru. "Yes. They're both *round* and *flat*. But never perfectly so. Never *utterly* round. Never *absolutely* flat."

"Is anything?" ZZ asked with a grin and a sparkle in her eye. "Perhaps we need a scientific opinion on the subject. Catree?"

Catree had dressed for the evening in a blue-and-orange tropical shirt, khaki shorts, and sandals; ZZ had no rules about formality, though she applauded style in whatever form it took. "I don't know about round, but the flattest—and thinnest—substance that exists is graphene. Carbon atoms, bound together in a hexagon pattern. Basically a two-dimensional material that's stronger than steel."

"Amazing," said Keene. "And *clearly* made by fairies."

He gave Oscar a superior look, as if he'd just declared checkmate in a game of checkers. Oscar saluted him with his glass and a single raised eyebrow.

"Not so much," said Catree. "It comes from graphite, the exact same thing we use as pencil lead. Know how they isolated the first samples of graphene? They stuck some tape—ordinary, transparent Scotch tape—to a block of raw graphite and pulled it off. They did this over and over, then looked at what they'd lifted off under a microscope. Eventually won them a Nobel Prize."

"Unbelievable," said Jaxon Nesbitt. He was grinning at her, and Catree was smiling back coolly. "The things you learn over dinner."

"I shall never look at a pencil the same way again," Keene declared. "Or Scotch tape. Or anything sticky or pointed, for that matter."

"Which brings us," said Oscar, "back to my original point."

"Untrue," said Jaxon. "Your original point was about fairy luggage loaded down with glitter."

"He's right," said Catree. "The sticky-pointy stuff came later."

"It often does," said Jaxon. They shared a look that spoke volumes—volumes with three great big X's on the cover, stored on a high shelf where children couldn't reach.

It's funny, what can come up at one of ZZ's dinners. She loves spirited discussion, exchanges of unusual ideas, information of any kind, but that doesn't mean her gatherings are strictly cerebral. Drink flows as freely as the conversation, and opinions are almost as welcome as facts—just don't be surprised if those opinions are challenged by someone who knows better than you do. We've never had an actual fistfight, but I've heard both insults and death threats, lewd suggestions and marriage proposals, crazed laughter and heartbroken sobbing. Intellect may rule here, but high emotion is always trying to storm the castle—which is just how ZZ likes it.

She'd noticed the chemistry between Catree and Jaxon, of course; ZZ's eyes are as sharp as her wits. "I'm so glad you could join us tonight, Catree; I like to say that science has a permanently reserved seat at my table."

"Thanks for inviting me," she said. "Looking forward to one of these feasts I've heard so much about."

"We'll make sure you don't starve, dear. But our hospitality isn't free; you don't have to sing for your supper, but you can't just sit there with your mouth shut, either."

Catree laughed. "Generally not a problem for me—you might even regret saying that."

ZZ snorted. "Ha! I regret very few things, my dear, and almost none of them are things I've said." She smiled warmly. "Now—in your professional opinion, what sort of bomb went off in my house?"

At a conventional gathering, that sort of bald-faced question would cause a horrified hush to fall as everyone struggled with what to say in response. But Keene, Oscar, and I were veterans of these dinners, and we reacted accordingly.

Oscar: "Bra*vo*, Mother. Now there's blood all over the salad course."

Me: "I was wondering the same thing."

Keene: "Are the pancakes ready?"

To her credit, Catree didn't freeze up, either. She nodded, slowly and seriously, then said, "Trinitrotoluene, absolutely. You can tell by the color of the smoke, and the smell. If it had been dynamite, the smoke would have been white and smelled a lot worse."

"Is that hard to obtain?" ZZ asked.

"Not really. It's one of the most commonly used commercial explosives. With some basic chemistry knowledge and an Internet connection, you could even make your own—though I'd advise against it. You let the nitrogen oxide levels get away from you during the nitration process and the whole thing goes exothermic."

"Boom?" said Max Tervo.

"Boom," said Catree. "But if you're smart enough to avoid home-cooking, it's pretty safe to handle. Shock- and friction-proof, so you don't have to worry about bumping it or dropping it. It actually melts at a really low temperature—about a hundred and seventy-seven degrees Fahrenheit—but doesn't detonate until it reaches three hundred and thirty-three degrees. That's still pretty low, though—a hundred and eighteen degrees lower than the ignition point of paper, for instance."

"You sound like a dangerous person to cross," said Jaxon.

"But a wonderful person to have as a friend," said Oscar. "I shall have flowers delivered to you, forthwith."

"Careful, Oscar," said ZZ. "You'll make Mr. Nesbitt jealous."

Now there was one of those frozen pauses.

"Also," continued ZZ, "a florist might have some difficulty in locating the truck she's currently staying in. I don't think they'll accept a license plate as a valid address."

"Um," I said.

"Well put, Foxtrot," said ZZ. "That's one of the things I love about you; you're always so well spoken. Except, of course, on those rare occasions that you don't speak to me at all, which I'm sure was a simple oversight on your part and won't happen again."

"Yes, ma'am," I said.

"Don't *ma'am* me, I took the brown acid at Woodstock. Put her in the room next to Mr. Nesbitt's, will you? I'm sure that's an arrangement that will suit everyone."

"Okay," said Catree. I'm pretty sure the stunned look on her face was identical to mine.

"Mr. Nesbitt," said ZZ. "Jaxon. Do you have anything to add?"

Jaxon's smile didn't have a lot of embarrassment in it. "There is, actually. I just want to say that all the secrecy wasn't my idea. Catree's the shy one, not me. Hell, I'll march out the front gate right now and give her a big kiss right in front of the paparazzi."

"What's going on?" Keene demanded. "Did I black out again? Dear God, did I miss the pancakes?"

"Yes," said Oscar. "A shame, really. They were all perfectly flat and perfectly round; I've already called Guinness."

"Well, at least there'll be beer," said Keene.

"I have every right to my privacy," said Catree, staring hard at Jaxon. "I don't care that you're famous, and I don't want to join you on the cover of a tabloid. I sleep with you because I have a weakness for eye candy and you make me laugh. Also, you're not stupid."

"That's the most romantic thing I've ever heard," said Oscar. "I may weep."

Yemane Fikru, who had been staring fixedly at a cherry tomato on his plate for the last five minutes, abruptly looked up. "Secrets. So many secrets . . ."

ZZ nodded. "Yes, and I'd prefer a few less of them. For instance: *Who killed someone and blew up my house?*"

Lucky Trentini, who'd been following this exchange with the rapt attention of a professional voyeur, cleared his throat. "Uh, I'd like to weigh in, if I may? First, despite the fact I had no idea my leading man was sleeping with my FX person, I do try to pay attention to what's happening on my set. Second, I really wish you had a butler because then we'd have at least one viable suspect."

Max Tervo spoke up. "It's not that we have any lack of suspects. It's that we have too many."

"Well then," said ZZ. "Let's narrow it down, shall we?" She picked up the remote beside her plate and thumbed a few buttons. The three giant flatscreens on the walls currently showing eighteenth-century paintings shifted from pastel landscapes to pages of documentation.

"This is the forensics report from the police report on the bomb," ZZ said. "Don't ask how I got it."

"How'd you get it?" asked Keene.

"I have lots of money. Now, Catree: These findings seem to agree with your assessment. But no trace of an explosive booster—like Semtex or C4—or a detonator was found, which has the investigators puzzled. They don't know how the bomb was set off. Their current theory is ambient heat from the fireplace itself, which is obviously absurd; no fires were lit that morning, and the fires from the previous night were long extinguished."

Most of us were desperately trying to read the report on the screen, except for Keene and Fikru. "What's happening?" asked Keene, sounding a touch desperate. "A minute ago we were in some sort of soap opera, and now it's an episode of one of the sciencey police shows. Am I a guest star?"

"Sssh," I said. "Relax. It's just a cameo, you don't have any lines."

"Oh, right then. Tell me when the pancakes arrive."

I don't always give ZZ enough credit. Yes, she's eccentric, and yes, the list of things she's interested in can change without warning—but when she really cares about something, she's a force of nature. She devours information the way a blue whale consumes krill, taking in huge amounts and sifting it for relevant information. Even though I'm her executive assistant and extremely good at research, it's the one area she rarely asks me for help with; she prefers to do it herself. I should have known she'd be investigating this as well, and that she'd be doing an amazing job. I may have talking spirits and shape-changing dogs on my side, but ZZ has resources of her own—she not only has lots of money, she has lots of friends. Smart, well-connected, powerful friends.

At that point the maid arrived with the main course. Everybody got a serving of beef Wellington with garlic mashed potatoes and pickled beets on the side—except for Keene.

He got pancakes. My boyfriend has an odd sense of humor, but he *does* pay attention.

We discussed the report while we ate, ZZ putting up fresh pages as we finished what was on-screen. The rest of them soon came to the same conclusion I already had: The bomb had to have been planted sometime in the night, after the evening fires had burned down.

"Who had access to the room?" Max Tervo asked. "Rolvink and Natalia, certainly."

"The maids, ZZ, and I all have master keys," I said. "None of them has gone missing—I checked."

"I think we can safely eliminate any of them as suspects," said Oscar. "Unless one of our household servants has an unsavory past I'm unaware of?"

I shook my head. "Shondra's very thorough when it comes to background checks. I trust everyone on staff. Anyway, the maids had all gone home for the night."

"Maybe they killed each other," Lucky suggested. "Rolvink plants the bomb, then Natalia kills him. She comes back the next morning and *ka-boom!*"

"A neat theory," said Max Tervo, "but untenable. Natalia, as anyone who's worked with her will attest, is squeamish in the extreme. She can barely stand to be around artificial gore, let alone the real thing. If, as rumor has it, the body was dismembered, then it couldn't have been her."

I nodded. "But why would Rolvink try to kill his lead actress—whom he also happened to be sleeping with?"

"Maybe she was pregnant," Jaxon suggested. "A sleaze like Rolvink would go pretty far to avoid palimony payments."

"Not possible," said Lucky. "Natalia can't have kids."

We all looked at him. "What?" he said. "Insurance companies demand to know all kinds of things before they'll cover a film shoot. Drug tests, medical history, psych evaluations. If an actress is going to quit halfway through a shoot because she's showing, they want to know. Don't blame me, I didn't make the rules."

"The bombing is too calculated for a lovers' spat," I said. "Natalia wouldn't blow herself up, and Rolvink was already dead by the time the bomb was planted. So how was the bomb planted in her room in the middle of the night, if they were the only two with access?"

I thought I'd figured that part out all ready, but I wanted to see who would speak up. There was at least one other person who knew how the bomb had been put into place, and quite probably they were seated at the same table I was.

We were all quiet for a moment. Then Max Tervo said, "The bomber didn't need access to the room. They only needed access to the chimney."

"Of course," said Catree. "Lower it down the flue on a line until it's at the right height. It's obvious."

"You could even send a thermometer down first," said

ZZ. "Make sure it wasn't too hot and you wouldn't be risking your life. All you'd need was access to the roof."

"In the middle of the night," I said. "After the fire in the study had gone out. Lucky, you were up fairly late, right?"

"Yeah, until around two, and I kept the fire going. I like a nice blaze, it helps me think."

"So the bomb was planted after two," said Catree. "And since the Catree is out of the bag, so to speak, I'm going to address the elephant in the room."

Keene glanced around nervously. "What, it's back?"

Fikru took a more careful look around. "No."

"I didn't do it," said Catree. "I have the know-how and I was no fan of Rolvink, but I didn't blow anything or anyone up—and I can prove it."

Jaxon nodded. "True. She was with me, in my room, from one AM to five. So unless anybody thinks we're *both* lying, we're each other's alibi."

"I withdraw my previous comment," said Oscar. "*That's* the most romantic thing I've ever heard."

Which sounded great . . . except I *knew* Jaxon Nesbitt had a good reason for wanting Rolvink dead. What I didn't know was how far Catree was willing to go to help him . . .

We talked things out a little more, but didn't come to any solid conclusions. Max Tervo, Yemane Fikru, and Lucky Trentini all maintained they were alone in their rooms after two; Catree and Jaxon had stated they were together. Keene, though his memory was still fuzzy, had been awake and outside the whole time, constructing his "enhanced" croquet field.

I'd verified Fikru's claim, and Max Tervo had been in the graveyard at the approximate time of Rolvink's death. Everyone else was still a suspect.

After dinner I went up to my office to finish some paperwork I'd been putting off. I knew I should really go home, but something was nagging at my subconscious. Whiskey had taken off on a mysterious errand, so I decided to go for an evening walk in the gardens by myself and tried to pry whatever it was out of the depths of my noggin.

I was so deep in thought I almost walked right into Lucky Trentini. Or rather, right over him; he was down on his hands and knees on the path, peering intently at the ground.

I stopped. "Um. Hi. Lose something?"

He didn't look up, just kept scanning the edge of the path. "No. Not exactly. I mean, I am looking for something, but it's not something I lost. Just something I haven't found, yet."

I frowned. "Can I help?"

"No!" He sounded more panicked than angry. "It's just—it's hard to explain. It's something I do every day I'm working on a film—during actual shooting, anyway. Started when I was just a production assistant."

"And what you're doing is?"

Now he looked a little embarrassed. "I'm . . . trying *not* to find a four-leaf clover."

"Really. Seems as if that would be easy to do."

"Like I said, it's hard to explain. It's just . . . when you're a PA, you often get stuck out in the middle of nowhere, with nothing but an orange vest and a walkie-talkie for company. So this one time, when I'm making sure nobody walks up a certain footpath in this forest, I start looking for a four-leaf clover. Just to, you know, pass the time."

"Did you find one?"

He sighed. "Yeah. Unfortunately."

"Um. I don't follow."

"Neither did I, at first. See, right after that it started

raining. And my walkie-talkie stopped working, and when I walked back to the shoot to get another one, a dog ran down the path I was supposed to be guarding and ruined a shot. Also, I got fired."

"That doesn't sound like your typical four-leaf clover story."

"Maybe not. But it got me thinking. About luck and probability and how superstitions get started. And I realized that the whole four-leaf clover thing is just a metaphor about probabilities. You know what the chances are of finding a four-leaf specimen in a field of clover? One in ten thousand. But all that means, in mathematical terms, is that something extremely unlikely just happened. Which meant, to my mind, that the string of bad luck that immediately followed my finding it was just as unlikely as a bunch of good things happening all at once."

I smiled. "So far, you're sounding pretty rational. You know, for a guy on his hands and knees looking for a four-leaf clover in October."

"Well, this is the not-so-rational part. See, I can be a little stubborn and a little obsessive, so I happen to know it took me exactly twenty-eight minutes to find that four-leaf piece of disaster. So the next time I was working on a film, I spent the same twenty-eight minutes searching for another one."

Whiskey started nosing around in the cold grass, too. [I wish I could help, but I doubt if they smell any different than the three-leaf kind.]

"Which I didn't find," Trentini continued. "But I didn't have a really crappy day, either. And after that . . . it kind of snowballed."

"So you devote twenty-eight minutes of every day you're filming to looking for something you hope you won't find?"

Now he looked both embarrassed and anxious. "It's worse than that. It has to be the *same* twenty-eight minutes every day. From eight PM to eight twenty-eight."

"Well," I said. "We all have our rituals." I hesitated, then added, "Maybe I shouldn't mention this, but—isn't talking to me screwing up your routine?"

"Kind of. But I looked at my watch when we started talking, and I'll add whatever time this conversation is using. I'm trying to be more flexible about the whole thing."

"Good for you. I'll let you get back to it."

"Thanks. Uh—don't mention this to anyone else, will you? I try to keep it private. Max struck up a conversation after dinner the night before the explosion and I had to fake a bathroom emergency to get rid of him. Luckily we were in the graveyard; clover's easy to find there."

"Of course. Our guests' privacy is extremely important to us."

When we left him, Trentini was studying his watch intently. Waiting for the exact instant to leap back into his specialized little zone of insecurity, hunting for something he didn't want to find. There was some sort of metaphor in there, but I had too much on mind to try figuring it out. Sometimes, you just have to leave other people's craziness alone.

Which didn't, of course, mean that craziness would leave you alone. Tango darted from beneath a shrub directly in front of me and skidded to a stop on the path. *<I've done it! I've caught the lousy son-of-a-dog that tried to wreck my production!>*

"You have? Well, that's . . . interesting. Who was the culprit?"

Tango stared at me intently, her tail lashing. *<Nazis!>*
Ohhhhhhhhkay . . .

19.

"Would you mind explaining that?" I asked.

<Okay, technically not Nazis, plural. Bring in the saboteur, Whiskey!>

Which is when Whiskey trotted out from behind a bush, carrying Unsinkable Sam by the scruff of his ghostly neck.

I stared. I blinked. I started to speak, and then stopped. Finally, I managed to get a few words out. "You're saying— hang on. You're saying this cat is a *Nazi*?"

<A Nazi spy,> Tango said.

"I hate to break this to you, kitty, but even the most dedicated spy would give up seventy years after the war ended. And the organization they served no longer existed. And, you know, they were dead."

Unsinkable Sam glared at me sullenly. *<Let me go! This is an outrage!>*

<Quiet, you. And no, obviously he's no longer an active spy. But he was during World War Two. All those boats he was aboard that went down? Not accidents.>

"That's—I don't—" I glanced helplessly at Whiskey. My life was a surreal environment *before* I learned how to communicate with dead animals, and since Whiskey and Tango showed up it had become even stranger. But this? This was a whole new level of weird. I was used to Tango's cat-centric views of any given situation, so her accusing a fellow feline of being a deep-cover German intelligence agent responsible for the sinking of several British ships wasn't as big a shock as you might think.

No, what I couldn't wrap my skull around was that Whiskey seemed to be endorsing this craziness. He was supposed to be the sane one, the voice of reason, the gently applied brakes to Tango's full-thrust wacky.

"Whiskey?" I said. "What's your take on this?"

Not surprisingly, his telepathic voice came through just fine even when he had a mouthful of cat. [I'm afraid I must concur. Sam was indeed doing his best to—*ahem*—torpedo the production. Tell her, please.] He shook his head, ever so slightly, and Sam swayed back and forth.

<*Very well,*> Sam spat. <*Yes, I was a spy. My name is Oskar, not Sam. I was tasked to gain access to British ships and report their positions. Once I did so, I left the ship and it was destroyed.*>

"But *how*?" I asked.

<*Humans are gullible and lonely. It was a simple matter to befriend the radio operator and tap out a simple signal when he was otherwise occupied.*>

Whiskey saw the look of disbelief on my face. [It's not as fantastic as it seems. The Nazis also had a program where dogs were trained to talk.]

"If this is the setup to an elaborate practical joke, I will make you both pay."

[The *Hundesprechschule Asra* in Leutenberg was an

institution devoted to teaching dogs how to count, talk, and reason. It existed from 1930 to 1945 and had Hitler's support. At one point they also had a cat.]

<That was Fritz,> said Oskar. *<We were in the same classes. He was clever, but softhearted.>*

I tried to put my brain into gear. "Okay, so you were a Nazi infiltrator during the Second World War. What does this have to do with Tango's production?"

For a moment Oskar didn't say anything. Then, *<I was simply having a little fun. It's in a cat's nature to play with their prey; I was trained to do so on a grand scale. I was . . . indulging myself.>*

[I fail to evince even the slightest iota of surprise.]

<Well, you messed with the wrong director, pal. Now you have to face the music.>

"Absolutely," I said. "Uh, what exactly *is* the music, here? Are we the music? Am *I* the music? Because I'm really not that well versed on what the penalty is for something like this, or how it gets enforced. Little help?"

[I'll take him to Eli. He'll decide on an appropriate punishment—which I imagine will include being banned from using the Great Crossroads for a while.]

"Yes, Eli. Good idea. Why don't you take him over there right now."

[I shall.] And with that, he was off, his prisoner swaying from his jaws. I almost expected Oskar to mutter, *And I would have gotten away with it, too, if it weren't for that meddling dog and his friends . . .*

"Okay, so you were right," I said to Tango. "But you still have a bunch of disgruntled actors to deal with. Hurt feelings, ruffled feathers. It's going to take a delicate touch to—"

<They'll come back or I'll fire every last one of 'em.>

Terrific. My cat, the living personification of the old Hollywood studio heads. I sighed. "Look, let me handle that, okay? I think I can smooth things over."

<Sure, knock yourself out. I have a rewrite to polish, anyway.>

Tango darted away. I sat and thought. By the time Whiskey got back, I finally had to admit to myself that whatever was nagging at me wasn't going to reveal itself just yet, and it was time to go home. Maybe some sleep would help.

Whiskey was strangely silent during the drive. When I asked him what Eli's decision about Oskar was, he wouldn't tell me.

"Why?" I said. "Is this one of those things you can't talk about? Is there . . . well, you know. A Bad Place for animals?"

[Hmmm? No, of course not. That's a human thing. What's going on with Oskar is more . . . complicated.]

"*More* complicated? Of course. Because the ghost of a Nazi cat spy trying to sabotage the graveyard theatrical production of a bunch of dead animals isn't complicated enough, obviously. Who's the actual mastermind behind this diabolical plot? The reincarnated clone of Godzilla's chiropractor?"

[Large radioactive lizards rarely need a chiropractor.]

"Don't think you can distract me by saying *rarely*. I know a radioactive red herring when it's waved in front of my nose."

[Nor are herrings generally any shade of—]

"Okay, okay. You don't want to talk about it, fine."

And he didn't. In fact, he didn't say much of anything, all the way home. Or between the time when we got there and I went to bed.

But I thought he looked worried.

*   *   *

I'd been experimenting with different ringtones, and when "The Lion Sleeps Tonight" started playing the next morning while I was putting marmalade on my toast, I knew it was Caroline. She didn't usually call me so early unless there was a serious problem, so I picked up right away. "Hey, vet lady. What's up?"

"I, uh, need you to come see me as soon as you can."

"Sure. What about?"

"Honey badger scat."

It took me a moment to process that she was talking about Owduttf droppings and not some new musical group; I was still working on my first cup of English Breakfast. "Oh. And this is urgent because?"

"Because of what I found in it. A watch."

"I see. Have you told anyone else?"

"Not yet. It's weird though, right? Why would someone throw that in his cage?"

"I don't know. Maybe Keene did it—he was on a real bender the other night."

Caroline didn't say anything for a moment. "Foxtrot, you don't think this is connected to . . ."

"What, the murder? No, of course not."

"It's just that I heard something about the body missing some parts. And the badger did get out that night . . ."

I sighed. "Okay, it's a possibility, but an unlikely one. He's more of an opportunistic predator than a hunter, right?"

"Technically, I guess. But that doesn't mean he isn't capable of attacking and killing something much larger than he is."

"Look, don't do anything until I get there, okay? We'll figure this out together."

She said she'd wait, and we hung up. I crammed the toast in my mouth, grabbed my thermos mug and filled it, collected Whiskey, and was out the door a minute later.

When we got to the estate, we went straight to the vet clinic. Caroline was waiting inside. She let us in and took us straight to her desk, where she pulled a small plastic bag out of a drawer. "I didn't touch it with anything but a metal scoop," she said, handing it to me.

I took the bag and held it up. The object inside was a little mangled, but clearly recognizable as a watch. The strap was missing, but Owduttf had probably chewed that part a little more thoroughly. The metal looked like he'd given it a good chomp, then just decided to swallow it whole.

Wait a minute . . .

I peered closely at it. Owduttf hadn't just given it a chomp, he'd bitten it right at the minute hand, punching the hand into the face of the watch hard enough to embed it. And, of course, stop it.

Right at eight twenty-two.

"Thanks for showing me this," I said. "You're right, we'll need to notify the police. I'll call Forrester and have him come down and get it. How's the honey badger doing?"

"Better than I am, I'm sure. Foxtrot, this is terrible. Did one of my animals *kill* someone?"

"I don't think so, Caroline. It seems much more likely he just found the corpse and . . . well, had a little snack." I didn't mention what else Owduttf had consumed; she'd know soon enough. Teeth are notoriously hard to digest.

I left Caroline and called Forrester as I walked back to the house. He said he'd be out to take a look right away.

I pocketed my phone after the call and said to Whiskey, "Interesting development. Doesn't give us time of death, but now we know Rolvink was alive at seven thirty

and dead by eight twenty-two. That means we can eliminate Lucky Trentini as a suspect; Max Tervo was with him
until just before eight, and Trentini was doing his unlucky-
clover thing from then until eight thirty."

[Unless he was interrupted by Rolvink. And perhaps
killed for it.]

"That's a disturbing thought. But even if Trentini was
crazy enough to commit murder over such a trivial thing,
there wasn't any clover in the area Rolvink was killed—
our gardener is too thorough for that. Lucky said he was
talking to Tervo in the graveyard after dinner. I guess
Rolvink could have found him out there . . . but then they'd
have to cross the yard where Keene and Oscar were playing croquet, and they would have been seen."

[True. As long as Trentini is telling the truth about his
clover-leaf obsession, it would seem he's in the clear. For
the murder, in any case.]

We went into the house and found Ben in the kitchen
preparing breakfast for the guests while Tango enjoyed
hers at her bowl.

"How goes the investigation?" Ben asked, cracking
eggs into a large steel bowl.

I poured myself a cup of tea from my thermos as I
talked. "Not so good. I've eliminated a few suspects, but
that's about it."

He grabbed a large whisk and started beating the eggs.
"Well, as long as you're making progress. Anything I can
do to help?"

I sighed, then went over and kissed him. "Just keep
everybody fed and me caffeinated. Oh, and if you could
talk to a few clouds and ask them about seeing anyone on
the roof the night of the murder? That'd be *super*."

Tango looked up from her bowl. <*Wait, he can do that?
Nobody told me he could do that.*>

Whiskey yawned. [That's because he can't do that.]

<Oh. Well, good. I go up there to be alone; I don't need random weather spying on me.>

I froze, my mug of tea halfway to my lips. "Hold on. Tango, do you spend a lot of time up on the roof?"

<Only at night. Why, is that a problem?>

"No, of course not. Were you up there the night of the murder?"

<Let me think . . . yeah, I was. Spent a few hours there, actually. There's a nice warm spot right next to the chimney.>

"The chimney," I said. "Okay, Tango, this is important. Did you see anyone up on the roof with you? Someone who put something *in* the chimney?"

She looked at me and licked a few crumbs of food off her whiskers. *<The chimney that blew up, you mean? Why, yes, Foxtrot, I did see somebody put something in there. It was a fat guy in a red suit. I was suspicious at first, but he said one of his reindeer had blown a hoof and he just needed to lighten his load. I didn't think it was worth mentioning.>*

"I'll take that as a no. Okay, now here's the really important part—when, exactly were you up there? When did you get there and when did you leave?"

<Gee, I'm not sure. Let me check the pocket watch in my vest—hey! Someone stole my pocket watch! And my vest!>

Ben shook his head and poured the eggs into a pan. "You know, you'd think cat sarcasm would never get old. And yet, it does."

"Come on, kitty, work with me. What was going on when you climbed up there?"

<Not much. Before then I was in the study, enjoying the fire and watching my fellow director edit. When he doused

the fire and went to bed, I went up to the roof. I could still see Keene working on his contraption, but that was it. Nothing much else happened until the zombies started milling around on the lawn. Keene was gone by then.>

Keene was up until at least five, when he was spotted by the film crew as they got ready for the day. The zombies were there by seven, when I arrived. "Tango, when did you leave?"

<I didn't come down until I saw your car drive up.>

"I got in around six, if that helps," said Ben. "Didn't see Keene or any zombies."

"The zombies were still in makeup at that point. But this doesn't make any sense."

"Why not?"

"Because if the bomb was placed in the chimney from the top, it had to have been done between two AM and sunrise; anytime after that, they would have been seen. But Tango says she saw no one approach the chimney in all that time."

[Perhaps she fell asleep.]

<Perhaps you're an idiot. You really think anyone could get with ten feet of me on a roof in the middle of the night without me waking up? I'm a cat, doofus. On my slowest, dullest, most impaired-by-anesthetic day, I'd still spot them before they got within scratching distance.>

She had a point. But if the bomb hadn't been planted via the roof, then how?

20.

"Our theory," Lieutenant Forrester said, "is that Maurice Rolvink and Natalia Cardoso each tried to kill the other, over a romance gone wrong."

We were seated in the study, having a cup of tea. When Forrester and I first met, he was cautious around me; since then, he's come to appreciate that I'm a valuable resource in my own right. This doesn't mean he'll tell me everything he knows, but he'll give up a few details just to keep me happy. He's realized that what happens on the Zoransky estate is worth keeping an eye on, and for that he needs me.

"Interesting," I said, taking a sip of tea, "but how? The blast originated in the chimney, so the bomb had to have been put there when the fireplace wasn't being used. Rolvink died some time between seven thirty and eight twenty-two, and there was a roaring blaze until around two AM."

Forrester shook his head. "We . . . haven't ironed all the details out yet. It's a working theory."

At my feet, Whiskey snorted. [Working? I believe a better adjective for that theory would be *unemployable*.]

"Thank you for the watch," said Forrester, getting to his feet. "If we can confirm it's Rolvink's, we'll at least know what happened to the head and hands. Animals have been used to dispose of body parts before, but the animal is usually something a lot more common—like a pig or dog." He glanced down at Whiskey. "No offense."

[None taken. I am a carnivore, after all—though I would never eat human flesh. Too much potential for awkward conversations in the afterlife.]

Forrester couldn't hear him, of course. And while I suspected the honey badger had done more than just consume some extremities, I wasn't going to tell Forrester that—not until I knew exactly what Owduttf was responsible for. "I'll let you know if anything else turns up," I said, getting to my feet. "Or, you know—is deposited."

I walked him to the door. "How's Natalia Cardoso doing, by the way?" I asked.

"Much better, actually. We took a statement this morning. She was a little shaken up by the news of Rolvink's death, but recovered quickly. She admitted to the relationship, but insisted there was no animosity between them."

I paused before opening the door for him. "Does she have an alibi?"

Forrester smiled. "Not as such. Which is why she's currently the prime suspect."

I waited all of ten minutes after he was gone. Then I got in my car and drove to the hospital.

Visiting hours weren't until later in the day, but hospitals are like any other large, busy business: They're run by people like me, used to juggling a dozen chain saws while tap-dancing and reciting epic poems from memory.

Sweet-talking a nurse into letting me pop in for a quick visit was really just a matter of convincing them I wasn't going to require any of their time or attention, after which I became invisible.

"Hi," I said, sticking my head in the room at the same time I knocked on the door. "Remember me?"

Natalia Cardoso was sitting up in bed, surrounded by flowers. She wore an elegant white nightgown that revealed a fair bit of cleavage, her makeup was carefully done, and her hair was immaculate. The look on her face when she saw me was the friendly smile of someone expecting to see a cherished loved one—which quickly crashed into a hard-eyed resignation when she recognized me. I was pretty sure I'd have gotten a much warmer reception if I'd had a professional-looking camera in my hands.

"Hello, Fandango," she said. "Did ZZ send you? I really shouldn't say anything without my lawyer present."

"It's Foxtrot," I said. "And no, ZZ didn't send me. Any legal wrangling will no doubt be done in air-conditioned offices with big boardroom tables and scary people armed with law books. I'm here strictly to make sure you're comfortable and if there's anything I can do for you. I see you got the flowers."

Yes, that was me. Sending flowers is second nature for a personal assistant; I have the numbers of every florist in a ten-mile range memorized and can recite most of their prices. I'd fired off a dozen bouquets to Natalia before she'd left the ambulance.

"They're very nice, thank you. But that doesn't mean I'm not going to sue."

I shrugged. "Okay. Like I said, not why I'm here. Actually, from what I understand, ZZ's not the one who should be worried about legal action."

Her cold stare grew icicles—sharp, pointy ones, aimed right at me. "That's ludicrous. I'm clearly the victim here."

"Oh, absolutely. But that's not how Forrester is looking at it. Don't let that small-town friendliness fool you; if he sees a way to close a case, he'll take it." I gave her the eyebrows-raised, know-what-I-mean-girlfriend look, which is surprisingly effective when used on people who don't have many friends. Natalia Cardoso didn't strike me as the warm and cuddly type.

"How could anyone think I'm responsible? I was the one who was almost blown up!"

"*Almost* is the key word there. As in, it *almost* makes you look like you got injured on purpose."

She looked stricken. It was an absurd claim to make, but that's the thing about human nature: Deep down inside, people believe that everyone else is just like them. Suspicious people think everyone doubts their motives, angry people think everyone's mad at them, greedy people think everyone's after their money.

But—personal opinions aside—Natalia had demonstrated what sort of immature, selfish behavior she was capable of. Which gave me a much more objective take on who she was, and by extension how she viewed the world.

In short: Natalia was conniving and selfish. Therefore, the idea that other people would falsely accuse her for their own selfish and conniving reasons was—to her—entirely believable.

"I suppose they'll try to pin Maurice's murder on me as well?" she said. Her voice was angry, but I saw a hint of fear in her eyes.

"I don't know. You were the last one to see him alive, right?" That was an educated guess on my part, but it made sense.

"How should I know? We were in my room briefly after dinner. He told me he had some things to take care of in town, and that I shouldn't expect to see him that night. Then he left."

I nodded. "Leaving you alone. Without an alibi."

"I was tired. I just wanted to get a good night's rest before having to get up at five AM." She glared at me. "Anyway, I don't need an alibi. There were plenty of people who wanted him dead, but I wasn't one of them. He *got* me this role."

True enough. "And I'm sure Lieutenant Forrester will figure that out eventually. In the meantime—how about I have some chocolate sent up? I know an excellent shop in Hartsville."

She frowned, a little puzzled by my abrupt turnaround. "I don't—"

"Look at it this way. An apology implies guilt, right? So any act of attrition by ZZ strengthens your case against her in a civil suit. Chocolate is *very* apologetic."

She thought about it, saw my point, and nodded ever so slightly. "Dark, please."

"Is there any other kind?"

I wasn't worried about Natalia suing ZZ. First of all, I'm a lot more knowledgeable about personal damages lawsuits than I let on, and she didn't have a case. Second, ZZ's legal team was so far out of Natalia's league that they weren't even playing the same sport. Natalia might try to claim some sort of negligence on the part of her host, but she wouldn't succeed; ZZ wasn't responsible for some maniac cramming a bomb in her chimney.

So who was? And how did it get there?

I thought about it on the drive back to the house, but it just didn't make sense. I was still thinking about it when I got out of the car and almost stepped on Tango. "Oh! Sorry, kitty—I didn't see you there."

<Obviously. Good news, Toots; my production is on track again. All morning long, my actors have been dropping by to apologize and say they want to come back to work.>

"That's terrific. I'm glad they're being reasonable."

<Reasonable? Well, it's true that the chance to work with me is a once-in-an-afterlifetime opportunity that any thinking being would jump at—but I think the real explanation is a lot simpler: fear.>

"Sure. You *are* fierce."

<Yes I am. But fair.>

"Always. Now, don't you have a show to prepare?"

<I suppose you're right. I'll see you later.> And with that she sauntered away, her tail in the air.

Whiskey was sprawled out on my office sofa, his usual spot. "Okay, mastermind, how'd you do it?"

He stared at me, innocent as a puppy. [Whatever do you mean?]

"You not only got all the actors to come back, you got them to apologize. How?"

[With Jim's help. He really is a very intelligent dog.]

"So are you. But it takes more than intelligence to soothe wounded feelings."

[True. One needs both empathy and a certain talent for manipulation. Jim has demonstrated both.]

"Ah. So you used a con man to alleviate the damage caused by an agent provocateur? Nice."

[Thank you. My strategy, since no one took Jim's pronouncements seriously, was to use that to our advantage. We went around and explained to everyone that both Jim and Unsinkable Sam were part of the production itself. Sam was supposed to instruct certain actors to react in specific ways to Jim's appearances; depending on how they did, they would be awarded with larger roles in the production.]

"I think I see. You told everybody that Sam went off-script."

[Indeed. Our explanation was that Sam misinterpreted his instructions; that he thought *prepping the actors for doom* meant trying to cause as much trouble as possible.]

I nodded. "And placing the blame squarely where it belongs. I'm guessing Sam is no longer in a position to refute any of this?"

[Not as such, no. And everyone else, once the situation was explained, was most gracious.]

"Even the squirrels?"

[Even the squirrels. The goats, though . . .] He gave a theatrical shudder. [Let's not talk about the goats. Ever.]

"Fine by me. How about we talk about the bombing, instead. I just can't figure it out."

[Yes, it's puzzling. Though I'm loath to admit it, Tango's senses are quite acute; if she says no one approached the chimney while she was there, then no one did. Nor would she lie about her whereabouts during the night.]

"No, she wouldn't. Which means nobody lowered it down the chimney—so how did it get there?"

And suddenly the answer came to me. Simple, yet obvious.

I grinned and pulled out my phone.

"Thank you all for coming," I said. I'd gathered everyone—well, everyone except Natalia Cordoso—in the study. "I think I've figured out at least part of the puzzle."

"Well done, Foxtrot," said Keene. He seemed a lot more clearheaded than he had last night, as did Yemane Fikru. "Whatever it is you've done, I mean. We're all ears."

"I'm not," said Oscar. "Not unless they've invented a sonic form of scotch, in any case."

"Go ahead, dear," said ZZ.

"Thanks, boss. What's been bothering me is how the explosives were placed inside the chimney."

"I thought we solved that last night," said Max Tervo. "They were lowered from above."

I shook my head. "Turns out that's not true. I have information from a reliable source that proves no one was on the roof that night."

I'd invited Shondra, too—she'd never forgive me if I didn't include her. "What source?" she asked.

"I can't reveal that right now, but where the information came from isn't relevant. What matters is that it pointed me in a different direction: down."

"Down?" asked Lucky.

"Yes. Our esteemed director was here in the study until two AM, editing footage on his laptop—but after that he put out the fire and went to bed. Which is when the killer entered the study and used something like *this*." I picked up the coil of metal cable at my feet; it looked a bit like a steel lariat and was surprisingly heavy. "A plumbing snake. It pushed the bomb up the flue until it was at the level of the second floor, where some sort of spring-loaded mechanism was activated to lodge it in place. In an older house like this, it's not unusual for two fireplaces to share a single flue—"

"Foxtrot," Shondra said. "I'm sorry, but that's not what happened."

I blinked. "Excuse me?"

"The report on the bombing clearly shows the blast was centered inside the second-floor chimney, right above the second-floor fireplace. While the fireplaces share a chimney, they aren't directly over each other; they're offset."

I smiled. "I know. I looked at the original blueprints; amazing what sort of stuff is archived on the Internet these days. The thing about plumbing snakes is that they have a crank or motor that not only makes the tip rotate, it also makes the whole thing flail against the sides of the pipe; I think that motion might have been enough to get the snake from one side of the flue to the other—"

"Foxtrot? Dear?" ZZ said, looking apprehensive. "I'm afraid that wouldn't work, either. The original flue was shared, it's true, but that's considered unsafe these days. We had a brick flue divider installed ages ago. Long before you came to work here, in fact."

And that was where I sort of ran down.

The bomb couldn't have been pushed up the flue; my theory had literally smacked into a brick wall. I was caught, center stage, under a single bright spotlight, and I couldn't remember my lines. Also, my pants had just disappeared.

"I," I said. "I, I, I. Don't. Know."

Everybody stared at me. I felt dizzy. I could feel every inch of skin on my body turning bright red and preparing to burst into flame.

"It's all right, Foxtrot," ZZ said. "You got it wrong. It happens. Now, I believe it's time for lunch; Ben has prepared a wonderful buffet, and I hope everyone will join me in the dining room." She got to her feet, nodded at me encouragingly, and they all began to file out after her.

All except Shondra, who waited until everyone had left until she approached me. "Foxtrot. You know I'm not the kind of person to say I told you so—but you should have come to me about this first. I could have saved you some embarrassment. I might even have had some ideas of my own to contribute."

"You're right. I'm—I'm sorry."

"This isn't like you. You're a terrific facilitator, which

means you know which experts to put where and when before getting out of their way and letting them work. I'm the expert, here. Right?"

"Right." I felt like sinking through the floor.

"So either you don't think I can do my job, or your own job is stressing you out so much you're starting to micromanage. I've seen it happen before, usually with new commanding officers; they're so worried they're going to make a mistake they feel like they have oversee every tiny detail. They get obsessed with control, and the more obsessed they get the more any tiny bit of chaos bothers them. It never ends well."

"It won't happen again." The classic excuse of the screwup.

"Of course it will. That's what life does. We can't see everything coming, and that's a good thing. The unknown isn't chaos; it's freedom. Try to remember that."

She met my eyes, gave me a serious nod, and left the room.

I think that made me feel worse than anything. Shondra wasn't so much angry at me as worried. Worried I couldn't do my job properly, worried that I was cracking under pressure.

Was she right?

I went and hid in my office. I didn't feel like eating. Whiskey sat with me on the couch and did his best to cheer me up, but it wasn't working.

Which is when Tango strolled in.

<Hey, Toots. How's everything?>

"Not so great, kitty. I just tried to solve the bombing case and got it wrong. Totally, completely wrong."

<Well, you're only human. Come on, I've got something to show you.>

I groaned. "Can it wait? I really just want to sit here and be depressed. And a snuggle from my favorite cat would be greatly appreciated."

She paced back and forth. *<We can snuggle later. Let's go, let's go!>*

I leaned forward, suddenly concerned. "What is it? What's wrong?"

She stared at me impatiently. *<Wrong? Nothing's wrong. Everything's just fine, which is why we should be going and not staying.>*

I frowned. "I'm not following."

<Yeah, I noticed that. Which is why you should get to your feet, which is a good start. Then we'll try the whole following thing, with me in the front. Don't worry, you'll catch on fast.>

"Okay, I'm not going anywhere until you tell me where and why."

<Isn't it obvious? My production is ready! On with the show! Let's go already!>

I stared down at her. "Tango. Did you not hear what I just said? I screwed up, in front of everyone. I'm worried and embarrassed and depressed and I am *not* in the mood to untangle another one of your disasters."

Maybe that was harsh. But I wasn't doing well, and I really needed a little emotional support. Tango's usually good at picking up on that, and providing as much comfort as I need. But at the end of the day, she's still a cat; and cats *can* be self-centered and arrogant and aloof. Usually that didn't bother me—but today I was the one in pain, and it did.

<Disaster, huh? That's not what you'll say after you see it performed. Which is gonna be as soon as we get ourselves down to the Crossroads.>

I leaned back against the sofa and closed my eyes. "No,

Tango. I am not up for this, not right now. I'm glad your little project has kept you busy, but I'm trying to solve a murder and a bombing. Stuff that *matters*."

Yeah, I said it.

I know, I know. There's that point when a disagreement becomes a fight, and I'd just crossed it. I wasn't just upset, I was angry. Not at Tango, but at myself; unfortunately, snapping at yourself doesn't really work.

So this is the part where the other person usually does one of two things: They either get all haughty and cold and leave the room, or they ramp things up by saying something nasty back. Either one would have been in character for Tango.

But she surprised me by doing neither.

21.

She stopped pacing. She sat down, curled her tail around her, and just stared at me for a moment. Then: *<Foxtrot. I have three things to say. First of all, I know you're not happy. I* always *know when you're unhappy.>*

"Kitty, I—"

<I'm not finished. The second thing is this: You should know better than to make death all-important. Painful? Sure. Necessary? Absolutely. The end of all good things? Nope. Don't lose sight of that. The third thing is that what really matters isn't how our lives end, it's what we do with them while we have them.> She paused. *<Like if you put a lot of time and effort into a theatrical project that you really, really needed someone to see. Also, all the actors are waiting for us and eventually they'll just wander away.>*

I sighed. "Okay, okay, I'm sorry. Let's go see your movie."

<It's not a movie, it's a play. I mean, you can't film spirits. Obviously.>

"Right. Obviously."

Whiskey had been oddly quiet during this exchange, but now he shook himself and jumped off the couch. [Excellent. Now we can see whether or not a feline has what it takes to bring a tale to life on the stage. Not quite the point of our original argument, but close enough.]

<Oh, you'll see, Bourbon on the Rocks. You'll see.>

[Was that meant to be an insult? Because the only insulting thing was your lack of respect for me in crafting it.]

<Oh, so now you're annoyed at my attempt to annoy you? Then my plan succeeded.>

Whiskey paused. [Well played. Shall we go?]

So I followed my cat and my dog downstairs, out of the house, around the house, and into the graveyard—which seemed to be completely deserted. Tango led me to Davy's Grave, where I was instructed to sit on the grave itself with the headstone as a backrest. I think this was more for Tango's comfort than mine, since she jumped into my lap as soon as I sat. The ground was hard and cold, but I'd thought ahead and brought a blanket with me as a cushion; I had a good view of a hill with a bunch of graves on and around it. Whiskey lay down beside us.

<Places, everyone! Aaaaannnnnd . . . ACTION!>

"In the beginning, there was nothing," a deep voice intoned. It was familiar, but I couldn't quite place it. "And then . . . there was *Tango*."

Midnight leapt into view from behind the hill, landing right at the crest. Hundreds of parrots exploded into the air behind him, a perfectly choreographed fountain of blue and yellow and red and green that curved up and to either side. The black panther posed regally, staring into the distance like a ruler surveying his kingdom, the parrots circling overhead giving him a Technicolor halo.

"But all was not well," the narrator continued. "The world can be a cruel place." Piotr the bear lumbered into sight, walking on two legs and wearing black horn-rimmed glasses.

"Glasses?" I whispered. "Where did he get—"

<Same place he got the unicycle. Ssshhhh.>

[You!] Piotr declared, pointing a massive paw at Midnight. [You are bad cat! I hate you! Eating my food and scratching my furniture—you can go live in street, bad cat!] He gestured dramatically with the other arm, and Midnight put his head down and skulked back the way he'd come, disappearing over the crest of the hill.

"Aww," I said.

"Her first life was short and brutal," the narrator intoned. "Scavenging for food, fighting other strays, always in danger. And then . . ."

Ever heard the sound of a bunch of deceased parrots imitating the noise of a car accident? I have. Screeching tires, crashing metal, stuck horn. Puts the *eeeee* in *eerie,* I can tell you.

"Her second life was longer," the narrator said, "but still fraught with difficulty."

A streak of black tore past me, right to left. Midnight, running with a gigantic rat in his jaws. A second later a pack of baying, barking dogs raced after him, clearly intent on taking his prize.

"But Tango had vowed never to back down from a battle, no matter how bad the odds."

Midnight and the dogs circled the hill. When they'd made one full circuit, Midnight put on the brakes and skidded to a stop right in front of me. I had a sudden craving for popcorn, but kept that to myself.

Midnight dropped the rat and snarled. The dog pack slammed to a halt and looked uncertain. Midnight gave a full-throated panther yowl, and the pack broke up and bolted. The rat played dead rather well, though I thought the tongue protruding from its mouth was a bit much.

"This life was much more fulfilling," the voice continued. "Tango knew both joy and sorrow."

The rat scurried away as Midnight flopped over onto his side. Half a dozen cats suddenly appeared from behind a grave and darted over to him. They crept between his front and back legs, nuzzled his belly—and suddenly I wasn't looking a full-grown panther; I was watching a domestic house cat feeding her litter. Midnight even groomed them as they pretended to nurse.

"Wow," I breathed, and I meant it. I'd never imagined Tango as a mother—she'd been fixed when she'd lived with me—but of course she had. She'd had five entire lives of her own before she ever came into mine.

"But every life comes to an end. And this one did, too."

The faux kittens all ran away. Midnight put her head down on the ground and closed her eyes for a moment—then opened them and sprang to her feet.

"In her third life, Tango found purpose. There was something out there in the world, something important. And she was going to find it."

Midnight stalked up the hill, her tail lashing back and forth.

"But no quest is without its perils. Tango faced them all."

Which is when Golden Cloud thundered over the rise. He was covered in monkeys.

"A monkey-pony?" I said.

<It's a metaphor. Quiet.>

Golden Cloud came to a stop. The monkeys clung to his mane, jumped up and down on his back, swung from his tail. Midnight put his ears back and hissed. Golden Cloud reared up on his hind legs and neighed loudly while pawing the air, a sight rendered only slightly less majestic by his coating of primates.

When he lowered himself back to earth, he began to stamp his feet and move backward slowly, in a circle around Midnight. The monkeys went nuts, climbing over and around every part of the horse as if he were a jungle gym, from the top of his head to the tips of his hoofs. It was dizzying, and ludicrous, and just a little terrifying.

When Golden Cloud had circled Midnight three times, he stopped. All the monkeys formed a line from head to tail, sitting perfectly straight and facing the cat. I almost expected them to do the famous hear-no-evil, see-no-evil, speak-no-evil thing, but there were more than three and what would the extra ones do? Smell no evil, fling no evil?

Midnight crouched lower and lower—then leapt, right over the horse and the monkeys. The monkeys never twitched.

Golden Cloud and his nimble riders trotted off. Which is when two schools of brilliantly colored tropical fish approached Midnight on either side, each stopping about ten feet away.

Midnight sat on his haunches, his head drooping. He looked weary and sad.

"But Tango did not find what she was looking for," the narrator said. "Not in her third life."

The two schools moved toward each other slowly, drawing closer and closer until their edges touched and they stopped, forming one big, shimmering neon curtain. I couldn't see Midnight at all.

The schools pulled away from each other once more. Midnight was on his feet again, looking wary.

"And in her fourth," the narrator continued, "she was beset by foes on all sides."

Which is when the rabbits attacked.

I've already described this scene—twice, actually—so I won't go into detail here, except to say that it went on for a long time and was utterly amazing. And while squirrels may or may not be evil, they are definitely the Bruce Lees of the rodent world.

Midnight fought them all. And though the battle was long and the enemies many, he emerged victorious. Exhausted, surrounded by the still-twitching bodies of his attackers, he stalked up the hill once more.

<Nothing will stop me,> Midnight declared. <There's no tree too tall to climb, no water too wet to dare. No claws or fangs or quills too sharp to deter me, no storm too fierce to prevent my progress. I will persevere, I will endure, I will triumph—for my goal is beyond price. Better than the finest catnip, softer than the softest bed, tastier than a sparrow soufflé with finely ground mouse bits. I will hunt it down, and wait outside its hole, and pounce on it. And then it will be mine.>

Well, Tango understood narrative structure: Give your protagonist an objective they really, really want, then throw obstacles in their way—one of which was the tendency of the main character to abruptly die every few minutes.

Which is when Topsy, the electric elephant, lumbered into view.

Topsy, believe it or not, was executed by none other than Thomas Edison. Her crime was killing her handler after he fed her a lit cigarette, but Edison was really just looking for an excuse to demonstrate how dangerous alternating current was; he was involved in something called the War of the Currents with Nikola Tesla, with Edison championing DC power over AC. Edison lost, but not before electrocuting a pachyderm and filming it.

Topsy was a prowler, and a scary-looking one at that. She was entirely black, still bore the chains she'd worn when she was executed, and voltage crackled over her skin, between her tusks, and over said chains. Which is why, I suppose, Tango cast her as a storm cloud.

"Even a lightning bolt could only slow her down," the narrator said. Topsy extended a long, black trunk, and a bolt of electricity zapped from it to a spot awfully close to Midnight. The panther flopped over and played dead.

<True story,> Tango murmured.

"Her fifth life was her most epic yet," the narrator said. "It was then she met her archnemesis: Yappy Dog."

The first time I met Higgins he'd arrived on Golden Cloud, an entrance I thought he'd never top. I was wrong.

Around the curve of the hill came a fierce little dog wearing a black cape that bellowed majestically behind him.

He was riding a flying shark.

[Grrrrrrr,] growled Higgins. [I will destroy you! Yap yap yap yap!]

<Never!> snarled Midnight. *<Neither you nor your sushi steed will bar my way!>*

And then they played tag. Well, it sort of looked like tag, because they were chasing each other all over the place. Two-Notch actually seemed intent on eating Midnight, which worried me—but when Midnight turned and leapt, knocking Higgins off the shark's back, she immediately lost interest and swam out of sight, her tail flicking back and forth lazily.

Midnight had pounced on Higgins as soon as he fell, and now had him trapped between two black paws. *<Where is your protector now, Yappy Dog? Gone, that's where!>*

[Mercy, mighty Tango! Please don't shred me with your razor-sharp claws and teeth!] Higgins trembled in fear. Either he was actually terrified at being inches away from a panther's jaws, or he was just a good actor. Either way, he was very convincing.

<Mercy? Where was your mercy when all I wanted was a nice, raw slab of salmon? Where was your mercy when you chased me out of that Japanese restaurant?>

[I was only doing my job!]

<Well, consider yourself . . . unemployed,*>* Midnight snarled, and bit Higgins's head right off.

I shrieked.

And then felt overwhelmingly embarrassed when I realized Higgins's skull was still attached and Midnight had simply engulfed the little dog's head entirely with his jaws. The panther lifted Higgins's limp, dangling body off the ground, then threw it to one side with a single violent toss of his head. *<So ends the reign of Yappy Dog,>* Midnight growled. *<Now it's time for some* sushi.*>* He stalked over the rise of the hill, disappearing from sight.

The sixth scene—or life, I guess—caught me completely by surprise.

There was a light in the sky.

It was noon on a cloudy, gray October day, but the light that shone down wasn't that of the sun. It was silvery, ethereal, unearthly. And it was getting closer.

I squinted at it, trying to make out what it was and what it was supposed to be. A bird playing a plane? A fish cast as a flying saucer? A luminescent octopus?

None of the above. It was a dog. A small dog, wearing a space suit.

It wasn't really a space suit, of course. It looked more like a padded harness attached with a bunch of leather straps and buckles. But I recognized the dog instantly: those perky brown ears, that single thin white stripe that ran the length of her muzzle.

Her name was Laika. She was the first animal to orbit the earth. And the first to die there.

She was a stray dog rescued from the streets of Moscow by the Soviet space program. They chose her because she appeared to be part terrier and part husky, and the scientists reasoned that a crossbreed hardy enough to survive a Moscow winter outside would already be used to extremes of cold and hunger. They picked her, in other words, because she was a survivor.

But she didn't survive. Something went wrong with her capsule, and it overheated. She only experienced space itself for a few hours.

Or so people thought.

Laika slowly descended, until she hovered only twenty feet or so over our heads. The glow coming from her body was like moonlight.

[You have struggled long and traveled far,] Laika said. Her voice in my head was soft, the Russian accent lyrical. [I know something of this. What you have been seeking is just a little farther. Do not give up.]

<*I'm so tired,*> Midnight said. It was hard to tear my eyes away from Laika, but I looked down and saw that Midnight was now standing with his front paws on the crest of the hill, staring up at the ghostly dog. <*Is it even worth it? So much suffering, so much searching. Is anything worth that?*>

[Oh, yes, Tango. It's the most valuable thing there is. You will see.] And with that Laika began to ascend once more. Midnight watched her go, his eyes full of longing.

A dog, from outer space. Just when I thought this wonderful, crazy, amazing place couldn't get any stranger, it surprised me. It revealed something that touched me deeply, and reminded me that what I did, even though exhausting, was worth the effort. And I needed that reminder;

I was so surrounded by the exotic and odd all the time that sometimes I couldn't see the enchanted forest for the talking trees. Maybe I needed some sort of touchstone, a little bit of wonder to carry around with me and remind me to look up now and then.

And that was the moment that I saw it: the little end of logic sticking out of the tangled mess that I'd been trying to unravel. I followed it as Laika rose higher and higher, and by the time she was out of sight I had a pretty good idea of what had happened . . . and how.

22.

I grinned. I beamed. I turned to look at Tango, and she looked pretty happy, too. *<I know, I know. A dog, right? But I had to go with that glow. Sure, plenty of spirits fly or swim through the air, but none of 'em had that certain quality I was looking for—oh, here comes the good part.>*

Which is when Whiskey got up and ducked behind a nearby headstone. He emerged on the other side, holding a small framed picture in his jaws.

It was a picture of me.

I recognized it instantly. It was a childhood photograph I kept at home, on my desk. I was six years old, and holding a kitten in my lap.

Tango.

I see that picture almost every day. I've owned it most of my life. I thought I took it for granted now, that long familiarity had eroded the deep emotions it used to evoke; but the sight of it as Whiskey gently placed it on a grave—upright—caused those emotions to surge forth as strongly as ever.

Midnight padded over. He looked at the picture, and cocked his head to one side—

"A kitty, Daddy? For me?"
"That's right, sweetheart. A kitty of your very own. Do you like her?"
"Look, she's rubbing against my leg! She likes me!"

Midnight put his head down and carefully rubbed his cheek against the frame. It fell over anyway, but he continued to rub his head against it. He started to purr.

Okay, I'd never had a ghost panther telepathically purr at me, but I'd been doing this mental-conversation thing for a while now, and something didn't sound quite right. There was something on top of Midnight's bass rumble, something resonating but not the same.

I looked down at my cat. She was purring, too. And as I stared at her, she ever so slowly blinked both her eyes at me.

<I finally found it, Toots. That perfect thing I'd been looking for. Took me six lives to do it, but it was worth the trip.>

Dammit, I hate movies that make me bawl my eyes out.
But I sure do love my cat.

That was pretty much it for the play. Written for an audience of one, it turned out, and that audience was pretty blown away. After it was over, all the actors came by to take a bow, and I made sure to tell each and every one what an incredible job they'd done. The narrator turned out to be Fish Jumping, which was almost as unbelievable as a canine cosmonaut. "You were terrific, FJ!" I said. "You didn't have a single outburst."

Fish Jumping preened himself proudly. *I didn't, did I? I think it was because I was so focused on remembering my lines. I have more than anyone, you know.* "Awk! Bragging bird! Bragging bird! Awk!"

"You earned it," I told him. "Higgins, that was quite a performance."

The little dog panted happily and wagged his tail. [Thank you. I did research the role rather heavily—I even talked to the original Yappy Dog. He had a much different view of the events than was portrayed, of course.]

"No doubt," I said.

Tango was still in my lap, purring contentedly, but she opened her eyes and glanced up at me. *<Story takes precedence over fact. Yappy Dog was more of a composite than a single character, anyway; I had to condense a lot for narrative flow and running time.>*

"And you," I said, pointing an accusing finger at Whiskey. "How did you manage to steal that picture and smuggle it out of the house and into the Crossroads without me noticing?"

Whiskey looked smug. [You expect me to reveal all my secrets? Let's just say that your usual laser-sharp focus isn't quite as . . . *coherent* first thing in the morning.]

I shook my head. "Both my partners, plotting against me. I'll never trust either of you again."

<Yeah, right.>

[I concur.]

Tango leapt from my lap, and I got to my feet. "Thank you both, so much. Whiskey, does your assistance mean you can finally admit that a feline is capable of organizing a theatrical production?"

Whiskey snorted. [Don't be absurd. First of all, that wasn't my original point; it was that dogs are better actors than cats. Considering your use of not one but two dogs in vital roles, I consider myself vindicated. Second, you never would have been able to stage that final scene without my help—]

Tango interrupted him. <*Apparently cats are also better at counting. Six dogs, not two; there were three in the pack that chased me. Which is still less than the number of cats I employed—seven—and last but not least, that wasn't the final scene.*>

[What do you mean? Clearly, it was.]

<*Nope. Since this is a biopic, there are certain conventions I can play with. You know, like having the actual subject of the film appear in the closing credits with an update. Only I decided it would be more innovative if I did something different. Fish Jumping, if you please?*>

Fish Jumping cleared his throat, then spoke again in his narrator's voice: "No life, however, is perfect. And despite the perfect happiness that Tango found in her sixth, an even worse opponent awaited her in life number seven: the distilled *essence* of irritation."

And that's when Pal trotted out from behind the hill.

One of his eyes was covered with a cardboard patch, on which was a crudely drawn blue eye. Australian cattle dogs already bear a certain resemblance to collies, which in this case had been enhanced by the careful daubing of mud on Pal's coat to mimic the brindle coloring of Whiskey's fur.

[You can't be serious,] Whiskey said, staring.

[I assure you, I am,] replied the imitation Whiskey. [In fact, I am never anything but. I believe my sense of humor is, in fact, entirely absent.]

<*Nice. Very *accurate*.*>

I didn't know a dog could look horrified. [This is preposterous,] Whiskey said.

[Indeed,] Whiskey Two agreed. [Preposterous in the extreme. Altogether ludicrous, in fact.]

Whiskey glared at his dopplegänger. [That is not what I sound like.]

[It is, in fact.]

[And stop saying *in fact*! I don't do that!]

"Hmmm," I said. "Well done, Tango. You've managed to annoy Whiskey to an amazing degree, while getting him to disparage the acting ability of a fellow canine. I'm still not sure which are better at acting, dogs or cats . . . but you're a natural-born producer."

[Indeed. In fact.]

[Stop that! Do you realize you're dangerously close to betraying your own kind?]

Pal struck a heroic pose, head up, gazing into the middle distance. [Not at all. For, first and foremost, I am an *actor;* a proud and lonely breed, a pack whose only leader is a fierce dedication to our craft—]

[Fine. Let's see how you like it.] Whiskey morphed into a duplicate of Pal, one without the eye patch and makeup job. [Ooh, look at me! I'm an actor! I'm good at pretending!]

[That's hardly accurate.]

[Look! Look! I can pretend my own tail is a squirrel!] Whiskey started spinning in a circle, barking wildly. [Curse you, tail-squirrel! I will catch you and prevent your evil plan to throw Timmy down a well! Again!]

[I refuse to dignify your pathetic attempt at mockery with a response, this statement notwithstanding.]

[Too late! There goes Timmy! Splishy splish splash! Tread water, Timmy, tread water!]

<*This may be the greatest moment of my life,*> Tango said fondly. <*My current one, I mean.*>

I laughed. "Yeah, this is pretty great. Now, just to round out the day, what do you say we go solve a mystery?"

* * *

I explained to Whiskey and Tango what I'd figured out, and what it meant. Then I sent them off on a very specific errand that would make or break my theory, and was ridiculously proud of myself when they found what I'd been hoping for.

After that, I went to visit Shondra.

"I am so, so sorry," I told her. "I should have talked to you from the start, but I'm hoping I can make up for that now." I told her—sort of—what I thought had happened. I left a few parts blank, and let her fill them in with her own conclusions; that might sound patronizing, but was actually pragmatic. I couldn't mention the paranormal elements, so I needed something else to stand in for them—and the whole theory sounded a lot more plausible if those suggestions came from a second person.

Because the theory itself was kind of wacky.

Then, once again, I convinced everyone to gather in the study. This time, Shondra stood next to me. "Hi, everyone," I said. "Thank you for the second chance." I glanced at Shondra as I said this, but she just stared back at me impassively. "I promise, what we have for you is more than just a theory—we have actual proof. It's a little out there, but bear with us."

"A bombing and a murder," said Shondra. "Two parts of the same case, or separate incidents that occurred on the same night? That's the first question. The answer is that yes, they were connected. It's the how that's complicated."

"What's always been problematic," I said, "is the how and when of the bomb being placed. Rolvink was already dead when it was put in the chimney, Natalia didn't blow herself up, and I have reliable information that no one approached the chimney from above during the night."

"*How* reliable?" Jaxon asked skeptically.

"Very," I answered. "But as I said before, where it came from is irrelevant. First, my source is not a suspect—and second, *the bomb wasn't placed in the middle of the night.*"

"Then when?" said Lucky Trentini. "It couldn't have been in the morning. Nobody had access to Natalia's room and anyone on the roof would have been seen by the crew on the front lawn."

"True," said Shondra. "Which means the bomb was planted some other time, when nobody else would have noticed—such as just after dinner. It was already dark out; no one was on the front lawn except Keene and Oscar, and they were absorbed in a game of croquet. Someone dressed in dark clothing and moving slowly could have crept onto the roof without being seen."

"But that's impossible!" ZZ said. "There was a blazing fire in the hearth—no one would have been crazy enough to lower an explosive into that. And if they had, it would have blown up in their faces!"

"You'd think so, wouldn't you?" I replied. "But that's exactly what happened. The bomb was lowered directly over a very hot fire, and it didn't go off until the next morning. Know why?"

Nobody did—or nobody was willing to admit it. I looked directly at Catree. "I see you have your backpack with you. Do you still have that thing you showed me the other day?"

She looked puzzled. "What, the zombie hand?"

"No. The *other* thing. The one that reminds you why you got into show biz in the first place."

She understood—and then she *understood.* "The aerogel," she said. She grabbed her backpack and dug out the container.

"Aerogel has many amazing qualities," I continued. Catree opened the container, took out the cube, and handed it to me. Once again, it felt like handling a solidified, square soap bubble. "Amazingly light, amazingly strong. But there's one particular quality it possesses that's relevant in this case: Even though it's over ninety-eight percent air, it's a very, *very* good insulator against two of the three kinds of heat."

"Which are what?" asked Keene. "Hot, *extremely* hot, and . . . tepid?"

"Conductive, convective, and radiant," said Fikru.

"Yes," I said. "Aerogel is so good at blocking heat you can put a flower on one side of a thin layer and a blowtorch on the other and the flower won't even wilt. That's conductive heat. Convective heat is hot air, which doesn't permeate through the gel."

"So the bomb was encased in aerogel, protecting it from the fire," ZZ said.

"We believe so," said Shondra. "Aerogel also shatters like glass if you overstress it, so it would have been completely destroyed in the explosion."

Jaxon Nesbitt, who had been lounging on the couch with his arm around Catree, suddenly looked distinctly uncomfortable. "Aerogel," he said. "Not a very common substance, is it?" He carefully didn't look at Catree as he said it.

"No," I said. "But it's not that difficult to obtain, either—once you know about it. Catree sees it as a symbol for science making magic, so she keeps it with her as a kind of touchstone. She showed it to me, and I'm guessing she's showed it to more than one of you."

Catree looked vaguely embarrassed. "Well, it's *cool*. Geez, now I feel like some kind of science slut."

I grinned. "Don't be ashamed—it *is* cool, literally. But one of the people you showed it off to started thinking about how they could use that to their advantage."

I tossed the cube back to Catree. "One of the details in the bombing report was that they couldn't detect any sign of a triggering device. TNT needs a booster explosive to set it off, but no trace of one was found. No fire was burning in the fireplace when it blew—so how was the bomb set off?"

Dead silence.

Shondra took a pair of evidence gloves from her pocket and pulled them on. Then she bent down to the satchel at her feet and pulled out a two-foot-long metal cylinder with a small box duct-taped to it. "With this," she said. "A blue laser."

"Where did you find that?" Max Tervo asked.

"In a tree," Shondra said. "One with line-of-sight to the mansion's chimney."

"This is basically a laser pointer on steroids," I said. "Easily obtainable via the Internet, and capable of igniting trinitrotoluene. The bomber climbed the tree, attached the laser, and aimed it directly at the top of the chimney. Must have been a little finicky, but if you took your time and used binoculars, you could do it."

Catree nodded. "Then you use a mirror to reflect the beam down into the chimney. Once you've got it lined up properly, you turn off or block the laser, and lower the bomb down the flue on a fireproof line. The explosion would destroy the mirror and the line, and the chimney would blow the pieces far away—like buckshot from a shotgun."

"But that would require two people, would it not?" Oscar asked. "One to lower the bomb and one to turn the laser on and off."

Shondra tapped the box taped to the laser. "Not if you used this. Programmable timer. Set it to go off for ten minutes every twelve hours, and you can use the first ten-minute block to align the laser. Wait until it turns off to lower the bomb, then leave and establish your alibi for the time people *think* the bomb was planted."

"The flashing blue light I saw that night," said Keene. "That's what it was."

"Yes. But up on the roof, the perpetrator made a crucial mistake."

"What?" asked Lucky Trentini.

"We'll never know for sure," I said. "My theory is that after placing the explosives, the bomber was startled by something. Something they saw, or maybe heard. It was enough to make them lose their balance—and fall to their death."

"Rolvink?" gasped Keene. "The murder victim was the bomber? But—"

"But there was no murder," Shondra said. "Only an attempted one—that of Natalia Cardoso."

"Why?" asked Jaxon. "Why kill his female lead?"

"Because principal shooting was already done," I answered. "And there's nothing the tabloid press loves more than a controversial death on a movie set. I thought the paparazzi showed up here awfully fast, and the reason they did was that they'd been tipped off. Rolvink dangled a juicy piece of bait in front of one of them, and he went for it. With the right kind of publicity, a zombie movie with a dead leading lady would have made him a lot of money."

"That's why he told us he was going into town that night," said ZZ. "He was planning on being in a public place with plenty of witnesses to establish his alibi."

I nodded. "I think his actual plan was to get arrested—being in a jail cell is about the best alibi there is."

"Ingenious," Max Tervo murmured. "But needlessly elaborate. Why didn't he simply use an ordinary timer on the bomb?"

"Why did he finance a movie about Sherlock Holmes fighting zombies?" I said. "It wasn't just the potential for profit. Rolvink had a flair for the theatrical, and he couldn't resist staging a crime that Professor Moriarty himself would have been proud of."

Yemane Fikru held up a single finger. "But the body was mutilated, wasn't it? How did that happen?"

"Yes," I said. "The missing head and hands. As it turns out, we did have a killer roaming the grounds—but not a human one. And in this case, he wasn't so much a killer as a scavenger." I told them about the honey badger, and how they'd been known to rob graves and hide body parts to eat later.

"But—an entire head?" Jaxon said.

I shrugged. "What can I say? He likes crunchy things."

"There's still one problem with your theory," Catree pointed out. "Rolvink must have used a ladder to get onto the roof. What happened to it?"

Keene cleared his throat. "Ah. That would have been me. While I have no clear memory of it, at some point I did use a ladder for my . . . creation. It seems I must have found it leaning against the house."

"So there you have it,", I said. "A devious plan by a devious man, who discovered that all the planning in the world wasn't quite enough when it comes to the goings-on at the Zoransky estate."

What I didn't tell them was I knew what Rolvink had to have seen that startled him so badly he lost his footing and plunged to his death: a ghost. Most people can't see them, but some—like Yemane Fikru—could. I wouldn't have pegged Rolvink as psychically sensitive, but then I wouldn't have pegged him as sensitive, period. And when Unsinkable Sam had first appeared, it was Rolvink who'd spotted him. I didn't know which spirit he'd seen on the roof, but it could have been any of the ones Yemane Fikru had sensed, or even Ambrose; the sight of a glowing blue-green sea turtle flying at you out of the night sky would boggle just about anyone, and Ambrose was fond of his nightly flyovers. I planned to do a little more investigating in the Great Crossroads to pin that detail down, but I was confident I was right.

"Well done, Foxtrot," said ZZ. "I understand now why Lieutenant Forrester isn't present. There's no one to arrest, is there?"

"Not as such," I said cheerfully. "However, there is tea and pastries, if anyone wants some."

The general consensus was that yes, tea and pastries were exactly what was called for, and I had Consuela bring them out. Then, when everyone was busy stirring and spooning and sipping, I took Catree aside to talk to her in the hall.

"What ZZ said about there being no one to arrest?" I said quietly. "That's not completely true."

"What?" she said, returning my stare. "You think I helped Rolvink? Neither aerogel nor TNT is hard to obtain—"

"I'm not talking about Rolvink. I'm talking about Jaxon, and what Rolvink was blackmailing him with."

The hard look on her face softened into understanding. "Oh. I should have known you'd figure that out. Look, he already told me what happened that night. It was a freak accident—okay, not as freaky as what killed Rolvink, but still nobody's fault. He panicked. Rolvink was supposed to drop the girl at the hospital, but he dumped her thirty miles away instead. Jaxon's just sick about it—he checks on her progress constantly, pays all her medical expenses anonymously. I've been trying to get him to go to the police and turn himself in."

I nodded. "Well, now you can *make* him. Tell him he's got two days; if he hasn't done it by then, I'll tell the press."

She could see by the look on my face that I meant it. "Wow. You *are* hard-core. You know how much he's going to hate you for that?"

"Better me than you, right?" I smiled. "Consider it a professional courtesy."

She smiled back, then sighed. "I'll tell him tonight. Thank you."

"You may regret saying that."

"Nah. I rarely regret anything." And with that, she went back to grab an extra-large mug of coffee and a plate full of French pastries to share with her movie-star boyfriend.

Ah, well. He did flirt with me at least once.

<*What I don't get,*> said Tango as we strolled through the Great Crossroads, <*is why you wouldn't let me be there when you explained the whole thing.*>

[I'd like to remind you,] said Whiskey, [that I wasn't present, either.]

<*That doesn't need an explanation, though. There's a glaringly obvious explanation, and it starts with the letter D.*>

"I didn't want Whiskey there because Yemane Fikru makes me nervous," I said. "He can see spirits, and he seems to know you're no ordinary canine. I thought keeping Whiskey out of the room just made sense. You, on the other paw . . . well, there's a certain piece of information I've been keeping from you. I didn't know how you'd react when I revealed it, so I decided to wait until later. Which is now."

[May I?] asked Whiskey, his eyes bright.

"Considering what Tango put you through, I think you've earned it," I said. "Go ahead."

Whiskey came to a halt. He sat and studied Tango intently. She watched him warily. [Tango. I'm afraid we deceived you as to the nature of the device you and I discovered in that tree. It was not, as we told you, an electronic remote control for a small robot spider designed to climb down a line and push a button.]

<It wasn't? But—but then how was the bomb in the chimney set off?>

[With a laser pointer.]

<What? No. No, that's not possible.> Her voice was horrified.

[I'm afraid so. Attempted murder . . . by the Little Red Dot.]

If there's one thing Tango holds sacred, it's the Little Red Dot. She fervently believes that one day, it Will Be Caught, and on that day many great mysteries will be revealed. She isn't sure what the purpose of the LRD is, or what it's supposed to teach; she just knows her faith in it is unshakable. Or was, until today.

<Blasphemy!> she hissed. <The Little Red Dot could never be used for evil!>

[And yet, it was. Maddening, isn't it?]

Her eyes narrowed. <The ways of the Little Red Dot have always been mysterious and frustrating. That's just its nature.>

[So you're feeling mystified and frustrated?]

<I . . . you're not . . . >

Whiskey nodded. [I see. I'll take that as confirmation. Thank you, Foxtrot.]

"That's it? After what she did to you? You're getting off light, Tango."

[Getting off light? If I were more inclined toward verbal gymnastics, I might take that as an opportunity for a pun.]

"Yeah, but you're not, so I'll have to run with it on my own. Getting off light? What are you, hooked on photons?"

<*I'm ignoring both of you. Hard.*>

[No, you're not. I've saved the best for last. The Little Red Dot that was used to set off the bomb? It wasn't even red—it was *blue*.]

<*That's it. I can't hear any more of this.*> And with that, she was gone.

I stopped and looked down at Whiskey. "You know she's just going to use the color as an excuse to dismiss the whole thing. She'll claim blue is the color of the feline devil or something."

[Yes, but in order to reach that point she'll have to question her entire belief system and consider the fact that she may have been wrong. There *is* no greater revenge—not to a cat.]

"Nicely done. Now, shall we get to work in tracking down the mystery ghost that caused all this?"

[There's no need, I'm afraid. I know exactly who it was—it was Oskar, aka Unsinkable Sam. While unable to bring down Tango's production, he did manage to send one more victim to their doom.]

That disturbed me. I'd been thinking of what happened to Rolvink as an accident—a well-deserved one, but an accident nonetheless. "You don't think he did it on purpose, do you?"

[It's worse than that, Foxtrot. I believe he may have been an agent for a greater evil, one that enlisted him for his skill at deception. I've been secretly investigating on behalf of Eli; I'm sorry I didn't tell you sooner, but when you've heard the full explanation you'll understand.]

I heard the flapping of ghostly wings, and an albino crow swooped out of the sky and settled on the cross-shaped headstone of a nearby grave. My other boss, Eli.

"Oskar's escaped," Eli rasped.

"What? How?"

"I can't talk about specifics, unfortunately. But some-time between Whiskey delivering Oskar to me and the cat going where he was supposed to go, he managed to slip away. And now we can't locate him anywhere."

That was even more disturbing. Though I didn't know exactly what Eli was, I was pretty sure he was a lot more than the ghost of a white crow. Anyone who could escape from him had to be bad, bad news. "So this wasn't the series of freak accidents it seemed to be? It was orchestrated?"

"*Exploited* would be a better term. Precarious events were encouraged to implode."

"Why? By who?"

Eli fixed me with a beady crow eye. "The Unktehilas, Foxtrot. They've returned."

Wait, don't go! There's more!

As a special bonus, I'm presenting this short excerpt from the script for *Sherlock Zolmbes*. Any gory bits have been edited out by my ace assistants Whiskey and Tango (by which I mean I read those parts out loud and altered them if either of my assistants began to drool. They are carnivores, after all). Enjoy!

THE SCENE: a spooky old graveyard. SHERLOCK HOLMES and his intrepid assistant WATSON are walking and talking.

WATSON: But I'm telling you, Holmes—that corpse I examined was precisely that—a corpse. But animated somehow, brought back to a semblance of life.

HOLMES: Nonsense, Watson. As a medical man, you must understand the sheer absurdity of what you're proposing. It's like saying a factory can still function once you've taken away all the machinery, stripped the wiring from the walls, removed the lighting, and dismantled the plumbing.

Behind them, a grimy hand claws its way free from the dirt of a grave.

WATSON: Then how was it done, Holmes? Answer me that.

HOLMES: All in good time, Watson. All in good time.

The ZOMBIE rises from the ground. Its (squishy parts) dangle from (some not-so-squishy parts. That doesn't sound dirty, does it?) It shambles forward, and (something repulsive) spews from (I'm just going to go ahead and skip this description, okay? It's a zombie. It looks gross and sounds scary and oh-my-gosh, the smell. Which in real life actually smells mostly like corn syrup, which isn't scary at all.) The ZOMBIE lurches forward, though neither WATSON or HOLMES has noticed it behind them yet.

HOLMES: There's always a scientific explanation, Watson. No, I'm more bothered by the mind behind this atrocity. A mind we're all too familiar with.

WATSON: Who are you talking about, Holmes? The only similarity I see to previous encounters with the purportedly supernatural is the Baskerville case—surely that's not what you're referring to?

HOLMES: Let us consider the facts, Watson. The choice of venue for the attack: a hospital, an environment you're intimately familiar with. The victim of the supposed revenant: a doctor specializing in diseases of the brain, and well known to you. And most important, the reanimated body itself: that of your beloved former nanny.

WATSON stops and puts a hand to his eyes. He is clearly shaken, momentarily overcome with remorse. The ZOMBIE reaches out and grabs him around the throat with both hands. HOLMES continues on, oblivious.

HOLMES: Mrs. Ogilvie, yes. All choices coldly calculated to invoke the maximum sense of horror and foreboding in you, Watson. Who would be so cruel? Who would deliberately attack my most trusted colleague in such a nefarious way? There can be only one answer, my friend: our old foe, Professor Moriarty. He is striking at me through you, for he knows how valuable you are to my investigations. With you hobbled by a surfeit of overwhelming emotions, Moriarty thinks he can diminish our effectiveness enough to ensure his success.

The ZOMBIE chows down on (eeewww. And I thought the last description was vivid. This one is a lot worse, and it goes on for at least half a page. Let's just say that Watson doesn't fare well, and afterward the zombie should probably consider going on a diet. Also, as a side note, Holmes is blathering on with his speech during this whole thing. I know he's self-obsessed, but deaf? Anyway, I really feel like someone needs to stick up for the spunky assistant here. Poor Watson.) HOLMES finally notices what's going on and leaps to Watson's aid. He pulls out a revolver and shoots the ZOMBIE in the chest, but when it has no effect he tries again, this time aiming for the head. The ZOMBIE's head (oh, for Pete's sake. This description is just completely gratuitous. It's like the scriptwriter is getting paid by the adjective, but only if the adjective is disgusting. The point here is that while shooting the zombie in the chest doesn't work, shooting it in the head does. This clearly bothers Holmes, who you think would be more upset by his best friend getting eaten in front of him.)

WATSON collapses to the ground. (Well, what's left of him, anyway. Though he looks surprisingly robust later on when he's trying to turn Holmes into Victorian steak tartare.)

HOLMES: Watson! Watson, hold on! Your wounds—they're mostly superficial.

WATSON: You're a terrible liar . . . old friend. Remember who you're speaking to; I know a fatal injury when I . . . encounter one.

HOLMES: I . . . you're right, of course. As usual.

WATSON: You must promise me, Sherlock. Promise me that if Moriarty brings me back as one of those . . . *things,* you won't hesitate to put me down.

HOLMES: I . . . yes, of course. I promise.

WATSON: It won't be me, Sherlock. No matter what I say, or do. You didn't hear the horrible things Mrs. Ogilvie whispered as she tried to . . . to rip out my throat.

HOLMES: That's . . . that's not going to happen, old man. I swear.

WATSON: I . . . never thought these would be my last words, Sherlock. You're . . . *wrong* . . .

HOLMES: Watson! Dear God, no!

WATSON dies. (Geez. A mindless zombie turns someone into a meal and the writer goes on for three paragraphs, but the most beloved sidekick in literary history expires and all he's worth is two lousy words? Assistants get no respect.)

MORIARTY steps out of the shadows.

MORIARTY: Oh, don't worry, my dear Sherlock. He's not gone—not really. The interstitial state is extremely short; it raises many questions about the nature of the soul and where, precisely, it resides. But as fascinating as those questions are, they must take a secondary position to more pragmatic matters; such is often the case with scientific research. Still, one gathers data when one can.

MORIARTY consults a pocket watch in his hand.

MORIARTY: There's some variation, of course, but considering his age, intelligence, and relative health at the time of his demise, I would say Dr. Watson will be returning to us right about . . . *now*.

The body in HOLMES's arms shudders. Its eyes open wide; they've changed, the irises now a vivid red. WATSON's mouth opens and an eerie moan issues forth. Horrified, HOLMES drops the body to the ground and leaps to his feet.

HOLMES: No! It can't be!

MORIARTY: But it is, my dear Sherlock. Your beloved Watson, back from the dead. Aren't you glad to see him?

WATSON lurches to his feet. HOLMES staggers backward, his face struggling with disbelief and horror.

MORIARTY: "When you eliminate the impossible, whatever's left—no matter how improbable—must be the truth." Have I quoted you correctly, Mr. Holmes? But what happens when the impossible decides to eliminate *you*? (By the way, this is the tagline for the movie. But you probably knew that the second you read it.)

ZOMBIES begin to erupt from the other graves. HOLMES keeps backing up.

MORIARTY: Come, Mr. Holmes. The earth is vomiting up its dead; where is your logic now? How does your vaunted intellect respond when confronted by the sight of your deceased comrade, on his feet and hungry for your still-living flesh?

The ZOMBIES lurch forward, WATSON at the forefront. HOLMES turns and runs.

MORIARTY calls after him.

MORIARTY: Yes, Mr. Holmes, run! Run as far and as fast as you can, for it is Death itself that nips at your heels!

END OF SCENE

(Okay, that's it. For real, this time. Go read something else.)

Read on for an excerpt from Dixie Lyle's next book

PURRFECTLY DEAD

Coming soon from St. Martin's Paperbacks

A war.

A *supernatural* war.

A war where one side tossed around tornadoes, blizzards, and thunderstorms, and the other could take on anyone's appearance and control your mind. Sort of like Vietnam, if you replaced the guys in helicopters with multiple clones of Thor and the Viet Cong with the cast of *Invasion of the Body Snatchers*. And threw in some hypnosis, just for fun.

The Vietnam conflict hadn't gone so well for the guys in the helicopters. Even without the evil-Jedi mind tricks.

"So," I said to my phone. "Why are you telling me? Is this a declaration of hostilities? If you want me to choose sides, I'm pretty much already committed."

"No, Foxtrot. I don't want this war to happen any more than you do," said Lockley Hades.

"Okay. I guess that opinion qualifies you as A) not insane, and B) a potential ally. Tell me more."

"I will, but for a more productive discussion we're going

to need more than just words. Skype would be better. I'll contact you tomorrow and we can continue this face-to-face."

He didn't ask for a number, but anyone that could pull that hidden area code trick probably didn't need to. I wouldn't have been terribly surprised if he'd pulled my Social Security number from his belly button—though I doubted that was why he wanted to see my face. "Hold on. If Maxine is an Unktehila, I'm going to need more information than just a warning. Is Ben in danger? Is Teresa? Why is she here?"

"Tomorrow." He ended the call.

I put my phone away. Both Whiskey and Tango were staring at me with worried eyes. I took a deep breath, and relayed what I'd just been told.

When I was done, there was a moment of silence. Tango was the first to respond. <*I'm not afraid of snakes. Let 'em come.*>

[*That's* your response? We've just been informed of a potential battle between two immensely powerful supernatural forces—with us in the middle—and the most vital information you have to offer is your own lack of common sense?]

<*Not lack of common sense. Lack of* fear. *As in, scared, not being.*>

"Yes, Tango, we get it. You're completely over your fear of snakes. Now, can we—"

<*Over? That sounds as if there was once something to be* over, *which there was not. Ever.*>

Whiskey growled in exasperation. [Fine. If we postulate that you are not now, nor have ever been, frightened in any degree by any sort of reptile that has ever existed, including but not limited to dinosaurs, mythical nine-headed monsters of the Underworld, world-devouring *Ouroboros* serpents or ninja turtles, *then* can we move on to a productive discussion of our options *vis-a-vis* surviving the approaching apocalypse?]

Tango sniffed in a disapproving way. <*Yeah, as soon as you calm down. We have important things to talk about, so stop making such a fuss.*>

Whiskey shot her a look sharp enough to shave with. [Indeed,] he growled.

I'm a multitasker. I get things done at the same time I'm doing other things, and the process works like this: thing one is important, thing two is *very* important, thing three is something I do all the time, and thing four doesn't matter much at all. I start doing thing three immediately because I can do it without thinking about it, and start thinking about thing two. If any of the things can be done simultaneously with thing three, I do that, and at the first possible opportunity I tackle thing two, now that I've had time to plan a course of action. While doing these things, there are always gaps, little moments where I have to wait for something to happen—a phone to ring, a file to load, a fuse to burn down—and during these gaps I work on thing one if possible and thing four if not. Got it?

Thing two, at the moment, was the impending war. Thing three was listening to the verbal sparring between my two partners, which I can pretty much tune out by now because I'm so used to it. In fact, while they're trading insults, I'm actually thinking hard about good old thing the second.

"We need to talk to Eli," I said.

[I agree,] Whiskey said.

<*You just had to go ahead and blurt that out, didn't you?*>

[You have a different opinion? What a shock.]

It was Tango's turn to glare at him. *<No, I think Eli needs to know, too. But since you said it first, I'm forced to . . . agree with you.>*

[How tragic.]

"This can't wait," I said, already hurrying down the path. Whiskey and Tango trotted to catch up with me. "Only . . ." I stopped abruptly, and so did my partners. "Something smells."

[*Everything* smells, Foxtrot. Well, almost everything.]

I smiled. "Good point, doggy. But what I mean is that the phone call I just got—and what we learned from it—has a decidedly peculiar aroma. When someone drops a piece of information right in your lap like this, they always have an agenda. They're pushing a button and expecting a response. A *predictable* response."

[Such as immediately rushing off to inform your superior of your news?]

"Exactly. Eli's hard to pin down sometimes, but he always shows up when I really need to talk to him. Maybe this is a way to draw him out in the open."

[In which case it's the *last* thing we should be doing.]

<But the Unktehila are master manipulators. They know we'd figure that out, so they actually told us to ensure that we wouldn't *go to Eli.>*

I held one hand up in the air and the other to my forehead. "Stop. This is how it starts—don't you remember what happened last time? The paranoia, the second-guessing each other, the mistrust?"

[You're describing a cat's natural behavior.]

<Yeah. What's your point?>

"We've got to be smart about this. We talk to Eli, but not directly; Whiskey, you get a message to him via afterlife channels, then come right back. We should have code words to ID each other that we only use telepathically—I don't think the Unktehila can read private thoughts."

I switched to thought mode myself. *My word will be, um, Whirligig.*

<Umwhirligig it is. Mine will be Tangotango-tango queenoftheuniverse.>

[Mine shall be A Total Lack of Surprise.]

<That's more than one word.>

[How observant of you. Are those blinders custom-made, or do you buy them in bulk?]

"Whiskey, we'll talk to Ben. Come back as soon as you can, and meet us in the kitchen. Go!"

Whiskey didn't even bother with a parting shot—when there's a job to do, he's all business. He took off into the darkness.

<I hate to be the pessimist of our group, but the phrase divide and conquer *might also apply right about now. I'd never admit it to Whiskbroom, but you just sent our muscle sprinting for the horizon.>*

"Whiskey can take care of himself. In a fight between him and another shapeshifter, my money's on the one who faced down an electric elephant. Which is him."

<Sure, but if I were the bad guy, right about now is when I'd go all monstery and eat you.>

I put my hands on my hips. "Well? I'm waiting."

She puffed herself up like a Halloween cat, but I wasn't falling for it. "Nice try. Come on, let's go talk to Ben."

She deflated and trotted along behind me, muttering, *<Oooooh, so confident. Maybe I'm just lulling you into a false sense of security, how about that? I could* still *be a monster . . . >*

I bit my lip, and refrained from answering.